THE
BLUE
SHOES

THE
BLUE
SHOES

Stories by

SAUL ISLER

POCAMUG PRESS™

Pocamug Press™
May's Lick, Kentucky
pocamug.com

Two of these stories have appeared elsewhere in a different form: "Seeing God" in the Marinscope newspapers, and "Paean to a Coconut Bar" in Hot Flashes 2.

Version 5/4/17

Library of Congress Control Number: 2017933733

ISBN 978-0998479002

For

Write Away

Thank you, fellow writers Sandra Smith, Brian Bland, Eleanor Howard, John Smith, Cynthia Rose Fairfax, Mark Saha, Dave Partie, Joshua Alper, Salle Soladay, Caroline Redekopp, Lis Caballero, Rosemary Sackett, and the rest of you for your patience, your prodding, your putting up with me.

Contents

Author's Note	ix
The Blue Shoes	1
The Bus to Selma	9
The 103rd Floor	14
Half a Man	25
Atop K'aala	37
I Want to Tell You I Love You	49
The Saving of St. Vince	55
The Refugiada	64
Isabella	78
The Sansei Sensei	88
Seeing God	93
Paco in Need	96
Shifted Passions	103
The Lesson	107
FilmArt, Ltd.	112
Finding AAA	118
The Vegetable Garden	122
The Night I Sang at the Met	129
The Answer	132
The Art of the Scam	136
The Clipboard	148
Natangu, the Wall	157
Morra!	162
The Witching Place	168
The Trial of Jimmy McCloud	173
The Interrogation	177
Theremin Man	182
Dear Nell	189
The Witches of Kimmelman's	193
The China Incident	196

Robert Jones 206
The Phone That Fell From the Sky 212
Please Turn Off the Lights 219
Paean to a Coconut Bar 224
The Critic 227
Sürstromming 237
Gargantua 241
Sitting In 257
Xerographika 265
A Brief History of Paper 277
A Note on the Type 281

Author's Note

Reading short stories is much like eating potato chips. One is never enough. Here you'll find a mixed bagful. Munch away.

These Blue Shoes stories range from a few pages to as many as fifteen. A few are autobiographical gleanings but nearly all are pure fiction, many ending with an O'Henryesque twist. Which is why I almost called this second collection of shorts "I'll Have Mine With a Twist".

It's likely these stories would never have been written had I not felt the figurative whip of necessity; the requirement that I write, write, write every week, as demanded by Write Away, a group of comrades I gather with weekly in Santa Monica. I dedicated this book to them and thank them again for their inspiration, willingness to laugh with, not at, my stuff, and their ongoing encouragement.

Finally, a special note of thanks to Write Awayer and pal, Brian Bland, who edited most of what appears in this book, culling out its infestation of typo, grammar and syntax cooties.

So now that this book is in your hands, settle back and slip into The Blue Shoes. I do hope they'll fit.

Saul Isler
Santa Monica, California 2017

The Blue Shoes
(For Anna)

Arabella Franceschi, born December 1, 1988, came out crying. Not so unusual; most children do. But Arabella Franceschi, from that day forward, cried for as long as two or three hours straight several times a day, every day throughout her first year. Her parents, David and Diana, though patient and loving, were beside themselves attempting to discover the unfathomable cause of Arabella's pain . . . if it was pain . . . and discomfort.

Their pediatrician, Trevor Allan, was equally baffled by Arabella's intractable condition. At first he passed it off as the mere means of communicating her needs. But her heaving, jerking, ongoing crying suggested that the source had to go far deeper. Colic, chronic earache, gastric upset and, later, the cutting of her teeth were, one after the other, ruled out as root causes. The distraught Arabella went well into her second year exhibiting the same constant crying shown during her first.

Lacking an answer, Dr. Allan wisely—and mercifully—suggested that as an experiment it might at least temporarily alleviate the distress of both child and parents if the latter would take a break from caretaking the former. Accepting the doctor's welcome advice, and frazzled beyond reckoning by now, David and Diana allowed themselves to plan a long-postponed, month-long vacation that would take them from Paris down the Rhone Valley through Provence to the French Riviera. And so, hiring a highly recommended nanny, a young woman named Ann Zelesky, to look after their Arabella, the trip was taken.

After a frantic week of sightseeing in Paris, David and Diana rented a hire car and began their meander south along the Rhone, with one of their overnight stops being the colorful, ancient town of Aix-en-Provence.

While in Aix, after a superb lunch of fried escargots and frites taken at a kiosk on the Rue Marseilles, David and Diana happened upon a small shop whose sign read *Maurice Chausseurs*. A shoe shop. Featured prominently on a pin-spotted pedestal in the middle of an otherwise dark window, as though it were a jewel in a Tiffany display case, was an exquisite pair of infant's high-top shoes of an indescribably rich shade, not quite navy or royal: more luminous than that, perhaps closer to azure. It was as if the artful shoemaker had mixed a bit of the French sky with a cupful of the Mediterranean Sea and thrown in a field of gentians to create such a nonesuch hue. They were dumbstruck at what they were seeing.

The Franceschis were seeing, for the first time, "The Blue Shoes."

Diana looked at David. David looked at Diana. No words were necessary; they had spoken to each other with their eyes. Hooked arm in arm, they marched right in to the little shop where they were instantly and profusely greeted by its proprietor, the eponymous Maurice Archambault himself, he being the only one in the shop at the time.

M. Archambault was a neatly dressed, corpulent, middle-aged man with a comically narrow pencil mustache that did not hide the fact he could easily pass for the increasingly popular actor, Gerard Depardieu. A voluble man, he, upon their inquiry, could not stop himself from offering a full history of the nonpareil—this was the very word he used—*chaussures bleues*, including the fact that the leather from which they were hand-crafted by Aubercy, the third generation of the finest shoemakers in all of France, came from Tanneries Haas, established in 1842 in Eichhoffen near Strasbourg, for many years now, supplier to not only Aubercy but to both Gucci and Louis Vuitton.

David, more than a little put out that prices were shown on practically nothing sold in this sun-drenched country, was almost afraid to ask the cost of the remarkable shoes. He did so nevertheless. M. Archambault pondered a moment, looking up, hand on chins, at his tinned ceiling as if the price were posted there. Then he informed David, in his fractured English, that he could not consider a sum under 1200 Francs—roughly, 185 American dollars. Or more than David was accustomed to paying for his own shoes. If David had been French, he'd have haggled. But haggling—for *these* shoes—seemed out of the question. He would pay the 1200. The shoes were indeed nonpareil.

If only M. Archambault could have known David's mind.

Diana looked at David. David looked at Diana. Only Diana knew that her questioning look would serve as the haggling her David was loath to do. She was the more practical of the two. And she was correct. This look, this hesitation, silently convinced M. Archambault to allow that, "For such a lovely couple as you, I might consider letting go of these fine shoes for a mere, shall we say, 1100 Francs."

Not much of a reduction. But a victory.

As if the shoes were some sort of Gainsborough of the footwear industry, the Franceschis were to call their singular purchase "The Blue Shoes" from that day forward. Feeling that their discovery was the highlight of their vacation, they might almost have opted to return home that very day to see how lovely the shoes would look on the tiny feet of their precious, if so deeply troubled, little Arabella. But they did not want to miss their bask on the Riviera.

Upon their arrival home, two weeks later, they found Arabella in Ann's arms, crying as usual, and with almost the same intensity they expected. Still, no matter what effort they made, they could not calm her down.

"The Blue Shoes!" blurted Diana. "Perhaps they'll distract her." Saying this, she unwrapped and slipped the "nonpareil" new high-tops on to Arabella's pretty little feet.

Then the strangest thing happened, even before Diana could lace them up.

Arabella, with a visible jerk of her head, stopped crying. What's more she visibly began to relax.

In fact, a rare laugh issued from her rosebud lips. And she remained in this calm and happy state until it was time, hours later, for her nap. But Arabella did not nap. She began sobbing again as soon as The Blue Shoes were removed before she was laid into her crib.

Diana and David looked at each other. Then they looked at Ann, who looked back at them. The three understood, at the same moment, that The Blue Shoes possessed a strangely leavening effect on Arabella's normally out-of-sorts disposition. And that their removal had an equal, opposite and corrupting influence on same.

As an aside, Ann Zelesky's ministrations had had a slightly improving effect on Arabella's behavior during the Franceschis' absence. Gratefully noticing this, they decided to take her on as Arabella's fulltime nanny. But, as for the crying, nothing worked its magic to stop it more than the wearing of—The Blue Shoes. Every day of the next year, Arabella wore—demanded in her way—The Blue Shoes. She wore them with white tights under a long blue dress printed with red and yellow nasturtiums, also from Aix. And with her favorite outfit, made by her mother: a pocketed, powder blue hoodie, piped in red and worn over elastic-waisted jeans, and topped by a slightly oversized Cleveland Indians baseball cap since the Franceschis happened to live in Cleveland Heights. And with everything else. And every day, for every hour she wore The Blue Shoes, she did not cry. Unless, of course, she fell and skinned a knee or bumped her pretty, copper-haired head.

Arabella was indeed an active child. Every day, as she learned to walk, and then to run, The Blue Shoes, though they were very well made, and very well cared for by Ann, became more scratched and scuffed, and more and more worn at both the heels and toes. And, all the while, Arabella was growing; growing right out of her treasured shoes. What would happen, then, when The Blue Shoes would no longer fit?

What *did* happen? Well, amazingly, nothing. Nothing at all. At age two-and-a-half, they no longer did fit. But it was as though, through Arabella's constant wearing of them, she became cured of the damnable affliction that had caused her anguished, round-the-clock and round-the-year crying.

Time to retire The Blue Shoes.

At first David and Diana thought of bronzing them. But that, of course, would hide their nonpareil, if faded, azure color. And, too—what were they thinking?—they could perhaps be worn again by a grandchild. So, after sending off The Blue Shoes to be expertly refurbished by the Aubercy factory, they retired them to the prominent mantel above their living room fireplace where they sat for years until David and Diana remodeled their home, at which time the iconic shoes were relegated to a shelf in Diana's sewing room. There they were eventually overlooked and then, though in plain sight, virtually forgotten, and, later still, tucked away for safekeeping.

And time passed.

Arabella, an only child, grew up to be loving, well-adjusted and outgoing; a delight to her parents, her nanny and to everyone who knew her. But, some time before the young lady entered high school, it became obvious that Ann Zelesky's excellent services would no longer be required. At which time the Franceschis decided to let her go. With, naturally, a large parting bonus and tears all around, mostly shed by Arabella who had hardly shed any since her third year.

Arabella went on to gain an MFA degree at the Rhode Island School of Design, become a fashion consultant at DKNY in New York, fall in love, then marry at age twenty-seven. She and her husband, Connor McPherson, a hedge fund manager, birthed a beautiful baby girl three years later. They named her Ophelia after the unfulfilled lover of Shakespeare's Hamlet.

Ophelia was perfect in every way—but one. Whatever mysterious malady her mother had suffered as an infant, Ophelia appeared to inherit. Arabella did her best to hide Ophelia's hopeless condition of non-stop crying from her own mother, but, when it became overwhelmingly clear, after just a few months, that the condition was chronic, and likely inherited, she phoned Diana in despair.

Diana took this news with equanimity, as was her way. She knew just what to do. The Blue Shoes, of course! They'd be much too large at first but—never mind—she was confident they'd serve their purpose. Now, where were they? The Franceschis had moved to a town home some years after Arabella's graduation from college, and had gladly ridded themselves of half the detritus they'd piled up over the years. But they would certainly never get rid of The Blue Shoes. Never, ever.

The couple searched everywhere for them. A second, even more thorough search turned up just the left shoe tucked away in a closet recess. But where was the other?

A third meticulous search was fruitless. The mate could simply not be found. They both prayed that the single shoe, plus as close a match as could be custom-made, might perform its task, as the pair had before. And so a local shoemaker made up a surrogate right shoe and both were sent to Arabella. But to no avail. The left appeared to be powerless without its original mate. And Ophelia went on sobbing as before.

In despair themselves now, the Franceschis renewed their search only to conclude that the right shoe was, for an absolute certainty, not in their possession. It was gone and that was that. What they did at last find, however, was the receipt for the shoes, pasted into a scrapbook Diana had made of their trip to France thirty years earlier.

The time of this finding was 10 p.m. According to the receipt, the store would not open until 9 a.m., in France. Which meant that David would have to wait until 3 a.m., Cleveland time, to call. He stayed awake, pacing and fidgeting, then made the call precisely at that time. And, miraculously, the first crisp words he heard were, *"Bonjour, Maurice Chausseurs, Maurice Archambault parlant."*

David's hand had been tightly clamped to his cell phone, his other nervously stroking the back of his head. "M. Archambault, is that really you? This is David Franceschi from America. Many years ago my wife and I bought a pair of children's shoes from you. Beautifully made, high- top blue shoes. Do you *possibly* remember us?"

Several seconds passed. Then: "M. Franceschi! *Mais oui! Les chaussures bleues!* They were—how do you say it—a single of a kind. What may I do for you?"

David blew out a long breath of relief. "M. Archambault, I would like to purchase another pair and have you overnight them to me. I do not care what they cost. Can you . . . are you able to . . . accommodate me?"

Another hesitation, a much longer one. "Monsieur, I am so sorry to report that those shoes have been discontinued. Aubercy stopped production of children's shoes perhaps a dozen year ago. But I do have an excellent selection of other children's shoes in exquisite shades of tan and brown, and even one in a most delicious shade of green."

Defeated, dejected, David interrupted M. Archambault, as the loquacious shoe merchant rattled off more of his inventory, to thank him and say goodbye.

Another fruitless search began, throughout Cleveland by David and Diana, throughout New York by Arabella and Connor, throughout the Internet by both. But nothing came close to the original. No one seemed to make such wonderful shoes anymore. They knew not where to turn. Three more days passed. Nothing turned up.

Then, on the fourth day, the Franceschis received a package from Fedex. Wrapped in brown Kraft paper, its return address noted only the name *Harkness*. It contained a hand-written note and—the mate of The Blue Shoes! No doubt of it.

David looked at Diana. Diana looked at David. Tears slowly formed then dropped from Diana's eyes as . . . the shoe firmly in her grasp . . . she fell into David's arms.

Recovering, David, through the tears welling up in his own eyes, pulled back and, over Diana's shoulder, inspected the neat, small script of the note, after which he asked Diana to sit down so he could read it to her.

Dear Mr. and Mrs. Franceschi,

I don't know where to begin except with an apology. I know what The Blue Shoes meant to you. But what you are likely not aware of is what they meant to me. Yes, it was I who took this shoe when I left you. The Blue Shoes were the only object that truly reminded me of the child I had so come to love—still do love so well. And, since I knew you would not part with them, I stole this one. I stole it. Please try to understand what got into me to do such a terrible thing.

I am so deeply sorry that I did not maintain contact with my Arabella. But I could not for fear that you'd somehow discover my theft. All I can say is that my heart was broken when I had to part from her. And I had to have a piece of her to hold for the rest of my life. And, finally, I came to realize—I knew—that I had no right, none whatsoever, to do what I did.

I ask for but do not expect your forgiveness.

The note ended with just a signature: *Ann Zelesky Harkness.*

David sat himself down next to Diana, tossed an arm around her shoulder as she looked at him with both relief and disbelief. Then he shut his eyes to better think about what he'd just read. Grateful as he felt, he was mystified about the remarkable coincidence of Ann sending the shoe just when it was most desperately needed. That might never be solved.

Did *both* of The Blue Shoes work their magic on Ophelia? Of course they did.

The Bus to Selma

The story had been building for weeks but, because of the war in Vietnam, wasn't yet at the top of the national news. The Reverend Martin Luther King, Jr. would march the fifty-four miles from Selma to Montgomery to protest the withholding of Negro voting rights. Dr. King, a recent Nobel Peace Prize laureate, was disgusted by President Johnson's refusal to speed up a voting rights act, and wanted to pressure Johnson to act.

The march, the first of three, took place on Sunday, March 7, 1965. With six hundred followers, not all of them black, marching behind him, Dr. King was stopped by a cordon of armed police and sheriff's men on the Pettus Bridge at the outskirts of town. The marchers, peacefully protesting, were brutally beaten on a day that came to be rightfully known as Bloody Sunday.

By the time of the next march, two days later, the world was watching. This time, mysteriously, the cordon dispersed at the bridge and appeared to allow King to proceed. But Dr. King, fearing an ambush and choosing not to put his people in harm's way again, called off the march, much to the dismay—and anger—of his followers.

Rushing to the White House to further plead his case, he was once again put off by Johnson. But, by now, the public outcry had helped enlist thousands of sympathetic whites throughout the country—from clergymen to ordinary citizens—to join hands with the original marchers on yet a third that would take place on Sunday, March 21.

And there was nothing more I wanted in the world than to be among the marchers, walking arm in arm with them.

Was I deluding myself? I was a draftsman, 31 years old, married, with two kids and a third on the way. And I was making $125 a week. Not the kind of money that would let me hop a plane to Selma. When I told my wife what I wanted so desperately to do, she not only thought I was crazy, she threatened to leave me if I did it. She feared not just for the destruction of our tight budget, but for the destruction of me; of our family. A family that could end up without a father.

I had no answer for her. It was something I had to do because, if I didn't, I knew I'd regret not doing it for the rest of my life. So I took a one-week leave from my job and I did it. My goodbyes to my kids were warm and fuzzy. I couldn't possibly tell them where I was going, only, afterward, where I'd been. But my wife could not warm to the idea. She wouldn't speak to me though, through her tears, she hugged me tight enough to nearly break a rib. After, she caved in and drove me to the Greyhound station.

It was 10:30 p.m. when the bus pulled out of that dreary station and headed due south. It would be a tedious two-day trip from my small Ohio town, one that would get me there on Saturday, the day before the march. I lay awake half the night, thinking about what might lie ahead in Alabama as we rumbled through Ohio and part of Kentucky. I dwelled on the satisfaction the march eastward would give me, not on the inherent danger represented by the rednecks who'd be glaring at us and shouting their hate all along Highway 80. Was I so interested in becoming part of history? No, my young mind didn't think that way.

So why, really, was I doing this? This I pondered as I stared, mesmerized and unseeing, at the endless telephone poles whizzing by. Why was I here? Because of an incident that took place when I was just a little boy.

It was the mid-forties, the war years. I was nine, maybe ten. A beautiful age if it was summer because you could spend all day every day with your pals doing anything you liked as long as you got home in time for dinner. Or you could do nothing. All we did was play baseball. Not the organized kind—there wasn't any—but the choose-up kind. We supervised ourselves in those days. By choice. There were no adults around, and none were desired. We'd play zones if only two or three showed up so that one would bat, the other pitch, the third, field. You'd get a homer if you hit it all the way to the street. A prodigious feat for a nine-year-old. An innocent game at an innocent time of life. But we kids weren't always so innocent.

We all lived in a gilded ghetto lined with three-bedroom brick homes occupied almost entirely by middle-class Jewish families like mine. It was a pristinely white suburb, typical of all in its day. It was a place where negroes were welcome. To clean our homes, to cook and launder for us, to tend our lawns. I actually felt sorry for them for being negro. Hardly knowing that some other people, in those days, felt sorry for me for being a Jew.

Negroes. My parents' generation called them, with impunity, *schvartzes*, the Yiddish word for blacks. No insult was intended, and if any were taken, we never heard about it. Black people were seen generally as good people. Many who worked for us as housekeepers, after years of service, gained status as beloved members of the household. Good people. But not, in our mid-century minds, you understand, quite as good as us. Remember: it was the forties.

With so much time to waste, we pals found ourselves not only playing baseball, we found mischief. Serious mischief. I can't recall who thought up the prank but, looking back, I'm pretty sure it wasn't me, though I was definitely up for it.

We'd often noticed an old negro man, a gardener working in the backyard of a home next to our corner ball-field. All that separated us from him was a hedge, easily high and thick enough to hide—and protect—three heartless little beasts like us. From a distance, we stared at the man edging, weeding, trimming, whatever. Then, suddenly, our leader laid out the plan that had been simmering in his miniature brain. We immediately agreed it was an ingenious plan. We'd do it.

The best plans are the simplest ones. We had no fear of it backfiring because there was no way this old dog could outrun a pack of foxes like us. Besides, he could barely see us through the bushes, or get through them if he tried. And the only weapon he had was a harmless-looking garden trowel, though we did suspect that he had a hidden knife, probably a long, switchblade model. He was, after all, a negro.

So here was Old Black Joe doing what he was underpaid to do. And there we were, three nasty little white schemers stationed in a crouch behind the bushes, ready to strike with a powerful weapon: the ugliest word in the English language.

The plan was underway. Our leader, a wiry little guy with glasses, counted us down. "Three, two, one . . ." and we let it out: "NIGGER!" And, just to make sure the poor man could hear us, we hollered it again. "NIGGER!" Heck, you could hear us all over the neighborhood. So what. We waited for our reward: an angry—dangerously angry—black man hopelessly chasing us with an eighteen-inch-long knife. Some of them had guns, too, you know? They must have.

But he didn't chase us. He did not chase us. Instead, he froze and looked up at the bushes. And I swear, thick as they were, he could see right through them, and I swear he was looking right at me, and I swear he could see right through me! And, while my co-conspirators sped away laughing and hooting, I froze, same as he had.

The look he gave me was like none I'd ever seen before—or since—on any man. It was a look of hurt the depth of which I believe I felt as much as did he. And still do. Who knew what a big hurt we'd put on him? *Or he on me.* And, instantly, the shame rose up within me. I was sick to my stomach with recognition that what I'd done was wrong. I didn't need a parent to inform me.

It was a seminal moment. Naturally I never told my folks about it but it's stayed with me ever since. It's as clear in my mind today as it was on that perfect—imperfect—day over twenty years ago. And, for twenty years, it has informed my sense of how I treat other people. All other people. It's made me raise my own kids to see every man underneath his color. And, by so seeing, to judge every man for himself, not for any other reason.

That ugly shout still reverberates in my head. No single word has a greater negative power, a power I chose to wield. But it turned out to be a word with the power to change me.

I like to think that we're all teachers. This man was mine though I never met him, never knew him, never spoke to him; except for that single, regrettable word. But it was he, with one look, who helped form me so I could help form my children, two of whom are about the age I was back on that fateful day.

So why, again, was I here? I'd have to say for penance. I wish that deeply hurt man were sitting here beside me. Not just so I could say I'm sorry, but to thank him for untwisting my young, unformed mind; for setting me straight about how I saw all men for the rest of my life.

It was, after all, that old man who put me on this bus to Selma.

The 103rd Floor

No high rise in America rises higher than the Willis Tower. It wasn't a badly designed building, but her Bauhaus training and temperament insisted on cleaner lines. Never mind that; she was here for another reason: The killing of Alfred Almquist, the man who'd murdered her Mikael.

How had it all come to this?

Thoughts of Mikael flashed before her as she waited what seemed like forever for the car that would take her to the 93rd floor. She remembered their cute but casual meet-up as sophomores at a lecture on structural methodologies at Umeå University in northern Sweden. He, from Askersund, a town of less than four thousand, the first in his farming family to attend college; Alexandra, an exchange student from Passaic, New Jersey; the long, heady nights of their post-graduate years, living and studying together, arguing over their design theologies, she, worshiping Gropius, he, devoted to Mies van der Rohe ... the frozen pizza and cheap rosé taken by candlelight at well past midnight ... the making of love, then being folded asleep together till dawn ... then graduation and their securing of jobs with competing architectural firms in Stockholm ... their fourth floor walk-up flat in Stockholm's *Gamla Stan*, its famed Old City ... the coming along of a son Mikael insisted on naming Axel, an anagram of Alex; and, a year later, their marriage by Mikael's father, a Lutheran minister.

There was that, all of their blissful life together. And there was the murder of Mikael.

And now there was this imposing edifice. Could she find her prey in it? What she knew of Almquist's whereabouts she had learned from his friend. She'd once seen the friend, Göran Persson, whom she hardly knew, talking with Almquist on campus, and once, later, in Stockholm. After the murder, she had put the police on Persson and he, with a misplaced sense of loyalty, told them nothing. But Alex would achieve what the police could not, even if she had to sleep with the little cretin, something which became unnecessary when he became so charmed by her that he spilled Almquist's whereabouts before her ever asking.

Alex's quarry had fled to America, a good place to lose himself in. He was working in Chicago, working in IT on one of the 110 floors of the Willis Tower. That's all Persson knew. Almquist's cell number and edress had changed. Likely his name as well. The fugitive meant to leave no trail.

Her search for his name in the building's directory had expectedly turned up nothing, and the reception desk had never heard of him. It being a Saturday, the building had emptied early so she couldn't ask anyone because there were hardly any anyones to ask. Then it hit her. The IT, of course. Information Technology.

"There must be nearly a hundred IT departments here, Miss," she was told at the information desk. "Did you mean the Willis Tower IT itself on 93?"

"I suppose," Alex said. That was as good a place as any to start. "You think anyone's there at this hour on a weekend?" It was already seven in the evening.

"Yes," was the clerk's answer. "It's pretty well automated, but they keep people on hand 24/7 because they serve the entire building."

"Thank you," said Alex, turning toward the upper bank of elevators. She realized that, if she were to get away with this, it was foolish to reveal herself to the clerk, but what else could she do?

When her elevator finally arrived it was empty. She stepped in and the doors closed. Alfred Almquist, damn him, was hidden up there in plain sight somewhere in this vast pile of steel, aluminum and glass. She had to find him. She'd declared a bounty on this repugnant monster's head and was determined to collect it herself. She took a moment to finger the new Ruger .380 nesting in her handbag. Small, but effective, its built-in laser would make certain that the man she wanted dead would be dead from a single, guided shot. Or two, or three or four. Alex knew she shouldn't be doing it this way but, damn the consequences, she'd locked herself into her decision.

She punched the button for 93.

As she rose, she began to re-think what she was doing. With Axel to raise by herself, did she have the right to do this? Better to put the authorities on Almquist. But she was no longer thinking straight, could not think straight, could not stop herself. This murderer *had* to die! And by *her* hand. Quid pro quo. She would take from him what he had taken from her. She was justified in doing so!

What's he doing right at this minute?. . . I'd kill him if he were in front of me now, but he isn't . . . He's here, this I know, I sense it . . . But he's a needle hidden in a 110-story haystack . . . Does he know I'm here? . . . How could he?

What had brought her to this irreversible pass? Her mind drifted back. She pictured her first encounter with Almquist. She and Mikael were at an art theater in Umeå, several years earlier. The man was sitting one row behind her and a seat to her left. She felt uneasy because she could sense his eyes staring at her, not the screen, throughout the film. She whispered her unease to Mikael who immediately turned and glared at the man. But, eerily, the man's eyes only slowly returned to the screen.

Moments later, Alex could feel them on her again and nudged Mikael. When the film ended, Mikael turned to Almquist, a giant of a man, a good six inches taller than him, and much broader as well.

"I don't know what you're doing," Mikael said, his jaw muscles tensed, "but you've made my friend very uncomfortable with your staring. I believe you owe her an apology." Mikael, a strong and wiry 5-9, had been a hockey defenseman throughout high school, and had been afraid of no one, with or without a hockey stick in his hand. But with his stick, he knew how to inflict harsh punishment.

The slack-jawed Almquist never said a word. He was wearing a rumpled, food-spotted black suit with a white dress shirt buttoned at the neck, and white sneakers. Expressionless, he ignored Mikael and began walking out. From his belt, sticking out from under his jacket, hung a slim leather holster apparently loaded with a slide rule, something that hadn't been seen on any campus since the blooming of the Computer Age, a quarter-century earlier. What was that about? There was something ominous about the damn thing. It looked oddly evil. Or was it just the man himself who looked both odd and evil? It wasn't just his outfit or even the four small ivory earrings looped through the top of his left ear. It was mostly his eyes, a shade of blue so pale they were almost no color at all, revealing nothing of what was behind them.

Mikael called after him again. "Hey, you, stop. I said you owe an apology to my friend!" But Almquist never turned back, his anachronistic slide rule swinging rhythmically from its holster as he slowly lumbered out.

Soon to reappear.

In the weeks and months that followed, Alexandra would see him often, always off in the distance, always staring at her, but never coming close enough to speak to her. Mikael had inquired and learned his name and who he was, a Computer Sciences major and a loner who appeared to have few if any friends. Mikael imagined him capable of shooting up a campus or a kindergarten full of five-year-olds. After repeated sightings by Alex, Mikael reported Almquist to the campus police, who said they could do nothing since he'd committed no crime. Wasn't stalking a crime? They shrugged him off.

Then, suddenly, no more staring giant. Had the police reached him? Whatever, he was gone. And good riddance.

Nearly a year passed without a sighting of the alien-looking Almquist. They now lived and worked in Stockholm's Gamla Stan, its Old City. They had more or less forgot about him; an ugly but momentary tear in the fabric of their hardworking but idyllic life— until he showed up one wintry day outside of Alexandra's building.

From her second floor office, she could see him standing stiffly across the street, looking up across from the entrance.

Alex was shocked, of course. Her first thought was an incongruous one. Did he still carry that sinister-looking slide rule? She couldn't tell because it was January and he was wearing a long black topcoat and black watch cap. Panicking for a moment, she called Mikael at his office just several blocks away. By the time he got there, Almquist was gone. Poof!

But, of course, Almquist would never be gone. This, they both believed.

He appeared two days later in Alex's underground garage as she was entering her car after work. His empty eyes were staring at her from behind a concrete post not ten feet from her, the closest he'd ever come. She locked her car doors and drove off before he could attempt to approach but she felt his cold eyes following her all the while.

Mikael, on learning of it, was incensed. He was ready to attend her twenty-four hours a day until he could resolve the matter, but Alex wouldn't have it. She wouldn't allow this strange man to disrupt —to *control*—their life like that.

But that must have been this strange man's purpose. He repeated his appearance a few days later after she'd exited a small *matvaror*—a grocery—in the Old City. But this time, for the very first time, he didn't just stare, he did approach her. And he spoke to her.

Almquist's reedy, high-pitched voice was grossly out of context with the grossness of his body, now ballooned to what must be well over three hundred pounds.

"Alexandra, please forgive me but I must tell you how I feel about you." She was too frightened to reply. "Alexandra, I have thought about you all these years and there is something I must now say to you." He hesitated, as a shy look came over his face. Alex, even in her fright, had to catch herself from feeling sorry for the man. His pitiful speech went on: "Alexandra, I love you. I know now that we were meant to be together. I sensed that the first time I saw you in that theater. Please tell me you can love me the way I love you, please,

Alexandra." His hands hung stiffly at his side as he spoke. The mono-tone speech sounded rehearsed. She thought it had been packaged for a very long time.

Alex finally found her voice. "I know your name, Alfred Almquist. I know it but I do not want to know you. You must stop this . . . this . . . *stalking* right now. Here and now, or I'll have you arrested, do you hear me?" Then, almost shouting, "Do you hear me?" With that, she walked determinedly away from the once-again slack-jawed Alfred Almquist. She looked back in case he was following her. He had not moved. His huge head was tilted far to the right, his face sagging in disappointment and his shoulders were shaking. He looked like he was crying.

That evening, after doing his best to calm Alex, the enraged Mikael stormed into the Old City police station, only to hear the usual: "We can't arrest him till he does something." But they did check their records and, while they found two Alfred Almquists liv-ing in the Stockholm environs, none remotely fitted Mikael's de-scription of him.

Wasn't this crazy man doing something? Wasn't he disrupting their life again? Mikael returned home to ponder his next move. He had to counter whatever insane intentions this man had. Never mind his size, he would bash his head in and kick his teeth out. How dare the sonofabitch!

But he didn't have to seek Almquist because Almquist appeared in the cobblestoned alley below their window the very next evening. The way he shouted Alex's name, pleading his love and begging her to come down and join him, Mikael was certain he was drunk or crazy or both. "Alexandra!" the giant shouted, "I love you. I don't care who knows it. Come down. I want to talk to you. I love you, Alexandra, I love you."

"Stay right there, Almquist," Mikael bellowed from the kitchen window he'd just slammed open. "I'll come down and you can talk to me." He looked around for a weapon, grabbed an old, black-taped hockey stick gathering dust in a closet and raced downstairs, only to find the alley empty. He called the police but they had to admit they could not find this Alfred Almquist. All the frustrated Mikael could do now was to set up his own vigil of waiting for the lovesick man to appear again.

The wait was only twenty-four hours. Mikael was ready with his hockey stick, stationing himself in his building's entry hall a dozen or so feet from the alley. It was snowing heavily, with wind-whipped snow gusting everywhere. Through the swirl, Almquist appeared like an apparition.

Mikael leaped out at him, his voice low, his words deliberate and carefully enunciated, the way he spoke when he was angriest. "You, you bastard, will now 'talk' to me and to me only." He advanced on the giant and, without another word, in his well-practiced way, two-handed the hockey stick up at him, catching him full on the side of his head, knocking his watch cap onto the snow. Blood gushed from Almquist's temple as he staggered back. But he did not fall. Mikael hit him again, with all his strength, this time full across his broad pasty face, crushing his nose, splitting his lip, drawing another gusher of blood. But, once more, the big man did not fall. Instead, a strange crooked smile broke through his newly-loosened teeth. He pulled back his topcoat to reveal the now-familiar holster hanging from his right side. As he lifted its top, Mikael could see the slide rule inside. With one swift motion, the giant withdrew it and thrust it at him in a single, seamless move, so surprisingly agile that Mikael never had a chance to parry it with his stick.

He stared at Almquist in stunned disbelief. Then he looked down slowly. What had just happened? What he saw was the end of a slide rule that had been plunged into his chest! What he could not see was the stiletto-like, seven-inch blade affixed to it, now buried in his heart. He looked up at Almquist, as if to inquire why as Almquist was still smiling his crooked smile. Mikael watched his own blood spurting through his helpless fingers, staining the snow a crimson red. Then he toppled over, dead. And with him toppled the life — the sweet, perfect life — that Alex and Mikael had been architecting for themselves since the day they first met in Umeå.

For the next three months, Alexandra had to take a leave of absence. She would not, could not work. She languished in their flat with the shades drawn all day, too bitter, too angry to cry, unable to accept the fact of Mikael's death. She drank too much wine while listening to Leonard Cohen, accompanist to the middle-of-the-night trysts of their college days. She would not answer calls, not even from her parents, and spoke to no one when she left the flat, which she did only to shop for food or, rarely, to take her Axel to the playground.

Finally, recovering enough to return to work, she began planning the revenge she felt she was owed. She would find Almquist and kill him herself. A capture and trial were too good for him. She applied herself to this singular task for the next two months, working enough only to hold on to her job. Her firm understood. Take some more time off, they said.

But the task was not an easy one. Almquist had left Stockholm, probably left the country. The police were just as stymied by his seemingly impossible disappearance. No one, in this day, can vanish so completely. They knew he'd worked in IT at a stock brokerage on the outskirts of the city, and possibly had now fled to America. But they knew almost nothing of his personal life other than what little they'd learned from Persson.

Which was all right with Alexandra. Persson had told her that Almquist was here, working in IT at the Willis Tower. That was enough. But, with his name change, his entire identity had disappeared from the data bases of every computer that sought him. A brilliant IT expert could do that. It was as if no man named Alfred Almquist ever existed. Not the Alfred Almquist Alex was after.

She could feel the car slowing as it reached the 93rd floor. When the doors opened, she staggered back and had to grab the rear rail to keep from falling.

The hulking form of Alfred Almquist stood before her, the crooked smile once more hanging on his face, the lethal slide rule still dangling at his side. She took immediate satisfaction in seeing the deep, still-red scar over his eye, the scar that Mikael must have inflicted. Dipping his head slightly to step inside, he tapped the screen of his hand-held and the car rose again.

Alex's heart now beat so furiously she could feel, even hear, the thumping of its blood in her brain. She knew instantly it was no coincidence that Almquist was there to greet her. He must have been following her movements from the moment she stepped into the Tower. She asked how he'd done so.

Again, Almquist's jarringly high, reedy monotone: "I hacked your phone, Alexandra. Locked onto its GPS app and followed you— all the way from Stockholm to Chicago, all the way up here."

The smile slowly morphed into a grin as the car opened at the Tower's 103rd floor Skydeck whose all-glass, extendable "balconies" offered tourists the "Ledge Experience." Their glass-floored view, 1300 feet up, was not for the acrophobic.

Almquist's words then softened. "Thank you, Alexandra, you've come to me at last."

A hard shiver wracked Alex. "No, Almquist, I've come *for* you," she said, her voice cracking as she withdrew her gun. Her resolve had, at least temporarily, overcome her mordant fear. If she wasn't a match for this monster, the Ruger was.

But he moved too quickly for her, folding her entire hand with the gun into his own, gently placing his other hand on the side of her face. She tapped 911 on her cell phone but he slapped it to the floor. She shivered again as he forced her into the nearest glass-enclosed balcony where he tapped his hand-held again. The balcony slowly began to slide out into the swirling storm beyond the Skydeck walls. The city lights allowed Alex to take in the sickening, vertiginous view below.

His bulk blocking her escape, he flung the Ruger to the clear glass floor where it clattered to a stop near her phone in the corner. Now her prey stepped back to admire his prey. He drew her to him. She could smell and feel his sour breath as he brought his out-sized face toward hers. His circling arms crushed her and his lips were now on hers. His tongue tried to force its way through her lips but her tightly clamped teeth barred it. Nausea was overcoming her. "Think, think!" her brain demanded. She opened her mouth and allowed his tongue to enter . . . then clamped her jaws together as hard as she could.

Almquist screamed in agony, shoving her against the outer wall. She'd bitten his tongue half off. He roared his anguish. The blood flew from his mouth, hitting both the wall and Alex. His release of her allowed her to dive for the gun but, before she could reach it, he brought his size fifteen boot down on her hand, sealing it to the floor. For a moment, everything seemed to move in slow motion. Then Almquist raised his head and let out a wolf-like howl, baying at a world that wasn't turning his way.

Recovering, spitting blood, he kicked the gun away and lifted Alex back up into his arms. Only, this time, there was no gentle touching. He unholstered his slide rule stiletto and held it to her throat. "Remove your clothes," he said, his words nearly unintelligible. "I want to see you do it."

She hesitated. He did not. His ham fist yanked her gauze sweater and silk blouse from her skirt and ran the knife up behind them. It came so close to her skin that it caught her bra. She could feel its cold steel between her breasts as her sweater, blouse and bra fell open. She could almost taste the rush of her adrenalin.

Beyond desperate, she flung her slashed clothes at his face. The move stopped him just long enough for her to duck under him and scurry out of the extended balcony. He wiped his bloody mouth with her blouse, then turned to pursue her. She had pressed the elevator button but who knew when it would open? He and his blade weren't more than a few feet from her when the door did open and she collapsed into the car.

But this time the car was not empty. She fell into the arms of two SWAT teamers who shoved her to the rear where a third immediately covered her with a flak jacket.

Almquist stepped back and surveyed the five armed men facing him. There was no expression on his face. "Drop your weapon," one demanded. He did not. "Drop it NOW, I said." The giant lunged at him. Bad move. A spate of bullets tore through his chest, neck and forehead, sending him crashing back into the already bloodied glass balcony.

Alfred Almquist was dead before he hit its floor. There was little left of his face except Mikael's scar. And his crooked smile. And his fathomless blue eyes staring upward.

An hour later at the police station, only half-composed, Alexandra asked the SWAT captain how his people happened to make their timely entrance. His answer: "Simple. We couldn't find him so we locked on you and you led us to him. Almquist wasn't the only IT genius around."

A wan smile appeared on Alexandra's face. Her first in months. It was over.

Half a Man
(For Abraham Verghase)

I met Mason Jessup in 2005. He'd been an infantryman IEDed in Fallujah a few years after the beginning of the war in Iraq. Shrapnel from the IED had sliced through the bottom of his spine, instantly making him a paraplegic who, for the rest of his life, would feel nothing from the waist down.

Mason was born in Appalachia, not twenty miles northeast of where he was now supposedly finishing his long rehabilitation at Towering Pines Hospital in Stone Break, Virginia. He arrived just before I became a resident internist at the Pines. I was taken on there after barely making it through both med school at St. George's University in Grenada and an internship at Carilion Memorial in Roanoke.

But it was Mason, as sad a package as he was, who later came to ignite my real awakening as a physician. This is his story. What he taught me motivated me to secure an additional residency at Howard University Hospital in Washington, where today, ten years later, at forty-one, I'm Howard's youngest-ever Chief of Internal Medicine.

Mason's widowed mother, Elspeth, influenced by good, store-bought whiskey administered by a passing tobacco agent, took up with the man, blithely abandoning the 14-year-old Mason and his seven-years-older, learning-disabled brother Ellis, while Mason was still in middle school. As the new head of his family of two, he had little choice but to quit school and work two, sometimes three, jobs: grocery clerk, delivery boy, 'bacco gleaner, whatever (he always looker older than his years) . . . to keep him and his brother in jeans and groceries. Luckily, their home—a two-bedroom shotgun shack—had been paid for in full by their frugal, if alcoholic, father who'd died in a Black Mountain coal mine cave-in a number of years earlier.

In his early twenties, Mason spent much of his time overseeing his hulking brother, Ellis. Ellis, always with a smile on his face, adored Mason, seeing him more as a parent than a younger sibling. He had a child's mind in a grown man's body. Still, in later years, Mason found time to run with the Hog-riding biker pack he'd formed as the Messengers of Hell, though, often as not, he divided his leisure time volunteering at the independent-living home that housed Ellis.

It wasn't until he found affordable long-term care for Ellis in nearby Johnson City that he left home to join the Army, winding up in Iraq where, within a year, he rose from being a fearless grunt to become a fearless platoon sergeant. His buddies took to calling him "Vince" because of his biker-born attitude of invincibility. A natural leader, he became the platoon's leader half a year later, when its first looey was snipered down in the suburbs of Baghdad. He swore that, once he was finished with this damn Gulf war—a war he, in his way, loved—he'd use the G.I. Bill to get himself a good education, one that would keep him out of the coal mines that had killed his old man.

When I first ran across the near-six-foot Jessup, he'd been at the Pines, like I said, for just a few months after vegetating in a VA hospital for over a year. He'd become a 140-pound shell of the 185-pound bodybuilder/biker he'd once been, and his head was not in a good place. Grim-faced, bitter and uncommunicative, he refused to do anything more than lie in bed and stare at a TV he wasn't seeing. It took me half a dozen visits before he'd allow me to roll him around the hospital grounds, then he'd open up only enough to spill the background I've just given you. Mason Jessup was no longer the hard-nosed, smooth-talking ladies' man he'd been before the shrapnel took him out. He hardly talked at all anymore.

Turned out that his paraplegia was the precursor of a far more serious problem. While in the VA facility, he'd developed an unremitting fever from a bedsore just above his buttocks. No one, including himself, paid much attention to it. Feeling no pain, he'd neglected the sore, stubbornly riding on it in his wheelchair and sitting upright on it. Soon, septic shock resulted from the sore's pus pocket release of bacteria, the beginning of rot, the resulting stench of which drove what few friends he'd made away. Eventually, the condition spread and the nasty bacteria began to eat through his buttocks, metastasizing into his pelvis where it threatened his circulatory system. As an internist—a GP, the first man you see—I'm first of all a diagnostician. I had to inform him that the immanency of blood poisoning throughout his system was placing his very life in danger, that a battery of tests and a long consultation with half the hospital's medical staff told me what I—and Mason—did not want to hear. I practiced what and how I'd tell him for half an hour before reluctantly entering his room.

Best way to go, I concluded, was straight ahead. I told him how his life was being direly threatened by the likely onset of blood poisoning; that he was now in a state of crisis and would need an immediate operation to save his life. "Say more, Doc. You think I could lose more than my legs?" He was doing his damnedest to be nonchalant, but fear had crept into this fearless man's eyes.

Though the question was expected, I've never had a tougher one asked of me as a physician. I now had to tell Mason that, after talking with a panel of the Pine's general surgeons, neurosurgeons, orthopedists, urologists, anesthesiologists and plastic surgeons, we concluded, unanimously and irrevocably, that he was a prime candidate for an extremely rare operation, a hemicorporectomy. The seven-syllable word had been as new to me as it must have been to Mason. It meant transection of the lumbar spine. It meant amputation of the entire lower half of the body below the belly button; a radical procedure first performed, unsuccessfully, in 1960, and only about four dozen times since. It meant a relentless regimen of sex hormone therapy to replace his testosterone, dietary training to avoid obesity, psychological counseling and extended physical therapy.

Mason accepted my words in eyeball-to-eyeball silence. Then, tight-lipped, he turned his gaze away and stared out the window for well over a minute, swallowing several times before slowly turning back to me, still gazing at him. The stunned look on his face morphed to one of uncontrolled rage. Directed at me? At the unfair world? At God? He looked as if he wanted to reach out and strangle me, the messenger who had just delivered the equivalent of a death sentence. Finally, incongruously smiling now, he said, practically in a whisper, "I'd rather die."

I wouldn't allow myself to back off. I had to convince him. "I'm telling you, Mason, if you don't go through with this you will die. I'll let you be for a while so you can decide, but you'd better do it fast because, if you say yes, we have to start prepping you and our people right away. I've already scheduled a staff briefing in an hour and the operation itself for tomorrow at eight a.m. You'd be first up."

I dropped an op consent form on his bed and started to leave but, before I hit the door, I heard his hoarsely delivered decision. Three words. "I'll do it." He signed the form, I took it and left. Then, seconds after the door shut itself, I—the entire floor—heard a long, despairing animal howl arise from behind it; a sound like I've never heard from another human being.

The next morning, precisely at 8:00, our team of eleven doctors, myself included as an observer, and eight OR nurses began the difficult, thirteen-hour procedure. Mason had been prepped, fully sedated and was lying face down on the operating table. Our orthopedist made his cut and sawed between Mason's upper lumbar vertebrae, after which the neurosurgeon immediately tied off the spinal cord and the nerves that emerged from it. The urologist ran the ureters to under Mason's right rib cage to an artificial bladder created from his small bowel. The general surgeon diverted his bowel and attached it to a colostomy tube placed high under his left rib cage. Then the final cut was made and the entire lower half of his body—half his bodyweight—his pelvis, genitals, buttocks, legs and feet, was separated from his upper body and lowered by two nurses into a waiting stainless steel tub below. All that was left was for the plastic surgeon to bring long anterior and posterior skin flaps from his back and his belly around to cover the bottom of what was left of poor Mason Jessup.

Mason Jessup's life was saved. But what kind of a life could it possibly be?

Not everyone survives a hemicorporectomy. Because of the possibility, still remaining, of deadly poison coursing into his system, Mason Jessup's survival odds, lower than most, were estimated at thirty percent.

But the operation went precisely as it was so carefully planned, and Mason did survive, emerging, however, in a state of deep depression that worked inexorably against his recovery. Upon seeing his lower half gone, he went into an expected state of mental shock, maintaining a stubborn silence for three whole days, finally speaking only to me and to one nurse he favored, MaryJo Brunner, who'd stayed by his bedside throughout. He saw no future for himself. His only thought—the only thing that seemed to keep him alive—was his concern for his older brother, Ellis; the thought of Ellis being alone. Ellis loved him and needed him and, in the same way, Mason loved and needed Ellis. Each, in their way, was very much alone in the world.

Months later, Mason, though still in a seriously depressed state, began to come around. But just a little. He was finally acclimating himself to the flat-bottomed leather bucket prosthesis that allowed him to remain upright on a flat surface. Still, if he'd been bitter about his paraplegia, he felt more so about being, as he now called it, "half a man." His innate intelligence could not reason away this fixed belief.

Several staff psychologists tried to reach him; each failed to elicit any kind of positive outlook on life from him. He claimed he had no life; no reason to live. Ellis, he must have sensed, would somehow be cared for, but he, Mason, who'd once been as fully independent as any man alive, could only conclude that he'd be fully dependent upon others for the rest of his life. He had never meant to be in the care of others, of anyone other than himself. At just twenty-eight, he no longer cared to live if he had to live this way. And he said so. His life, he felt, was over and he begged me, repeatedly to help him find a way to end it. I, of course, had no choice but to refuse him.

What I did find for him, however, was Elizabeth "Lizzie" Carpenter. And I didn't have to look far because Lizzie was a patient of mine. She lived in town but, born poor in the hills of eastern Kentucky "nearabouts seventy years ago," she, for all her days, had called herself "nothin' but an edicated hillbilly." She was strong-minded and as strong of body as a two-year-old heifer, but she was stricken from birth with severe hypertension. Still, she had willed herself, with hard work, to attain a BS in Physical Therapy at Bluefield College, and had quickly become the area's best independent contracting PT. Her superior ability in her field was readily acknowledged, especially by the PT staff at the Pines. She's been at her trade now for forty-two years and counting, having established her own fully equipped facility, CPT, the Carpenter Physical Therapy Clinic, twenty years earlier.

Though she'd been a comely woman who'd had many opportunities to marry, she never quite got around to it. Simply "never found the time for that nonsense." She was too busy learning and plying her unique, highly personal therapy methods, and building what she had learned into a viable business that pulled in a steady flow of clients from three surrounding counties and beyond. Hers was a destination clinic.

Lizzie, on the outside, was tough as new leather but, once you got to know her, was marshmallow-soft inside. At five foot even and 155 pounds, she was a stump of a woman, swore like a marine, looked like an upended concrete block and made you feel like one had fallen on you if you were a client who failed to measure up to the high bar she'd set for you. When the Pines' PTs couldn't get anywhere with a recalcitrant patient, they'd invariably call in Lizzie Carpenter. With Mason, she was the obvious PT choice.

And the "love affair" began. The day they met, Lizzie, with arms folded across her ample chest, sat opposite Mason in a stare-down that lasted over two minutes before either spoke.

"What's your name?" said Lizzie, at last.

"You got it on your chart," snapped Mason. "Why'd you have to ask?"

"'Cause it's the usual way to start a friendly conversation."

"What if I don't want no conversation at all? What if I don't wanna be bugged by people like you. What if I just wanna die? You got a therapy for that?"

"Look, Mason Jessup, you were a paraplegic and you thought that was the worst thing that could ever happen to you. Then you became a hemi and you thought *that* was the worst thing that could happen to you. And now you want to die?"

"What's your point?"

"What's my point, buster? Just this. Why, *knowing* more than most men what the worst things in life are, would you want the worst thing of all—to *die?*"

"Jeezus, lady, you sound like them fuckin' shrinks."

"You know something, Mason, you're right, I do. So let's can the conversation, we're both here to work."

"I don't feel like workin'."

"I don't feel like workin'," she mimicked. "Lookit, fella, I'm a PT, a physical therapist, not a psychotherapist. I don't give a good goddamn what you feel like or why you feel it. You and me is gonna stop this chit-chat and start working together to turn you back into the kind of whole human being you used to be. But I can't do it unless you're fully willing to cooperate. Ever hear that word? I've studied your case history and I know you been fighting everyone who wants to help you. Whatever, you might's well know that I don't feel half as sorry for you as you feel for yourself. You want me to give a damn about you, you better start giving a damn about yourself . . . about getting yourself whole again. But the first thing you gotta do is *want* to get whole again. Is any of this penetrating your thick skull?"

A tiny light began to show in Mason's hooded eyes. "You used that word 'whole' a coupla times just now. Maybe you didn't notice, lady, but I am half a man. Not even half a man. You got that?" But these words were said without Mason's usual conviction, without his usual belligerence.

"No, I don't 'got that' at all. A man ain't a man just 'cause he got no legs. Or no pecker. Your being a hemi don't make you less a man.

A man *is* what a man *does*. Now, are you gonna do or are you not gonna do? I ain't got a lot of time to waste with a lousy attitude such as yours."

The light went out of Mason's eyes. "With all due respect, ma'am, go to fuckin' hell," he said, softly, slumping as he turned his face and spun his body away.

Lizzie got up and started to leave. But she stopped at the door and turned back to him. "You were a body builder, weren't you?"

"Yeah, what of it?" This was said through gritted teeth.

"What if I told you that you could become one again?"

"Hah! An old lady's gonna turn me into a body builder." Again, there was little conviction in his voice.

"You think I'm shittin' you, Mason?"

Mason paused. Maybe to allow images of the weight lifter he'd once been to seep into his addled mind. "You could make that happen?" he said. He'd turned and was looking straight at Lizzie when he said this.

"*You* could make that happen," Lizzie replied. She knew she had him now.

"And just how the fuck would I go about doin' that?"

"I told you: by working your ass off at my place, just down the road. Lemme know what you decide," she said, over her shoulder as she left. She knew Mason wanted to talk some more, but now he'd have to do it at "my place."

Mason was quiet for a while. "Maybe I'll think about it," he said to the now-empty room.

Three days later, as Lizzie was working with a hip-replacement client at her clinic, her assistant, Violet Thomson, a tall, town girl, strongly built and passing pretty, pulled her aside. "There's a Mason Jessup on the line, Lizzie. Wants to make an appointment, but only with you. Can you handle him?"

Good question, Lizzie mused to herself. "Set him up for tomorrow morning at nine. I don't want him cooling off."

Next morning, Mason, as he requested, was delivered to the clinic. He made Lizzie no promises. "I'll try," was about all she could get out of him. So it started slow. And stayed that way for the better part of three months. Partly because of Mason's awkwardness in acclimating himself to the PT equipment and partly because of his self-consciousness, but mostly because of his native intractability. He had no real conviction. He couldn't see much point in it. He'd show up irregularly and do his exercises half-heartedly. But he never gave up altogether because, with all his complaining, giving up was not really a part of Mason Jessup. Or never used to be a part of him.

Lizzie did all she could think of doing. But, while it wasn't her way to feel discouraged like Mason, she did feel discouraged. She was almost as ready as he to throw in the towel, and he seemed very ready. Until, one day, Violet brought her a picture she'd taken of Mason doing his "half-assed stretches," as Lizzie called them. Violet had photo-shopped the picture by putting Mason's head on the body Arnold Schwarzenegger had in his Mr. Universe days. The new Mason/Arnold looked ludicrous. But Violet's snap of Mason had caught him in a rare smile and the total effect was kind of charming in an odd way. Lizzie, distracted over her clipboard when Violet showed her the doctored picture, gave her permission to show it to Mason.

His first reaction, sitting in his wheelchair, was to go crimson in the face. "Dammit, girl, you gotta a lotta fuckin' nerve makin' fun of me that way!" he said, as he ripped the photo in half. But he looked like he wanted to eat his words when he saw the downcast look on Violet's face as she heard his words.

"Mason, I am so sorry. You're right, that was a stupid thing to do. But I sure didn't mean you no harm. I only did it to get you to laugh a little. I'm sorry, I really am, Mason." She started to cry and ran out of the room. For once, Lizzie, standing nearby and watching this scene unfold, was too dumbfounded to say a single word. Why had she let that little filly do a stupid thing like that?

Mason stared at the two pieces of the photo lying next to him. He picked them up, held them together and stared at them some more. Then he slumped and turned from Lizzie. She could see that he too was wracked with silent sobbing. He was doing his best to hold back his tears while hiding his face from hers. She left him to be on his own and went straight to her tiny office. She'd seen her clients break down like this before. Often it was the beginning of something good.

But she had all she could do—tough old "Lizzie Borden," as her staff sometimes lovingly called her—to keep from bawling herself. Dammit, I ought to fire that girl, she said to herself, even while blaming herself as the one who'd let Violet show him the stupid photo.

A half hour later she heard a knock on her door. Probably Violet wanting to apologize. But it was Mason, who had wheeled himself over. He had a strange, determined look about him, one that Lizzie had never before seen. "I'm ready to work," he said.

"Huh?" she said.

He repeated his startling words.

The new workouts started brutally, only to get tougher as they progressed. But now, for the first time, the progress was rapid. Mason's lifts, curls and reverse curls were carrying more and more weight as the days went by. There was no bending because there was nothing to bend, no toes to bend to, so he could do little more than turn his body, arms outstretched, as far in each direction as he could while his base was firmly planted in his bucket, locked into a fixed, socketed base designed by Lizzie. What else did he have to work with but his arms?

Soon, he was doing the same, but, this time, holding increasingly heavier weights. In doing pushups, he began by simply raising his body vertically, as far up as his arms would let him, meaning that he was lifting only his seventy-pound body weight, ten reps per set. Then Lizzie designed a leather contraption that fit over his shoulders. It allowed him to bear weights on them so he could lift increasingly more poundage. He wore this device again when doing pull-ups on an overhead bar. And bought his own weights and had a removable pull-up bar installed in a door opening at home so he could work out there as well. He hadn't worked out this hard in his old body-building days, but had more reason to do so now. For the first time since the operation, he was sweating like a fat man in a sauna.

With his new can-do attitude, Mason now virtually haunted Lizzie's place five, sometimes six days a week, spurning her well-intended advice to rest a day between workouts. Once he got the hang of things, he trained, as if possessed, relentlessly. At the end of a year he looked a lot more like the old Schwarzenegger than the listless "half a man" he'd been. With his reappearing abs, pecs, biceps, triceps and lats—what there was of him looked even better than in his army days. But then, why not? What else did he have to work with? By now he was feeling good enough about himself to look in a mirror and joke that "I look like a suitcase with arms." He also liked to boast about his "four-pack."

It was about then that I became interested in the progress the military had been making with exoskeletons. Originally designed to enable combat soldiers to do heavy lifting, exoskeletons were now being developed privately to replace lost limbs. I informed Mason that, in the near future, it might be possible for him to employ exoskeleton legs, making him whole again. And tall again. No longer, in his coinage, half a man.

It was also about then that Lizzie Carpenter was hit with her first, not entirely unexpected, heart attack, fortunately a mild one. Which is why, at her milestone seventy-fifth birthday party, she shocked no one by informing us of her impending retirement. But she did shock us all by announcing that the new name for her venerated clinic would henceforth be Carpenter-Jessup Physical Therapy, Incorporated.

Mason had discovered an entrepreneurial gene within, recognized first by Lizzie who decided to make him a junior partner. He had both the smarts and the deep desire to run such a clinic, and what better clinic to run than the one that had saved his life. He was a natural, his inventive mind virtually spitting out ideas for improved equipment, for add-on areas offering aerobics and yoga and Pilates, for expansion to, maybe, Johnson City. He even talked of franchising.

He was everywhere, the half of him, running around in his wheel-chair which, no longer mechanized, was a low racing model. He'd first used a crude plywood board with spinner luggage wheels, then a custom-made snowboard with wheels he could remove so he could also slide—even slalom—recklessly down Black Mountain in winter. These varied modes of transportation became a common sight that few any longer seemed to notice.

The clinic thrived and, six months later, Lizzie made her full retirement official. During her farewell party at the clinic, Mason noted that he'd now have a "not-so-silent partner." His gooey speech included remarks about how Lizzie had become more his mother than his real mother. Tears flowed down every cheek, including mine. It ended it with a heartfelt, "Thank you, Mom."

But Lizzie's face, when she wasn't wiping away her own tears, wore a troubled look. Unless she was barking orders, she wasn't much of a speaker. But she was able to tell us that she was searching for a word stuck to the tip of her tongue. A name. Everything stopped as she rushed to her files to pull out Mason's old client folder. Riffling through the many pages of his history, looking for the account of his tour in Iraq, she found what she was looking for. She rushed back to the room and to Mason who, like everyone else, was still standing open-mouthed at her sudden disappearance.

She stuck out her hand to shake his and, with her two hands locked in his, all she said was, looking straight at him, "And I thank you, Vince."

No one knew, until she explained it later, what or who she was referring to. But Mason did.

The invincible Mason Jessup. No longer half a man.

Atop K'aala

"The Pacific is a very large body of water. How did you manage to find this particular dot on the map?" said Einar Rasmussen. A hulking, bearded man, nearly two meters in height, he was sitting slumped in a cross-legged position on a rattan cushion. His slow way of speaking failed to disguise his agitation.

"You mentioned Candle Island in the account of your final circumnavigation in 1972," I replied. "You indicated it was an important find, yet you wrote almost nothing about it; a paragraph or two at most. You may agree that your treatment of it was rather abrupt."

"You observe well, Herr Solheim. I did not reveal the island's whereabouts. In truth, I meant to mislead my reader so that I might return, as I did, to spend the rest of my life here in study, meditation —in peace. Undisturbed, I might add, by a maker of films who *would* reveal my whereabouts."

I shrugged off Rasmussen's last comment. "You were not easy to find, sir. I did so mainly by deduction, then by relying extensively on technology. But, in the end, I had to fall back upon my own instincts. Where, I asked myself, would I have gone from the last place you named before the world swallowed you up? Are you aware that the world still believes you to be dead?"

"Let them," he shrugged. "Say more about these confounding instincts of yours."

"Herr Rasmussen, Here's *my* truth. I have spent the last two months visiting no fewer than twenty-two of the Pacific's most remote islands to locate you. But I found your Candle Island less by instinct than by sheer good fortune. I stumbled upon you."

My honesty brought an unexpected smile to his deeply creased and jaundiced seventy-eight-year-old face, impressively framed by a full head of yellowed white hair that fell to his wide shoulders. Einar Rasmussen had been honored many decades earlier as a world-famous explorer. He was made a Knight of the Order of King Haaken, Norway's highest civilian award, given for meritorious service. He even had an island named for him off the west coast of Australia. But he never bothered to show up for the awarding of his knighthood because, true Viking that he was, he was too busy sailing the high seas in his Lady Solveig, named for his late wife who died in those same south seas of malaria.

Rassmussen stared at me for the longest time, as if to decide whether to kick me off his tiny island or allow me to remain. Shaking his head (in regret?) he picked up a wood clacker sitting on the table next to him and rattled it noisily. A young man, whose name, I was to learn, was Tam Tam, came trotting through the low door of the thatched hut. He wore only a multi-colored loincloth. Rasmussen gave him an order in a native language laced with Norwegian. Tam Tam returned minutes later with a pitcher of a warm, bittersweet beverage that turned out to be slightly alcoholic and oddly delicious.

There was no toasting of my arrival. We sipped our drinks as Rasmussen continued to eye me in silence. I would love to have known what was going through his cautious mind. This famous explorer has been unheard from since the publication of his sui generis memoir thirty-four years earlier, written before but published shortly after his disappearance. Reading it all these years later, something in it told me that he was not only alive but must have returned to that briefly mentioned island of his. Wanting to know if my quirky instincts were correct, I had to find him. The world would welcome the story my cameras would tell.

"You said you wish to do a film, Herr Solheim, a documentary about my life on Candle Island. I'll admit I'm impressed with the tenacity that got you here. And your being a fellow Norseman sits well with me. The fact is, I meant to write of this place myself but, failing to do so all these many years, my ambition began to fade, as ambition will in a clime like this. Also, as you can readily see, I have not been well for many years, and do not believe I have long to live. So I will make a bargain with you. You may tell my story. But, for reasons of my own, you will not release it to the public until I have died. Have I your word on that?" he said, offering me his gnarled, out-sized hand.

"You have my word," I replied, without hesitation. Judging by the firmness of his handshake, the world might have a long time to wait for my doc. Rasmussen, in a better mood now, invited me stay with him in adjoining quarters during the filming, but that I had one week to complete it and would then have to leave. This was not a man who enjoyed the company of others.

The next morning I set up two Canon XF200 HD camcorders under a pair of low, spreading palms in front of Rasmussen's hut. One was fixed, looking over my shoulder at him, the other, mounted behind his shoulder looking at me. The interview was shot entirely in natural light. The film is still in the editing bay but I've tran-scribed Rasmussen's narrative here, uncut. Of the hundreds of inter-views I have recorded, this was the strangest by far.

After my journey of nearly twenty-two thousand nautical miles I could think of nothing but returning to Candle Is-land. To my knowledge, no white man had ever set foot there before me. A certain something about it had intrigued me. Not simply its indigenous people—a tribe of six hundred small, friendly-seeming, dark-skinned pygmies—but some-thing else; a presence unknown to me. A mysterious, per-ceived presence calling me back.

I called the place Candle Island because of its long nar-row shape and tapered northern end at which rises a moun-tain named after their first king, K'aala, perhaps two thou-sand meters high. The Candlari believe that their god, Ko-ganilui—He Who Lives in the Cave—resides up there, but they won't climb K'aala for fear that they will be confronted by this god and be punished with death for the way they live. The Candlari, I should inform you, are polyamorous, and were once known to be cannibalistic.

To appease Koganilui, they sacrifice one of their youths each year, alternating between male and female; they burn them alive on a huge bonfire at a respectable distance from the foot of K'aala. I've urged them to cease their barbarous practices, but who am I, after all, to stop them? Yet for reasons unknown to me, they see me as something of a demigod.

So, for my own protection, I have not discouraged this belief. But neither do I ever forget that this is their land, not mine—their laws, not mine.

I'd felt from the beginning that the mystery of my attraction to this idyllic island could be solved only by discovering what lies atop K'aala. To reach its lofty peak I'd need to trek through jungle containing who knows what sort of wild beasts, then climb almost unscalable crags and boulders. And though I'm an atheist through and through, and skeptical to begin with, even I had misgivings as to what I'd find up there. But finally, my curiosity overcame my concerns, and so I planned the journey.

Unfortunately, nothing I could say or offer would convince even one man from the island's three villages to accompany me, so great was their fear of Koganilui. Thus I was obliged to begin the trek alone; twenty kilometers through near-impenetrable virgin jungle, then the scaling of the mountain itself, well over a kilometer high and mostly straight up. The first fifteen K were easy but as the foothills began to rise, the luxuriant growth became thicker, the trees higher, the occasional marshes deeper and less passable. As I approached the last K the next day, the crowns of the trees were so interwoven that, though it was only mid-afternoon, it seemed as if I were in a deep twilight. Tired and aching, my machete arm nearly falling off, I was forced to camp there for the night.

After dark I was assaulted by screeches and howls and

roars I'd never heard at the other end of the island. At one point I stared at a pair of bright yellow eyes staring back at me. Fond of hunting, I wasn't concerned because I was aiming between them with a .416 Rigsby big-game rifle with shells as long as a cigarette. The eyes belonged to a ferocious-looking wild boar that simply trotted away when I let off a shot in the air. What point in killing it when what I was hunting was not necessarily of this earth?

Rising the following morning later than I'd meant to, I reached the mountain's foot at eleven o'clock and began my climb, having found it necessary to leave much of my gear behind. The halfway point, over half a K above me, took nearly two more hours to negotiate. Nearly exhausted, I rested for an hour, had some lunch and continued. While the rest renewed me and I was acclimated to the climb by now, I had to admit that manning the tiller of a forty-six-foot ocean-going sloop was much more to my liking than climbing vertical mountains. But the going leveled off a bit and became easier as I passed the tree line and neared the summit.

It was true twilight when I hauled myself over the last stubborn outcrop of granite, only to find not a summit but a shelf of sorts, about forty meters across, ending at a sharply rising wall at the foot of which was an opening that suggested a cave within. The home of He Who Lives in the Cave?

I was at last able to stand upright on solid flat ground for the first time since that morning. Looking to the west I watched the sun sink, like a foundering ship, into the Pacific It was a sunset so radiantly magnificent, with its twisted strata of red, pink and blue clouds it nearly made me weep.

My plan was to spend the night up there then explore the cave, if there was one, the next morning, let the gods be damned. Pitching my tent, I built a small fire, fried up some more of the pig meat, yams and goat cheese the Candlari had offered me for my climb. Then I fell, completely spent, into one of the deepest sleeps of my life, notwithstanding my anxiety over what might lie ahead.

I was awakened at half past nine by the sun beating upon my face. I'd slept twelve dreamless hours. Refreshed and ready for whatever might come next, I breakfasted on bacon, powdered eggs and Candlari banana bread.

Concentrating my gaze on the depression in the cliff forty meters opposite me, I could now readily see that it was not a depression but indeed the entrance to a cave. This I approached with trepidation. "Hallo!" I hollered, several steps into the imposing tunnel that lay behind it, hoping an echo might suggest its depth. But I heard no answering reply. Was I being too tentative? I strode on briskly, pretending I wasn't concerned with what I might find. Stopping fifty meters in, I spied a freshet of water tumbling down the wall to my right. One taste led me to gulp down almost a litre of it. Cold water had never refreshed me so fully.

To further echo-test my progress, I hollered another hallo and banged my canteen against the rock wall, each time hearing deep, hollow reverberations, suggesting a long path ahead, a path that was slightly rising. The light of my torch told me the tunnel's cross-section was gaining size. I continued on for at least twenty more minutes, a near kilometer by my estimate, before turning a corner to find a large room of perhaps ten meters square and two meters high. Unexpectedly, it was lit by a soft glow whose source I could not determine, especially since it appeared to have no openings to the outside.

At the room's opposite end was a naturally formed platform of a few square meters, rising below a small alcove whose opening was a reflection of the cave's entrance. Drawn to it, I mounted the platform and peered into the alcove. As I did this a beautiful and unearthly music rose to my ears, similar to the compelling minor key progressions of a loving-kindness metta chant.

In the low light of the alcove I could see nothing but vertical lines of shimmering light, much like those that rise from an asphalted road on a hot summer day. That was all it took to tell me that there was someone . . . something? . . . in this cave with me. Something, I intuited, that belonged here, even as it struck me that perhaps I did not. What was its true form? A frisson of foreboding caused in me an involuntarily shudder, and I could distinctly hear the beat of my now-racing heart. This, I convinced myself, must be the presence I sought, one I knew I must confront. If it didn't speak to me, I must speak to it.

I waited a while but all I could hear was the continuing music. My mind raced to think of an appropriate question, but all I could utter was, "Whoever or whatever you are, please reveal yourself." In response, a low rumbling came from the tunnel that continued deeper into the cave, a sound not unlike the distant rumbling of an earthquake. This all seemed beyond reality. Wait! Could it be that some false Oz-like wizard was behind this mystery—a Candlari shaman perhaps?

Screwing up my courage, I turned my plea into a terse command: "Reveal yourself!" But no answer was forthcoming so I began to frame another question. Before I could finish, a voice arose from the core of wavering lines, now under-lit by an eerie blue light. The voice was itself hollow and resonant, as if coming from within the tunnel's bowels. And, to my great surprise, its words were clearly spoken in our Norwegian language: *"Hvorfor er du høre?"* "Why are you here?" Apparently this presence was capable of speaking any language directed at it.

The question, in spite of its wizardly quaver, was stated in an unthreatening manner, more conversational than divine, thus setting me somewhat at ease. "I have come here," I replied, without hesitation, "because I have long believed a mysterious presence has existed on this island, drawing me here. Now, it seems, I am correct."

"Are you now?" said the voice. "How do you know that? Some things are unknowable . . . cannot be known by the likes of man."

Was the voice mocking me? It suggested no image of the face that might be behind it, nor did its odd timbre reveal whether it was feminine or masculine. I asked it, "How much of the truth about this island will you reveal to me?"

"How capable are you of accepting the truth?" it replied, with equanimity.

"How can I accept your truth until you *have* revealed it?" said I.

"What makes you a worthy recipient of my truth?"

"What?!" I said to myself. Then, to the voice: "Are you going to keep answering my questions with your questions?"

"A question well asked, Einar Rassmussen," said the voice. "But I must ask you one last question. If you are willing to—"

"Who are you?" I interrupted. This god, this personage, whatever it was, knew my name. What else did it know about me? I was impatient and at my wit's end. "What are you? Are you Koganilui, god of the Candlari people? Or are you something more? Do you claim to be the one *true* God?"

I heard the rumbling deeper in the cave again. There was a hesitation, caused, I surmised, by the impatient lowering of the eyes behind the voice. "I repeat," it said, at last, "if you are willing to first hear my question, then answer it, I will then reveal what you wish to know."

Should I give in? Will this damnable presence, like some high Buddhist priest, ask the unanswerable? Some koan, say? Identify, say, the sound of one hand clapping? Or a tree falling in the forest? What was this nonsense? But how could I get an answer without offering one? "Ask your question," I said.

"I have already asked it. Why are you here?"

I was, it must be obvious to this quizzical presence, exasperated. "And I," said I, "have already answered it. It is because a presence . . . perhaps yours . . . drew me here."

"You are correct, Herr Rasmussen. But why do you suppose it was you, of all people?" said the voice, becoming now more serious and forceful. "Do you have any idea why you alone, of all the people on earth, were chosen?"

"I alone? No, I did not know that. And chosen for what? You are confusing me. How could I know that? But wait, you said you would ask only one question and now you have asked several. I insist that you reveal yourself!"

The presence began to laugh a deep masculine laugh that suddenly and magically morphed into a clear, tinkling feminine laugh. What was going on here? And then I realized that something about the laugh was oddly familiar. Before I could plumb my mind further for its provenance, the blue light from which it emanated wove itself into the holographic image of a human figure, not half a meter high, shrouded in a long white robe. I was, of course, stunned beyond belief. My poor eyesight made it necessary to drop to my knees for a closer look. Though this spectral person had its hands over its mouth—I suppose to hold back more laughter—I knew suddenly what . . . *who* . . . I was looking at.

I was face to face with my beloved Solveig!

My heart leaped. "Solveig," I cried, "is that you?"

"Yes, my Einar. And no," she replied. "Yes, it is I, but in soul, not in body." She smiled her Solveig smile. The same crookedly beautiful smile that captured and captivated me all those many years ago.

"You asked why I was here," I said, "but first I must ask why are *you* here?"

"So many questions, my love. Please forgive me for teasing you that way. I was so overjoyed at your finding me that I wanted to extend this precious moment. But you looked so comically confused I could not take it further. To answer your questions, asked *and* unasked, this mountaintop is where I came to reside—to be resurrected—after I was taken. Why here, I cannot explain. I never believed I could reach back for you but somehow I was able to, or allowed to, if only to provide you with a sense of where I was.

"I've always felt your presence," I said. "It's what drew

me here. Now I know that." Solveig then demanded my version of what she had always known: the story of, my feelings about, my lonely life lived without her. I spent the next two hours telling her, and expressing my unbounded joy at finding her again. Finally, I got around to asking about, ". . . this business of Koganilui—are you one and the same?"

"Yes," she admitted, a sheepish grin coming over her comely face. "Did you not think it strange that Koganilui arrived here shortly after you did?"

That coincidence I hadn't recognized. "But why did you create him?

"I do have limited powers," replied Solveig. "Enough to perform a few minor feats. You knew the Candlari were once a cannibalistic people. To allay anything happening to you in case they acted again that way, I conjured such as a typhoon out of a cloudless sky, or the rumbling of an earthquake from this cave atop K'aala. They eventually came to associate these happenings with their undue behavior, especially if it involved threatening you. They did not believe it was you who could create such miracles or fearsome happenings but they would take no chances, choosing, rather, to see you as a demigod—and Koganilui as their real god. It was they, not me, who created Koganilui out of fear of retribution. I simply confirmed their belief. Which proved that man can create a god as surely as God has created man."

"So it was you who have looked after me all these years."

"Just as you always looked after me, Einar—and looked *for* me."

"Had I known you were here," I replied, "I'd have come to you much sooner."

Again, I was greeted by Solveig's tinkling laughter.

As Rasmussen's plaintive tale came to an end, his head fell to his chest. He appeared as weary as he must have felt at the top of his

K'aala climb. I could only stare in amazement at him and at what I had just been told.

Determined as I was to retrace his footsteps, I would first have to return, properly equipped, to do so. My simple face-to-face interview wanted to be followed up by my own journey to the top of K'aala to see and film what was actually up there. But something was gnawing at me. It was the man's insistence that he wouldn't let me release my doc till he was gone. What was that all about? I finally asked him, point-blank.

He pondered the question a short minute. "Because, young man, anyone hearing my story would mock me in total disbelief. They might think, for example, that the water I discovered and drank in the cave was some sort of hallucinant; that I am a total fraud, a mere constructor of stories. Do even you believe what I've told you?"

"Yes, I do," I replied, uncertain if I did or did not. And less certain that Rasmussen believed my answer.

"Will anyone else believe me? Or believe *you* after you've shown your film?"

"I hadn't thought about that, sir. But it should not matter if no one believes you. Or me. I will document what happened. That is what I do. You and I may be seen to lie but my cameras and my mics do not. They will see and hear the truth and reveal it."

"They will see and hear what they see and hear," snapped Rasmussen, as he rose from his chair. "Others will interpret it as they will. I know what I saw and heard!" This last was said with such vehemence that the old man fell into a rasping cough he could not quell for fully a minute.

When it subsided I asked my few questions remaining. "Did you, sir, continue to visit the cave?"

"I did. But Solveig recognized my failing health and suggested I bring her to my home below. Which I did. She is with us here as I speak."

An eerie feeling came over me. I thought it impolite to look around so I said, "If you don't mind my asking, Herr Rasmussen, where, specifically, is 'here'?"

The old man, smiling half a smile, took my arm and guided me into the hut behind us. While looking at me to see my reaction, he pointed to a shelf at his right. The only object on it was an urn painted in colors that, I was told later, by Tam Tam, were those Rasmussen saw in the sunset that first evening atop K'aala.

This last gesture was made with a weary finality that told me our conversation—and my five-day visit—was at an end. I spent the rest of the day packing up my equipment. Next morning, after offering my heartfelt thanks and goodbyes, I left on the chartered sailing craft that had brought me to this remarkable isle.

Two months later, my financing in place, I returned to the island with a small film crew. I was deeply saddened to learn from Tam Tam that Einar Rasmussen died shortly after I had left, and was cremated, at his own instructions, on a funeral pyre three days later, as was the island's custom. Every man, woman and child of Candle Island was present to honor and celebrate the life of their beloved demigod.

"What became of his wife's urn?" I asked.

"He wanted it placed on his pyre with him," answered Tam Tam. Within two days, after an unbelievably arduous trek, my crew and I were at the cave's entrance. We examined it fully, of course filming along the way. We discovered the freshet of water, the large room further in and the alcove. But there was no rumbling, no hollow voice, no wavering blue light.

I made my film, but what I sought, hoping to reveal it at its climax, I never did discover.

So what really did happen—atop K'aala?

I Want to Tell You I Love You

My name is Lionel Wasserman. You may have heard of me. Maybe not. I'm seventy-one years old. I live on a tad more than social security in a rent-controlled efficiency that almost overlooks the Venice boardwalk. I've been in my place now for thirty-two years. It's got all I need: a bed, a desk, a stove, a bathroom. And my portable keyboard, a reliable old Roland F20. What I do here is—don't laugh—I write songs.

Been writing songs all my life. Mostly ballads. You don't hear them much anymore—I mean ballads, not my songs. Well, you don't hear my songs at all anymore. *Edna, Please Don't Leave Me.* Never heard of it, right? How about *Lonely Moon Over Philadelphia*? Or *Still Waiting for You at the Bus Stop*? Yeah, they're love songs, songs about broken love, unrequited love, love that never happened or if it did happen it ain't happening anymore. If you could read the memoir I almost got published, you'd understand why I write what I write.

Those songs? Though they didn't do too well, I did get them published. It was through a music agent, a friend of mine. Well, an acquaintance, Phil Weinstein, who had an office on Ventura up in the Valley. He worked alone back then except he had a secretary he was always screaming at, who also happened to be his wife, Edythe, spelled the fancy way with a Y in the middle and an E on the end. But that is neither here nor there. Edythe, who always called me "Wasserman," was a real looker and I kind of had a thing for her. I would have said something to her about how I felt, but, you know, she was married. Which is also neither here nor there because all of what I'm telling you happened a long while back.

Anyhow, I just wrote another song, good enough to make me think I have a real chance to sell it. But I don't have an agent anymore and I know that these days you can't get near a music house without one. Which is why I took a shot at knocking on Phil Weinstein's door again just a few weeks ago. Only he's not Phil Weinstein anymore, he's Phillip Winston. And he's not in the Valley anymore but on, pardon me, Camden Drive in Beverly Hills. Edythe's not with him anymore either, just this empty head up front with a suspiciously large bust. I identify myself and my purpose and Phil comes out to see me—after making me cool my heels in his outer lobby for maybe an hour. He invites me back to his corner office that practically needs a golf cart to get you there, which tells me . . . screams at me . . . that he's doing better these days.

So he offers me a cigar. I decline, asking if maybe he has a joint instead. We laugh. Me, sincerely. Then I see his eyes pleading with me to state my purpose, he's got better things to attend to. Okay, I tell him about my song and he asks me to play it on his piano the size of my apartment. I remind him I'm not much of a singer, I'm a composer of songs, then I tap out the notes while I half sing, half speak the lyrics.

He sits there when I'm done, swivels his leather chair away from me, ponders for a minute, takes a huge drag on his Churchill, exhales a few rings, swivels back and says, "You know something, Lionel, that is a lovely song. If you'd come to me just sixty years ago, when I was nine, I'd have known just what to do with it. I still do."

He's trying to be funny, I know, but I'm not laughing.

He continues to look at me, picks a shred of his cigar off his teeth with the manicured nail of his little finger, inspects what he finds, then says. "You got any hip hop or something? Some crossover C&W maybe. I'm doing a lot of Thrash and Christian/Reggae these days, you got anything like that?"

Fucking smartass. "Yeah, well, no, Phil, I don't have any of that," I say.

"Just what do you got?" he replies. Phil once actually spoke good English. Now he sounds like the "artists" he represents.

"I just gave you what I 'got,' Phil. A song. A good song. You don't like it, just say so, I won't trouble you anymore."

"I don't like it, Lionel. Goodbye."

Harsh!

Anyhow, the other day I find a corner on the walk a block south of Muscle Beach, and I start playing a few of my better oldies on my portable keyboard, trying to pick up a little change, while my pal Eddie "Highpockets" Rollins riffs along on his sax behind me. Eddie's a good guy. Once played with Dizzy and Charlie Mingus. Now he's a drifter living in his orange and yellow Vanagon on the beach. He still blows a pretty good tune when he's not lost in a cloud of his own making. Meanwhile, I'm hoping someone in the crowd steps out, drops a double sawbuck in my sombrero and says something like, "Say, fella, that was swell. We may have an opening for you at the Orpheum." Yeah, yeah, I suppose my daydreams are fifty years old like my music, because there's no crowd for someone to step out of, except out steps this tall, wiry guy I've seen who does a three-card monte thing off of a traveling TV table. Tall Wiry puts his face close to mine and tells me this corner is his and I better get the fuck off it. This is very discouraging to me.

So I pack up my keys and leave and, just as I'm turning the corner for home, thinking about that can of Campbell's Beef and Barley soup I've been saving for lunch, I see this sort of down-at-the-heels but really fine-looking woman, slim, smooth-skinned with a thick, silvery white braid hanging down her back. She's maybe in her sixties and she's got a card table set up against the sea wall, selling sketches of the boardwalk regulars. I mean really terrific india ink drawings almost like they were photographs. And damn if one of them isn't of me.

I have to stop and ask this really fine looking woman how she came to draw me. She explains that she's seen me before, playing my songs on the walk, liked my face, didn't want to interrupt me and just decided to draw my picture, and is it okay? I say sure, be my guest, maybe you'll make me famous. But all the while we're talking she is smiling a smile I would have to call a knowing smile. So I finally have to ask, "Why are you smiling?"

"Don't you know me, Wasserman? I'm Edythe!"

"Oh, Jeezuz!" I blurt. "Edythe! With a Y in the middle and an E on the end. Phil's wife. Edythe Weinstein, right? "

"Wrong. Edythe Weinstein Templeman Abernathy Schwartz. Phil was three husbands ago."

"But you just said four names. What's with the Schwartz?"

"That's the name I was born with. And will die with. I dumped them all, the bastards, but we still talk. Barely. I don't burn bridges. How you doing, Wasserman?

"Me? I'm getting by. How you doing?"

"How well *can* I be doing? You got eyes?"

I said, "I got eyes for *you*, Edythe," not knowing why I said that because I don't usually say things like that. But, having said it, I kept on in the same vein. "I always did. Man, you look great." She blinks at me like she doesn't hear me. I hope I didn't upset her. So I change the subject. "You still keep in touch with old Phil?"

"I told you we still talk."

"Well, you know something? Major coincidence. I took myself to see the man not two weeks ago. By bus with *two* transfers!" I tell her the whole story. And add: "Anyways, it made me think about you, Edythe. I was kind of disappointed you weren't still out front."

"C'mon, Wasserman," says Edythe, "that was then, now is now. You said you had a new song. You always had a new song. And most were good, I know. Phil never knew squat about good songs, just about which passing bandwagon to hitch his miserable behind to. His timing was always better than his taste. Now, can I hear your new song?"

"What, now? Here?"

"Yeah, Wasserman. Now. And here."

"But Eddie, my sax guy, split and—"

"Now. And here."

"A capella?"

"Yeah. No. Set up your keyboard and play it *and* sing it."

How can you argue with a face like that? I set up my board and get ready to sing my song. Just for Edythe. It's called *I Want to Tell You I Love You.* "You really wanna hear it, Edythe?"

"Yes, Lionel, I really want to hear it."

Now it's Lionel. Just when I'm thinking she's never going to stop calling me Wasserman.

What the hell, I sing it:

I Want to Tell You I Love You

VERSE #1:
I want to tell you I love you,
I've loved you for such a long time.
I want to tell you I want you,
I want . . . to put it . . . to rhyme.

CHORUS:
The words won't come, I'll think of some,
I think, in fact, of many.
They enter my mind, then I leave most behind,
And suddenly I can't think of any.
Except to say I . . . love . . . you.

BRIDGE:
When I'm near you I stumble,
I don't know what to say.
I want to tell you I want you,
But I just . . . can't find . . . a way.

VERSE #2:
I want to tell you I love you,
I've loved you since I was three.
I want to tell you but I'm afraid
That you . . . will laugh . . . at me.

CHORUS:
Oh, the words won't come, I'll think of some,
I think, in fact, of many.
They enter my mind, then I leave most behind,
And suddenly I can't think of any . . .
Except to say I . . . love . . . you.
I love you.
I love you.

So I'm finished. I even take a deep bow, dusting the ground with my Dodgers cap. Edythe stands there on the Boardwalk. Does she think it's just another of my corny tunes? Nobody's around us. It's just her and me. Her hands are placed, one on top of the other on her chest and her head is cocked at about twenty degrees. And she's crying. She's crying. I grab my cowboy handkerchief from around my neck and wipe the tear rolling down her still smooth cheek.

She straightens up and says, her sweet voice cracking a little, "Who did you write that song for, Lionel?"

And then it hits me, the truth of it. With full force. Well, the truth I'm feeling right now. I'm looking at the ground when I say it, and she has to ask me to repeat it because I say it so softly the first time.

"I . . . I guess I wrote it for you, Edythe."

Another tear rolls down her cheek. "You really do have eyes for me, don't you, Lionel. You just said it. So why didn't you say it way back when?"

"Aw, Edythe, you know why. I wanted to but, you know, you were married."

"Yes, Lionel, I was married," she says, her head bobbing in a manner that suggests she's regretting her past. All of it.

"What's wrong, Edythe?"

"Nothing," she says. Then she says, "You live around here?"

"Yeah," I say, "just around the corner."

"Show me," she says.

And I show her.

The Saving of St. Vince

Now that I'm retiring from the Plain Dealer with a local Pulitzer after a "stellar" career (the cake says so), I can say, since you asked, that the most important piece I ever wrote—at least, most important to me—was, oddly, the very first I ever wrote. But it wasn't for the P.D. The first time I saw my Joe Barnett byline in print was in one of the early Cleveland Magazine issues back in the mid-seventies.

I had a thing for thrift shops back then and was determined to do a complete review of the fifty-some, spread throughout the city. The magazine liked the idea and the forty-five hundred words I eventually submitted, and my career as a journalist began.

But this is really about a little old lady in a great big thrift shop in the then decaying east side part of town named after its main streets, St. Clair and Superior.

I spent a month scouring Cleveburg's 'hoods, rummaging through mountains of rummage—research, call it—to find what I could honestly declare the single best thrift, the one with the most and most valuable of the coolest clothing, furniture, books, household goods, you name it. Stuff. I hit every Goodwill and Salvation Army, and every church-run and privately owned shop in town. And, in the end, one did rise above the others. Literally. It was the now, long-since-relocated St. Vincent de Paul's, a four-story high ex-factory crammed like a hundred grandma's attics, a place you could get lost in for a day and come out furnishing your entire home, filling every drawer in it. For real cheap.

The opening spread of the piece was a photo of me next to an acquired pile of a jean jacket, a pair of bell-bottoms, two or three books, a Parcheesi set and a set of dishes. Its caption read, "I got all this junk for $2.78!"

The checkout station at St. Vince's—that's what everyone called it—was presided over by a woman who couldn't have been five feet tall, a dervish of energy who had to be somewhere north of 80. After I'd decided on St. Vince's, I returned to interview her at length, finding Marina Yurchenko to be one of the most charming women I'd ever met. Her husband, I learned, had been killed in an industrial accident many years earlier, and she lost her young son, a suicide, not much later. She lived with her only other child, a mentally disabled daughter, Irena, just a few blocks from the store. Her life was wrapped up in caring for Irena. And in St. Vincent's, the poor church next to it and especially the store which served the neighborhood. I'd been told by the clerks there that Marina was deeply beloved at both, a kindly, charitable, pious and matriarchal figure to all who knew her, and a sharp businesswoman in the bargain, even now, at her advanced age.

When I told her the article would be coming out the following week and I'd named her adored St. Vince's the best thrift in Cleveland, she practically broke into tears, grasping my hand in both of hers, and kissing it. "I don't know how to thank you, young man," she said, her voice cracking, "but you have done God's work in choosing us. I am going to light a candle for you this Sunday and say a novena for you."

My grin must have revealed that this would be a first for me. What she didn't know is that I've never had a candle lit for me and I've certainly never been blessed with a novena. Maybe because I'm Jewish. I had no reply. Partly because I was choking back my own tears. I'd just been doing my job, I felt I'd done it well, and I knew I'd made the right choice in naming St. Vince's, so I was feeling pretty damn good. Not knowing what else to do, I hugged Marina in thanks. She then told me I reminded her of her son who would have been just a little older than me had he lived. Which choked me up even more. I began to see Marina Yurchenko as a sort of mother figure to me.

The day after the article came out, my ego insisted I drive past the store to see what my first-ever words in print had wrought. And, sure enough, the place was packed, not a parking spot within two blocks. A six-foot-high sign, crudely made, had been posted across the front window: "St. Vincent de Paul: No. 1 in Cleveland! Cleveland Magazine." And under the Cleveland Magazine reference, in smaller letters, was my name, Joe Barnett. Next to the sign the whole story had been clipped from the magazine and Scotch-taped in place. But seeing the line of people waiting to enter the store was almost better than seeing my name in print. The power of words. I was pretty full of myself just then. Though it was too busy to buck the line and go in to see Marina, I caught a glimpse of her sitting on her wooden stool up front, smiling, as always, directing traffic and glowing, probably at what had to be the non-stop ringing of the cash register next to her.

So I waited a few weeks before returning to collect the acclaim I'd likely get not just from Marina, but from the entire St. Vince staff. I was a sucker for that then, still am now. The place was busier than I'd ever seen it, but there was no Marina mounted on her stool. I pulled a staffer aside, identified myself, then asked if this was maybe Marina's day off, but the young woman, apparently recognizing me from earlier visits, looked at me and ran off crying. I was beginning to think the worst.

Another clerk, an older woman, now sat behind the counter, a Mrs. Bailey, as she introduced herself. "Mr. Barnett?" she asked. She was holding an envelope, staring at me, It took a while before she could say more. And when she did, she gave me the worst. Marina Yurchenko had suffered a heart attack nearly a week before, lingered three days while recuperating from a quadruple bypass operation, then died. A mass would be said for her the coming Sunday and the funeral would take place after the service, would I wish to attend?

I was too stunned to reply. The thought sneaked into my mind that the novena-worthy excitement I'd generated with my story might have had something to do with Marina's attack. I did my best to dismiss it. I thanked Mrs. Bailey, held up both my hands because I didn't want to hear anything more, and started to half walk, half run, out of the store, rubbing, then banging my forehead in disbelief.

"Wait, Mr. Barnett," called Mrs. Bailey, as I was about to jerk open the door. "Mrs. Yurchenko—Marina—handed me this envelope in the hospital. It had your name on it."

"My name?" I said, spinning around to face her.

"Yes. I was there visiting her and she handed it to me. She said she didn't know how to reach you at the magazine. She said it was very important that I get it to you. Very important. I'm thankful you stopped by, Mr. Barnett. Here." And she handed me the envelope, which I jammed into the side pocket of my jacket before rushing out. I don't remember if I even thanked her.

I sat in my car a few minutes with the letter in my hand just feeling the weight of it, begging to be read. What could be so important to Marina Yurchenko that one of the last things she did in her very full life was to write a message to me, of all people. To thank me? She'd already done that in spades with the candle and novena. I stared at the envelope with my name printed on it in her shaky hand. It had some heft to it and it bulged a little. I opened it.

It wasn't a letter at all. It contained two pieces of hand-cut cardboard taped around a key with its head covered by a thick piece of plastic on which was stamped the number 108. It had to be to be for a locker or some kind of bank box. On one of the cardboards was a brief, shakily inked note: "Identify yourself to Mr. Borwin at the St. Clair Branch of Cleveland Trust. Bless you. And forgive me." That was all it said and it wasn't signed. Forgive her for what? Cryptic. Writing it couldn't have been easy for her. The poor woman must have known she was dying. And that I'd soon show up at the store. Which must be why she gave the envelope to Mrs. Bailey to bring back to St. Vince's for me.

It took me exactly six minutes to rush over to Cleveland Trust. I burst through the doors and looked around. I saw a private office, a glassed in cage maybe eight feet square, along the far wall. Approaching its door, I could see the name *Richard T. Borwin* carved into a triangular wooden prism sitting atop the office's gray Steelcase desk. I walked right in. The man behind the desk looked at me like I was a bank examiner making a surprise call.

"Mr. Borwin, I'm Joe Barnett."

The troubled look on his sallow face disappeared as he rose and came around the desk to greet me. He was a skeleton wearing a shiny blue, chalk-striped suit with pants that stopped two inches above the top of his brown cordovan shoes. "Mr. Barnett," he said, smiling now, "I've been expecting you."

When I stuck out my hand to shake his, my driver's license was already in my other hand to confirm who I was. His handshake was active, but weak and moist. He examined the license like he was authenticating a baseball autographed by Bob Feller. What had Marina told him about me?

"Have you anything else to show me?" he asked, smiling again as he said it. If this was some kind of game, he was obviously enjoying it. I showed him Marina's key. By his nod and continuing smile I could tell he recognized it. He then bid me to follow him to a vault behind the tellers' cages, where he made a fuss of fiddling with the combination on its steel door. Leading me to a row of the largest strong boxes, each the size of a milk crate, then to the box that carried a number matching the one on my key, he inserted his own key, one of many on a retractable key ring attached to his belt. Turning it, he then instructed me to insert my key and do the same. I complied, pulling out the strong box. Still smiling, he left me and closed the vault door after instructing me to press the red button next to it when I wanted to leave.

I did as instructed. The box must have weighed twenty pounds. I needed two hands to lift it onto an oak table in the center of the room. Raising its lid, the first thing I saw was a thick, business-sized, wax- sealed manila envelope, Scrawled across it was, "To Whom It May Concern." It was sitting atop a bottomless pile of stock and bond certificates, which I quickly leafed through. Mostly blue chips. Pepsi Cola, General Motors, General Electric, like that. Some were dated as far back as the 1940s. The share amounts of the stocks were mostly in four, sometimes five numbers. Without reading the letter,

I slipped it into my breast pocket, closed the strongbox, locked it back into place, walked back to the door and pressed the red button. Borwin opened it immediately, still smiling, almost as if he had been standing next to it all the while. He walked me to the front door of the bank, likely disappointed that I didn't choose to reveal the box's secrets to him.

"I trust I'll see you soon again, Mr. Barnett?"

"I nodded without saying a word as I smiled back at his smile. Then I left and headed straight to my place above the sprawling Flats that bordered the Cuyahoga River, downtown. I needed time to inspect the letter. The damn thing,like Marina's earlier envelope, was burning a hole in my addled, overworked brain.

I won't read you the letter. It was seven pages long. But I will give you the gist of it. A bit of it was Marina Yurchenko's history with St. Vince's, telling how she'd lost both a son and a husband and was now raising a young daughter, Irena, stricken from birth with hydrocephalus—water on the brain.

But most of it was . . . a confession.

As a young widow she'd spent three months volunteering at the thrift store before being taken on full time. She took to the job like it was created for her. Within a year she was named its manager. Within another, she took it from a small, single-floor storefront operation to being one of the largest, most thriving thrift stores in Cleveland; a source of jobs for the neighborhood, and much needed revenue for St. Vincent's Church, among the poorest in town. Many employees and St. Vince parishioners took to calling her "St. Marina." But not to the humble woman's face.

Marina had a bent for making money. Trouble was, she was making it for herself as well. It began by her skimming a few dollars from the till each day. And then more than a few dollars. She did it at first because she herself was poor and had chosen to support Irena by boarding her at a private school for the developmentally disabled. By the time she'd squirreled away enough funds to cover Irena's yearly expenses, her skimming had become a habit. One that netted her well over $25,000 a year. That shortage was somehow overlooked because St. Vince's, under her management, kept growing and doing better.

Her take amounted, in the thirty-eight years she'd been taking, to a little over one million dollars, almost all of which she invested in those blue chip stocks and bonds. Even with some setbacks, they had more than doubled in value. Her "milk crate" at Cleveland Trust held no less than two million in not just securities but a stack of mortgage holdings as well.

What did she want me to do with her two mill? First off, she prayed I'd set up a secret trust fund to support Irena for life. Why me? Because God had told her He would send her a stranger she could trust, someone she'd been looking for all her later working life. Me. A stranger she could trust.

The bulk of the money, she said, was, of course, to go to her church. Directly, and without bringing in an attorney to complicate matters. I was simply to place all of her papers into the hands of St. Vince's longtime priest, Stanley Novotny — Father Stan to all who knew him. He was a good man, she said. He'd know what to do with it. Finally, her donation was to remain anonymous. As proud as Marina Yurchenko might have been of her largesse, she was equally and deeply ashamed as to its source. She knew how highly she was thought of in the parish, not as she would be as a benefactor of the church, but as she already was: the guiding light of its thrift store. It was her reputation as the latter that she wanted to remain unsullied. I don't know if it was a need for eventual confession or maybe a vestige of ego, but Marina did note that I could reveal her story if I promised to wait twenty-five years to do it.

The letter was dated just two weeks before she died. It was accompanied by Marina's hand-written will, spelling out the terms of its distribution. It was witnessed by Borwin, he of the now-understandable nonstop smile. Did he suspect anything? If so, could he be trusted to remain quiet? Had she slipped him a stipend to do so? I wasn't going to waste time thinking about it.

The September sun was beginning to set as I sat in my efficiency, reading the letter twice, then taking an hour and a half to ruminate over it while working my way through half a pack of Kents and four, maybe six fingers of Jim Beam on the rocks. Then I took another half hour just to think some more. When I was done thinking I slipped the letter back into my pocket, left to grab a hamburger steak at the Theatrical, went back to my digs, watched the tail end of a losing Indians game and went to sleep.

I did not sleep well.

Next morning I returned to Cleveland Trust and went through the same routine with Mr. Smiles. This time, anticipating my needs, he pulled out a neatly folded, heavy canvas bag, the kind the Brinks people use, and handed it to me before I could think to ask for it. After filling it with the contents of Marina's strongbox, I hightailed it over to St. Vincent's Church, a dark, sad-looking pile of dirt-and-smog-encrusted sandstone over on St. Clair Avenue.

Father Stan. Maybe in his sixties, was big all over; big man, big voice. At the mention of Marina's name, his welcome grew. I could tell he was anxious to talk about her. But his interest seemed to be as great in the bag I was carrying as it was in me. His eyes drifted to it all the while I was talking to him.

Still, the big man did exude warmth. I could see why he was so well-liked by his parishioners. He'd immediately walked me into his small, spartanly furnished office and offered me a drink, an inexpensive scotch, which he made seem like this was the normal thing to do, never mind that it wasn't yet 10 a.m. I reluctantly accepted it because it seemed to be the right thing to do. Then I got right down to telling him the story I've just told you, explaining that, per the terms laid down in Marina's letter, I would be using a fourth of the money to establish a trust fund for her Irena, the balance going to St. Vince's Church. And I stressed the fact that it had to be anonymous.

Father Stan motioned to pour me another drink but I put my hand over my glass to stop him. Which didn't stop him from pouring another for himself. After downing half of it, he puffed out his red-veined cheeks as he pondered what he'd just heard, his huge head wagging from side to side all the while. He looked half pleased, half stunned. And completely uncomfortable.

"You know, Joe," he said, after a long silence, "if I accept this gift for the parish it seems to me that several laws will have been broken, not the least to say, God's. Marina—I'm having a hard time accepting the fact—stole this money. What other way is there to say it? And we, in accepting it, would then become—what's the legal term?—an accessory after the fact. Wouldn't we be seen as criminals ourselves, both legally and morally?"

"It's true," I replied. "Depends, I suppose, on who, besides God Himself, knows about the source of the money. Marina, of course, can't be prosecuted since she's no longer with us. And the parish would only be accepting money that belonged to it in the first place. Where's the crime in that? And if she'd come to you in the confessional, mightn't you have told her to simply return what she'd stolen before handing out her penance?"

Father Stan's massive hand went to his face and massaged it a while before answering. "You do have a point, Joe. Maybe it's best to just accept the gift and leave it at that. I'll make my own penance to God."

"Maybe it is best," I offered. "And, for my part in it, maybe I'll speak to my rabbi." Father Stan offered a rueful smile. As I rose to leave, I said, "I know you'll do the right thing, Father Stan. I plan to myself. But just remember," I added, looking at him over my glasses, "once an investigative reporter, always an investigative reporter." His grin bloomed bigger than mine.

And with that, after losing my hand in the big man's hand while shaking it, I left.

Marina? Her daughter, Irena? Father Stan? They're all gone now. But St. Vince's thrift store and the church? They're both alive and thriving today. What's that? The Pulitzer? Oh. That was for what I've just told you. Marina Yurchenko's story. The one I had to wait twenty-five years to tell.

The Refugiada

If you read the New York Times you know my name, Peter Corrigan. My column appears every Sunday in its Review. I've been traipsing around the world, mostly in the Middle East and sub-Saharan Africa chasing down stories of man's substantial inhumanity to man. Most recently I took myself to Guatemala to report on the plight of the refugiados, the refugees fleeing their Central American homelands because of political pressure or gang and drug wars decimating the citizenry, chasing the victims north to the United States.

This mass exodus was an old and ongoing story until President Obama and Mexico's President Nieto gave a nasty new twist to it. The two set forth a new policy of sending the refugiados back to their homelands "to protect them from the dangers of an illegal border crossing," never mind that the dangers of being sent home were far greater. It's one thing to take your chances on surviving in the desert, quite another to risk brutal torture or murder by your own countrymen.

So there I was in little Ixtapec, in the Mexican state of Qaxaca, a staging town for *La Bestia*, The Beast, the freight trains crowded with northbound refugiados. It was there that I figured to hear stories no one else would listen to; stories I could then tell to my readers who would listen.

On one rainy evening, I found myself in a church meeting hall full of refugiados telling their woeful tales. One of them, a bedraggled but articulate girl who couldn't have been sixteen, was beginning to speak when I entered. Before I could focus on what she was saying,

I was struck by her subtle beauty, so much so that soon, after staring at and listening to her well-told story for twenty minutes, an offbeat thought crept into the back of my mind. The girl's name was Valeria Vasquez. She was the first I chose to interview at the end of the evening. Here's what she told me in her lilting, if halting, schoolgirl English. Forgive me, I've turned it into readable prose.

I was born in Ciudad Guatemala—Guatamala City— where my family and I came to be on intimate terms with poverty. I lived with my older sister, Antonia, and my father, Manuelo, in a two-room, tin-roofed shack built by him in a slum at the city's edge. There are sixty thousand souls packed into this steep, mile-long ravine known as *La Limonada*.

Four years ago my father wanted nothing more than to move his daughters away from the squalor of the Limonada. He feared that its gangs would prey on us even though we were at the ages of just twelve and fourteen. But his meager earnings as a part-time butcher in a small mercado provided us with little more than food and basic clothing. In the Limonada one was fortunate to find any work at all. Many young men preferred to make their way as members of the numerous gangs that thrived there. These Limonada gangs were able to govern themselves and govern us because it was and still is a place where even the police refuse to go, or they look the other way, with outstretched hands, when they do enter.

Dante "Paco" Alvarado, at nineteen, was the leader of such a gang, *Los Merodeadores*—The Marauders. He was handsome, strong and well-built, but he was ruthless as a leader. He always walked around in a clean, white undershirt to show off his muscles. I knew of him in our neighborhood; everyone knew of him and feared him and his gang. He got what he wanted because he was able to take what he wanted. And what he wanted, from the first moment he saw me, *was* me.

My father has told me that, even at the age of twelve, I showed promise of being a beautiful woman. I was taller by far than most Guatemalan girls, the gift of my beautiful mother (I only knew her through photographs) who died giving birth to me in the very shack where we now lived. I was slim and straight-legged. and people sometimes stopped and embarrassed me by staring at me. I had high cheekbones and large, deep-set hazel eyes and my father's mestizo nose, aquiline almost. My lips were full and my skin was the color of milk chocolate. My father often said to me, "Valeria, you are *unico en su clase.*" One of a kind. And he always made certain that he said the same to Antonia, who is beautiful also. My father is very nice to us. He is a very good, hard-working man when he can find work and he is very proud of me and Antonia.

When Paco first saw me, he gazed straight into my eyes. Even then I was nearly as tall as he. He stopped me and backed me against a wall. "You," he said, "I have not seen you around here before. What is your name?"

I stared him down and was not forthcoming in my reply. I knew who he was and, though I was frightened, I said to him, "I do not wish to speak to you."

I wanted to run away from him but he sneered and laughed a wicked little laugh before pinning my arms to the wall. He was too strong for me to break away. "Listen to me, little one. When I speak to you, you will answer me. Once more, what is your name?"

I remained silent until he began to squeeze my arms so tightly that I cried out in pain, and had to tell him my name. Though I was still frightened, Without thinking, I kicked at his groin, but he twisted out of the way before my foot could reach him. I thought this would make him very angry but he laughed instead.

"I like that, Valeria Vasquez," he said. "You are *luchado-ra,* a feisty young thing. And a very pretty young thing."

"Too young for you," I spit back at him.

"That is for me to decide," he said, with quiet arrogance, "and here is what I have decided. You are to be the girlfriend of Dante Alvarado, how would you like that? You do know who I am, don't you? I am Paco Alvarado."

"Yes, Paco Alvarado, I do know who you are and that is why my answer is still that I want nothing to do with you and your rotten Merodeodores."

I do not know where the courage to say this came from but as soon as I said it, the look of amusement on his chiseled face changed. The blue veins on his forehead popped out as he tightened his jaw. "Think about it tonight, little one, and do not be a foolish girl. I can find out where you live." With that, he squeezed my arm again and pinched my cheek so hard it turned red. Then he spun around and walked away toward three of his gang members who were grinning broadly at the tableau they'd just witnessed. They whistled at me, and one of them called me a *puta*.

That night, about to tell my father what had happened to me, I suddenly chose not to. I did not want him confronting this very dangerous Paco Alvarado. The next day Paco approached me as I left our home. "Have you reconsidered my offer, my little Valeria?"

"Yes," I said, "And the answer again is no, absolutely not, and I am not *your* Valeria."

"Then, little beauty, it is no longer an offer, it is a demand." Once again, his fellow Marauders stood in the background. I knew that, by my saying no, he had to say something like that to save face. And then the offer that became a demand now became a threat, a horrible threat.

He clamped my arms as he had done before, then brought his sweaty face close to mine and snarled at me in a hard, low voice, "You will do as I wish, Valeria, or I will kill your sister, do you hear that? Do not think I will not." He released me and began to walk away, then stopped and turned around. Pointing a finger at me, he said, "I do not play games, little one. I want an answer now!"

I could only stand there in shock and shake my head. "No!" I screamed, as I ran away.

In your country a threat like this could put a man in jail. But there were no police to complain to. I once more feared informing my father because he, like Paco Alvarado, was hot-headed and would confront him and I could not let this happen. I did not know what to do. I determined that it was best to run away with Antonia but, with no money and no knowledge of the outside world, we did not know where to run or how to run. I thought I could make excuses to this Paco to stall him off until I could form a plan, but when he approached me yet a third time, and I once more refused him, he stormed away without saying a word, making a gesture at me that I did not understand, but dreaded nonetheless.

I confided in Antonia about Paco's advances and she said that we must, after all, tell our father and make our plans for perhaps the three of us to run away together.

That is what we were discussing the next day after my father left for work. When Antonia looked out our front window and saw two of Paco's *secuaces*, his henchmen, approaching. They banged on the door and shouted for me to open it. When Antonia refused, they kicked it in and entered. One of them said to me, "Are you coming with us?" I could only shake my head no. The other then rushed over to me and held me from behind with his arm around my neck, while the first casually walked over to Antonia, snapped open a switchblade knife and rammed its six-inch blade into her stomach as I was made to watch, horrified.

The pair walked out laughing as if nothing had happened. I immediately called for an ambulance but, before I could hear its siren, Antonia, my only sibling, was dead. Her murderer had pulled a sheet of notebook paper from his pocket, wiped his blade with it, then, smiling, floated the sheet onto her dying body. It read, through Antonia's blood that was now soaking into it, *Tu padre sigue.* "Your father goes next."

Though my distraught father wanted to go after Antonia's murderer with his meat cleaver, I talked him into doing what I thought was the right thing. He made a police report. But, after the police carefully took down everything my father and I said, nothing more was done. We never heard from them again. That was how the law was applied inside the Limonado.

Fearful that my father's life was in danger, even my own, I became, the very next day, the girlfriend of Dante "Paco" Alvarado; one of several in his "harem." As such, I was not ever allowed to leave his headquarters. My cell phone was taken from me so I could have no contact with my father or the police. I was now living less than a mile from my home but neither my father nor anyone else knew where I was or even if I was still alive. It was as though I had fallen off the face of the earth.

I was made to perform any act ordered by and for Paco, and, at his command, for other members of Los Merodeadores as well, as their reward for special services to him. When I did not do so to his complete satisfaction, I was beaten. One time, when Paco caught me trying to run away, he whipped me repeatedly with his heavy keychain, its ring of keys still attached.

My living hell of a life became more than I could bear but I did bear it for over four years because I felt I had no choice, I was a prisoner. Then, one day, as Paco's guard happened to fall asleep when the gang was off on its evil rounds, I slipped the guard's cell phone from the table in front of him and ran out the back door. Knowing that Paco would head directly for my home to find me, I phoned my father and had him meet me behind the market where he worked.

I had not seen nor spoken to my father in all these years. He had no idea where I was, thinking that I had been kidnapped and was now missing or dead like his other daughter. He was a broken man. When he saw me, he embraced me in tearful silence for a full minute. But there was little time for this touching reunion. He handed me a paper sack filled with Guatemalan quetzels—a large part of his savings—and another of *perujos con carne*, baguettes filled with meat, and then went with me by bus to the rail yards at the northern outskirts of the city. There, with tears still in his eyes, he watched me and dozens of other fleeing citizens, climb atop La Bestia heading north.

My journey to freedom was a slow and difficult one. It took me first across the Guatemalan border to this sanctuary town of Ixtapec. Once here, I made inquiries and was directed to a man who specialized in arranging passage to and across the U.S. border at a town called Socorro, just east of El Paso, Texas. His manner was harsh, reminding me of Paco's, but he turned out to be okay, although he didn't mind crowding me into the rear of a canvas-covered truck, along with nine other refugiados, and a huge pile of watermelons under which we had to hide all the way to our destination.

When we arrived we were shocked to learn of the new "protective policy" that erased the leniency of previous policies. We were immediately rounded up and sent back to Ixtapec where we were staged for return to what, for most of us, would mean death or torture by gang or by government. That was yesterday, and here I am today, telling you my story. I do not know where to go from here. I cannot allow myself to be sent back to the Limonada, to the Merodeadores. I do not know what to do.

Valeria seemed to understand who I was, that I was someone in a position to help her. She insisted on showing me the scars inflicted by Paco Alvarado. It looked like three angry entwined rivers running diagonally up from the middle of her back to her right shoulder. I asked what had become of her father. She said she once did reach him, but the connection was bad and she was only able to say where she was and that she was safe for the moment. He informed her that Paco had warned him that, if he did not present his daughter, he would be tortured until she did return. He promised Paco he would do as he was told, then instantly fled to protect us both.

For some time Manuelo had been ill with, she believed, some form of cancer, though he would not admit this to her. That was why he had not been able to leave Guatemala. But he had found refuge in a small village up in the mountains, out of cell phone range, and was himself safe for the time being. Valeria would not tell me the name of this village because she no longer trusted anyone. And barely trusted me.

I had listened intently to her story, knowing that thousands like it were not being listened to by any authority who could or would do something about them. I finally was able to impress upon Valeria the wisdom of letting me inform the world of her predicament. I did this by convincing her that she would serve as a perfect example of how wrong the Obama/Nieto decision had been. I told her that she, through her story, could help stop or at least reduce refugiado deportations.

But something else was troubling me. I knew my column in the Times would be preaching to the choir. It was a message that needed to reach a larger audience, not just the progressive readers of the Times. It needed to be told to a public that had never heard the word refugiado. This was on my mind later that same night while I sat alone, downing a few Del Cabos in a cantina next to the church meeting hall. That's when the idea rattling around in my brain earlier that day began to take form. What if—just what if—this obscure young girl wasn't just a one-shot deal, a few dozen column inches? What if, instead, this feisty young woman could somehow speak from a broader platform than the one I represented, and, importantly, on an ongoing basis? What if I could bring her back with me to New York where I could introduce her to the broader media so her story could be spread by them? Valeria Vasquez as the sixteen-year-old poster girl for the plight of the refugiados? Why not? Would it be exploiting her? Yes, it would, but for the right reasons.

Valeria carried herself well. If a little on the shy side, she showed a lot of spunk. She was motivated to tell her story and so what if her natural beauty would likely gain as much attention as her words. Would people listen to this innocent-looking Guatemalan girl telling her not-so-innocent story? I was convinced they would and that Valeria could carry it off. Or at least I'd pretty well convinced myself that evening. After one more Cabo I was certain of it.

I met with Valeria the next morning over breakfast. First, I reassured her that I'd do my best to delay any official attempt to send her back to Guatemala. How, I wasn't quite sure. "How do you see yourself a year from now, Valeria?" I said, before I began to lay out my scheme.

She stared into space and gave off an involuntary shudder. "If I am back in the Limonada I will be dead," she said. "Or as good as dead, a zombie." She actually used that word. "I would want to kill myself."

My turn to shudder. "Look," I said. "I want your story to go beyond my telling. What if I told you that part of my effort to gain your freedom involves my taking you to America, to New York City, where you can tell your story to other media. I would do this because I want your story to go beyond, way beyond, my newspaper.

Valeria's unblinking eyes told me she was absorbing what I was saying. She got it, and if she also got the need for gravitas as a spokesperson, well then, so much the better.

"But how can you make such a thing happen?" she asked, wide-eyed.

"I happen to know a few people," I deadpanned.

I watched as what I'd just proposed sank in. Valeria sat silently for a few moments, straightened up in her chair, and said, "I will do it, Senor Corrigan." This was the first time she used my name. Then she stuck her hand in mine to seal the bargain. "But," she added, with furled brow, "what exactly will you have me do in America? Where will I stay?" She said this like the wary adult she'd quickly grown to become at the hands of Paco Alvarez.

"Good questions," I replied. "I'm not sure yet what you'll be doing —I haven't mapped it out yet—but I think I know where you'll stay." I immediately called my girlfriend, Karina Carlson, and laid out the short version of Valeria's story. I knew what KC's heart-of-gold response would be. For at least the short term, Valeria could stay with her in her oversized Tribeca loft.

I spent the rest of the day banging out my column for the following Sunday. It featured Valeria's story, along with several more I'd gathered at the meeting where I'd met her. I made only a passing reference to Valeria's beauty, and, of course, did not mention any plans I had for her. I hated to admit that a picture could be worth more than my deathless prose, but I did make certain to include, with my communiqué, half a dozen cell-phone shots of her, including one of her scarred back. The one they featured three columns wide was of her lovely face.

That piece drew more mail than any of my columns this year.

Five days later, after I'd massaged a few hands and called in several favors, I had the papers in hand to spirit Valeria past the local authorities and fly her to New York. Accompanying her, I saw myself, in spite of myself, becoming her guardian and mentor. Giggling, she called me her *duenna*, an older woman acting as a chaperone. Me, Pete Corrigan. A duenna.

Karina was waiting for us at JFK, whisking us off through the sound and fury of Manhattan to her loft. Valeria, her mouth wide open all the way, was too awed to speak a word. Once installed, we decompressed over an everything pizza. Karina listened to Valeria's story this time in her own words, not mine. As she told it, she exhibited, on request, the ugly chain scar that ran along her otherwise smooth back. Afterward, Karina sat in silence, slightly nodding her head in disbelief.

I broke the silence with, "So, Karina, I plan to contact a lot of media friends to spread Valeria's story around. You've got some too. Any suggestions on where to start?"

"Where do I work, Peter Corrigan?" she said, looking straight at me while folding her arms.

"You're a V-P at Elite Modeling," I replied, innocently.

"And, knowing you, Pete, you're hardly unaware of Valeria's natural beauty, her perfectly beautiful, beautifully perfect face, right?"

Valeria reddened at Karina's bold statement. I finally got it about the smile growing on her own beautiful face. "Oh. Right. Are you suggesting that Valeria could be a model? Say more."

Karina said a lot more, to both of us, but mostly to Valeria. "Look, I work for the most important modeling agency in New York. I see beautiful young women walk through our doors every day. I believe that you, Valeria, can compete with them. Sixteen is a good age to begin. As a model, you could speak up for your cause and become the spokesperson that Pete thinks you'd be so good at. But there is a little problem. Your back. You'd need a good plastic surgeon to repair the damage done to it. Would you be up for that?"

Karina might as well have been speaking Russian. Valeria, more than a little overwhelmed, looked at Karina sideways and asked her to repeat all she'd just said. She knew what a fashion model was but did not seem to understand what being one had to do with her or with her dire situation. Nonetheless, after Karina went over her little speech again, a smile, a very small but beautiful one, graced Valeria's now-tilted oval face. Surely she must have been aware of her own beauty. If she said nothing it was because she was thinking, visualizing the picture being presented to her by Karina. Her silence tacitly bade Karina to go on, which she did, laying out her thoughts on how to generate a career for Valeria, one that would allow her to tell all about the refugiados of Central America.

"I don't expect you to say yes right away, Valeria, but please tell us what you are thinking."

"I am thinking that you offer me a great opportunity. And my answer is, yes, I would like the chance to become a model. But there is one thing I will not do and that is that I will not have my scars removed."

Karina swallowed before speaking. All she could say was, "Why, Valeria? You can't be a model with . . . with that disfiguration."

"But it is exactly my 'disfiguration,' as you call it, that I would want everyone to see. If they see that, they will believe what I have to say. People do not always listen to models. They would listen to my scar."

I'd been watching the two like a spectator at a tennis match. Suddenly, it was Karina who was speechless. Me, too. It was hard to believe these wise words were coming from such a young girl. But this was a young girl with a psyche made older and wiser by the life she'd lived.

It was finally Karina who spoke her thoughts out loud. "A model with a scar on her back? Could that happen? Beauty and the scar, juxtaposed. Really? Can Valeria make it happen? Why not? Can *I* make it happen? We can both try."

And Karina did try, and was successful, setting up an interview with Elite for the next afternoon, preceded by a morning at the hairdresser for a simple straight cut with bangs of Valeria's long black locks. Her natural poise, her perfect, proud stature and her lovely face all worked together to make her interview and photo shoot a success. Some of the photos, as directed by Karina, who was committed now to Valeria's young wisdom, were three-quarter shots taken from the rear, exposing the sinuous scars on her back. In walking the runway, her awkward turns in a backless Vera Wang gown, sharply limned her scars. She would get used to walking in Laboutin heels, but could the fashion world get used to seeing the vicious carvings of Paco Alvarado?

It could and it did.

Thus Valeria's cause was made and her career as a model was launched. Surprising even Karina, Valeria quickly gained supermodel status.

Suddenly, she was working almost every day, in the studio and on the runway. Her face, but even more so her now-familiar back, in combination with her words, became the foundation of her fame, thanks largely to the nature of the social media. Eventually, half the world—and not just the fashion world—knew who Valeria was and what she stood for. But, just as her fame was rising, she was advised by Karina to change her name because another older and very popular model was named Valeri. One wag at Harper's Bazaar had come up with a new name, a single name that would become as well-known as that of Iman or Kate or Gisele. Valeria Vasquez would then and forever be known as—ViVi. Cap V, small i, cap V, small i.

Everything was changing for her. ViVi was becoming more of a household name than mine. But it was her story, not her lovely face, that evoked an invitation to the White House during Obama's waning days as president. She told it, alongside Karina and me, at a private dinner with the Obamas and their daughters. Noticeably impressed by what she had to say, President Obama had another sit-down with President Nieto of Mexico, a conversation that resulted in the removal of the restrictions they'd put on her and thousands of other refugiados like her.

This was a fairy tale that could not happen. But it was happening, unfolding at the lightspeed of today's electronic media, so virally fast that the strain of the demands on Valeria's instant fame was beginning to tell. Though Karina and I were doing the best we could to alleviate her worries, that was not enough.

At the heart of her concerns was the well-being of her father, Manuelo. She feared more than ever for him. The rules for political refugees had changed for the better, and she had helped change them. But the Limonado had not changed. Her father was out there somewhere and, though not in the Limonado, she worried that Paco and his henchmen would seek and find him, torture him as retribution for her fleeing, or hold him in ransom for her return. Or had they done so already? Was he even alive? In spite of repeated attempts at reaching him, she had not been able to do so in all this time. She did not know if he was still in the mountains and could not use his phone, or had been captured by the Merodeodores and hauled back to the Limonado. And, if he could contact her, why had he not done so by now? At sixteen years old, Valeria Vasquez—the supermodel ViVi—was close to having a complete mental breakdown.

So there was one more string for me to pull. Actually, a whole set of strings. I contacted Ned Vickers, American consul in Guatemala City, and then an old friend, Arturo Colon, managing editor of the city's largest daily, *Diario de Centro América*, and, through their combined efforts, was able to arrange a covert operation I was not at liberty to report on, to even reveal, until and unless it succeeded. And it did succeed.

A week after Valeria's return from the White House to New York, where she was still staying at Karina's loft apartment, we threw a seventeenth birthday party for her there, inviting several Elite models and staffers. Before having her take a whack at a birthday piñata, we blindfolded her, spun her around and aimed her in its general direction. With a stout stick in hand she half stumbled toward it and began a swing that was caught in mid-air—by the hand of her father, Manuelo. With his other hand he pulled the blindfold from her eyes. Her scream of *Papá!* as she looked into his moist brown eyes, filled the room. She leaped into his waiting, butcher-strong arms and stayed there, not letting him go.

Tears were shed. Hardly just by the two of them. Then, before resuming the celebration, the rest of us excused ourselves from the room.

Isabella
(For Maritza)

"Look, Walt, thanks for the invite and I'd love to fly down. But fact is, dammit, I'm more than a little tapped out."

"I have an idea," said Walt.

"No, seriously—" I started to say.

"No, no, Stevie boy, I've been thinking about this awhile. I can't get up to the reunion—not since I broke my hip—so I mean to bring the reunion to me."

Walt, my best friend, has always foisted quirky ideas on me. What did he have in mind now. "Explain!" I said.

"You kind of pulled this reunion together, right? Has it really been thirty years since we graduated high school?"

"It really has. So?"

"So you're going to be my guest down here then take pictures and go back and tell the guys all about me at the reunion up there and it'll be like I was actually there."

"Grand idea, and thanks, old pal, but you didn't hear me—"

"No, Steven, you didn't hear me. I said 'guest.' Now please don't do your injured pride bit and stammer me a no. Is your passport up to date?"

"Yes, but—"

"Good. Don't go away. I'm going to buy you a ticket."

Cali, Colombia? Why not? Hard to refuse. Great chance to hang out with Walt. In a country—a continent—I've never been to before. So I said yes, what else could I do?

As I watched Walt on Skype, he booked my flights by phone in under ten minutes.

Two days later, after a seven-hour leg from L.A. to Panama City and a short hop from there down to Cali, I came through Customs at Aragón Airport near midnight to see, standing out from everyone else, my hulking, six-foot-three pal, Walt, a big grin adorning his square face as he leaned on his cane. He was wearing a baseball cap with a hand-lettered STEVE sign taped to the front of it. After the fist bumps and hugs we took a 45-minute cab ride—Walt doesn't own a car, says Cali cabs are cheaper—to the magnificent condo he shares with his Colombian wife, Teresa, in the Melendez district, next to the University of Valle and Unicentro, a sprawling shopping center in an upscale part of this modern/ancient city of over two million. Though I'd never met Teresa, the greeting she gave me was just as warm as Walt's.

Before I could sit down, Walt, owner of a civil engineering firm, handed me an Excel chart blocked out with just about every hour I'd spend there. He and Teresa meant to show me every corner of his adopted city in the next week. Knowing how I loved martinis, which were relatively unknown down there, they'd bought the fixings and had me mix some for the three of us. The heavy-handed way I make them, we all got loosened up for whatever was to come. Walt and I drifted back to our high school days. He was the big sonofabitch tackle who chased the bad guys from the No. 3 hole so I could get through. Always made me look like a better fullback than I was. But that was a long, long time ago.

First up, next day, after a tour of the city, was a homemade dinner at Astrid's, one of Teresa's two best friends. The three of them —Teresa, Astrid and Isabella—had playfully taken to calling themselves "Las Supremas" after the singing Supremes. Astrid and Isabella, two handsome single women, are professors at the University. The meal was superb: a native chicken-and-potato soup from Bogota called ajiaca. Before it was over, they all made me feel like I was one of them, part of their family of friends.

But I couldn't concentrate on the meal because I could not take my eyes off Isabella. Something struck me about her from the moment I saw her. Her beauty, yes, but more than that. A gentleness and a certain vulnerability in her lovely green eyes. When she told me, conversing after the meal, that she'd known from Teresa that I was a writer, and was impressed by the little she'd seen of my work, she had me. She asked about my novels and short stories but, for once, I only wanted to talk about her, to know more about her. She'd traveled throughout the world and was about to spend a few months of her upcoming hiatus in France and Spain. She's dean of the Faculty of Arts at the university, the youngest in its history. And, nearest I could tell, she was ten, maybe fifteen years younger than me.

I tried to be sociable, talking to everyone at the table, but I wanted to be alone with Isabella to talk with her privately. Which did happen. Just before we left, I found myself beside her for fifteen minutes on Astrid's balcony where she opened up a little more. I learned she's been divorced for some years. I didn't have time to learn much more but had quickly come to feel comfortable in her presence. And, at the same time, boyishly giddy.

So here I was—what's that antiquated word?—smitten. Within minutes! Over a woman who lived in another country on another continent over three thousand miles away, a woman I'd known for exactly two hours and I was leaving in less than a week. And she was May—well, maybe June—and I was September. The perfect love story.

I saw Isabella a few days later, but again it was with Walt and Teresa and others at a party at La Matraca, Cali's famed salsa nightclub, and we had only a noisy half hour alone during which I couldn't say what was on my mind because there was just too much going on.

Later in the week, the Supremas and I—Walt, with his bad leg, couldn't make it that evening—went to another nightclub to dance to Cuban music on my farewell eve. I sat opposite Isabella but we could hardly hear ourselves over the throb of the music. I wasn't able to tell her anything of what I was feeling. As far as she knew, I felt nothing more for her than I did for the other Supremas. We were all friends now, nothing more, never mind that I sought more than mere friendship. The kiss I got from Isabella that night was more a goodbye to a friend than a hello to a relationship.

Walt's a lucky man to have his Teresa. I had no one of my own. Amidst hugs from him and near-tears from her, I left the next morning, basking in what had been and even more in what might have been.

Great trip. One week, and now it's over. First day back, I taped a hazy photo I'd taken of Isabella to the hutch over my desk. A foolish thing, putting that face there. Who was I kidding, imagining there could ever be anything between us?

What was I looking for? In my hopeless way, I'm still grieving for the only woman I ever loved, now dead these seven years. What the hell was I doing, thinking anything about Isabella? And why was I mooning over the picture of a woman I'd known for just a few days, hours really? But these had been, for me if not for her, intense hours during which I had all I could do to keep from calling her now and letting her know my feelings. About a woman I'd likely never see again, one who probably hadn't felt for me anything of what I felt for her.

I paced my office floor. Andy, my cat, started pacing with me. I knew why he was pacing. It was past his snack time. But why was I? I looked at my watch. Five forty-five p.m. Fifteen minutes till my personal happy hour. I was looking for words and needed my martini for them to come, the words I would write to Isabella so they'd be more perfect that any I could speak. Why, suddenly, did I need a drink to write when I never needed one before? Maybe because I've convinced myself that I've never met a woman like Isabella. Or the woman I was imagining Isabella to be. Where was this coming from, Steven?

The little hand up, the big hand down, I poured. And sipped. And waited. And the words came.

Dear Isabella:

I'm writing to thank you for the lovely time you and your "La Supremas" showed me in Cali. I didn't know I'd ever dance like that again. I really appreciated the warm hospitality you all showed me and . . .

And what? I killed what I'd written. I paced some more, finished my martini and sat myself back down at my computer. It had to be direct. And brief.

My Dear Isabella,

I must admit that you have been on my mind since I left Cali.

We had so very few hours together. More like moments. But moments which meant a great deal to me. We talked of our backgrounds, of writing and the arts in general, of . . . cabbages and kings. And I felt we could talk into the night, which I believe we would have if we'd had the chance.

I don't know any other way to say it, Isabella, than just to say it: I have feelings for you. I won't say more to avoid saying the wrong thing, and may have said too much already.

But I will add that I miss you.

And would love to see and be with you again.

Steven

I looked at what I'd written, re-read it several times, made little corrections and read it yet again. I did a little more pacing, came back to the letter and moved the cursor up to the red dot in the corner, ready to kill again. Hovering there a moment, I dropped down to *Send* and tapped it. How else would she ever know where I stood? How else would I ever know where she stood?

I didn't have long to wait for Isabella's reply. It hit my in box the next morning. I stared at its highlighted name before opening it. Was the quick response a good sign? Would it be a new email or an easier to send Reply? What would be her answer?

Just open it, you idiot. It was a Reply.

Steven:

I sat up quite some time last night thinking about what you had to say. And, though I was flattered by your unexpected feelings about me, I don't see the person in me that the words you expressed saw.

Yes, Steven, I enjoyed our time together too. But I cannot truthfully say they led me to the place where you profess to be. I'm in a relation-

ship now, I would have told you that, but it isn't going too well and I'm uncomfortable even considering another right now. But please do not take that as a sign of encouragement. That is not what I intended.

You must recognize the obvious barriers between us, Steven, our different backgrounds, nationalities, our literal distance apart, and the fact that we know almost nothing about each other. As for our age difference, I presume it's about fifteen years, though I wasn't thinking about that as we conversed.

Were such differences to be overcome, I am not yet ready to leave the relationship I'm in, and must repeat that I'm certainly not ready to begin a new one.

I conclude then that we have begun a friendship, nothing less, but nothing more. Should you visit Cali again I would welcome you, of course, but not if I were to be the main purpose of your visit.

I do hope you will understand.

Isabella Justina de la Fuerza

She'd opened the email with a colon after "Steven," not the more intimate comma. Bad. But she used my first name twice in the body of the email. Good. But she signed it formally with her full name, not just the more meaningful Isabella by itself. And why did she have to say she "certainly" wasn't ready for another relationship? Couldn't she have said she was not yet ready? This did not bode well. But why was I trying to analyze the most honest and straightforward email I've had in months? A collection attorney couldn't have made his purpose clearer. Isabella is all right with just being friends. And will be happy to see me again only if she is not my main reason for coming.

Okay, I get that.

Swell.

You know what, Steven, I told myself a week later, still unable to think of a response capable of penetrating Isabella's "obvious barriers," you will dream of this woman for maybe another week, then you will stop dreaming, then forget her name, then forget her altogether. Stevie boy, she was right about those barriers. It was a lark for you, nothing more. For Isabella it was nothing at all. You became friends, that's it, that's all she wrote. You'll get over it.

Another week passed. I still dreamed vividly of Isabella. I did not forget her name. Isabella Justina de la Fuerza. I loved her name rattling around in my still-smitten brain. Two more weeks passed. It was coming on a month since the visit. There was nothing more to say to her. It was over. I knew this. Clearly.

No I didn't. I was about to write her again. I sat down and tapped her name into a fresh message. And then a little sound told me an email was just in. I took a peek. Jeezuz, it was from Isabella.

Steven,

Alfonso—he's my boyfriend—has discovered your email. I caught him looking at my computer. Though I had made it clear there was absolutely nothing going on between you and me, Alfonso didn't believe me. He is a terribly jealous man. Unreasonably so. Which is only one reason why we—he and I—have not been getting along. I write to you now to warn you that he has said he means to travel to Los Angeles to seek some kind of revenge upon you. This would seem an empty threat, but you do not know Alfonso as I do. If you should hear from him, or learn somehow that he has followed through on his threat, please take all precautions to protect yourself. He often carries a concealed weapon.

I would not have contacted you at this time, Steven, if the situation had not warranted it. I am concerned for you.

Isabella

Huh? Alfonso? So that's the boyfriend's name? And he's coming for me? With a *concealed weapon?* Coming to do what? Nothing ever happened but a little conversation. What kind of tangled goddamn web have I woven? And I wasn't even out to deceive, though, now that I think about it, I'd love to have done exactly that. Anyhow, her email was signed with the friendlier Isabella. But I think she was being exactly that, friendly, nothing more. So, what's next, Steven? Are you really going to pursue this madness? Or are you going to run from it?

Isabella:

This Alfonso of yours must surely know that I wasn't aware he existed when I first met you, then emailed you. I didn't really mean to bust up any kind of an actual romance. I guess he has my email address and, by now, probably my actual address. How big is this guy? And that concealed weapon... would you happen to know if he has a permit for it so he can pack it in his luggage? I'm not worried, I'm just saying.

Steven

The next email I got from Colombia wasn't from Isabella.

Steven—

¡You bastardo! If I could afford a plane tickets I would like to come into your home and strangle your neck like a pollo. Isabella is my woman, do you hear what I am saying? You must be leaving her alone or I will break both your feets.

Don Alfonso Miguel Antonio Huerta del Norte

Holy cow! Well, at least the guy was too broke to fly up here. But before I could even think of a response, I heard from old Al again.

Steven—

I am the happiest to say that my cousin, Marvin, who lives in Covina in California and has his own car, has consented to avenge the wrong that you has done to me. You may be expecting him in the very soon.

Don Alfonso Miguel Antonio Huerta del Norte

This guy must get awfully tired of signing his name. I needed to talk to him right then and let him know just where I stood.

My Dear Alfonso:

Surely you must realize by now that, when I first wrote to Ms. De

la Fuerza, I was unaware of your relationship to her. But now that you're threatening me with strangulation and the breaking of my feet, I think you should know that your inamorata doesn't really care for you all that much so whatever you had in mind for me will all go for nothing when she tells you to buzz off, buster.
  Steven
  P.S.: I have a green belt in karate.

The minute I hit Send, I knew it was a mistake. Why did I have to provoke this man? Why did I just have that second martini?

A half hour later, the other shoe was dropped by Isabella, who must have been BCCed by the lovely Don Alfonso, who then must have forwarded my answer to her.

  Steven:

  I am very upset with you. By what right did you have the effrontery to inform Alfonso that I no longer cared for him and would tell him to, in your words, "buzz off, buster?" I had only said that Alfonso and I were not getting along. I'm afraid you are in real trouble now because Alfonso's cousin Marvin is not a man you'd care to deal with. Though he is about your age and retired now, he was once a world champion at what you call prize fighting. His name, should you want to Google him, is Marvin Hagler.
  Isabella

Marvin Hagler? MarvinfuckingHagler? C'mon! He was only one of the greatest middleweights in the history of the game! And now suddenly he's a cousin of some crazy guy in Colombia? And he's going to come rapping on my door? I remember that face in the ring. He could look my door down!

  What now, Steven?

  Well, nearly six months passed. And nothing happened. Former World Middleweight Champion Marvin Hagler did not come a-rapping on my door on behalf of his cousin, Don Alfonso Miguel Antonio Huerta del Norte.

Hagler's being his cousin must have been a lie Al told to both Isabella and me. Creative, I had to admit.

What did come, though, was another invitation from Walt, insisting that, considering the fabulous week we'd had earlier, it was time for a return to Cali.

"Thanks, I'll think about it," I lied. I was still sort of broke. "By the way, how's Teresa doing?" Then it just fell from my mouth. "And how's Isabella?" I could feel myself flush at my own mention of her name. Did Walt know about Isabella and me? What am I talking about? There is no Isabella and me. I doubted if she'd told Teresa about our quirky correspondence.

"Funny you should single her out, Steven. I was just about to tell you it was Isabella who suggested the return visit."

"Really, Walt?" I replied. What I'd somehow kept myself from saying was, "Are you fucking kidding me?"

"Really. It was at a dinner party at our place. She'd come alone and she brought up your name. Wondered how you were doing. I said I hadn't heard from you in a long while and she said it would be nice if you could visit again."

"She said that?"

"She said that."

"Did she say why?"

"No."

"What else did she say?"

"What else? Nothing else. Figure out its meaning for yourself."

"What meaning? Doesn't she have a sort of boyfriend?"

"He's history, pal. And apparently you're not."

I could picture the smug grin on his florid face.

"Walt," I said, "Can you really handle me for another visit?"

"Cretin! I just invited you. It's on me again. C'mon down."

"I'm there," I heard myself say. My mind pictured my lovely Isabella.

And the unlovely Don Bunchanames. He's probably still hovering around. But with my new moves, he'll never see me coming. He'll never know that two weeks ago, I earned my second degree brown belt.

The Sansei Sensei

Some fancy drug store. Has the nerve to call itself an apothecary even though it's crammed with high-end wine, wristwatches and something called "sundries." But in Brentwood it's an ... apothecary. I'm Wolfe. Abel Wolfe. Private Investigator. Chasing the disappearance, maybe the abduction, maybe the murder, of a karate student at a nearby dojo. I've been sent here by a tip from my pal, Chief of Detectives Eddie Ohara. Eddie says the drug store owner is a person of interest, a guy name of Sesuwa Sessei. Eddie wants me to nose around and give him my take on Sessei. What's a drugstore got to do with a dojo, I ask Eddie. Sessei, he informs me, also happens to own the dojo. He's supposed to know something about the disappearance.

"What do you mean, *supposed* to know?"

Eddie sounds like he's holding back. "We think he may have been the one who made her disappear."

"How so? And who's 'her'?"

"'Her' is the missing student, Helen Barton, who worked at this apothecary, and was last seen leaving a class at the dojo. We put two and two together and still come up with two. Maybe your arithmetic is better."

We bandy our usual insults and, half an hour later, I'm at the apoth ... the damn drugstore, and it has a long line at the prescription counter. I plant myself in front of the line, ignoring the whiney old bag behind me, but I don't see any male type persons of interest at the window. A sweet-faced young thing asks what I want. "A chat with Mr. Sessei," I say, showing her my grump and my badge.

"I'm afraid he's off today."

Swell. "Where might I find him?"

"You know him?"

"'Fraid so. I owe him money." I wave my wallet at her to show how sincerely I want to pay it.

"Oh. He's at his dojo. Brentwood Martial Arts. Five blocks—"

"North." I finish her sentence. "I know where it is."

"Did you wish to fill a prescription, sir?"

"Not one you could handle, sister."

Minutes later I'm facing Sesuwa Sessei. Posh place, this dojo, lined with thick wall-to-wall mats. He's a small man, maybe five-six, all muscle, not a pinch of fat visible. He's wearing one of those white things bound with a black belt and he's in a wide stance, rocking and stretching, hardly sweating. I'd just watched him beating up on three students who are not only dripping, but are on their collective back gasping for breath.

I offer my card and ask for a private confab. He directs me to his small office in the back, sparsely but tastefully furnished with pricy Knoll, including a double-wide chaise. It reeks, oddly, of patchouli incense. Looks like an executive suite but smells like a hippie crash pad from the seventies. Sweet little domain.

"I guess you're the Sensei here," I offer, flashing my complete knowledge of Japanese.

Sessei smiles. "I'm not just a Sensei, Mr. Wolfe." I stare at him, blankly. "I am also a Sansei."

"Sansei?" I need to control this conversation. I'm looking for a lead on a missing, maybe dead, girl. But, not knowing what the hell he's talking about, I say, "Meaning?"

"I'm a third generation Issei . . . a *San*sei. What's on your mind?"

"Wait a minute," I say. "You're a *Sansei* Sensei. Makes no sense, I—"

"My grandfather was born in L.A.," he interrupts, fingering his bonsai. "Which makes me a Sansei, a third generation Japanese-American. My father is second generation, a Nisei, so was my grandfather, first-generation; an Issei."

"I see."

"No, I said Issei. Also a Sensei. But not a Sansei Sensai."

"You don't say."

"I do say. An Issei Sensei, so I'm a Sansei Sensei."

"Which makes your son a . . . ?"

"Yonsei. And his son will be a Gosei."

I sigh. I've lost the handle here. "Are you anything else?"

"Yes. A yakuzaishi; an apothecarian."

"So," I say, "Sesuwa Sessei is a Sansei Sensei yakuzaishi grandson of an Issei Sensei, father of a Nisei, whose son is a Yonsei, the Yonsai's son, if, say, he has one, being a Gosei. Did I say that right, Mr. Sessei?"

"Perfect, Mr. Wolfe. And do you know we Sesseis were once fierce samurai?"

"No, sir, I did not, and I thank you for the instructive tutorial, sir, but, if you don't mind I'd like to ask about Helen Barton. You recognize the name?"

"Should I?"

"She lives with her family who haven't seen her in five days. She works—or did work—at your drug store and she is or was a student of yours at this dojo, last seen leaving *here* exactly five days ago. Yes, Mr. Sessei, you should recognize her name." Shoot from the hip, Wolfe. "Did you have anything to do with her disappearance? Like, possibly, killing her?"

My blunt question does not shake him up. "No," he says, not changing the deadpan look on his round face.

"She was your girlfriend, wasn't she?"

"What makes you say that?"

"A set of photos taken in this very room," I reply, waving my cell at him. I'm bluffing, of course. Lying in my teeth. But it's amazing how a lie can sometimes bring out the truth.

"You're lying." He says. "Show me the photos on your phone."

"Not my phone, I meant hers. The police have it—but they don't have her. Selfies on it show the two of you together in positions that are more Kama Sutra than Karate. And neither of you are wearing one of those white things—or anything else."

"A *gi*, Mr. Wolfe, the white thing is a *gi*. The more you talk, the more you stick your foot in your mouth. Or perhaps I can do that for you." He's smiling now, not of the happy variety.

"They found her phone in the alley behind this place," I continue to lie, "and now we need to find her. You can follow me down to the station to see the photos or you can talk to me here and tell me what you know. Your choice."

"I'd like to play poker with you, Mr. Wolfe. You don't lie very well. You have no photos because there are no photos. Yes, of course I know Helen. I was just being cagey with you as you are being with me. She did work for me and is a student here. She's a troubled girl but she's never been my lover and I had nothing to do with her disappearance. Why are you lying to me?"

"To see if there's any truth in the lie. You've already told me more than you might have if I hadn't lied. So just what more can you tell me about the missing Helen? What might have troubled her?"

"Genealogy is my guess," he said.

"Explain."

"Helen told me she's been diagnosed with a rare, genetically transferred disease of the lungs called *hai no encho*, well known in Japan since the 1800s. She did a genealogy study and learned that her grandfather was Japanese, which, incidentally, makes her a Sansei. She was told that its best specialist practiced in Kyoto. Not wanting her family to know anything until she could determine the course of the disease—or if she actually had it—she asked me for a loan and flew over to see him. That's where Helen is now. Alive, I hope, well, and hardly missing. Would you like me to call her right now to prove what I've just told you?"

Hearing the ring of truth, I promise the old scoundrel in me that I'll tell no more lies. Well, not, at least, to Sessei. "Make the call," I tell him.

He does. After speaking to Barton awhile, he hands his cell to me. I inquire after her health. In tears, she says she's just received a clean bill. Then I make her promise to relay the news to her folks immediately. "Of course," she promises.

Case solved.

I thrust my hand out to the yakuzaishi. His smile, now smug, has returned. He looks at my hand a moment before taking it. "And may I say, Sansei Sensei Sessei, *Gomenasai.*" I remember the phrase from the old song. It means "I'm sorry."

He shrugs his broad shoulders. "And I accept your apology, Mr. Wolfe." Grinning now, he fakes a chop at me.

Seeing God
(A True Story)

Having seen God just once, I thought it worth dog-earing that page in my life: 7:15 p.m., Sunday, March 20, 2011.

Okay, I'm sipping my preprandial martini. About a third of the way through, while reading, I get to thinking about the Saturday volunteer walks I'd been taking each week the past dozen or so years with the mentally or otherwise disabled residents of Cedars of Marin in Marin County where I lived at the time. They were a lovable bunch whom I'd often thought about recruiting as characters for a mystery novel in which they'd work together with our small cadre of volunteers to solve some diabolical crime. Maybe I'd call it "Murder at the Cedars of Marin."

But this time, instead, a picture came to mind of something I'd seen every Saturday for all those years at Cedars and yet had taken little notice of before, nor had I given it much significance.

When we volunteers would arrive to lead the residents on their walk, we'd find many of them already gathered out front to greet us with high fives or hugs, and often thank us just for being there. There was no pretense to these expressions of love and gratitude. They were honest feelings honestly expressed because those who expressed them had no guile, none whatsoever. Their "agenda" was simply to take their walk and stop at the convenience store along the way for the weekly treat they would buy with the few dollars allotted to them. But those moments of greeting went to the heart of what motivated us to do what we did, year after year. It was a greater reward—a sop for the soul, you might say—than we could possibly receive any other way. These residents were, in fact, doing more for us than we were for them.

So I'm sitting there that Sunday evening, sipping my drink, when another thought shoves both my mystery novel and that scene of greeting aside. I suddenly visualize another scene that always took place between the fifteen minutes we volunteers would arrive and the moment we'd begin our hour-plus walk.

What I see, in the midst of our group, is two of the Cedars residents, unable to walk with us, being picked up by their parents for their Saturday outing.

First, there's longtime resident, Eleanor Powers—I'm not using her actual name—who is . . . who defines the very word . . . happy. Inspirationally happy. So much so that she makes everyone who knows her happy. Tiny Eleanor, perhaps in her sixties, is somewhat mentally challenged, quite bent, but uses her walker energetically, and with aplomb. When I'd see her, walkering herself to her parents' car, I'd always say something like, "Hi, Eleanor, how ya doin'?" And she, with her huge, beautiful smile, would always reply, "I'm wonderful! Thanks for asking." And she'd usually add something like— not the least bit banal coming from her—"Isn't it a beautiful day?" And the way she'd say it . . . and just to be in her presence . . . it became a beautiful day even if it was raining. Eleanor's parents, easily in their eighties, readily recognized us volunteers just as we recognized them, and we'd say or nod hello to each other.

The second resident, Lena Williams, another Cedars long-timer, even smaller than Eleanor and about the same age, can walk, barely, but is severely disabled mentally, cannot speak and is not able to openly acknowledge the presence of others. And every week, her mother, perhaps in her eighties, would arrive when we did to pick up her Lena for their day together.

God is coming; stay with me.

So there I am, thinking about these stunning scenes of familial love I'd been witnessing every week, writ on my mind with invisible ink and revealed, that Sunday evening, by the heat of my gin, and yet about which I had given so little thought before. And that's when it occurred to me that it's time I walked up to Mr. and Mrs. Powers and Mrs. Williams, introduce myself properly, and tell them what an absolutely exquisite thing their love of their child had been to observe all these years.

I even worked on appropriate words to say to these remarkable parents because I wanted the words to be right: "Though I know you don't need me to tell you this, you have something very special in your daughter. And she has something very special in you. And the thing that's so special is . . . love. God has blessed you all."

And so, come the next Saturday, I said something close to these words to each of them. Ending with that odd—coming from me— "God has blessed you all."

God? Who am I—who was this devout atheist—to have invoked the name of someone . . . something . . . in whom, in which, I did not believe? In which I *professed* not to believe. What had prompted me to even think of, much less speak the name of, God, and insert Him into this stunning tableau?

And then it smacked me in the face.

I had seen God. And God was not a robed and bearded deity who resembles man and resides in heaven. I had seen God in the love of these aged people with familiar faces but who'd been relative strangers to me, and me to them, for years.

I had seen God not for one rare moment, but every Saturday for many, many years. And I guess I was too blind to recognize Him. I had seen God in the love these parents had been showing to their child, a love exhibited by the simple act of being there; in one case, a mother's and father's love in being there for their Eleanor, who could so eloquently speak her thanks for my "Hi, how ya doin"; in the other, a mother's love in being there for her Lena, who could not speak hers.

An epiphany? I don't know. Maybe all I saw, on that Sunday evening in 2011, was a beautiful and unique expression of love. But I will swear to you that I saw God. And that time—I did recognize Him.

And when I did, I burst into tears. I sobbed at the very beauty of what, at last, I was given to see.

Paco in Need
(For Pablo)

"Hey... Hola!" I called down to the man standing below my second floor balcony. He was sifting through our apartment building's trash dumpster for cans and bottles he could turn into cash. Slowly turning his face, mostly hidden by his sweat-rimmed cap, he gave me a resigned look that suggested he was once again about to be shooed away from what might be seen as trespassing; as some kind of theft. But that wasn't how I looked at it. Doing what he did, he was doing the world a recycling favor and maybe making a small living for himself and his family.

"Can you use some clothing?" I said, not sure he understood English. He shook his head, yes, so I tossed down a shopping bag stuffed with things I'd outgrown or was tired of wearing. He picked up the bag and gave me a nod of thanks. There was a certain dignity in the way he held himself while finishing his sifting and the stowing of his loaded bags into the trunk of his faded Mitsubishi coupe—about ninety in car years—before he drove off.

For several months now he'd arrive Saturday mornings about seven, so that maybe once a month, when I had a bag of clothes, an old lamp or toaster or something, I'd hear him rummaging in the dumpster and, often half awake, stumble to the balcony to toss or lower my stuff down. He seemed pleased to get it and it made me feel good to give it. No big deal. Win-win, like that.

Then, one Saturday morning, just being me, I asked him,

"What's your name?" The dark look I got suggested he didn't have papers and was uncomfortable with the question. "Just your first name?" I added.

"Paco," he replied, reluctantly.

"I'm Desmond. Des. Do you have a family, Paco? Kids?"

I guess it was the right question because he held up four fingers and grinned. A quick change from his first distrusting look.

"How old?" I asked. I was thinking maybe I could collect some stuff for his kids from my friends.

"One son, three daughters. Danny, seventeen; Mariah, fifteen; Dahlia, eight; Riley, four."

This he said mostly in serviceable English and with much pride in his voice. I wondered where that "Riley" came from but didn't ask. I didn't ask about his legal status either because I'd come to like the man, or, I should say, respect the man, and I didn't feel it was my business to inquire.

One Saturday, several visits later, though I had nothing for him, I stepped out on my balcony to say hello and we got to talking. He told me a little about himself and his family. It wasn't comfortable talking from above so I came down to meet him face-to-face and shake his hand. He pulled off his grimy glove to do so. The grip of his big, leathery hand was hardly as tentative as the attitude he'd shown me when first we met.

I don't know what that face-to-face meant to him but, after a Hola from above several Saturdays later, he replied in kind and then motioned to me to come below again, saying, "Por favor, sir." I came down, of course, wondering what he had in mind.

He had plenty.

It took some verbal stumbling, but here's the gist of what he said. Yes, he had been doing his best to make a living selling the recyclables he collected every day, but the price for them was dropping rapidly and he was very concerned that he could no longer earn enough to feed his family and pay his rent and keep his car running. But, he hastened to say, he was managing; he'd saved a few dollars. His only luxury, he admitted, was to take his family on Sundays to the soccer grounds at the park near him because his children loved the game, and his wife, Marta, would then lay out a spread of roasted chicken and churros for a picnic. They lived in a two-bedroom apartment in East Los Angeles—"East Los" he called it—and he drove about fifty miles every day making his rounds. Though I welcomed his new openness with me, I sensed there was a purpose to what he was telling me.

There was.

Reticent as he had been earlier, Paco Alvarez now told me that he felt he could trust me enough to ask a large favor of me. He appeared, at once, to be both hopeful and pained.

"Go ahead, Paco," I said. Was he about to hit me up for a loan? In a second I would feel guilty for thinking that.

"Mr. Desmond," he began—he insisted on calling me Mr. Desmond or sir—"I must tell you that I am an undocumented immigrant." He said this as though he had practiced the speech he was making. "They call me an illegal alien and say that I have no legal right to be here and maybe I don't. But I feel that you will not report me as such and, sir, I have an important question for you." He waited to see if I would accept his question, his confession. I could think of nothing other than to open my hands to him, inviting him to continue. Which he did. At length.

"Mr. Desmond," he said. "I am a hardworking man. But I do not have a job, a real job. If I could find a real job, then I could get a green card, you know what that is?" I nodded. "Good," he said. "But I cannot even ask for a job because then they ask me, well . . . you know." I knew. "Anyhow, If I could get a green card I could stay here in America—a place I love, you must understand." I understood. "Then I could become an American citizen which is what I want more than anything in the world. And then I would be able to vote and I would gladly pay my taxes and I could send my children to school without fear that they would deport me and—"

I had to stop him. "Paco, I do understand. I wish that for you too. But why are you telling me, an old man, this? What is it you think I can do for you?"

Paco's darkly handsome, thinly mustached face fell. His head went to one side. "I thought maybe you could find a job for me—any kind of job except this . . . this . . . what I am doing."

Here's the gist of what I told him. I'm a draftsman. An old one, past eighty and pretty well retired. My specialty is patent drafting —making drawings of inventions for patent attorneys the old-fashioned way, with T-square and triangles, with compass and dividers, with Rapidograph pen and India ink. I'm among the last of my kind because draftsmen now do their work exclusively by CAD . . . Computer Aided Design. But I've kept a few old clients because they like the personal service I provide and appreciate the art inherent in the drawings I make by hand. Still, I explained, with so little work of my own, what kind of work could I find for him?

Paco listened with great patience and even greater interest. He wasn't scratching his head though he looked like he was about to. "You could teach me, sir," he replied."

"But nobody wants drawings the way I make them anymore," I protested. "You have to know a computer to be a draftsman today." Then I changed the subject. "I'll show you what I do, wait here—no, come on up with me. And he did, readily, and I showed him samples of my hand-drawn plates, and he was in awe, without words to express it. His eyes, eating up my drawings, glistened with compliments.

"I know a little how to use a computer, sir," he said, excitedly. "I learned this at the library. I go there many times and they teach me. They have classes and I like to learn. But don't you have to know how to make these patent drawings of yours before you can make them on a computer, is that not right?"

He had me there. And he had me again when he drew a worn, folded sheet of lined, loose-leaf paper from his pocket and showed it to me. It was a beautifully penciled sketch of a cat staring out of a window. "This is Pepe, my cat. I draw it."

"Paco, this is beautiful. If you want to be a draftsman it helps to be something of an artist too, but to teach you drafting, I don't know . . ."

"Nobody wants my cat drawings, sir. I—"

I stopped him again. "Paco, please call me Desmond. Or Des, not 'sir' or 'Mister,' just as I call you Paco. Okay?"

"Yes, sir . . . Des-mond. Anyhow, these patent attorneys, they will pay me for my CAD drafting, right? I will be a good CAD draftsman if you will teach me to draft, to do what you do. I will bring you a basket of fresh fruit every week if you are willing to teach me."

All the while, I had to admit that the man had every right to ask. He wanted to get ahead. I had always wanted my kids to succeed me, but they weren't interested, and I don't blame them. I was practicing a dying art. I mean, just how do you succeed in an esoteric field like patent drafting these days? Hardly by handcrafting drawings in India ink. Not anymore. But this humble man Paco had the answer. First, learn drafting. Then learn patent drafting. Then CAD—computer drafting.

Paco was both logical and relentless. So I said yes to him. Yes, I would teach him, yes, I would give him three months of lessons and then we would know if he were meant to be a draftsman.

What else could I say? But just what was I getting into?

Paco Alvarez, every Saturday morning after that memorable conversation, with his gym bag full of my cast off old drafting instruments, and before even glancing at our dumpster, tapped on my door. For our one hour—sometimes, when we were really at it, two hours —he would work over his board with me looking over his shoulder. With less and less looking over required as time passed.

As he learned . . . quickly, as I'd suspected . . . I came to eat a lot of oranges and mangoes instead of the chips and crackers I loved. I lost four pounds in the process, so we both benefitted from my lessons.

Paco had a natural talent combined with a keen, three-dimensional mind that any good draftsman or artist must have. He understood as well that, in laying out drawings of an invention, the draftsman must quickly grasp the heart of the invention—that which sets it apart from other inventions—and disclose it with the most revealing orthographic and perspective views, and often with complicated exploded perspectives. Paco got it. Right away. His mistakes were rarely repeated. He truly was a natural.

So at the end of the three months I handed him an old, non-working electric pencil sharpener. "For your 'final examination,' Paco, I want you to draw this," I said. "I want a perspective, a top and bottom plan view, a left and right side, and a front and back as though it were for a design patent. Then I want you to take it apart and add as many auxiliary views and cross-sections as you think necessary to fully disclose it as though it were for a utility patent. Finally, you must give me an exploded perspective showing all its parts. You have one week to do this. Any questions?"

He shook his head rapidly. "No, Mr. Desmond. I will do it," he said, furiously jotting notes in Spanish. He inspected the pencil sharpener a moment then placed it in his bag. Instead of the frown I expected, there was a shadow of a smile, a confident one, under his mustache. If my Mechanical Drawing 101 professor had asked me that, I'd have vomited.

The following Saturday Paco brought the sharpener back, stripped and rebuilt . . . and, incidentally, working again . . . along with no fewer than seven plates of drawings as beautifully thought out, drawn and inked as those it took me a year's apprenticeship to make half as well, and nowhere near as quickly. As I studied them for the rare mistake I was able to find, Paco studied my face. When I finished I looked up and said, "Paco, my *brilliante*, on your final examination I am giving you an A-plus." Which I then swashed with a red felt-tip pen on the cover of his submission, then signed. To complete the ceremony, I pulled an envelope from my pocket and handed it to him. "And here, sir, is your 'diploma' from the Mr. Desmond School of Patent Drafting."

"Diploma?" he said. He looked confused as he murmured his thanks. He was grinning now but didn't seem to know what to do other than stare at it.

"Well, aren't you going to open it?"

He blinked and opened it. Immediately he did a double-take as his eyes went wide at what he was seeing: a check for three thousand dollars. Before he could say anything—and before any tears could be shed by him or by me—I said, "That is a loan, Paco, not a gift. It will cover your tuition for a year-and-a-half CAD degree program at the

Southwood School of Design, not far from where you live. With my recommendation, you won't have any trouble getting in. I expect you to pay me back from your wages when you get your first job. Congratulations!"

He stood there, stunned, then took my hand in both of his and shook it till I thought it would fall off. And he hugged me—my first of many to come—before racing out to report the news to his family, completely forgetting to collect his cans and bottles.

All that I have been telling you? That all happened nearly three years ago. Paco Alvarez did just fine at Southwood. But he never did get a job. Never looked for one. Instead, on the day he graduated, he officially opened his own firm, Alvarez Patent Drafting, working out of his small apartment, then out of an office. A nice one, too. And he's doing just fine; more than fine. He's already repaid every penny of that three thousand dollar loan, including ten percent interest that I never asked for, but he would not allow me to refuse. Not only that, but he's so busy now with his computer-generated patent work that he sends me his occasional overflow which, though I'm now approaching my mid-eighties, I'm able to do almost as well as Paco. And still love doing as much as I did on the first day I did it, over sixty years ago. And, frankly, I can use the money.

I'm often invited to Paco's Sunday picnics because he insists I'm part of the family. And recently I attended the sumptuous wedding of young Danny where his dad made "Papa Des" get up and tell the whole story I've just told you.

Then Paco spoke: "Without Papa Des there would be no wedding like this. Without my friend Desmond I would still be collecting cans and bottles."

"I don't think so, Paco," I said.

Then I sat down.

Shifted Passions

I'm Lute Garrison. Maybe you've heard of me. You haven't? "Lute, the Chute?" No? Well, me and my team are in the Drag Racing Hall of Fame. No small feat, I assure you. Some say there wouldn't be any sport like drag racing if it hadn't been for me.

That moniker, "Lute, the Chute?" I was always the first to pop my drag chute—the one that helps brake me so I don't fly off the end of the track—because I always seemed to be the first one over the quarter-mile finish line. I liked finishing first.

Anyhow, I got an odd phone call a couple months ago from a young woman. I'd like to tell you about it because, at sixty-four, I don't get that many from them. This one was from a Sherri—or was it Cherri?—Milliken, who said she was with "Crossover," an AARP eMagazine that featured "intimate interviews" they called "Elderviews." Cute. She was doing a story about famous people who, later in life, shifted passions to endeavors that had nothing to do with what had made them famous like, as she mentioned, George Foreman, the former heavyweight champ who has his own barbecue grill company. At first I thought it was just another phone hustle. And she sounded so much like a little girl that I wasn't even sure I was talking to a grown-up. After she introduced herself she happened to ask if I tweeted.

"You mean do I tap out those messages with the octothorpe in front of them?

"Huh," she replied. "What's that?"

"It's a hashtag."

There was a long hesitation before she said, "Could you spell it?"

"Sure," I replied. "H-A-S-H—"

"No," she interrupted, "I meant 'octothorpe.'" She didn't get it that I was teasing her.

So I spelled octothorpe, feeling a little smug that I could fold a new word into her empty brainpan. Well, if she wanted to interview me, what the hell, I invited her over. I'm glad I did because she was a real looker, a blond with those Radio City Music Hall chorus girl legs. She kind of looked like the young things in hot pants who used to hang out near my pit at all the race tracks. Those were the days! But somehow the interview didn't go quite as I thought it would.

Here's how it did go, best as I recall.

"So, Mr. Garrison, you started out in a two-car garage, right?"

"That's close. It was a one-car garage."

"Right. And a year later you were at, what you were once quoted as saying, the 'top of your game,' one of the fastest-rising—"

"Wait a minute. I never said that. A year later I was still at the bottom of my game. But a few years after that I was hitting the finishing line first almost every time."

"Finishing first. An interesting way to put it, sir. I suppose you did see yourself as needing to finish first." Then she put down her notebook for a minute and stared at me with what I'd have to call slack-jawed awe. "What was it like, Mr. Garrison, I mean *really* like," she asked, "to be first, to be the true pioneer in one of the most important endeavors of our time?"

"Pioneer? Now that, young lady, is truly an interesting way to put it. I don't know if it was 'one of the most important endeavors of our time,' but yeah, I guess I was a pioneer. As an inventor and engineer, I pretty much had to start from scratch. In the beginning my prototypes just wouldn't perform the way I first designed them."

"You said you were an engineer, sir, right?"

"Right," I said, "An automotive engineer." But she didn't seem to hear me because she was too busy scribbling notes and inspecting her next question on what looked like a three-page list.

"And you used your prototype to build your team into one of the best ever in its field, right, sir?"

"Right. I guess so." I was getting a little annoyed with the "sir" bit. Why do you keep calling me sir?" I asked. "And why do you keep saying 'right?'"

Again, she acted like she hadn't heard me. "It's obvious," she said, "that no one has ever put solar power to better use than you, Mr. Garrison."

"Solar power? Are you pulling my leg, Sherri? You think solar power put me over the finish line in under four seconds? If I had to rely on solar power I'd never have made it to the *starting* line! My power was supplied by X16 oxygenated fuel. That's what powers a dragster."

Whatever I had just said stunned the poor girl. Her writing pad dropped along with her well-formed jaw. "Why are you looking at me like that?" I said.

"Please tell me you're Knute Garrison, Mr. Garrison. You are, aren't you?"

"*Knute* Garrison? I'm Lute Garrison. 'Lute, the Chute' Garrison, if you're into drag racing."

"Drag racing? Lute Garrison?" she brought her pretty little hands up to cover her even prettier red face with its pretty little red-lipped mouth. She looked like she was about to cry. And she did. "Mr. Garrison, sir, I am so embarrassed. I was told to interview *Knute* Garrison, the inventor of the solar panel and CEO of SolTeK Industries. I Googled him and researched him on Wikipedia and I must have hit a wrong key and, oh my god, please forgive me, sir, but . . ."

I reached out and put my hand on her shoulder to steady her. "I do forgive you. It's okay. I forgive you, Cherri."

"Sherri," she corrected me, through tear-stained hands.

"See, Sherri?" I said, "it's easy to make a mistake like that. So I've forgiven you, it's your turn to forgive me."

"But—"

"Forget the buts. You're human. No big deal. But, since you're here, consider this. Lute Garrison is not exactly chopped liver. You need a story, I got one. And not half as boring as solar panels."

Cherri—Sherri—collected herself, wiped her gorgeous, almond-shaped emerald eyes, picked up her notepad and said, in a small voice, "Well, I was going to ask what you were doing now . . . what your passion was now . . . now that you're not covering America with solar panels." She half laughed and half hiccuped, and I laughed with her.

"How about 'now that I'm not setting America's dragster speed records?'"

"You're making fun of me," she said, pouting a pretty little pout.

"No, Sherri, I'm not." You were making fun of yourself and I like that in a woman—in anybody. I wasn't sure if it was the beating of my sympathetic heart or something happening a little lower that made me want to reach out and hold her, call me a dirty old man. "Look, kid," I said, repeating myself, "I'm not making fun of you. Go ahead and ask me about my 'shifted passions.'"

"Okay," she said, perking up at my encouragement. "I suppose you've given up drag racing, ri—?" She caught herself before she could finish her usual tag word, and she smiled a smile that melted me.

"Yes, Sherri, I gave up drag racing some time ago."

"Then just what is your passion these days?"

I told her, we talked about it, I brought out a pitcher of iced tea and some excellent butter cookies I'd just picked up from the artisan bakery down the street, and we kept on talking for another two hours.

Sherri Milliken's interview, incidentally, never made it to AARP's eMagazine because she quit her job that very day, and now she works for me at the passion I've shifted to.

What passion is that? Didn't I mention it before? I'm a pornographer. I always wondered what AARP would do with that.

The Lesson

Shadrack P. Nelson had taught writing to aspiring Masters candidates for more years now than he cared to remember, even though conventional wisdom suggested that writing couldn't be taught. But try telling that to his boss, Jacob Browning, flamboyant dean of Jefferson University's famous Writers Program.

Shadrack, of course, agreed with the dean, an old friend from his student days at Jefferson. He knew that if he couldn't teach writing he'd have no career at all because, as an author, the only book he'd ever sold was his second, a mystery called *What Doesn't Kill You*. It had reviewed well, securing his staff position. But that was over thirty years ago and—thank God for tenure.

A poor student himself, an indolent English major, he'd progressed, not by studying but by his gutted out ability to write extemporaneously on demand. And accurately predict when such demands would be made so he'd be sure to show up in class, something he rarely did otherwise.

Shadrack—Shad to his colleagues, even to his graduate students—leaned to fiction. The voracious reading of it, the rare writing of it, the love of teaching it. Particularly the art—to him, the science—of the mystery, a genre about which he could trot out the knowledge he'd gained by suckling upon the oeuvres of Conan Doyle, Maugham, Stoker, Hammett and every other nineteenth- and twentieth-century mystery writer from Poe and Dostoevsky to Graham Greene and Stephen King.

On one perfect Monday morning in mid-September, Shad Nelson was teaching the first day of a course listed as "Whodunit 401: The Noir Writers." Having designed and curricularized it a few years earlier, it was now in the category of sign-up-early-or-lose-your-seat. Fully fifty-two MFA aspirants packed the tiered seats facing him. Following a perfunctory welcome, Professor Nelson dug in.

"Look to the left and right of you," he said. What you see are hopeful writers, right? Wrong. Let's reverse the calendar to, say, March 13, 1941. Each of you is a detective. A shamus. A gumshoe. A private eye who's just been hired at fifteen simoleons a day plus expenses, and two cents a mile for the use of your battered 1931 Hudson coupe, got that? Okay. A sincere-looking blonde slithers . . .without knocking . . . into your fourth floor walk-up office in the Acme—"

"Professor Nelson!"

What the hell? The professor's young student assistant, Sharon Donohue, looking deeply troubled, had just rushed through the door nearest the lectern. She was wearing short white shorts and a baby blue, off-shouldered blouse that revealed an attractively deep cleavage. A red ribbon held her hair in a loose ponytail and her feet were encased in a pair of blood red cowboy boots. A large tattoo of a yellow rose tinged with red adorned her right forearm. Every pen writing, every finger tapping on a laptop or notebook, the very sentence the professor was speaking, stopped.

Shad Nelson's lips went tight. "What is it, Ms. Donohue?" he demanded, his hands outstretched in a can't-you-see-how-busy-I-am pose.

"I'm so sorry to disturb you, Professor," blurted the distraught Ms. Donohue, "but it's your wife. She's been trying to reach you but you didn't . . . I guess couldn't . . . pick up. There's an emergency at home and—"

The professor's face went white. "Hold it, Sharon. Slow down, it's all right. I'm certain it's—never mind, just please say what you have to say."

The students looked at each other in wonderment as the comely assistant explained that Shadrack's wife had tried to reach him to say that their cockapoo, Maizie, had run away again and could he please rush home.

Shad's eyes rolled. Up. A look of anger came over his heavily-bearded face. He smacked his forehead, abruptly dismissed Ms. Donohue and turned to his students, most of whom had not yet closed their wide-open jaws.

"Excuse me, people, I apologize for this embarrassing interruption," he said. "I almost forgot what we were discussing. Can someone remind me?"

They all looked at each other again, not sure what to make of the jarring scene that had just played out. A hand went up in the fifth row. It belonged to Adam Singleton, an exchange student from Jamaica. "Shad, mon, jus' wot de hail was dot all about? Is dot girl kiddin'?" The room exploded in laughter.

Waiting for it to subside, Shadrack said, "I'm pleased you asked, Mr. Singleton, because I was about to ask all of you the very same question—but without the lovely tang you just put upon it. What, indeed, was that all about? What all of you just witnessed—and I stress that word, witnessed—was a charade. My lovely wife and I do not own a 'cockapoo' or any other breed of canine. The whole tableau was a sham to detect if you detectives can detect; if you private eyes can see."

Once again, the students looked at one another, this time in confusion. Their professor explained. "I beg you now to use your imagination. You couldn't have come this far without it. So let's now assume another scenario, that my assistant, Ms. Donohue, was my supposed wife, betrayed by moi, her rotten, philandering husband who, she'd just learned, had bedded not just the baby sitter but her best friend as well."

"Takes a whole lot o' imagination, suh." This, from Mr. Singleton again, generating another laugh, a slightly uncomfortable one.

"I'll pretend I didn't hear that, Mr. Singleton. Back to Ms. Donohue acting as my supposed wife. Let's say she was holding a Ruger semi-automatic pistol in her hand, which she used to shoot me dead. I'd have had her do that but didn't want anyone to panic at the shot and call 9-1-1. We are a college campus, after all."

Another laugh. Shad Nelson had their full attention. All were leaning in, practically falling off the front of their chairs.

"All right, you budding shamuses, you now have a murder case to solve. As trained detectives you'll have absorbed details important to solving it, so you probably want to ask questions about what you saw. Well, my friends, I'm not going to entertain any. In fact, though we still have twenty minutes remaining, I'm going to dismiss you. I'll see you two days from now. Solve this 'case.' With answers, not questions." With this, the professor walked off the stage, leaving his dumbfounded students looking at themselves for a third—or was it a fourth—time. Most left the room, a few stayed behind to jot or tap out notes.

Two days later, the class reconvened. Shad looked slowly around, then spoke. "Today is your first blue book test of the semester. The more perspicacious of you will take that as no surprise. The test has only ten questions. It regards what transpired here on Monday. All of you were witnesses. Often, witnesses are not questioned till several days after the event they witnessed. So I wanted you to have a few days to let the details sink in or, for some of you, to have them fade. You needn't, after all, solve this case because I never gave you its full scenario. What I do want to see is what you can remember, or anticipated the need to note, what you saw. You may be sorry if you didn't. But that, in itself, is a lesson you won't forget. Enough said, I'll leave you to write, which, as I recall, is why you enrolled here."

With that, Shadrack stepped back to a portable whiteboard, rolling it to the front of the stage where he spun it around to reveal the ten questions. "You have fifty-five minutes. You may begin now," he said, as he made his exit.

Here's what the board read:

1. Describe, in one detailed paragraph, what you saw here two days ago.
2. Before the interruption you were called detectives. What else were you called?

3. As a detective, what were you to be paid per day, including extras?
4. On what floor was your detective office?
5. What was the year and make of your car?
6. After the interruption, why did my supposed wife want to kill me?
7. What was my supposed wife wearing?
8. Describe the color, style and adornment of her hair.
9. What other distinguishing features did she have?
10. What type of gun did she use?

Fifty-five minutes later, Shadrack returned to his rostrum. "Stop now, pass your books to the left and one of you bring them forward."

While the blue books were making their way to the front, Shadrack P. Nelson spoke again. "You're not really detectives, are you?" he said, rhetorically. "But if you're going to make a living as a writer of, say, detective stories, you're going to need the powers of observation of the best private eyes in the business, real and fictional. Whatever genre you choose, the more you remember of what transpires around you—the more detail you observe and file away in your memory banks—the better you'll do, not as the detectives you're not but as the writers you hope to be. That's your lesson for today. I'll return your blue books on Friday. I doubt you observed as well as I know you'll will in the future.

"Class dismissed."

FilmArt, Ltd.

Delmore P. Philmont, practically from his cradle days, loved movies. Particularly the early forgettable ones that gained such cachet in the twentieth century, the B movies and noirs no one's ever heard of. He'd see upward of two hundred a year, making it understandable that his career path would lead him to become a respected Hollywood film editor.

Philmont's work demanded that he stare at, first, celluloid images, later, digital ones every day, millions of them. But, sharp critic that he was, he came to see far more than a story being told. He saw cinema art comparable to what one would recognize in a museum or gallery, or on a concert stage. Oddly, the film he first saw as true art was an obscure Harold Lloyd two-reeler talkie called *Gadzooks!* in which the irrepressible anti-hero finds himself dangling over the side rail of a window-washer's platform outside a thirty-story-high building. The POV fascinated Philmont, inspiring an unusual idea: projecting just such films against just such buildings.

The idea percolated until, a year before his retirement at sixty-two. His closest friend and colleague, Dean Armiston, was an extraordinarily talented cinematographer who knew more about what made cameras tick than Bell and Howell combined. Philmont put his ambitious concept to his friend and asked if he could come up with a projector that could deliver a clear image to the entire side of a skyscraper. Armiston, in his reticent way, lifted his shoulders and palms and said, "Why not?" They shook hands as equal partners and,

112

within six months, Armiston had perfected the prototype, which he named *Projectron.*

Philmont began inspecting L.A.'s tallest buildings—or rather the sides of them—downtown, at Century City and throughout metro L.A. including the San Fernando Valley. As congenial as he was glib, he convinced managers of not just the residential but commercial buildings which most appealed to him, that his free "projections," as he first called them, would provide their properties with helpful publicity and increased sales by drawing huge crowds. He secured signed contracts for his deals while carrying rarely more than twenty dollars in his pocket.

Lining up his first few buildings, he incorporated his little venture as FilmArt, Ltd. and was ready to project its first films, but for a slight problem. FilmArts' development fees had left both him and his partner broke. Actually, beyond broke. They were nearly half a million in debt and hadn't yet opened their magnificent Projectron's shutters.

Philmont had anticipated that FilmArt could be floated on the revenue from ads that would be shown along with their films but the catch was that they first had to prove they could draw large audiences that would warrant ad fees. Well, thought Philmore, they weren't expected to make money in their first year so, a couple of second mortgages on their homes later and the pair were in business.

Philmont's master plan was to open with *Gadzooks!*, the same Harold Lloyd film that had inspired his venture, followed by an old Bogart noir, *Dead Reckoning*, then later blockbusters like *2001* and the *Star Wars* sagas. Armiston insisted they'd need to hire a publicist to make certain that crowds would be drawn, but the shrewder Philmont, did not want to spend more money they didn't have, nor draw any publicity before the first showing for fear that the law would find a way to stop them. He insisted that they'd simply run their first feature unannounced, sit back and just see what would happen. And he was a believer in word-of-mouth, especially as it didn't cost anything. "Project the film and they will come," he said, paraphrasing his favorite sports film.

And my, how they did come. When the Projectron, housed in a

nondescript, well-used panel truck fitted with a second-hand Dolby theatrical sound system, threw its first images up against L.A.'s tallest skyscraper, the U.S. Bank Tower, appropriately situated on Hollywood Boulevard, precisely at 8:00 p.m. on October 19, 2016, all hell broke loose. Curious people gathered on the sidewalks, which soon were filled, forcing the crowds into the streets where many cars had already stopped to see what was going on. The wide street quickly came to resemble that rush hour parking lot known as the 405 Freeway. The black & whites were helpless to untangle the mess that resulted, even though the laughing crowds were mellow and well-behaved.

The next day's coverage of the event proved a publicist's dream. Everyone was talking about what the Times called "The mysterious film that appeared hundreds of feet high yesterday evening, unexpected and unannounced in the very heart of Hollywood." "Return of the drive-in!" shouted the Times. "Who needs TV?" asked the Hollywood Reporter.

So Delmore Philmont decided to project *Dead Reckoning* the very next night, this time downtown against the L.A. City Hall itself, on Spring Street, just to see if he could get away with it. And the crowds gathered and the streets filled and the law makers and enforcers were stymied once again, mainly because, while they approached and questioned Philmont and Armiston at the center of the ruckus, they could find no law being broken except the misdemeanor of creating noise pollution, because, as yet, there was no law preventing films from being projected against the side of a building. Nor were any permits required. This wasn't a paid event, it wasn't a parade, it was free and, as yet, totally lacking in anything seriously prosecutable, not even the enterprising "Popcorn Pete's" trucks that popped up alongside the movies. FilmArt had no deal with them (though they meant to in the future).

The "as yet," of course, had to come. First off, extra safety forces had to be called in to control the growing crowds attracted by the projections. And free movies for the masses did not exactly sit well with the theater owners who wanted to sue someone, anyone, but had no grounds. Their lawyers were stymied by the fact that became apparent. Such free movies created a loophole in all the laws they could uncover because their "freeness" proved to be Philmont's other stroke of genius. Had he charged even a dime, it all might have gone against him.

So, while the forces of City Hall—on which side 2001 was being projected—debated the legalities of such showings, and while the theater owners were railing against the distributors who were railing against FilmArt, the movies went on against the sides of both of Century City's Century Towers, against the new Wilshire Grand Center, still under construction, against One World Trade Center in Long Beach and against 10 Universal City Plaza in the Valley. At the same time, the pressure to quash the showings was growing, especially after an injunction was filed by the attorneys for the theater owner's association.

But when news of the injunction was made public, a heartening thing happened. Word of it spread rapidly through the social media. Within a week nearly 100,000 petition signatures were gathered on FilmArts' behalf, both on the street and electronically. The people wanted their free pop-up movies—for which they'd invented the name "Slabs"—and would boycott the theaters if they didn't get them. The owners chose to ignore the petitions and press on with the injunction, threatening criminal charges and a civil suit. The petitioners responded in force with a call for a "No Show" weekend during which they not only boycotted theaters but picketed the largest of them, marching in front of them with signs demanding "Free Movies or No Movies!" and "Slabs, not Crabs." After the second weekend of the boycott, the loss in ticket sales by the theaters had grown to an estimated $1.5 million. The injunction and threat of a lawsuit was quickly withdrawn. As for the noise pollution, the ingenious Armiston created a free app that allowed their projected film's sound to be synced on a cell phone.

As for the building owners, they were noticing a sizable uptick in traffic and sales at the many businesses within and near them, businesses which, in many cases, they owned or whose space they leased. And when the theater owners came to realize that the films being shown were not first run, FilmArt was no longer considered a threat to them.

Philmont and Armiston were still broke and deeply in debt. But, while this deeply worried Armiston, Philmont, the true entrepreneur, was not fazed. As anticipated, with little cash but attractive stock options, he hired a small but highly effective crew to organize a group funding campaign and a sales crew to sell ads that would be projected before each Slab showing. The money rolled in and, within a year, the burgeoning company was nearly solvent.

Meanwhile, FilmArt had expanded its showing of Slabs—now a registered trademark rapidly becoming a brand—to San Francisco and was moving north to Portland and Seattle, and east to Las Vegas, Phoenix, Dallas, Houston and Denver, with the Right Coast next on the agenda, including, down the road, the Big Apple. Within another year, dozens of Projectrons, well protected by patents, were doing their thing throughout America, and every city with a twenty-story building was clamoring for their very own Slabs®.

Every city but New York itself. FilmArt had gone public with great fanfare in March of 2018, but hadn't yet hit New York City with its showings. What Philmont intended he accomplished on the second anniversary of FilmArt's first Slab showing. That was to show his first Manhattan Slab on the very day FilmArt was listed—with FA as its stock symbol—on the New York Stock Exchange. And there, on the balcony overlooking the Exchange floor, at precisely 4:00 p.m. on Friday, October 19, 2018, the proud Delmore P. Philmont, with his old pal, Dean Armiston at his side, brought the hammer loudly to the closing bell. At eight o'clock that same evening, fittingly, *Wall Street*, the movie, was projected on the front of the Exchange at 11 Wall Street. And New York quickly fell in love with the Slab. As did, shortly after, Europe and the Pacific Rim countries.

FilmArt had gone big in a very big way. So big that, two years later, NBC/Universal, owned by Comcast, made Del and Dean an offer they couldn't refuse. Six point three billion.

And so the pair retired, only to form the FilmArt Foundation, dedicated to the spread of free movies for the masses and the establishment of the FilmArt School of the Film Arts, offering education in that high art form free to any student who couldn't afford it.

Finding AAA

I was lost, as usual. And desperate. Yet still unwilling to face my locatory disability. All right, my total inability to find my way. Please don't misunderstand. If I sound over-the-top, I'm being literal. I'm a dedicated commuter. I drive eighty-five miles each way every day to my job at Glidden as its turncoat. That's what they call me at the Glidden plant, and I'm proud of it: The Turncoat. But not the kind you're thinking of. I am the nonpareil expert in my field who can, with a prolific hand, turn a coat of paint into a silken gown. What I don't know about paint can be poured into a half-pint can with plenty of room at the top. And which is why I—and only I—am trusted to paint all the rooms and the walls—yes, interior as well as exterior—and the ceilings and home furnishings you marvel at in all those Glidden TV commercials. Half a shade off and the commercial would be ruined, would never pass the demanding approval process that our professional color consultants demand of us.

But, if painting is my forte, my downfall, my armageddon, is my sense of direction. I can't, I cannot, seem to find my way to work each day. I know that repeating the route should make the task easy, but, as yet, I haven't been able to repeat the route with anything resembling consistency. I can't find yesterday's route today. I have an iPhone and consult Siri regularly, but—can't explain it—I (like her, occasionally) get lost nonetheless. And when I reach the city where our plant is I become the most confused. And when I need to get to our test-painting studios, forget it, I'm totally lost. I'm afraid

I have—no, I *do* have—what our company psychologist has labeled destinophobia, or the fear of seeking my destination, an affliction that seems to baffle the psychologist as much as Siri baffles me or is often baffled herself.

It had come to the point where my job was threatened. No matter how early I might start out in the morning, I would become lost and would arrive late, often relying upon street people for directions, some of whom had come to know me because I'd stopped them so often, and some who would actually misdirect me simply for their own amusement.

You might ask why I never moved close to my job so I could maybe walk to work. I'm sorry but that just wouldn't work because I get lost walking too, and if—when—that happens it would take even longer to reach my job.

Well, one day, I came across one of those street people I'd never seen before. He was standing less than a mile from the Glidden offices. A one-legged man wearing a soiled dashiki over OshKosh overalls. The man—Columbine Pendragon by name—took pity upon me when I stopped him for directions, and was quick to admit that he was as direction-afflicted as me.

"In all honesty, my friend," he said, "I haven't the slightest idea how to get to Glidden. But," he added, "I believe I have the solution to your problem." His wild eyes looked to his left and right, surreptitiously, as if he were about to impart the secret of life. Then he grabbed my lapels and pulled me halfway through my side window so he could whisper a single word into my ear that—I will tell you right now—came to change my life, to make my fear of reaching my destination as nothing. As *nothing!* The word?

"AAA."

Well, maybe that's not a word. But that's what Pendragon said on that fateful day, pointing out AAA's direction to the east, then changing his mind and pointing to the west. "AAA," he repeated, with true earnestness. He then drifted off into the swirling fog that so often graced the shores of the Cuyahoga River on late autumn mornings.

I was never to see Columbine Pendragon again. But that word, or whatever it is, stuck with me. AAA. I forgot work that day. I had to seek it out. It took me two more hours to find it and when I finally did—I found myself. There its sign loomed, neon-lit, piercing that fog so symbolic of the one from which I was about to emerge. AAA. I sensed an epiphany.

Approaching the door, salvation overcame me; I dropped to my knees and wept. Once inside I was guided by an understanding counselor to their meeting room upstairs. I could see others, obviously suffering as was I, kindred bottom-of-the-barrel spirits standing on the porch outside the meeting room, drinking coffee and smoking. A gong sounded and they came inside and seated themselves. I sat in the last row, an emotional wreck, ready to listen, not knowing but nonetheless readily willing to give myself over to whatever was to come but not yet ready to insinuate participation.

Their leader called them to order and had them recite, in unison, a touching prayer. The leader called it the Prayer of the Lost Ones. It went something like, "God, grant me the ability to accept the fact that I cannot find my way, the courage to seek my way nevertheless, and the wisdom to know when I am totally lost." After free maps and travel guides were given out, a motivational speaker came forth and told, with great passion, the story of how he'd once been lost and now he was found through adherence to the tenets of AAA's hallowed "Twelve Steps of Finding Oneself".

What could this be about? Members, some of them wearing 40-, even 50-year pins in their lapels, recited, in turn, each one. "We admitted we were powerless over our misdirection—that our lives had become unmanageable; We came to believe that a power greater than ourselves could show us the way and restore our sense of direction; We made a decision to turn our misdirection over to GPS as we understood It; We made a searching and fearless inventory of the maps in our glove compartments; We admitted to GPS, the exact nature that turned us left when we should have turned right; We're ready to consult more maps to remove the detours we have taken; We asked GPS to show us the true way; We made a list of all the people we repeatedly asked directions of, and made amends to them for all the trouble we caused them; We took a personal inventory and promptly admitted we took a wrong turn; We sought, through prayer and meditation and the conscientious use of Triptiks, to understand where we were headed." And, finally, "We promised to stop at a gas station and ask directions whenever we are lost."

I got it! It was as if lighting had struck me. I was on the way to finding my way. But it was to be a long and arduous journey. A month later, attending daily meetings and giving repeated witness by describing the meandering routes I'd taken to reach the depths of my confusion, I was called forth and given my thirty-day coin, a small AAA bumper sticker and a cupcake with my name on it. I received loving hugs from just about everyone in the room before I tore myself away, tears rolling down my cheeks, and staggered out the wrong door to affix the sticker to the trunk of my old PT Cruiser, just above the peeling "Harry's Cherries" used car dealer decal.

I was certain that I'd find my way home. I felt that I *had* found my way home!

I would never lose my way again. Not with the support of AAA. Not now. Use it or lose it, that was to be my guiding principle from now on.

Before leaving the parking lot I pulled to a stop. A faint song struggled to reach my ears. I rolled down my window so I could hear it more clearly. My fellow acolytes—now my AAA friends—were on the porch again, smoking and singing *Amazing Grace*. The words floated down and cloaked themselves about me. The lyrics linger with me still:

> *Amazing GPS, how sweet the sound,*
> *That saved a wretch like me.*
> *I once was lost but now am found,*
> *Was blind, but now I see.*

The Vegetable Garden

The three men, all well into their seventies, congregated daily behind Mermelstein Towers, one of Miami Beach's few remaining outposts for retired Jews and any other religion or color who might possibly be interested in joining them to play gin rummy or mahjongg or to garden or just to plain schmooze, the latter of which is what these three men did more than anything else they did.

Mermelstein Towers is but a single tower and, at five floors, is hardly towering. Nor were any of the three men sitting on its designated smoking gazebo way off to the rear of the grounds. Morris "Moe" Fingerhut, the tallest, at five-seven, was enjoying the long silence occasioned by the fact that he, Abel Schneider and Ben "the Schemer" Hurwitz, were basking behind the tendrils of smoke rising from the last of the cigars Moe had snuck back from a recent trip to Toronto to visit his daughter, Cheryl.

These cigars, it must be noted, were not ordinary cigars. These were the finest in the land of their origination, that being Cuba, and the cigars being Cohiba Behike BHK-2012s, costing, if you please, five-hundred and forty two Canadian dollars the box of ten, gifted to Moe by his son-in-law, David Foxman, a private investment firm CEO doing, should you ask, very well.

The six-inch Cohibas, ring size fifty-two, were now, stripped necessarily of their gaudy bands, down to a single, yet still amply satisfying, inch.

"Well, that's it, boys," said Moe. "That's the last of the Havanas. But these days we can just pop down to Cuba and grab some more."

Moe stopped speaking and let out a sigh. "I wish," said he. "Just one of these Cohibas costs more than a couple boxes of our Dutch Masters. So I guess that's the end of that."

"No, it isn't," said Ben, now applying his ill-fitting dentures to the dead, saliva-soaked stub in the corner of his generous mouth. "I got an idea."

"Bennie, the Schemer," chimed in Abel. "You always got an idea. Your last little scheme was to bet on a nag called "Running Esther" because Esther was the name of your third wife. Cost you twenty simoleons which, by the way, you didn't happen to have on your person that particular day and, don't forget, you still owe me."

"Thursday we get our checks, Abel, you'll get your money," said Ben. "But here's my idea. A box of say, twenty of those Cubans costs —what did you say, Moe, about six hundred Canadian? Well, I happen to have a cousin who happens to know the trainer of a gorgeous gelding name of 'Pete's Pride,' going off at 40-to-1 today at Hialiah. Hershey says that the trainer says this horse is way overdue and—"

"Wait a minute, Bennie. If this horse is so damn overdue, why's he 40-to-1?"

"Never mind that. At 40-to-1 if we, each of us, put down, say, fifty apiece we'd snag over eighteen hundred smackers, enough to buy not one but *three* boxes of these lovely Cuban Cohibas." Ben's tips and his ideas of how to cash in on them arrived with a frequency equal to the trips he made to the bathroom, engendered by his enlarged prostate.

"You know something, Bennie boy, if you were as good at picking the ponies as you were at math, youda been smoking *your* Cubans long ago, not Moe's."

Moe heard none of this badinage between his two best buddies. He was, instead, enraptured by the sight of three frantic mockingbirds trying to chase each other from a feeder hanging off a corner of the gazebo. He could not take his rheumy eyes off them. He jerked himself to an upright position in his lounger. "I have a thought," he announced, unaware that he was overriding Ben's limp idea.

Moe's ideas were rare in coming, but most often worthwhile. He, Abel thought, was worth listening to. And so, Abel stopped and listened.

"I was fascinated watching those birds fight over the seeds in that feeder," said Moe. "Then the thought struck me, all of a sudden, that seeds are the answer."

"The answer to what, Moe?" said Ben. "What was the question?"

"Shut up, Bennie," said Abel. "Go ahead, Moe."

"You want Cubans, here's what we do. We, all of us, go to Cuba —I'm being serious here—not to *buy* cigars which are just about as expensive down there as in Canada, but to, uh, liberate the seeds that grow up there to become Cubano cigars."

"What do you mean, 'liberate'?" cried Ben, "isn't that stealing?"

"Shut up, Bennie," repeated Abel. "Let Moe talk."

"Stealing is just a word, Benjamin. It's not stealing if we should, say, become curious tourists visiting their tobacco fields and some seeds should accidentally fall into our pants cuffs. Tobacco seeds are very small. I figure if we wear pants with, say, two-inch cuffs we could get maybe half a pound in each cuff. That's three pounds in six cuffs. Probably enough to seed a half-acre tobacco garden."

"How do you know that?" said Ben.

"Jeezuz, Bennie, I'm trying to make a point here. I don't know that. You ever hear of estimating?"

"But where would we plant these seeds of yours?" asked Bennie.

"The Towers is very proud of its tenant garden, right? So we create our own plot here. You see that big untilled piece next to the azalea bushes? We get permission to turn it into a big vegetable garden."

"Vegetable garden? Didn't you just say—"

"Shut up, Bennie."

"We plant, say, cauliflower, artichoke, lettuce and maybe some sunflowers, like that," replied Moe. "And, in between, we plant our Cuban tobacco, *ferschtay*? No one around here has ever seen tobacco grown, they'll think it's just another vegetable. Rutabaga or something."

"I dig," said Abel.

"Damn right you'll dig," said Moe. "And plant and water and weed."

"Then what?" said Abel.

"Then we harvest the whole schmear and lay the tobacco leaves on a guy I know in the Calle Ocho, in Miami; the cigar-making district. His name is Jaime."

"Hymie? The guy's a yid?" blurted Ben.

"Yeah, Hymie, Ben," replied the very patient Moe. "but he spells it J-A-I-M-E. Jaime Esteban. He's from Cuba. He's the best cigar maker in the business. We cut him in to shut him up. Then, if all goes right, we got Cubanos for life. Enough maybe to do a little side-selling at, say, twenty, maybe thirty, a pop. I'm not saying we could get rich, but who cares when we're smoking Cubans ourselves?"

Was this a good idea, better than any of Bennie, the Schemer's? Apparently Abel, and even Ben, thought so because a week later, passports in order, the trio of septuagenarians boarded an Air Key West flight to Havana. The morning after they arrived at the barebones, three-star Vedado Hotel on Calle 0, they hailed a passing taxi, a 1987 Buick Century station wagon in brushed-on pink and maroon, sporting Chevrolet hubcaps on three of its wheels and none on its fourth. Its driver, a man of few teeth who introduced himself as Rafael, spoke no English but was hand-gestured to understand that these Americanos wished to visit a tobacco field. The nearest was in Pinar del Rio, well over a hundred kilometers to the west. A deal was struck and, forthwith, Rafael and his Buickful of alte kockers was on its way to observe Cubanero gatherers at work. Within an hour of their arrival at the fields, they were done with their task: the surreptitious emptying of the world's finest tobacco seed pods into the suspicious looking two-inch cuffs of their Docker chinos.

Fearing spillage, they moved carefully during the return trip to their hotel.

The day after their return to Mermelstein Towers, the "Sunshine Boys," as they liked to call themselves, got busy potting their precious seeds to start them indoors. A month later, the trio were on their replaced or otherwise arthritic knees, planting their precious seedlings in their new vegetable garden's rich, fertile soil, along with seeds of cauliflower, artichoke, lettuce and sunflowers calculated to hide their struggling tobacco plants in case someone actually could identify them. Who knew that none of the vegetables did well in the hot, southern climes of the Sunshine State.

Three months later, their camouflaging cauliflower, artichoke and lettuce, fighting valiantly to survive, began to wilt. But the sunflowers, those daisies on steroids, had grown as tall as a man and had blossomed gloriously.

Along with them, the little seedlings of tobacco, lying in their shadow, also flourished. The Sunshine Boys watered and weeded and otherwise coddled their fledgling plants for months until they began to spring up into hearty, healthy, living things. Their leaves were a light green in color, but getting darker as the weeks passed, suggesting a certain richness of flavor. At last they begged to be plucked and cured and later rolled into the real thing, *Havana cigars* to be end-cut and wooden-match lit and moved about the mouth and smoked and tasted and smelled and observed as they shortened themselves. Like concubines, they existed to deliver nothing but endless pleasure; and later, perhaps—who knew?—they might deliver endless profit.

After harvesting, the curing took eight weeks, hanging under the blistering Florida sun on the laundry line behind the home of Abel's nephew, Roger Ginsburg—who also would have to be cut in on the scheme. Then came the day when the curing was done and the leaves were gathered and bundled and a test batch was toted off to Jaime Esteban, who anticipated the receipt of the leafy swag every bit as much as the three old Jews who, like the Magi, were delighted to lay it upon Jaime's tobacco-stained bench as though it were frankincense and myrrh. But it was something better yet: Havana Gold.

The leaves of this first batch were carefully swathed in ever-so-lightly moistened muslin in a roll ten feet long by a yard wide. Before Moe placed the roll on the bench, Jaime rushed to the front of his shop to hang a "Closed" sign in his window.

Then, with great ceremony, he began unrolling this treasure. When a few feet of the roll was laid out, he plucked a leaf from the muslin, smoothed it out and wiped it dry with a clean linen towel. Withdrawing a magnifying glass from a cubicle filled with the instruments of his craft—his molds and knives and cutters—he held the glass to his eye, and focused upon the leaf before him.

"What are you looking for?" asked Ben, the Schemer.

"Shut up, Bennie," came the usual rejoinder from Abel.

Jaime, after applying his practiced eye, now ran his brown-stained hand over the veins of the leaf. He rubbed the leaf between his juxtaposed forefinger and middle finger and his thumb. He brought the leaf up to his nose and sniffed of it deeply then tore off a piece, the size of a playing card, and put it in his mouth and tasted it. And stopped. He'd been bent over his stool, but now he straightened up and simply sat there, eyes closed, for what felt, to the three wise men, like an hour, but which could not have been for more than fifteen seconds. And then, smiling an enigmatic smile, he turned to them and spoke.

"What did this Rafael tell you when he brought you to the field that grew this tobacco?"

Moe, whose ear was better attuned to the subtlety inherent in such a question, even when spoken by a non-native speaker like Jaime, detected quotes around Jaime's mention of the word "tobacco." He suddenly feared a conclusion he wasn't certain he wanted to hear. He knew he was expected to be the one to reply to Jaime. And so he did. "Rafael told us these were the seeds of the finest tobacco crops in all of Cuba—in all the world. Are they not? Don't play games with us, Jaime, tell it straight."

"I play no games, mi amigo. If these crops were tobacco, would he have shown them to you, an American? Have you any idea how guarded my countrymen are about their tobacco crops? Do you think they're not aware of what respect and awe a Cuban cigar is held in the world?"

Moe did not have an answer because he was pretty sure he knew the answer. "Are you saying Rafael was playing games with us?"

"I'm not saying anything," said Jaime. "I'm just asking questions of three naïve Americanos."

Moe was running out of patience. "Jaime, dammit, just tell us what you have to tell us."

Jaime looked left and right before answering. Then he looked directly at Moe before complying with his demand. "Have you ever seen a Cuban spinach leaf? Some varieties look a lot like tobacco. Have you ever tried smoking one?"

A long silence followed.

"What's he talking about, Moe?" said Ben, breaking the silence.

"Spinach," replied Moe.

"Is he saying that this is—"

"Shut up, Bennie!" This time the speaker was Moe.

The Night I Sang at the Met
(A True Story)

On April 16, 1966, one of the most memorable nights in Metropolitan Opera history, I was on stage for the gala closing of the Met's old MetOpera House in New York. And I sang. I sang at the Met.

Sort of.

There's a story behind that bold statement, that boast, one that began twelve years earlier in 1954. In my twentieth year, during a summer-long recuperation from a serious leg operation, I spent a great deal of time honing the patent drafting craft that still helps feed me in my eighties.

On Saturdays I'd while away my drawing hours in my attic office listening to the MetOpera radiocasts and gradually falling so in love with them that, several years later, I volunteered to become a supernumerary—a spear carrier—for the Met when it came to Cleveland on its annual summer tours. My five dollar stipend barely covered the cost of parking but the experience was priceless, being able, backstage, to stand, cheek by jowl with the great tenors Pavarotti, Domingo, Franco Corelli, Jan Peerce and Robert Merrill, along with mezzo Marilyn Horne and basso Jerome Hines; and the eloquent sopranos Roberta Peters, Dorothy Kirsten, Renata Tebaldi and my absolute favorite, Joan Sutherland. Heady days, those nights at the Met were for me. And I did this for thirteen years until the Met could no longer afford to travel.

My first walk upon the Met boards was as a Nubian slave in that grandest of grand spectacles, *Aida*. My entire body was virtually painted in a dark brown makeup that took a dozen showers to turn my skin back to white. But, for a while there I kind of felt like Ralph Ellison's *Invisible Man*.

Two memorable incidents occurred the night Dame Joan did her nonpareil Lucia di Lammermoor. When she completed her famous "Mad Scene" aria, *Il dolce suono* (The Sweet Sound), I, standing backstage, was so enthralled I could not keep myself from bellowing out, Brava!"

The Met's elegant thaumaturge, its famous director, Rudolph Bing, standing near me, looked like he wanted to throw a spear through me. He nonetheless allowed me to remain backstage.

Earlier in the evening I was backstage for another memorable moment that took place between the acts. Sutherland was to do an entr'acte aria to allow time for a major scenery change. I quickly volunteered myself and a friend, a fellow Nubian, Bob Ruggles, to stand behind the curtain and open it for her entrance. As she stood there so regally, between us, Dame Joan, waiting for her entry cue, got to picking at her teeth with her fingernail. Finally finding what she was looking for, she dispatched it with a flick of her finger, then said, in her notable Australian accent, "There, I got the dirty bugger!"

With that came her cue, we opened the curtains, she stepped through and made, to quote Rodgers and Hammerstein, "the sweetest sound you'll ever hear." And, right behind her, throughout, were Bob and I, awaiting her final note so we could reopen the curtains for her return to the place where she'd nailed that "dirty bugger!"

But my crowning MetOperatic achievement came upon that most historic of all Met nights in 1966, the closing performance of the old MetOpera House on 39th Street. While maybe twenty or thirty supers were required for Met performances in Cleveland, the New York venue used as many as one hundred fifty. All, I was to learn, were regulars, many of whom made a living somehow on a paltry twenty dollars per diem.

There was nothing more in the world I wanted to do than super among the Met luminaries. Every star in the Met's firmament would be doing an aria. But no auslanders like me were allowed to super on that very special evening. So I wrote to the director of supernumeraries, Stanley Levine, whom I'd come to know over the thirteen years I toted the Met's spears, shields and torches. I pleaded with him to allow me to super that night, and he finally gave in. A few days later I flew to New York for that purpose only. He informed me I was the only non-New Yorker ever allowed to partake as a super in Manhattan. And certainly the only one there for that night of nights.

In the huge underground dungeon that served as the male supers' dressing room, I found myself in a situation I'd never been in before. It quickly became obvious that, of the hundred-plus men in the room, I was perhaps the only one who was not . . . gay. A very strange feeling, indeed. Who knew? But I was game to carry on. This was the Big Night and I was damn well going to be part of it . . . even if the only straight part of it.

So, came my big moment. I was standing in a phalanx of maybe twenty Roman soldiers carrying, yes, spears. Backstage, just before our entrance, our highly animated "captain," was entirely taken with the electric excitement of the evening. Literally jumping up and down in anticipation of our entrance on stage, he said—an exact quote—"Let's, all of us, just *prance* onto stage!"

I took this as my panicked cue to speak up from my position near the phalanx's rear. Believing my choice of entry to be an arbitrary one, I raised my hand and said, "Excuse me, but I don't prance, I march." And when our cue came, march I did, the only carrier of a spear *not* to swish onto the stage of the venerable old opera house on its gala final night; the night when the audience tore down the curtain after its final drop. And I came home with that most precious of keepsakes, a program signed by many of the great Met stars.

But wait. That's not all I did. Standing there, spear rampant, during a famous tenor's singing of yet another famous aria, I, baritone hummer that I am, hummed along. Loud. Not, of course, loud enough for Sir Rudolph to hear. But I did it.

I sang at the Met.

Sort of.

And I got paid for it.

The Answer

There was no place in the world better to live and raise your family than Mercerville. Nothing could duplicate it. It had once, in the late 1800s, been a backwater village until a farmer, Tom Mercer, great grandson of the town's avuncular founder, Amos Mercer, while drilling a water well and waiting for osmosis to do the heavy lifting, struck oil. The first of Big Oil.

Within a few years, Mercerville became the heart of the state's burgeoning oil industry. The moon that rose each evening over Tom Mercer's extensive ranch—that's what it was still called even though there were more wells on it than cows—beamed down on what was now the country's third largest oil reserve. Word had it that you could shove a sharp stick into the ground and you'd get a gusher.

Years went by and things just kept getting better for Mercerville and the Mercer clan. A billionaire now, wealthy beyond his desires, Mercer turned to other pursuits. He became a kingmaker in politics until he tired of the game, tired of pouring his millions into candidates who turned out to be more charlatan than statesman. And he'd already heavily funded educational reform, especially in technology and the sciences, particular passions of his.

But Tom Mercer wanted to do something of universal import, something far beyond politics, even beyond educational reform. He had his eye on outer space. A dedicated conservative, wary of government intervention, and now of government altogether, he established a privately held corporation, Mercer Interstellar Exploration, quickly to become known throughout the world simply as MIX.

Tom Mercer's specific purpose? To reach out to other galaxies; to learn if there was anything like human life out there that might occupy a near-duplicate world similar to our own; a concept that consumed him. Everything that science and technology had learned in its accelerating knowledge of the universe pointed to the fact that there were such worlds. He believed in them, he believed they existed. His dedicated quest would be to find them.

The search became an obsession. Tom Mercer would not rest, and would not rest the funds of MIX, until he could prove that his surmise was correct. He'd already established a world airline and was now embarked upon the design and manufacture of interstellar aircraft capable of exploring worlds beyond any known currently. How else to prove his dream a reality? He poured MIX's billions into interstellar communications devices that operated around the clock, sending out messages in every known language. The messages were straightforward. First, "Are you out there?" Second, "Are you a peaceful people?"

More years went by. Messages were received. Or they seemed to be messages. If they were, they were in no language decipherable to man. For all that Tom and his scientific minions knew, they might have been the noise made by universes colliding. But, while he believed they were out there, his doubt was growing. And, as oil was becoming less and less important as a world fuel, his income was, for the first time ever, tapering off. By 2034, oil was seen as an energy source that had seen its best days in the previous century. Today it was all about the power of the wind and the sun. And the rebirth of nuclear power during the presidency of Donald Trump. The land was now covered by far more wind and solar farms than oil wells. And nuclear plants were once more beginning to proliferate.

Within the next two years, with a world-wide depression entering its eighth year to add to his woes, Tom Mercer was down to his last million. His educational foundation was defunct. MIX was nearly bankrupt. And he was about to go the same way personally. Just as troubling, the world was too wrapped up in its own woes to be concerned any longer with life on planets other than its own.

So Tom dropped out of public life. He'd reached his late seventies now and was in failing health. His wife of forty-eight years had died the year before of ovarian cancer. Alone now, he himself was battling not only prostate cancer but a deep depression that had settled in after his Molly had passed.

All he had left was a ranch that no longer sprawled, as he'd had to sell off most of it to pay for his wife's, and now his own growing, medical expenses. Unable to get about without the use of, first a cane, then a walker, then a wheelchair, he spent most of his waking hours on the wide front veranda of his home, his only companion a yellow mutt, Rusty, and a male nurse. His children, having lost the opportunity to live off his vast fortune, had more or less forgotten him. This added no little to his depression.

A few months later, now confined to a wheelchair, he was sitting where he always sat at the north end of the veranda, the one with the best view of the rolling hills spread out below. The few neighbors who dropped by anymore, agreed that Tom's mind was beginning to go. It wasn't, though. The reason they thought this was because he claimed that what he was doing, staring out at the hills beyond, was looking for "visitors." "From where?" they asked. But his only answer was a smile. If they pressed him on the matter, he would only say, "Out there."

And, sitting there a week later, the space ship he was always expecting landed not a few hundred yards from the veranda. It was elongated, not disc-shaped like a "flying saucer," and was only about thirty feet long. And it had no visible means of propulsion. It likely had dropped from a mother ship still way out there. The landing was smooth, a coasting glide that took out a healthy swath of cornfield, narrowly missing a donkey-like pump jack oil well, one of the few still operating. Tom, expecting its appearance, sat quietly, waiting for its doors to open.

Five minutes later, they did. Two people, a young man and a slightly older woman, both dressed in rather attractive space suits, appeared in the hatch and waited for a set of steps to be lowered from the spacecraft's slick black fuselage. They descended and, with tentative steps, approached Tom.

To Tom they looked very much very much like himself when he was younger. They carried no visible weapons. A good sign. All he could think of was that all of his efforts to reach beings from another planet—or was it another galaxy?—were finally being fulfilled. He hadn't felt better—or happier—in years.

The pair stopped at the bottom of the veranda's six steps. Just yards now separating them from him, sitting comfortably alone in his wheel chair. They stared at him for a long minute. Then the woman ungloved her hand and held it out in greeting. In perfect English she said, "Hello, my name is Captain Elizabeth Townshend and this is my partner, Lieutenant Eric Killebrand. May I ask your name?"

"Tom. Tom Mercer. I've been expecting you, Captain Townshend. I'm pleased you've finally arrived."

"Well, we have after all," She said. "Our navigator seems to have done an excellent job because we have landed precisely at your doorstep, Mr. Mercer. We felt, knowing your efforts over the years, that this was the appropriate place to set down. And we'd like you to know that we've come in peace."

Tom was immensely pleased to hear this. Especially as these creatures were easily two times his height.

"This is a great day, Tom Mercer," she added. "For your world and ours."

"I could not agree more," replied Tom. But just what world, might I ask, have you come from?"

"I thought you knew that from the radio messages we sent," Captain Townshend replied.

"We have received no messages," said Tom. "At least none we could decipher. Apparently the ether scrambled your words. So, again, I must ask, from where have you come?"

Captain Townshend's reply: "Why—from Earth."

The Art of the Scam

I was desperate. *Desperate.* Tapped out. Every damn Chris Bellman scheme lately, gone up in smoke. Not a good place to be for someone who makes—made—a decent buck living off the scheme. Or, calling it what it is, the scam. Yeah, I'm a con man, okay? Hey, we all gotta make a living.

So I woke up on a recent Monday, hung over and my mouth tasting of cow pie. I slumped half an hour in the shower, pulled on my Walmart jeans and poured out my 99-Cent Store Fruito Flakes, after which I booted up my Mac, the most valuable thing I still own. Beside my iPhone and my '06 Corolla.

What came up? Nothing? Not one personal email. Just the usual heartfelt messages from Nigeria, Benin, Ghana, Togo, Cameroun and Senegal offering me untold millions if only I would offer the sender my own unmade millions. Why do they waste their time sending such trash? A child could write a less ludicrous, more convincing email. Then the thought hit me. Slammed into my medulla like a bullet train. These people need to learn how to put a decent scam message together. And who better to teach them the art of the scam than me?

"I hope to meet you in good healthiness" one of them offers. "I must discuss something of the uttermost urgent with you," tries to say another. A third, Reverend Sister Patricia Orphan, greets me with "Hello Beloved One. I do sincerely apologies for my intrusion of your privacy since we haven't meet physically before," before offering me $6,000,000. These people don't mess around with anything less than seven figures.

I'm sure you get the idea. So isn't it time I taught these poor souls how to put a real letter together? A real scheme/scam? Never mind that I dropped out of junior college, I speak proper English and know enough to sign scam-mail with an acceptable western name, one that doesn't start with Ibn. And if my spelling isn't perfect, my tongue, though cleft, is made of .999 fine silver. I know how to handle the English language.

What I need is to go over there and kick some ass. Set up some kind of a what? An institute! A seminar given by an institute. With a scholarly notebook thrown in. But let 'em know what they're in for. And don't be afraid to call it what it is: a scam. *Art of the Scam Institute.* No, a little too direct. *The American Institute for Enrichment Presents the Art of the Scam.* That'll chase the few straight-arrows likely to show up and make trouble. What the hell, it's only the scammers I'm after. If it takes one to scam one, then straight-talk is the straightest route to making it work. Send a well-worded invite out to every scammer who's tried to scam you. Wait for the chickens to roost then pluck their every goddamn feather.

So I got to work. First thing needed—surprise!—was cash. Hard cash to get me to where? To Lagos, naturally, the former capital of Nigeria and the current Capital of Scam. A few thou would buy my ticket and leave me a few bucks to set myself up in some kind of hotel conference room. I didn't have a few thou so there went the old Corolla.

And I needed a friend. Easier to line up than cash.

When Delta set me down in Lagos, jet-lagged and exhausted, I instantly headed for its finest hotel, the Wheatbaker, five bills per night plus another five thou for conference room rental, food service, set-ups, the rest of it. I couldn't cover my first night but they didn't know that so they greeted me like the wealthy American I was clothed to be as I slapped down my Amex Gold, the only valid plastic from my well-shuffled eighteen-card deck.

The teaser email I'd sent earlier to the 817 scammer edresses I'd amassed in the past two years read:

THE AMERICAN INSTITUTE FOR ENRICHMENT
INVITES YOU TO
A FREE THREE-DAY SEMINAR ON . . .

THE ART OF THE SCAM
CREATING THE KILLER APPROACH
AND HOW TO COLLECT BIG ON IT

The inside read:

Wharton Professor Edmund "Dr. Email" Entwhistle, PHD in Economics from Harvard and Wharton, will personally reveal the secrets that have made him (and can make you) a multi-millionaire through his patented method of Enhanced Email Solicitation and Recovery.

Dr. Entwhistle personally guarantees that your close-to-zero close rate will rise to a minimum of 20 percent after you have attended his free seminar. His guarantee of success is included along with a free AIE manual outlining his patented ARR method of Assured Remuneration Retrieval.

Space is extremely limited so sign up now for this free three-day seminar. To reserve your place, send only a nominal registration fee of US $20.

Along with additional promises of instant riches, I included the boilerplate: the date, time, place, special hotel registration rates, funds transfer number and other details.

Did it work? Before I even boarded my flight, I had 217 reservations solidly booked, thus $4,340 to pad my previously hollow Amex account. A good beginning.

Anyhow, I slept for six straight hours on arriving, waking up in time for dinner, before which I made all the arrangements for the conference room, meals, notebooks, literature, signage and the rest. But I needed a local I could count on to make the gears mesh, so I asked the boy who brought my tray who he thought was the most important person on staff. "Garmone Yumbo," he said, without hesitation. "Our concierge. Nothing happen here unless he make it happen." I tipped the boy a sawbuck for this intelligence. His resulting grin was wide enough to reveal at least a hundred teeth as he bowed himself out of the room.

Disappointedly, I found Yumbo half asleep behind his lobby desk. In his maroon and crème uniform he looked more like an organ grinder than a concierge. But he awoke fast when I waved a Franklin under his oversized nose. "How may I help you sir," he said, in a near-soprano voice, eyeing my hundred-dollar bill.

I spent the next half-hour with Yumbo, downloading my demands for the following day's conference set-up, including lunch and dinner for 200-plus attendees, distribution of materials and a million more details. "Make it happen right and you'll earn another hundred," I said.

Garmone Yumbo made it happen right. The next morning, my seminar opened precisely at 9:00, after a "getting-to-know-you" breakfast that I stayed away from to build the mystery of who I was.

This was to be a near-solo performance. The stage contained only a small, rostrum which became pin-spotted after the lights were dimmed to darkness by my new personal assistant, Yumbo. My prerecorded voice intoned, "Ladies and Gentleman, Dr. Email, the honorable Harvard Professor of Economics, Edmund A. Entwhistle." I stepped to the rostrum, placed my hands on its sides and stared into the audience for a good fifteen seconds as if I were examining their credentials. I was wearing a brown Harris tweed jacket, sharply pressed, dark tan gabardine slacks, a blue button-down oxford shirt and a red bow tie. The quintessential professor.

"Please bring the lights up," I said, before opening my brief speech. "I'd like to see what several hundred millionaires-to-be look like." When the light rose I saw 284 people, most of them men, skepticism visible in their hooded eyes and arms-folded posture. Many looked to be high rollers there to become higher rollers. Most did not. I recognized Armani and Versace suits or decent-looking knock-offs of the same. Many of the men wore caftans, djellabas, keffiyahs and turbans or fezzes. Some of the few women wore hijabs. I spotted several Rolexes and Louis Vuitton bags. Phonies? Wouldn't surprise me.

"I don't mean to insult you," I said, "but I should have opened by saying 'Hello, losers' because if you were winners like me you wouldn't be here. Still, I am delighted that you are. My name, Dr. Edmund A. Entwhistle, is my *real* name." I paused for a laugh that never came. "I'm also known as Dr. Email." Again, no reaction. "I am . . . a scammer."

I waited. A buzz went round the room. I'm sure that words like these had never been spoken to them. "But," I added, "I am not here to scam you. I'm here to teach you how to be a scammer like me: a winner. I'm here to teach you how to scam the other guy, the mark. That's my honest admission. That's why I offer you my words of wisdom.

"Who's waiting for yours? No one, right. Again, isn't that why you're here? You get no responses to the garbage you float out there in the ether waves? Well, you'll get plenty after you leave here in three days of the hardest work you may ever have done. You give me three days and I'll give you a lifetime of wealth. A big promise, sure, but one I mean to prove beyond the doubt of every one of you."

I stopped speaking. I looked around. I saw an audience that was now looking at itself. With unfolded arms. They weren't mesmerized yet. But they soon would be. They soon would be mine.

"Now, if any of you are shocked to hear me call myself a scammer, then you don't belong here. I *am* a scammer. *You* are a scammer. Say it. 'I am a scammer.'" Hesitation. Then a few voices said it. Obediently, but softly. "Say it!" I repeated. "'I am a scammer.'" Now, half the room said it. Louder. "Say it," I demanded, at the top of my lungs. And they—the whole room—said it. Shouted it. At the top of their lungs. "I am a scammer!' Repeat it," I cried. And they—with me directing them like a maestro—repeated it, again and again. "I AM A SCAMMER!"

"Okay," I said, softly. "Now we know why we're here." The laughter that followed warmed the cockles of my scheming heart.

I turned my back to them for another few seconds, then turned around like I'd just arrived on stage and purred, "Ladies and gentlemen, the American Institute for Enrichment welcomes you to the world's first-ever gathering dedicated solely to . . . THE ART OF THE SCAM!"

My greeting was met with a small round of instant applause, then another wave of it, this from the entire audience, now rising to its feet.

Time to take them to the movies. "Fellow scammers, now I have a treat for you. Some brief excerpts from two films. I hope you're not too terribly shocked because both illustrate the undying art of . . . the making of . . . love." An amused murmur went through the crowd, shifting in its seats, as the lights dimmed and a projection screen rolled down behind me. I tapped my handheld.

The excerpt from the first clip was from a poorly made porno film. It was crude, badly written, acted, and lit, and too anxious to get down to its raw sex. Without comment I segued into the second clip from the stunning Korean film "The Handmaiden." It depicted two nude lovers in an artful embrace, beautifully shot in soft light. It left out nothing as it left my audience squirming and gasping.

"What you've just seen," I said, "was yourselves making love to your marks in the first clip . . . and yourselves making love to them in the second *after you've learned how to 'make love' in these three days!*"

The murmur—this time much louder—was of approval, with more applause following.

I spent the next half hour outlining all the ground I'd cover in the next two days. I made promises. Guarantees. I told them that, if they paid close attention, they'd likely average a $50,000 take in the month following the seminar, and that would be just the beginning. I mentioned my latest bank deposit, rummaging around in my pocket to then wave a deposit slip with my name on it, forged, of course, in case anyone insisted on seeing it. I asked them to guess the amount stated on it. Guesses ran to a few hundred thousand. I modestly admitted that the number was a mere $75,000. A little reverse steam. My last *real* deposit slip was for $150.

By now I felt I had them. But I wasn't dumb enough to believe I had *all* of them. "Now I'd like to hear from the skeptics among you," I said. "I know you're out there."

The first comment came from a swarthy man with a charming French accent. "What you do—what *we* do—is that not against the law? How do we know we're safe here. How do we know if government officials aren't here among us, monitoring what you're saying?"

"They may be, my good fellow. Who breaks more laws than them?" Broad laughter. "The fact is, sir, no one is breaking any law by being here. Not me, not you. It is no more illegal to disseminate information and to absorb it than it is to sell a hash pipe, as opposed to selling hashish. What you do with this information is up to you. Now, before you leave these premises, three days from now," I changed the subject, "you will be on the road to riches, a road, if I'm guessing right, that most of you have never traveled." Another buzz as these overblown words were being digested.

"My friends," I went on, "As they say in my country, let's get real. I suppose my inbox has heard from most of you. And let me tell you, you don't know what you're doing. You do not know what you are talking about. You don't even know *how* to talk. For most of you, every message you've ever sent—by the thousands, I'd guess—has been trashed." Heads were nodding. "Be honest now. Raise your hand if you've closed as many as half a dozen deals in all the time you've been in business."

About a dozen hands went up. "Really?" I said. "Maybe you should be up here instead of me." Another laugh. They were softening. "Well," I said, "for the rest of you, you losers, all that is about to change. Three days from now you will know precisely how to word a message that will yield as much as—or should I say as little as—a twenty percent return on the hundred or thousand or hundreds of thousands of emails you send. Three days from now—even before you leave here—you'll be sending emails that will be opened, not deleted. And responded to. And will yield, ultimately, cold cash. How much response? Twenty, thirty, as much as forty percent. That's up to you. Worth thousands? Why not millions? Or nothing if you continue sending what you're sending, or if you don't choose to work your bony tails off during these three full days with me.

"This, understand, is not a mere speech, it's the prelude to a workshop, and I stress the word 'work.' Over these days, you are going to work, and if you work hard enough to absorb the secrets I'm about to reveal to you, you *will* be on that road to riches. You *will* be sending messages to English-speaking people who *will* view you as an English speaker. You've been emailing them as foreigners, but it is you who have been the foreigner to them. You will speak, through the messages I teach you to compose, as though you were one of them. That is necessary if they are to trust you. And I will teach you how to be trusted and how to make the all-important, the critical, close that leads to—the drop; the cash that goes from them to you."

"You said this was a free seminar, Entwhistle. What is in it for you?" came a shout from the rear. Heads turned to face the man who'd interrupted.

"Good question, sir," I replied. "Deserves a straight answer. I'm not an altruist. The answer is that I will exact ten percent of every net dollar I teach you how to earn, *after* you have earned it. Which means if you are so thick-headed as to earn nothing, you will owe me nothing and we will have wasted each other's time. But if you should wind up owing me, say, $10,000, that could only mean you've already pocketed $90,000. You win, I win. A win-win situation. I take a reasonable ten percent commission, you take the rest. Is that not reasonable? I might have charged you several thousand for this seminar. But I didn't. It's free because I'm confident that I'll make plenty *after* you've made yours. Any other questions?" I was pleased to see many attendees staring the man down.

A distinguished-looking, light-skinned, elderly man in a Keffiyah and skull cap arose slowly. Yumbo placed a mic in his hands. "I am Ebeneezer Erdoni Mugabu, sir. Yes, your fee is fair for what you promise, but scamming, as you call it, just as it is your business, is ours as well. What makes you think we'll pay you or even give you a fair accounting of our earnings?"

"An even better question, Mr. Mugabu. Am I pronouncing that correctly?" He nodded. "Thank you for bringing it up, sir. I'll be frank with all of you because I am one of you. I don't fully trust any of you to either provide a true accounting or, worse, pay me a dime that is due me. I'll make out fine if even half of you pay me."

A hush fell over the audience. Then Mugabu, still standing, began to slowly and rhythmically clap his hands.

"Why are you clapping?" I asked.

"Because you are not shoveling the usual bullshit," said the man, who pronounced it "boolsheet." A roar of laughter was followed by everyone clapping. Apparently they approved of my straight talk. Obviously the likes of me was new to them. When the clapping stopped, Mugabu said, "So just what *do* you propose, Dr. Entwhistle?"

"Well, as I have noted, there is not always honor among thieves. But I will take a chance on you if you take one on me. I mentioned that I expect you to earn a minimum of $50,000 in your first month following this seminar. In the front pocket of your notebook you will find a document titled 'Escrow Agreement.' It is there for your protection, not mine. Please take a moment to glance at it."

A minute later I continued. "You are looking at a document that asks you to place, by wire transfer, ten percent of your assured $50,000 in your escrow account by midnight tonight. That is to be the institute's $5000 commission, my fee, if you will, which you have agreed is fair. Per the terms of the escrow, if you have not netted your assured $50,000 by the thirtieth day following this seminar, the $5,000 will revert back to you, not to the institute. It will have failed you and you will owe it nothing, even if you've taken in as much as, say, $49,000. Thus my commission will be released to the institute only when you have hit your $50,000 mark. I will, of course, expect an accounting from you. There must be honor among thieves." Another laugh. "If you choose not to enter this protected escrow, you will not be expected at the next two days of this seminar." No laugh. "Are there any further questions?"

The silence that followed was deafening. A man arose in the second row. He was a tall, thin man, well-clad and soft-spoken. "My name is Herman Golowayo, Dr. Entwhistle. You have indicated that you cannot trust us. How indeed are we to trust you? What is to stop you or this institute of yours from absconding with our funds? To scam us, so to speak?"

I was about to answer when another man, at the end of a row farther back called out, "Dr. Entwhistle, allow me a suggestion, please. I may be able to answer Mr. Golowayo's question better than you." The man, speaking near-perfect English in a deep, slightly English accent, was perhaps in his sixties, skin so black it was blue. He was short and very round but impeccably dressed in a three-piece suit and a Panama hat. "I am William A. Serafin, recently retired as senior vice-president of the National Bank of Liberia."

A few chuckles went up from the crowd. They'd heard such claims before. Why would a bank officer be at a conference like this? But then, several such esteemed financial officers were in attendance. Everyone makes money his own way.

Serafin continued his statement. "Your former president, Ronald Reagan, once said, 'Trust and verify.' What I propose is even better. For us, not for you, sir. We, well most of us, trust you, of course. But I suggest that we set up our own escrow in a bank of our own choosing, perhaps the very bank where I sat as vice-president. I can have the escrow completed before evening falls, with the wire transfer number being issued, of course, by the bank, which will hold all funds. I do hope you understand why I suggest this."

Another stunned silence. Then renewed clapping, even some cheers and whistling. All were waiting for my reaction. I stood there awhile, my mouth half open. Then I threw up my hands in surrender. "I guess that would suit me, Mr. Serafin." Serafin corrected my pronunciation of his name. "Uh, now that this little matter *and* the means of my institute's compensation has been decided, isn't it time we began to address *your* compensation—and how to attain it?" A ripple of quiet laughter. "Okay, let's move on to the introductory content of this seminar. Please open your notebooks to chapter one, page three, entitled 'The Message as Messenger.'"

I lectured until noon, rarely referring to the notebooks which I'd cobbled together with gobbledygook garnered from half-a-dozen out-dated self-help books. I knew we wouldn't be going that deeply into them.

Before lunch, as I walked through the hotel's lobby, I noticed a small group of men and a few women attendees who'd left the morning session early. They were checking out, quitting the seminar. I did my best to ignore their dirty looks. Can't win 'em all.

At lunch, the table where ex-banker Serafin sat was being visited by several dozen seminar attendees enthusiastically shaking his hand to the point that he was hardly able to finish his meal.

From two o'clock until five I continued to lecture, stressing the structure of the hook in the perfectly constructed email message, and the ensuing close. I offered a "perfect" email and deconstructed it, line by line, demanding that, for their homework this evening, they write one of their own for me and my "staff" to "grade." After breaking to rest for an hour in our rooms, we took over the entire lounge for cocktails. Again, I spotted Serafin being greeted warmly by a large circle of men patting him on the back. More were surrounding him than me. Same way at the dinner that followed. There was a rush to fill his table of ten, not mine. It was obvious they trusted him more than me. Toasts were made, several by Muslims who apparently were ignoring their proscription on alcohol. A few toasts were made to me but far more to the new hero, one of their own, William A. Serafin.

So be it.

The dinner ended about nine, myself and most attendees adjourning to the crowded lounge. I was approached there by several men asking endless questions about the material in the their notebooks. Serafin was still busy doing the sign-ups he'd been doing all afternoon. He kept his distance from me. It wasn't until eleven that I returned to my executive suite. I poured myself a nightcap then strolled out on my terrace to stare at the near-full moon and enjoy what was left of the balmy Lagos night. I hadn't long to wait before I heard a near-midnight knock on my door. Actually two knocks, skip one, then three more. I opened the door, greeted the man standing before it, let him in and poured us both a glass of vintage Veuve Clicquot champagne.

"Well, Mr. William A. Serafin," I said, to Billy "Bone Man" Barker, the closest friend I had in the world, "Have you something to report to Dr. Entwhistle?"

Billy was doing his best to contain himself and speak in the officious, practiced, Englishy baritone he'd used earlier in the day. "I bring you an excellent report, my good doctor. Of the two-hundred-eighty-seven attendees at today's seminar, fully one-hundred and ninety-seven have properly and fully subscribed by wiring their requisite funds to William A. Serafin's special escrow account in the National Bank of Liberia, a.k.a. our newly opened Bank of America checking account in Brooklyn Heights."

"That's nice, Billy," I said, suppressing a grin. "Gimme some numbers."

"I hear you, Christopher. Five thousand times one hundred and ninety-seven equals nine hundred and eighty-five thousand. Simoleons, Chris. USD. That's, give or take, half a mil apiece."

Christopher Bellman smiled at Bone Man Barker. The "B&B Boys," as they were known, growing up.

"What do you suppose we were selling down there, Billy?" I said.

"Our scheme? Pie in the sky? What?"

"No, sweet William, we were selling trust. Or, rather, erasing distrust. That was the key, the hook. I knew they would never trust me, that's why I needed you. As Serafin, you became one of them. Or so they believed."

"But you'd think those guys would be too smart to fall for a scam like this."

"They're scammers themselves, Billy. But look at the crap they put out. How smart can they be? Truth is, ain't nobody easier to scam than a scammer."

"I get it," replied Billy, ruminating about what I'd just said. "I get it."

"Well, what you'd better get now is packed, man. We have a plane to catch in two hours."

The Clipboard

Three years into the Reign of Trump, as it came to be called, Muslims were no longer simply unwelcome in America, they were, by law, being deported, but first being detained indefinitely behind walls topped with razor-wire in internment camps, officially called "holding zones."

And the promised wall across all 1933 miles of America's southern border, contrary to the disbelieving wishes of half of the country, was nearing completion at a cost of $47 billion, courtesy of the American Treasury, not the Mexican people who, by this time, were ready to declare a second Mexican-American war, supported by America's northern neighbor, Canada. Most of the rest of the free world were in sympathy with both of America's neighbors.

Abdoul-Haziz al-Akhbar, a Libyan-American living peaceably for thirty-two of his forty-seven years, was, like all Muslims in America, deeply unhappy with his lot. He had just received notice that his assigned internment number, 2023357, had just been called and he was to report within a week to a train that would convey him cross-country to Holding Zone #17, situated twenty-five miles southwest of Milford, Delaware. He would be held there, along with some 27,000 other Muslim-Americans for as long as a year, or sooner if President Trump could successfully thwart Congress's objections to the deportations. This illegal incarceration is something he'd been able to do almost at will since he took office in January of 2017.

Abdoul-Haziz, an only child, had seen his father, Ibrahim, abandon him and his mother, Nabila, to return to Libya where he was recruited into a faction reputedly connected with ISIS. While at Duke University on a hard-earned scholarship, Abdoul-Haziz, who by then had taken on the name Abby Allerton because he wanted no connection to his father, learned that his mother had contracted cancer. He dropped out of his studies temporarily to care for her. But Nabila died within months, leaving him with nothing but a broken-hearted memory of the only person he'd ever loved.

Allerton had a keen mind but, because he was noticeably short at five foot three, pear-shaped and prematurely bald, and because of the blotched skin and permanent pinch of his face, he was unattractive to women. Always something of a loner, he never dated—never even tried to date—and had given up hope of ever marrying. And now, having lost both his parents, his permanent resident status having been revoked and facing internment before deportation, he'd taken on a mood of deep bitterness that would define him thereafter.

For Abby Allerton, this expulsion was a pivotal point in his wavering allegiance to his country. He had graduated Duke at the top of his class, attaining masters degrees in both chemical and electrical engineering, after which he'd built a burgeoning career at Dupont's famed R&D Center in Palo Alto. He'd been a good and conscientious citizen and voter until this monster, Trump, had bullied his way, first beyond the morass of mediocrity that represented the Republican Party in 2016 then, stunningly, past Hillary Clinton at the polls. But now Allerton was ready to throw over any remaining feelings he had for a country that wanted to throw him out, to banish him. Nothing of his contributions seemed to matter. As a Muslim he was being treated like a common criminal who would be sent back to live in a country he did not know or care about, the country of his detested father.

He hated this President Trump. Hated him. If he could not reach him directly to wreak some kind of revenge, he would find another way to assuage this hatred. And he could not forget that it was America that had put Trump in office. Thus his anger over this travesty was now applied equally to both his president and the country that was putting up with him, that was meekly following his führer-like dictates. What had America—Abby Allerton's America— come to?

Two years earlier, Allerton had been reached by an ISIS cell based in Richmond, Virginia, ironically in the very shadow of the nation's capitol. It must have been his father's doing. They knew of his background and were seeking his help in planning and carrying out their terrorist mayhem. Straight off, they wanted him to make bombs for them. He turned them down. But, though his loyalty to his country had been strongly shaken, he decided to withhold knowledge of having been contacted by them. That however was before Trump began making good on his promise to rid America of bad Muslims by getting rid of all Muslims. Now his livelihood, his home and homeland, his entire way of life were being ripped away from him by this monomaniacal dictator. Still, he was not ready to cooperate with the likes of ISIS. Not yet. But he was ready—*finally* ready—to act for himself.

A solo act of terrorism? The loner Allerton was capable of it. More than just capable, he'd begun preparing for it almost daily, mulling it over in his scheming mind during these past six months. He would do this not for ISIS but for himself. And for the three million other Muslim- Americans no longer welcome in this so-called "land of the free."

A bomb. It had been forming in his hyperactive brainpan for months. But this would be no ordinary bomb, no amateurish, easily detectable, back-packed cigar box crammed with colored wires and sticks of dynamite. This would be a very smart bomb impossible to recognize as such but lethal enough to impart a fatal wound to the side of, say, a Boeing 777, taking down all its three hundred passengers in its death spiral to the ground.

Would he fear being among those passengers? He was a deeply religious man who believed his ultimate reward from life would await him in his afterlife. He'd made himself buy the seventy-two waiting virgins meme. But, for Allerton, that was beside the point. He had a Statement to make.

He understood that, once his deportation orders were issued, the only plane he'd be allowed on would be the one transporting him to

Libya. He was already on a no-fly list of millions of others like him who would soon be rounded up and placed on buses and trains headed for internment centers. Which was good enough reason to make and place his bomb. Let America and the heinous man it elected president, know that its Muslim citizens would not take such debasing treatment without retribution. As for the morality of what he was planning, he'd think about that too. Maybe there was a better way to seek revenge. But, at the moment, the bomb was filling his addled head.

Allerton would rely upon the Occam's Razor principle that the best approach is the simplest one. He meant for his bomb to be simple and basic in both content and structure to lessen the chance that anything would go wrong.

He chose to use the deadly explosive Semtex, a malleable, waterproof and odorless explosive, reddish to brick-orange in color. Since its increasing use by terrorists, a taggant has been required in its manufacture to give it a distinct vapor signature that would aid in its detection. Semtex is set off by an electric charge sent through it. In its pure state, it resembles the popular toy, Silly Putty. But Semtex is no toy.

Allerton's idea was to add chemicals to the Semtex to harden it so that it could be molded into innocent-looking objects. After trying a dozen solvents, he chose a cyanoacrylate similar to that used in the various super glues. Adding a sodium bicarbonate-based deodorizing agent to kill the scent of the taggant, he also introduced various coloring agents to change its pinkish color to a medium shade of mottled brown.

Ingeniously, he molded this substance into what not only resembled a simple, nine-by-twelve-inch office supply house clipboard; it would actually become a more than serviceable clipboard after the riveted-on addition of a standard clipboard clip, in this case, one removed from a board he bought at Staples. Its Staples logo, embossed on the clip, he reasoned, gave the whole affair an even more innocent-looking appearance. To the board's clip he removably affixed a small, rectangular pencil sharpener. On the board, below the clip, he tacked on a patch of removable paper that read "Free Pencil

Sharpener Included!" with an arrow pointing to the sharpener. The finished product couldn't be distinguished from any of the innocent ones it resembled except for the fact that it was nearly twice as thick; thus twice as effective in achieving its nefarious purpose.

What couldn't be seen on cursory inspection was that the "pencil sharpener," while it was actually capable of sharpening a pencil, was actually a hollow, lead-lined plastic box containing a miniature computerized radio receiver from which hidden leads were attached to the composition "wood" of the board itself, completing a simple electrical circuit. To detonate the clipboard/bomb, one needed only to "phone" the programmed receiver—the pencil sharpener—and tap out the proper coded signal from an actual cell phone anywhere in the world.

Of course, Allerton would have to test his clipboard bomb. For this, he chose the Inyo Mountain wilderness, a remote area due east of Fresno near the eastern border of California. Hiking five miles beyond the reach of any vehicle, he placed a boxed, "loaded" clipboard next to a three-foot high boulder nestled in a copse of evergreens. Standing behind a large sandstone boulder himself, a good hundred yards away, he made his "phone call" and punched in the pre-arranged code: 3494-1. The resulting boom deafened him for a few moments as it echoed off the nearby mountains. Tracking back to ground zero, he saw that the explosion had left a pit about eight feet across and five feet deep. The smaller evergreens surrounding it had been leveled for another ten feet. And the boulder was gone, smithereened to dust. Repeating this set-up a few dozen yards away, he detonated the second clipboard/bomb. Same satisfying result. Amazing what a clipboard, the equivalent of six sticks of TNT could do. Within days he made ten more of his "Angels of Death." That's what he called them: Angels of Death. Abby's Revenge.

Six days after completion of his boards, Allerton was due at the train that would take him east. If he didn't show up, they'd come after him. He'd sold his modest two-bedroom home and wrapped up his quotidian affairs earlier, after which he made his goodbyes to the few friends he had at the Dupont lab. All that was left was to place his clipboard invention on a passenger flight. Or several on several flights. All that was left was to make his Statement, one that would be heard round the world.

But what statement did he really want to make? Whatever it was, it had to be made soon. He wanted to wake up his adopted country to the iniquities it had allowed its president and its citizens to inflict on Muslims, on all its so-called "illegals." But he needed to act, and act quickly. Did he actually mean to take out hundreds of innocent airline passengers? Was he the fearless terrorist he'd set his mind to be? This was no time to be questioning himself like this. For the next two nights he slept hardly at all.

He could not conceive of a way to get his bombs onto an airline's planes. He'd have to come up with a better plan. And he did, after yet a third sleepless night. He would plant his bombs, all ten of them. But not on passenger planes. Instead, he would send his clipboards in individual packages to different destinations by way of Fedex Air so that different planes would be used to carry each. If the packages were inspected by X-ray, or even randomly, for some reason, by hand, they'd likely pass inspection. After all, how harmful could a clipboard be, especially if its wiring was hidden behind a lead foil-lined *pencil sharpener*. Once the bombs were aboard, he would make his calls and tap in his sequential detonation codes. The plan appeared perfect. Odds were that most, if not all, bombs would explode while the planes were in flight. Too late for Fedex to stop their flights.

The lives of perhaps a dozen crew members, not hundreds of passengers, would be sacrificed, and maybe a billion dollars worth of planes and their contents would be lost. Air shipping in America, even the entire world, would then grind to an extended halt. Yes, some bombs might be stopped and likely an unfired bomb would be traced back to him. But chaos would have been let loose in the land and throughout the planet, and his message would not just have been sent, but loudly received. And wasn't he ready anyhow to meet his maker and his afterlife rewards? To millions, he would, in fact, be a hero, not just an unwanted and despised traitor.

Allerton had carefully checked expected shipping times for Fedex two-day air service. He determined that the mid-point of a given flight would average nine hours from drop-off at the nearest

Fedex shop, the one on El Camino Real. The next day he brought home from there ten Fedex boxes and shipping forms, filling out the latter with fictitious names for sender and receiver, but with real addresses in major cities like Minneapolis, St. Louis and New York. The boxes were ten by fifteen by three inches deep. In each he placed one of his lethal clipboards along with a crosswords magazine as though it were a gift from the sender. Every board was packed with pillows of bubble wrap to keep it from being damaged before it could do its damage.

The following morning, Friday, he took the pile of boxes back to the El Camino Real shipping center. The place was crowded. He had to wait nearly fifteen minutes before he got to the counter. Five minutes later, the boxes were sitting in a soiled cloth cart behind the unsmiling clerk who'd processed them. Receipts in hand, Allerton noted the time as he left the center: 9:58 a.m. By his measure, his messengers of death would be in the air, on the way to creating their own form of Armageddon, by approximately 5 p.m., Pacific Time. Zero Hour.

From the center he took a leisurely drive to a Starbucks, sat for an hour with his coffee, then proceeded to the mosque he usually attended in Palo Alto. It was not quite time for *dhuhr*, the mid-day call to prayer. No more than a dozen men were standing around there talking to each other. All the while he had the eerie feeling that they knew what he was up to. He dared not speak to anyone because he did not want to call attention to himself. Instead, he drifted off to a corner and there he offered his personal prayers, first that he was doing the right thing, then for the success of what he planned. He stayed for the *jumu-ah* prayer, then drove directly to his home, had a light meal and watched an hour of TV news. After, he eased himself into his reading chair and waited, cell phone in hand, for the five o'clock hour to approach.

He had plenty of time to change his mind. But he did not change his mind. The more he thought about what he was about to do, the more set in his resolve he became. He stared at his cell phone, watched the tiny numbers indicating the time turn from 6:58 to 6:59 to . . . 7:00. Then, with great care, he tapped in 3-4-9-4 . . . said a quick prayer . . . and added the final, fatal number, 1. He could visualize the explosion and the plane falling, possibly in pieces. Then he tapped in—no hesitation at the end . . . 3-4-9-4-2. He did this mechanically until he'd entered the final numbers: 3-4-9-4-1-0. Then he walked into his kitchen and microed the piece of KFC chicken he'd brought home for his dinner and proceeded to eat it, along with a small cup of cole slaw. After dinner he returned to his chair and waited, his hands folded in his lap.

It didn't take twenty-four hours for a phalanx of white panel trucks, some with the letters FBI on them, a few with SWAT, to rush up his driveway and come to a skidding halt. He'd given them what was, essentially, a road map to the place. At the time, he was sitting on his small front porch, again with his hands folded in his lap. He gave no resistance to the men approaching him.

Abby Allerton, the former Abdoul-Haziz al-Akhbar, for his part in blowing seven Fedex planes out of the air, and three still on the ground, was convicted of ten separate acts of terror against the United States of America. His indictment included the accusation of eighteen premeditated murders. For these acts and murders he was sentenced to life in prison without the possibility of parole. He would serve his term in San Quentin, ironically just fifty miles from Palo Alto where he had hatched his diabolical scheme.

Three weeks after arriving at the Q, as its inmates called it, he was found lying dead and mutilated on the Q's exercise yard. A tape-wrapped prison "shank" was left sticking out of his gut. No inmate could be singled out to be charged with the killing.

President Trump completed his term but was not re-elected. His Muslim and Hispanic containment policies, in great part due to Abby Allerton's disastrous act of terror, were seen to motivate more than mitigate terrorism in America. Trump was succeeded, in 2020, by Elizabeth Warren. President Warren saw to it that his "holding zone" internment camps were plowed under. His wall, never completed, was reconfigured into the longest mural in America, painted mostly by immigrant artists of Mexican descent, most of whom had no papers. For their efforts they were rewarded with American citizenship.

Some came to call the wall "The Welcoming Wall." Most called it The Eighth Wonder of the World.

Natangu, the Wall

Who could have known that the Kenyan child, Natangu Odembre, would be an NBA basketball prospect when he was born? Though his mother was very tall at five-ten, Natangu was just eighteen inches long and barely five pounds at birth. His father didn't know him at all. He was from another Maasai village, unknown in Natangu's village, and had walked out months before the infant was born, never to be seen by Natangu again.

Natangu was something of a reluctant learner and seemed destined to be nothing more than a goatherd, the only occupation for which he exhibited a propensity. But his future was repurposed when, at fourteen years, Natangu Odembre reached the height of six foot eight and was discovered by an Israeli coach, Meyer Levine, barnstorming his team through Africa.

Five years later, Natto, as Natangu came to be known in the world of professional hoops, stood at seven-foot-seven, just two and a third feet below the rim of the basket, which he could easily touch while standing flatfooted in his size nineteen basketball shoes. He was the tallest man in NBA history. Ripley's was ready to enter him as such and Madame Tussaud was making inquiries. Quite a ball of wax Natto would be!

Additional nicknames came Natangu's way. A sports writer dubbed him "Tree," another topped that with "Sequoia." Yet a third one called him "Kilimanjaro" after the highest mountain in Africa.

But the one that stuck was that given him by Meyer Levine who was now his agent and mentor. The name? The Wall. You see, Natangu, not particularly fast, was not your typical giant who couldn't get out of his own way. In fact, he was best at getting in the way of others. Graceful, actually, and very agile for a big, big man, he was uncannily attuned to where the man he was guarding was headed and, anticipating the man's jump, he was there, like a wall, to block the shot. His 5.4 shot blocks per game still stands as an NBA all-time season record, nearly two more than the previous record. That's eleven points denied.

What's more, Natangu had a natural bent for knowing how the ball would come off the rim; thus he averaged well over ten rebounds per game, and was always among the league leaders. His thirty-two rebounds in a single game against the Chicago Bulls is a modern day record—even if it couldn't touch Wilt Chamberlain's fifty-five from a bygone era.

At the offensive end, Natangu wasn't the dominator he was at the other end. But his hook shot close to the basket, earned him a double-double nearly every game. That is, at least ten rebounds and ten points per game.

And nothing got a greater roar from the crowd than his slam dunk alley oop where a guard would throw the ball above the rim and Natangu would grab it, often in one huge hand, and stuff it through the hoop. At this point his head was a spectacular two feet above the basket. Picture yourself dropping a balled up scrap of paper into a waste basket; that's what Natangu seemed to be doing.

But there was one thing that he could never quite get the hang of. The foul shot. Extra tall players like him were fouled often; maybe ten times a game. That means that he'd have the opportunity to score as much as twenty points at the line. But, while others averaged maybe eighty percent accuracy, Natangu was averaging less than fifty. And it wasn't for lack of trying. Teams began to intentionally foul him in the fourth quarter just to keep his teammates from shooting.

He'd stay late at practice shooting as many as a hundred foul shots. He realized that his scoring average would rise from around ten to at least fifteen per game if he could just find the basket from the line. No coach seemed able to find it for him either. He'd wear out two ball boys and could hardly lift his arms after these endless sessions. When he approached the line during home games he'd often hear boos, causing him, understandably, much embarrassment. He began to fear coming to the line.

His mood, after a long practice, would have to be called despondent. It seemed the more he practiced, the worse he became. He began to think that practice itself was making him worse. He was digging a hole deeper than he was tall.

But Natangu was a star; some would argue, a super-star, a recognized and perennial All-Star, maybe even headed for the Hall of Fame. He had no fear that his foul-shooting would affect his tenure on the team, nor his mounting millions of salary. Still, his defect affected him deeply enough to see the team's psychologist, which, by now, every team had.

"No," said Dr. Emerson, after thoroughly examining the contents of Natangu's size eight and one quarter skull, "I can assure you it's not your brain that's your enemy. You're normal in every aspect. I don't usually conclude this but, you need a coach or someone to look at, well, the way you shoot your fouls. It may have to do with your release or your stance at the line or—I'm hardly qualified to say."

Thanks, Doc. For nothing, thought Natangu. Another coach. He'd been there, done that. Square one, coming up.

Next day, an off day and the arena now empty, Natangu was back at the foul line, throwing up one shot after another, not half of them finding the net.

"Try putting your feet closer together, son." The words came echoing from the shadows a few rows up from the far corner of the floor.

"What? Whadaya mean?" replied Natangu.

"Your feet. Plant them under your shoulders. Your stance is so wide it's restricting your release. Try putting them tight together then, if that doesn't work, spread them a little, but not nearly as much as you normally do."

Natangu did not recognize the voice. Who the hell was this guy?

The arena was dark. Only the court floor was lit. He peered into the corner and could barely make out a tall, thin man, maybe six-four, leaning on a push broom. A custodian? "Who are you?" he called into the dim light.

"Never mind that. Just try a few shots with a narrower stance." The words were spoken with enough authority to stop any more questions from Natangu. Natto squared himself to the basket. Then he drew his feet together and tried another shot. And missed yet again.

"A few inches closer. And keep your left foot a little ahead of the right," said the man with the broom. "Better stability. And put a little more arc on the ball."

Natangu, having nothing to lose, did as the man said. The next shot bounced on the rim and dropped in. Hardly a miracle.

"That's better," said the voice. "Now relax and take a deep breath before you shoot. Do that every time you shoot."

"Why should I listen to you?"

"Four-four-two, that's why."

Natangu recognized this as his current percentage of foul shooting success. Call it failure. He had nothing to lose but that losing percentage. He brought his feet a tad closer together, planted the left a bit ahead of the other, took a deep breath, let it out, relaxed and . . . shot. This time the ball swished through the net. He did it again with the same result. And again and again. He made five straight before missing, and made four in a row after that. He kept at it, making thirty-eight of his next fifty throws. But when he finally turned to thank his new foul-shooting coach, the man with the broom was gone.

Well, after all, this was just practice. No pressure. Could he do this in a game?

He could and he did. Making several foul shots in a row gave him the confidence to keep making them. The next game he had eight chances at the line—fourteen free throws—and he missed only two. The game after that he made nine for ten. Best of all, he not only shut the home crowd up, he opened them up to cheering every time he stepped to the line. He was to slip a little after that, but would level off at a respectable seventy-four percent for the rest of the season. No one was intentionally fouling him anymore.

Three weeks later, on a rare night off, Natangu got a call from his mother whom he had moved into her own apartment in Philadelphia where he played for the 76ers. "I have some, well, rather odd news for you, Natangu. Some news I was not certain I would pass on to you. But I knew somehow you would want to know. I received a call from your father's sister. She told me that he just, well, passed on. I didn't even know that he was still alive. I had totally lost track of him."

Natangu didn't know how to react to this. He hadn't thought of his father in years, didn't know him, didn't even know his name because his mother would never tell him.

"When did this happen?" asked Natangu.

"Three days ago."

And where, Amai?"

"Strangely, right here in Philadelphia where he must have been living. I had no idea. Do you suppose he ever saw you play?"

Natangu was stunned into silence. Choking back tears he was finally able to say, "Yes, Amai, I believe he did."

Morra!

It was the summer of 1951. A typical Cleveland Heights summer. Most of my high school pals were, like me, Jewish. And always, naturally, looking for adventures outside our gilded ghetto.

Just down Mayfield Road, at the northern edge of the Heights, was the Hill, the Little Italy neighborhood where we'd go for the best pizza at Valentino's or Presti's. Its other intriguing attraction, besides the coloratura arias floating out from half the Little Italy homes? The Cleveland Mafia was headquartered there and we got off just reciting the names of its "bosses," the capo de capos who'd lived there: Vincent Miletti, John "Pickles" Ponti, James "Four Fingers" Licavoli and Angelo "Big Ang" Sangiacamo.

Though I can't recall how this particular adventure started— likely a desire to live dangerously—we drifted down Mayfield into the Hill and got friendly with a bunch of Little Italy guys our age, and came to hang out with them all that summer.

They'd lay a little Italian on us, we'd press a little Yiddish on them. Lots of laughs. We broke bread and drank dago red with them in the alleys, and, soon, they, in the friendliest way, referred to us as Yids, Hebes, Hymies or Sheeneys, nothing worse, and we'd call them wops, guineas, dagos. Lovingly, of course. They invited us to roll bocci with them at Alta House, their community gathering place, and they taught us Morra, the fingers game.

Ah, Morra. And don't forget to roll your Rs when you say it. I'll explain it because it's the most important part of this meandering tale.

In Morra, two players face each other and throw out a handful of fingers simultaneously—none to five digits—while each hollers a number between one and ten in properly inflected Italian. Thus: *uno*, *due*, *tre*, *quattro*, *cinque* (my favorite), *sei*, *sette*, *otto*, *nove*, *dieci*.

If the total of the fingers thrown by both players does not equal the number called by each, the call is a draw, and they continue playing until one player hollers, say, "*Sei!*" six, while throwing out, say, two fingers, and the other shouts, say, "*Sette!*" seven, while showing, say, four, the first player wins because he called "*Sei!*" six, and the total of fingers thrown was two plus four, six, the number the first player called. Sounds complicated. Isn't.

Well, we studied those Italian numbers, memorizing them quickly, perfecting their pronunciation, working harder on them than we'd ever worked on a language in school. And we practiced the game so we could keep up with our "guinea" pals. And then, it was important not just to know the numbers and spit them out at breakneck pace—a round could take as little as two seconds—but to throw out your fingers in a manly fashion. You could fling them down like you were proudly revealing a full house; you could backhand them, as if challenging your opponent to a duel; you could uppercut them. Every man had his own proud and singular style.

This went on all that balmy summer until we got almost as good at Morra as the Italians. Played it just as fast, too. We even began to learn their quirks; their "tells," the little ticks or habits that reveal what they might call. And, naturally, they came to learn ours. For example, we might know that one player liked to call *quatro!* maybe every third time. But we never truly *knew* the calls or the number of fingers that would be thrown.

It was, till then, the best summer I'd ever spent. Especially because I'd made a bunch of new friends. A lot like us. But not exactly.

But you know how it is. The summer passed. We graduated the next year and went on to college and into budding careers, quickly drifting away from the Hill gang, soon forgetting their names, if not their faces. Still, it had been a summer to remember.

Now it's maybe twenty years later. The early seventies. Most of us are already married, myself included. Some have moved away, but I chose to stay not just in Cleveland, but on the Heights in my third home there, a renovated carriage house at the top of Mayfield Hill overlooking Little Italy. So I still get to the Hill often and it still has the best Italian restaurants in town. And definitely the best pizza.

And Little Italy has the Feast, its annual, mid-August Feast of the Assumption, begun in 1898, celebrating the assumption of St. Mary, though I never did learn what it was she assumed.

The Feast is the biggest, baddest festival in town. It begins with the parading of a huge plaster statue of the beloved saint, carried on the shoulders of a horde of local men. People rush into the street as it passes, pinning singles, five, tens, even twenties on her skirts, all to support the church on the Hill, Holy Rosary.

This is certainly no ordinary festival. Sure, there's plenty of great, homemade food, live music, arts and crafts booths, the works. But there're also card tables where you can lay down a few bucks for a juice glass full of scotch or play Over & Under, or shoot craps all day long.

People walk around with open bottles, not just of beer and wine, but the hard stuff, not even bothering with a brown bag. In no time, half the crowd is staggering like they're at an Italian wedding. It being August, it gets steamy hot and, inevitably, fights break out.

Where's the constabulary? Everywhere, most of the cops being Italian, many from the Hill. They break up the fights, of course, patting the participants on their fannies and sending them on their way. But they somehow never seem aware of the gambling. Or the booze, practically flowing down the gutters.

It may not appear to be a safe place on this day, but it is. If, of course, you're white. The black community happens to also border upon Little Italy, but, by tacit agreement, that border is never crossed. Never. Not without serious consequence to any black man, woman or child foolish enough to cross it.

But I, being certifiably white, have chosen to visit the Feast on this sweltering August day in 1971, along with a few buddies from the old days. An hour in, we're beginning to feel the chianti or the few beers we've had with our pizza. The sun is merciless. The temp has climbed to near ninety, the humidity, through the roof. The Hill is packed and the tension, hanging low in the still air, is palpable. Trouble awaits, ready to be summoned.

Walking near the church, I spot something I don't want to see. Three young, black kids, maybe in their mid-teens. Jeezuz, what the hell were they thinking? Hadn't anyone told them they should be ten miles past anywhere but here? Especially on this, the day of the Feast? They look scared as hell and are ready to bolt, but a crowd of young men, many my age, not just teens like them, have surrounded them and are menacing them. It doesn't take a minute more before the N-word begins to fly.

A big guy, about my age, steps forth, winnows out two of the kids by their shirt-fronts and starts to scream more of this filth in their faces. He's about to take both apart when it hits me. I actually know the guy. It's Frankie Sangiacamo, a distant cousin of ex-capo "Big Ang" Sangiacamo. He's one of the "pals" who taught me Morra back in the day. I'm good with faces but how I even remember his name, I don't know. What I also don't know is where I get the guts, to step out of the crowd and volunteer to put my face into his and say, lightly, "Frank? Frankie Sangiacamo? You remember me? How the hell you doin', man?" A brilliant opening, but it's all I can think of at the time. I guess I'm a little buzzed from my Rolling Rock. Make that Rolling Rocks.

Big Frank looks—what's the word—befuddled. And mightily pissed off. I've cut off his action. I've disrespected him. The outcome may be catastrophic.

I talk fast. "Hey, man, I'm Mel Horwitz. C'mon . . . *Morra! Uno, due, quattro!* Hey, Frankie, we spent a whole summer with you guys once, maybe twenty years ago. You gotta remember that."

Back then, Frankie had always seemed one card short of a full deck. I doubt if he ever found it. Right now he looks big-time annoyed, enough to drop the kids and take me on with the ham fists hanging at the end of his thick arms. This is a notion I have no notion of complying with. Especially since he has half a dozen guys standing behind him who'd pay to be in his place. My two pals are now looking very pale, even with their inherited dark skin.

"Yeah, Horwitz he says. "I remember you." His fist is in my face. "Now get outta my way or I'll—"

"Hold it right there, cowboy," I say. "You wanna use your fist, I'm gonna show you how." This, coming from my fourth good beer, not my good sense.

"Yeah, little Yid, I'd kind of like that," he replies, letting go of his other fist's grip on one of the black kids' shirt. He squares around to me. His goombahs are grinning by now, eyeing me and my buddies, anxious for the good fight to begin.

Somehow, Frankie's "Yid" didn't have quite the friendly sound it had in the old days.

My hands go up and out in front of my chest. "I don't know what you're thinking, Frankie, but here's what I'm thinking. When I mentioned using your fist, I meant we should play a little Morra. You remember Morra, don't you?" Before he can say a word, I offer: "I challenge you to two out of three rounds. Shouldn't take more than a few minutes. I win, the kids get a pass out of here. I lose, then, whatever you had in mind for them, you can lay on me. You up for it?"

Why am I doing this? This guy can grind me to powder.

Frankie's lumpy face says he wants to skip the preliminaries and take on the kids, me and both my friends. But his friends are shaking their beer-filled heads now in anticipation of watching a good Morra match with what has to be a great outcome. Entertainment, followed by Big Frank kicking my head in. What can Sangiacamo say but— encouraged by his pals—yes?

So we go at it. A circle forms around us. A crowd forms around our circle. The cops are looking the other way, except those looking to see a few good rounds of Morra; and the pasting that's sure to follow. Three of the goombahs are holding onto the three black kids. The others slide behind my pals to make sure they won't exit before the festivities are over.

My task ahead fortunately clears my addled brainpan. Frankie and I are both leaning forward, each with our right fist behind our back. We open, as one. I holler, "*tre!*" he bellows "*otto!*" But the total of our fingers doesn't match our calls. Try again. He comes back with an uppercut of "*sette!*" as do I. But our fingers total eight; another no-go.

Then I fling out three fingers to his four. My repeat of "*sette*," seven, matches his clever repeat of the same. And we do total seven; a tie. On goes the game, no winner yet.

We must both must be thinking higher numbers now because he slaps down a bold "*nove!*" to my "*otto!*" He shows five fingers, I show four. Total: nine. Whoops! He wins the first round.

Next call for him is "*due!*" to my "*cinque!*" Our fingers total five, so it's taken me just three seconds to tie the match. I always loved *cinque*, but no sense gloating over my win. Would that the immediate past be prologue to the future. The final round: coming up. My hand is sweating. As is the rest of me. Drenched. Not just from the humidity.

I'm doing my damnedest to recall Frankie's old tells. And one finally comes to me. When he loses a round, he likes to go for a low number. Back then and, apparently still, because, sure enough, he barks out a backhanded "*due!*" to my "*uno!*" A single finger sticks out from his huge fist, and waggles as if to demand a matching single finger from me. And, just to be funny, he's using his middle finger. Ha, ha, ha, the joke's on him. The fist he's staring at has . . . *no* fingers extended.

"Your one and my zilch, zippo, nada, nothing, Frankie, appears to total *uno*! I win, pal." Not a brilliant idea, taunting him, but I can't help myself. His prognathous jaw is hanging open.

But, if he's in despair, I'm in ecstasy, at least as relieved for myself and my pals, as we hurry ourselves away. Those not-so-foolish black kids had slipped away in the rising excitement of the moment, free at last because, on that fateful summer day in 1951, a full score of years ago, I met a bunch of Hill guys who taught me that sweetest of games, Morra.

Cinque!

The Witching Place

"Nevologist?"

This was the one-word question by which I opened my conversation while standing outside the Dutch door that, ajar, bore that unusual word. The door opened upon a small emporium I'd happened upon in my meanderings about the *Gamla Stan*, the famed Old City in the heart of Stockholm. I was in Sweden to attend a seminar on a new, disease-resistant strain of apples developed by two Swedish botanists.

The woman who answered my question spoke perfect English, as most Swedes do. She was sitting well back from her door so I could not see her face. "I read nevuses—birthmarks," came her soft reply. I came up to the door. She was of a nondescript age, tall and gaunt, and wrapped in a heavy shawl over a long, colorful dress hemmed with the signs of the Zodiac. Her dark complexion, unusual for a Swede, led me to believe that she might be of mixed blood, or perhaps a pure-born Gypsy. "Would you care for a reading?" she monotoned, without a smile or other enticement.

Intrigued, I said yes without wavering. Which surprised me, as I have little if any interest in the predictive arts. But I thought about the dark red, irregular mark just below my right shoulder. It's in the shape of a human being with a vestigial arm reaching upward toward a circle. Not a birthmark, it's a tattoo of my Tantalus Orchard's trademark, devised as a representative form of the mythological Tantalus himself, forever condemned to reach for an apple that would pull itself away as he did so. As did the water beneath him as he reached down to quench his thirst.

I grow and market my apples, mostly Honeycrisps and Braeburns, and some experimental Fujis, as having "the most tantalizing taste of any apple grown by man." Thus the Tantalus logo. This might be amusing, I thought. Would she recognize my perfidy? Would she know the difference between a birthmark—a nevus, or whatever she called it—and a . . . tattoo?

All the walls of the perhaps ten-foot wide shop were hung with dark green velvet drapes, making the place, which smelled pleasantly of sandalwood, appear even smaller and more confining than it was. Along the walls were ancient wooden showcases filled with incense, rune sets, tarot cards, crystal pyramids and an endless array of what one expects to find in a shop whose window sign reads *Den Förhäxande Plats*—"The Witching Place."

But as soon as I entered, the frivolity of my purpose evaporated. And suddenly I felt an odd sense of anticipation, a feeling that I was about to learn something of importance about myself. I now felt embarrassed about the trick I'd meant to play on this imposing woman. How could my tattoo possibly fool her? And so I hesitated entering, as I was no longer certain I'd be pleased with the outcome of my doing so. This no longer seemed a game I was playing.

The woman introduced herself by her given name only, Helga, and motioned me to follow her into a back room barely able to contain its small table which held a lit candle, the only lighting there. Two worn Thonet armchairs sat, opposed, at the table. Before we began, this Helga pointed to a cardboard sign hanging on the wall behind her chair.

"Readings: 400kr" it said. Nearly fifty bucks. A rather stiff fee, but I immediately laid the notes upon the table. As soon as I did, she whisked them into the open vee of her dress.

No preliminaries, no nonsense. "You have a nevus you wish me to read?"

Reluctantly, I nodded my yes, adding, "It's on my shoulder."

"Let me see it."

I removed my jacket, unbuttoned my shirt and pulled it back off my left shoulder. Staring at the mark for some time, she did not appear to recognize it for what it was, acting as though it were a birthmark. And maybe acting was all she was doing. Whichever, I did not like the frown growing upon her long face.

Leaning in until her eyes were but a few inches from the tattoo, she touched it with two fingers of her right hand. As she did so, I felt my shoulder grow warm. And could almost swear that an eerie green light began to emanate from the mark. For a moment at least, it actually seemed to glow.

Her eyes closed as she allowed her fingers to rest upon the mark, as if reading it, for nearly a minute. Then she pulled back her hand, folding it into her other hand in her lap. No word came from her as she meditated for another minute, her eyes still closed.

I felt extremely anxious, wanting to believe that this was all an act, a ridiculous joke. Of course it was. Mumbo-jumbo. And I was ready to bolt. Who was fooling whom, here? A joke indeed, except that I could not explain where the heat, rising from my tattoo, was coming from. I broke the silence. "Tell me what you've—" But she extended her palm to stop me before I could finish my words.

More silence. Another minute passed before her eyes came open. No longer looking at my tattoo, she was staring off into the distance. Without a word, she reached into the opening of her dress, removed the bills I'd given her and laid them on the table.

And finally she spoke. "You may not believe what I am about to tell you because I sense that you do not believe in me. If that is how you truly feel, you are welcome to take your money and leave now. Further, if you do trust me and remain, you may not be pleased with what I have to say."

An odd construction of words for a woman who'd earlier seemed pleased to take my money. Not pleased with what she had to say? I'd never heard of a—call her what you will—a fortune-teller offering to return her fee. But now I had to hear her out. "Keep the money," I said. "Just tell me what you've found."

Without touching the bills she said, "I have never come across a nevus such as yours. It is extremely rare. But I do know what it means." She stopped speaking and looked directly into my eyes. Not until I made a praying motion with my hands, imploring her to explain her observation, did she do so.

"You bear the Mark of Tantalus," she said, so softly that I had to ask her to repeat herself. Which she did. Then, leaning back, she again folded her hands in her lap.

Just when she looked as though she would continue her explanation, I stopped her. I could not help but reveal myself. "This is all nonsense. Of course I 'bear the Mark of Tantalus.' But it's not a birthmark. Tantalus is the name of my apple orchards. An artist put that mark there. It's my logo, my trademark. You 'read' my *tattoo!*"

Helga—if that was her real name—did not immediately reply. But she was not in the least nonplussed. In fact, a smile slowly appeared upon her lips. "Nevus or tattoo, regardless. Did you feel the heat generated when I touched it?"

She had confounded me. Nonplussed myself now, I replied, "Yes, I did." I awaited her explanation.

"What do you know of Tantalus?" she asked. I knew of the Greek legend and repeated it. And explained how it inspired me to name my orchards for it. A lark, nothing more.

"Were you aware of the genealogy of Tantalus?" Genealogy? I shook my head. "Tantalus was himself a tragic figure," she went on. "He was the progenitor of the most tragic figures in all of Greek mythology. His daughter, Niobe, saw all her twelve children murdered, and was condemned to cry for the rest of her life. His son, Broteus, went mad. His grandson, Agamemnon, was murdered by his wife, Clytemnestra's lover. Agamemnon's children, Electra and Orestes, in turn murdered Clytemnestra. Your mark, placed there by an artist or by God—it does not matter—will not serve you well, sir. I can say no more other than to offer a warning. Beware of the heat of the Mark of Tantalus." I was dumbfounded. "Please leave me now," she said, while turning away from me as though I'd been cursed.

Had I? Of course not! Cursed by a mere tattoo? What a fool I'd been to enter this maddening salon. We did not bid each other goodbye. I arose and left.

Three days later, the strange incident still lingering upon my mind, I sat, before take-off, in the holding area at SAS, tapping away on my laptop. After waiting in an endless line, I found myself, at last, passing through the boarding door.

As I did so, I sensed a tingling below my left shoulder. Touching the area, I felt a bit of warmth. By the time I'd strapped myself into my seat, the mark was growing warmer.

My flight took off, then the plane foundered and, with no warning, crashed into farmland less than a kilometer from Arlanda's runways. Fortunately, though I suffered severe injuries, I was not among the forty-two, out of 217 passengers and crew, who died in the crash. But how fortunate was I to be on that flight at all?

Did Helga know something she wasn't telling me? I'll visit her again—as soon as I'm released from the hospital.

The Trial of Jimmy McCloud

It was reported that James "Jimmy" McCloud of Yates Center down in Jepson County, Kansas, had murdered his brother Jonas; had stuck a nine-inch chef's knife into his gut and then into his heart in, as they say, cold blood. And no exonerating circumstances had yet been uncovered. The case appeared to be of the, as they also say, open and shut variety.

The trial went forth and, though Jimmy had pleaded Not Guilty, the judge, Absalom Jackson, came to instruct the jury that they must find James McCloud guilty of first degree, or premeditated, murder; second degree, or unintentional murder, or find him innocent.

Jimmy's court-appointed lawyer, Tory Withers, who incidentally had passed the Kansas bar less than a year before (after two failed tries), argued the case weakly. For that and for other reasons, the trial lasted but three days with the jury ready to deliver its verdict after just two hours of deliberation.

A little background here: Jimmy and his identical twin brother, Jonas, born seconds apart thirty-two years earlier, lived together in a ramshackle bungalow on the outskirts of town. They'd inherited the small, two-bedroom home from their mother, who'd died of uterine cancer only two months earlier. Their father had abandoned the three of them when the boys were infants.

Here are the facts, heard by the jury, as delivered and attested to by Jimmy McCloud, who was at once fidgety, while also acting in a way that could only be perceived as cocky, on the stand. This was as noted by a zealous Kansas City Star newspaper reporter, known for his tendency to sensationalize whatever he wrote. Such reporting, it was thought by many who attended the trial, seemed to further deprecate Jimmy's already shaky case.

On the day of the murder, Jimmy told of being at home, specifically, at their kitchen sink washing dishes. They had argued earlier that day over whether the home should be kept or sold. Jimmy, a compulsive gambler, wanted to sell, to cash out his chips, so to speak. Jonas thought this to be blasphemy—an insult to their mother's memory. He insisted on keeping the home, even offering to buy out Jimmy's share. But Jonas was unemployed at the moment and had no ready funds with which to back up his offer.

When Jonas, standing behind Jimmy, reacted strongly to the names Jimmy was calling him, a scuffle broke out, escalating quickly into a fist fight. What happened was this: Jonas, even more volatile than his brother, spun Jimmy around and punched him in the face several times before his strong hands enveloped Jimmy's neck and began to choke him. Jimmy, holding the knife he was washing at the time, admitted that, " . . . at this point I lost it." His words. He was, per his testimony, " . . . in fear of my own life. So I stabbed Jonas in the stomach."

Had Jimmy stopped at that single thrust, argued the prosecution, then, even if the wound it caused was a mortal one, the stabbing might have been justified as having been done in self-defense. Or at least, defensible as manslaughter, having been done on the spur of the moment. But, it was further argued, Jimmy then chose to continue his thrusts, stabbing his already dying brother in the heart. Not once but, according to the Jepson County coroner's report, no less than four times.

The prosecution insisted that the several minutes or more it must have taken Jimmy to further consider his act of murderous mayhem and then systematically carry it out, constituted an act of certain premeditation. It demanded a finding of first-degree murder.

Jimmy's attorney, Withers, argued that there was never a preconceived intention to commit an act of murder in the first place, that when the brothers awoke that day they had been at peace with each other and, in fact, rarely fought.

What Withers would never know—what no one except the brothers knew—was that Jimmy and Jonas McCloud, practically from birth, hated each other. Withers' summation, however, was as flimsily presented as his arguments, not so much regarding the facts he was defending, but for the nervous manner in which he defended them. His disconcerting facial tic, noted by the Star reporter, did not help his client.

The jury, perhaps because of Withers' weak defense, accepted the logic of the prosecution's premeditation argument. Thus it came as no surprise that the jury saw the murder as premeditated, and found James "Jimmy" McCloud guilty of murder in the first degree. And he was taken away, sentence to be delivered within two days.

When Jimmy was returned to court, he had a strangely benign look on his sallow-complected face. It was as if he knew something the Judge didn't.

"James McCloud," intoned Judge Jackson, "you have been found guilty of murder in the first degree. I hereby sentence you to imprisonment for life in the state penitentiary at Leavenworth, Kansas." An approving rumble went up from those who had attended the sentencing hearing. The Star reporter, who had hounded Jimmy in print throughout the trial, noted later that, " . . . as the prisoner was being led into custody, he appeared to wear an inscrutably unrepentant half smile."

And well he might have.

Within a month Jimmy, after firing the hapless Withers, and acting on his own behalf, with the help of a jailhouse lawyer, filed a writ of habeas corpus with the court. The writ was granted by Judge Jackson, curious to know what the prisoner had up his sleeve. Why was Jimmy there? To argue the simple fact that . . . they had arrested and convicted the wrong man.

"Your Honor," said Jimmy McCloud—or the man the judge and jury had been purposely led to believe was Jimmy McCloud—"I wish to inform you that I am not James McCloud, I am Jonas McCloud, James' twin brother. In short, I'm afraid you arrested the wrong man. I admit to having lied to the officers who arrested me and again, on the stand, I lied to you, sir, and to the jury as well. I told you I was

James when, in fact, I am Jonas. Legally, I expect I'm guilty of perjury—but nothing more, Your Honor, and I step down. That's all I got to say."

Judge Jackson was too stunned to offer an immediate reply. "Mr. McCloud, I must admit that *I* hardly know what to say. If you can prove that you are actually your brother—well, that's not exactly what I mean. I mean that if you can prove you're Jonas McCloud, then obviously we *will* have arrested and tried the wrong person. That does not, however, preclude the fact that we must now try you, Jonas McCloud, for the murder of your brother, James. Do you understand what I'm telling you?"

"I understand it perfectly, Your Honor. But you cannot try me again because you've already tried me. I—my body, my person—have been tried and found guilty on this very same stand. You therefore have no legal right to place me here again. That, sir, would be, in the eyes of the law . . . double jeopardy."

The proverbial pin could be heard to drop. That very day, Jonas's trial for perjury was set for three months ahead. Jonas McCloud walked through his loophole and out of the court as a free man.

Jonas was of course convicted on the perjury charge, and was made to serve six years in prison, after which he became free to live out his life in the home he loved . . . alone and without his detested brother James.

Or was it the other way around?

The Interrogation

"What're you having, Dad?"

"I think a pastrami and swiss and an egg cream. You?"

"A Cobb salad. So what's going on with you?"

"You really want to know?"

"Yes, I really want to know."

"I met a woman, Mims."

"You didn't! So that's why you asked me to lunch?"

"No, I like your company. Isn't that enough?"

"No. I want you to tell me about her."

"I just did."

"No, you didn't. I've heard that trope before. Tell me more. I mean, did you *just* meet her?"

"I've known her for nearly two months. Remind me what a trope is again."

"Never mind. You little devil, you. You never said a word."

"I'm saying now."

"Sounds serious. Please say more. Do you like her?"

"Of course I like her. Would I be with her two months if I didn't?" (long pause)

"Don't you go silent on me, Dad. I'm listening."

"Okay, okay. She's—a very nice person. A—I think she said—a Presbyterian. Or maybe a Methodist, whatever. But a devout atheist and a screaming liberal like me. Was twice married, once divorced, once widowed."

"How old?"

"Seventy-six. A year older than me."

"A cougar."

"Very funny."

"But, Dad, you've always been attracted to younger women. Mom was twelve years younger. Your last 'girlfriend' was—what?—twenty, twenty-five years younger?"

"I'm done with that *mishigas*, Mims. Look, I wasn't looking for anyone. I went to the Getty for a lecture on Frank Gehry's architecture. Gehry himself did a slide show. You know how I love that stuff. And I got to talking to this woman who happened to be sitting next to me and I suggested we have coffee afterward so we could discuss the lecture and she says, skip the coffee, let's have a cocktail, which we did. Next thing you know, I ask her to dinner and—we're, well, we're seeing each other. And talking—a lot."

"Talking? That's it?"

"Talking."

"Sooo—are you attracted to her for more than her architecture?"

"Well, Mimsy, I have to admit, she is well constructed."

"Now who's being funny? What's her name? Does she have family? Is she working? Tell me *everything*."

"What's to tell. Her name is Christine Abramovitz."

"What? Quite an interesting tag. I thought you said—"

"I guess she likes Jews. Both her husbands were Yids but she never converted, *nu*? She has four kids, all living back East where she grew up in Manhattan. Nine grandkids. She moved to LA because her second husband got a job here in the Industry. And died here. She became curator of an art gallery on Melrose, then retired last year as its manager."

"So, Dad, you dabble in art, she ran an art gallery. You met in a milieu—an art museum—a place you love at a talk about a subject you both love. You sound like you have a little in common. You love food. Does she? Does she, uh, cook?"

"I've gained three pounds since we met."

"She cooks. Wait a minute, Dad. Are you telling me all this because you're attracted to her in a way that you'd like to, maybe . . . uh . . . uh . . ."

"Stop uh-ing me, Mims, I'm not thinking about that. Well, maybe I am, but, hey, if she's up for it—"

"Father mine, I'm talking about marriage. What are you talking about?"

"Uh . . . uh . . ."

"Right. Are you sleeping with her? You are, aren't you? Get that silly grin off your face."

"Daughter mine, it's none of your business."

"You are, aren't you?"

"Sleeping. Cuddling. What's the difference? We're holding on to each other for dear life."

" Okay, Dad, I get it—I understand."

"But do you, Mimsy? Can you? Can anyone of your tender years understand?"

"Please, Dad, I'm forty-two tender years old. Of course I understand. And I'm happy for you. What does she look like?"

What does she look like? What do I look like? Does it matter? Why don't you ask me what it feels like to be with her? Maybe I shouldn't have told you about her."

"Dad, I'm sorry, please don't get upset. I didn't mean—"

"I know what you meant. You just wanted to know who she is. Christine is a good person, that's who she is."

"C'mon, Dad, are you thinking of marrying her? I don't want you settling again. You've been through enough pain. I don't want to see you hurt. So maybe you can understand why I want to know more about her. In the end, if you agree that she's right for you, then I'll think the same. Well, I think I will. But it's your turn to understand me. I want to protect you. That's the only place I'm coming from. Don't jump on me for this, Dad, but you've made some mistakes before. They've hurt not just you but me, so maybe I can get to meet this Christine before you go any further? I promise you this, if I see that she cares for you, truly cares for you, I know I'll like her. I think if she cares for you, she'll care for me too. Oh, Dad, I love you way too much to see you get hurt again."

"I know that, babe. I've always known that. I love you, too. But I can't erase the fact that I've made some mistakes before. Plenty.

You remember that last woman, the one I met in the nightclub?"

"I do. And I recall what you said about her. That you were coming from the right place but were looking in the wrong place."

"Right. Truth is, I'm a little scared of my feelings for Christine. Scared that I may be making yet another mistake. But, you know what, Mims? I really think you'll love her."

"And why is that? Do you?"

"What? What did you just ask me?"

"Were you not listening? Or didn't you want to hear me? All I said was, do you love her?"

"I heard you the first time, Mimsy. Funny thing is, I never really asked myself that question. I need to think about that awhile."

"Well, I'm asking now. You don't know if you love her and you're maybe thinking of marrying her?"

"Who said I was?"

"I said. You said, too."

"Okay. Yes. I'm thinking."

"Of marrying her?"

"Yes. But I'm only thinking about it."

"'Only thinking about it.'"

"Yes. I think so."

"You *think* you're thinking about it?"

"I'm knowing. Okay?"

"Knowing? Now it's knowing? What is it you're knowing? I repeat, Father: Do you love her?"

"My God, Miriam, I told you I never asked *myself* that question."

"So *I'm* asking. I'm repeating myself too, but I'm asking. Do you love Christine?"

"I'm still thinking. Is that okay?"

"No."

"'No,' she says. Then, you know what? I do love her. I love her, Miriam. I do. And thanks for asking, because if you hadn't—I might never have realized it."

"So you do love her. Good. Lunch. Tomorrow. *With* your Christine Abramovitz. Twelve noon at the Archer Grille on Fourth."

"What? What? I can't remember all that. Send me an email."

"A text okay?"

"I don't know how to text."

"Yes, you do, Daddy. Daddy?"

"What?"

"I love you."

"You already said that."

"Yes, but I'm repeating myself again. I love you."

"Yeah, yeah, yeah."

Theremin Man
(for Donny)

This was the third reel of costly film wasted because, while the light was perfect, the sound was way off. Way, way off. It was already 1931. The talkies were an established art form—though it may be a stretch to say that. But it wasn't the actors who were causing the problem.

It was the sound of the theremin, its spooky permutations of low and high notes, then yet higher ones, crescendoing to a climax that the director, the incomparable Tod Browning, knew weren't even close to what was demanded. Everyone else on the spanking new Sound Stage 12 knew it, too.

Browning's now-gutteral "Cut!" came through the megaphone nearly twenty times that endless afternoon in May, its sound itself rising with each upward climb of the theremin's dismally dissonant notes.

The film's new star of Dracula, Bela Lugosi, was playing Bram Stoker's vampire even better than he'd played it four years earlier on Broadway. Legendary was a term he'd soon rightfully earn. Some said that Paul Muni, who'd first been sought for the role, would have been better. But time was to prove that Lugosi, who was paid just $3500 for the six-week shoot, was the definitive count with the over-size canines.

The rest of the cast—Helen Chandler, David Manners, and especially Dwight Frye as Renfield, who becomes a raving lunatic slave to Lugosi's Count Dracula—all fit their parts as though born to play them. Everything—every*one*—was perfect.

Except the damn theremin.

The idiot hired to play the thing just could not hit the right notes. It was important that the instrument be recorded on the set as it was meant to limn the atmosphere in which the actors could more authentically perform their roles. But, by now, Lugosi himself was ready to drain the musician's blood. The theremin, even if prerecorded to be added later, was seen to be a major player in the film. It would set the background, the pace, the true mood and feel of the film. Most important, it would provide the leitmotif for Count Dracula. But this bum made its weird notes emerge as a wobbly roller coaster frequently running off the tracks.

And then . . . and then . . . a young grip, rolling a dolly laden with electric cables, happened by the distraught Browning's elevated director's chair, just as the man had dropped his leonine, beret-covered head into his hands in despair. The grip stopped, hesitated, then boldly whispered into the director's ear, "I know who can play it."

Enraged at the abrupt words, especially coming from a lowly grip, but at wit's end, Browning jerked himself upright to pounce on the interloper, spitting out, "Who the hell are you and what in damnation are you talking about?"

"Leon."

"And who in hell is 'Leon'?" screamed the director.

"Leon *is* theremin, sir."

"Leon *who*?!"

"Leon *Theremin*, sir. He invented the instrument."

Browning practically fell off the chair. "I thought the guy was dead," he said. But he was just covering himself. He'd never even heard of Leon Theremin. And the idea would never have occurred to him to seek the obvious, the very man who'd dreamed up the damn thing. It was simply one of those overlooked glitches that can and often do bloom into disaster in the burgeoning new film industry. A Hollywood thing, nothing more.

Dismissing the grip, Browning bellowed, to no one in particular, "Get me Leon Theremin," And, immediately, the studio turned into a kicked-over anthill. But not the grip, Donny Aros by name. Cowed yet standing his ground in front of the great Browning, he softly offered, "He's my uncle."

"Well, why, for pete's sake, didn't you say so?" bellowed Browning, his normally pink face darkening to deep red.

"I'm new here, sir. I didn't think it proper to speak to the director. And because, well, we don't exactly get along, my uncle and me. I haven't seen him in years."

"Well you're going to see him now! You know where to find him?"

"I think so."

"Don't think, just do it! Find him. Now. I'll give you till exactly five tomorrow to put him in front of me. Otherwise, don't bother to show up here again." The auteur being the auteur.

"Would that be five a.m. or five p.m., sir?"

"Don't get smart with me. Five p.m. Now get going."

It was true. Donny hadn't seen his uncle in ten years. Not since Theremin divorced his aunt, his mother's only sister, Amelia. The man was a genius, no doubt of it, but he was also a curmudgeonly hermit who'd paid no heed to his wife, spending all his time in the laboratory he'd made of his garage, tinkering with his electronic apparatus while holding the world—especially his family—at bay. All Donny remembered of him were the sounds—spooky sounds he'd never heard before—constantly spilling out of the dilapidated garage behind Leon Theremin's home in the sparse hills north of the Hollywoodland sign.

When the twelve-year-old Donny finally ventured to sneak a look through the garage's smudged window, all he could see was his uncle standing before a strange device that looked like a wired steel box with a rod rising from its right side. The man was playing the instrument—if that's what it could be called—somehow without even touching it. In fact, it could be said that he was "conducting" the box, just as a symphony orchestra conductor would do, waving his hands in a maestro-like fashion, in a way that seemed to control the sounds coming from the box. When Theremin finished, Donny was so deeply impressed, so awe-struck that he began to clap.

Theremin, noting Donny's presence, became enraged at his spying nephew, picked up a hammer lying near the box and threw it through the window, sending shards of glass into Donny's face and causing a scar across the bridge of his nose that Donny bears to this day. His Theremin scar, he calls it.

That was the last that Donny ever saw of his deeply anti-social uncle. Neither regretted the estrangement. Donny's Aunt Amelia divorced Theremin less than a year later. And now Donny was charged by the famous director, Browning, with collecting and delivering this difficult man and his strange apparatus within a day. His career depended upon it. Theremin's too, though he could hardly be aware of it.

Donny didn't believe that his Uncle Leon—no longer his uncle—would be interested in anything Hollywood had to offer him. He wasn't even sure he could find the man, he was that odd a duck. But he turned out to be easy to find. The first music shop Donny hit the next morning happened to have a theremin on display. The owner was reluctant to give out Leon's whereabouts but acceded when Donny explained, straight-faced, that he was the inventor's nephew and Leon's sister was dying. The owner sympathized with Donny, directing him to a tenement in Inglewood, a ramshackle affair that looked more like an abandoned warehouse—or his old garage—than a residence.

Donny peered through the grimy, barred window but could see nothing inside. There was no bell so he rapped and waited, then banged on the door when there was no response. Finally an unshaven face loomed in the window before the door opened. Donny recognized it as Theremin, now looking like an old man.

"What do you want?" said Theremin, glaring at Donny.

"I'm Donny Aros, your nephew, Uncle Leon."

"Yeah, I remember you, Denny. Denny, the spy. What the hell are you doing here?"

"Donny," corrected Donny.

"Denny, Donny, I said what do you want?"

"I want you, Uncle Leon."

"I'm not your uncle. Not any more. Scram! Get out of here!"

"The moving pictures want you, Uncle Leon. I work in the moving pictures and the picture I'm working on desperately needs a theremin player and no one plays the theremin like a Theremin, right?

"What of it, kid? I'm not interested. Beat it."

"But—"

"I said beat it. Amscray! You understand English?" With that, Leon Theremin pushed Donny back from the doorstep.

"You've got to listen to me, Uncle Leon," pleaded Donny. "If you —"

But his last words were cut off by the slamming of the door.

Desperate now, and with half the day gone, Donny rushed back as fast as two street cars could rush him to the Laemmle sound stage. Finding the chief sound engineer, Milt Howard, in his booth, Donny demanded a recording of the off-key theremin player's magnum opus. Howard balked, but caved in when Donny explained the urgency of his plea and the outcome to his own career and of the film itself if Howard didn't come across.

Howard came across.

Back across town, this time by cab, went Donny with the recording, a device to play it on, and another device to record what Donny intended to record. All of it stuffed into a bulky suitcase he could barely lift. The time was already four o'clock when he arrived back at Theremin's.

He knocked on the door. No answer. He knocked harder. Still no answer. He shouted his uncle's name. The answer he got from deep within was, "Get lost, you pest!"

But Donny wasn't about to get lost. He set up the playback equipment and began to hand-crank out the disastrous theremin notes, turning up the volume to near full. In a few minutes, shouts began to rain down on him, from the tenement next door, to knock off the goddamn screeching. He now turned the volume up to max, dodging a tomato and a bucket of water thrown at him by Theremin's irate neighbors. This went on for the next seven minutes. Until Theremin's door finally swung open.

"Where the hell did you ever get that pile of crap?" said Donny's uncle. Donny fast-talked an explanation, detailing the situation and stressing the urgency of time to produce some *real* theremin music: played not just on but *by* a Theremin.

"Uncle Leon, do you have a recording of your theremin work I could bring back to the studio."

"No, kid." But an odd look began to fill Theremin's craggy face. Accompanied by ten seconds of silence. Followed by something that almost resembled a smile. And he spoke again: "I know—barely recognize—the piece that's being played. I can't allow my instrument to be played like that. You, Donny, you'd better jump into my truck as soon as I can gather my equipment."

An hour later, Theremin's beat-up, 1918 Model T two-seater flatbed pulled up to the studio gate. The time was 5:18. Donny identified himself to the guard and explained the situation once again. But the determined guard said, "No dice, kid. Mr. Browning's strict orders. He said if you ain't here by five, you ain't comin' in, that's it!"

"But—"

"Get lost, kid." Seems like everyone wanted him to get lost. But he was well aware that Browning would exit through this very Gate 4 at six o'clock sharp, as he did every day.

And at six o'clock sharp, there he was, in his shiny yellow Deusenberg roadster, a silk scarf rakishly tossed around his neck as he approached the gate. But this time he was greeted not just by the befuddled guard, but by a sight that had startled everyone within eye-sight and ear-shot of the gate.

There stood a tall, disheveled, long-haired man, standing perfectly upright on his truck's flatbed, conducting a . . . a box sitting on —another box, an upended orange crate. A steel box with a rod rising from its right side and a rounded steel antenna projecting from its other side. And from the steel box emanated the weirdest, eeriest, strangest, most frightening, but perfectly *on-key* sounds ever to soon star in a major motion picture.

When Leon finally lowered his hands after his twelve minute concert, 150 pairs of hands came together, along with the first "encore" ever heard from the man in the Deusy, followed by shouts of "Bravo" from the gathering of actors, grips, best boys, studio execs, writers, extras and others who'd rushed up to hear what they'd never heard before. Truly a concert played on a theremin. *By* a Theremin.

There's a reason why they call the original *Dracula* a film classic. And the reason is not just the man who plays the bloodthirsty count.

Dear Nell

Dear Nell,

I'm short. Very short. "Height-deprived" as the politically correct folks say. I know that telling you this is not a very good way to begin a serious letter but it's important that I mention my height for a reason I'm about to explain. So important that I've put a great deal of time and thought into this letter—the first I've written by hand in years.

Look, Nell, we've been corresponding for some time. I put down in my Match.com profile that I was "quite" short. You, like—I must admit—many others, responded nonetheless. Most responses either never mentioned my being short or were apathetic or just plain *pathetic*. But you came right out and said that—bless you—size doesn't matter, it's the kind of person you are that matters.

And that, Nell, really got to me. Your response was so well-written, so full of wit and humor, so accepting and kind that I did something I never thought I'd have the nerve to do. I emailed back that I'd love to meet you. I assumed, from your wonderful emails—well, I guessed—that you were maybe pretty short yourself, maybe five feet or maybe even four-ten. Am I right? You never said.

Was I fortunate or just plain lucky to draw your response? Or was your reply fortuitous; was it serendipity that connected us?

189

Whichever, we began a regular correspondence and found—I hope you agree—that we have a lot in common, you and me. Not just liking walking on the beach or a good, home-cooked meal or we both like honest people, but your love of traveling and of movies and especially your love of reading, all three things that, as you now know, I love as well. I can easily picture us having a picnic of maybe home-made fried chicken and a peach pie while sitting under a huge elm tree way up on a countryside hill, then you just lying back while I read a good story to you. Even one I might have written myself. You said you really liked the short stories I sent you.

Well, back to my profile, I of course included a photo, but it was only a head shot. Now I have to admit that, in a way, it was a lie. Oh sure, it was a real photo, and that really is what I look like, but if I'd posted a full- length photo of me, you'd know the real truth. What I'm trying to tell you, Nell—and right now I want to apologize for leading you on, and I surely hope you'll forgive me—is that I am a little person.

You and the rest of the world would call me a "midget" or what I am not, a "dwarf," but I prefer being seen as a little person because, other than being shorter than other people, I am a person just like you and everyone else.

Nell, I am four feet, four and a half inches tall. But I hasten to say that I am "normal" in every other way. Yes, I had no business not making that very clear in my Match.com description of myself. I admit that I deceived you and every woman who responded. They would be unforgivingly upset at learning of this, just as I'm certain you are, but I'm hoping you'll be understanding enough to at least forgive me (though I hardly deserve forgiveness) without hating me. I must tell you that I am ashamed of myself for my deception and again apologize for it.

I will certainly understand if I never hear from you again, Nell. But please try to remember me not for my short stature, and I hope not for the way I've deceived you, but for whatever it was in our correspondence that made you feel good. Maybe for those stories I sent you, especially the one about the guy who met the girl of his dreams through Match.com. As for me, I will always remember you.

I guess, by now, that I must sound pretty darn pitiful, so I'll stop and simply say . . . Goodbye, Nell.

Yours very truly,
Harvey

The very next hour, Harvey received this reply:

Dear Harvey,

You're an idiot. But a nice one. And not as good a liar as you think you are because, yes, I do love to read, am very good at it and was therefore able to read between the lines of nearly every email you sent and even the wonderful stories you wrote. I knew you were trying to tell me that there was something about you that was different. You often said things like, "I'm not like other people," or "I have a different perspective on life than most men."

I, of course, couldn't know that this "difference" you were intimating had to do with your height, which, yes, I took to be maybe five foot four or something. But I quickly came to know that you were different, and my intuition told me that I might not only accept that difference but I would somehow appreciate it and maybe even love it.

What if, Harvey, you were deaf or blind or, worse, a paraplegic or had muscular dystrophy or some other debilitating condition? Would that make you less of a man? Not to me it wouldn't. It is your mind that I like; your pleasant manner and your gentleness in the way you say things. Emails—I'm sure you know this—can say an awful lot.

And you know something, Harvey? Your telling me about yourself before letting it go so far that I would be shocked if and when we somehow met in person tells me that you're a far more honest man than you think. It takes a lot of moxie—I think that's the word—to reveal something you think will cut you off from a relationship you really want to have. And if you think otherwise, then you really are an idiot.

Harvey Mueller, I'm not busy Friday night. I live at 401 Apple

Court, Apartment 201 in Fairwood Heights, exactly three and a half miles from you according to Google Maps. My phone number, once again (you haven't used it yet) is 620-331-6770. Would 6 p.m. work for you? I know of a terrific Italian bistro nearby, if you'd prefer to go out. The best risotto you've ever tasted. But I'd rather cook a meal for you first. I shouldn't reveal the menu but you may appreciate it more if you can anticipate it. I do fried chicken and peach pie very well.

With much admiration, and with anticipation of meeting you,
Nell

P.S.: I thought you might like this photo of me. My friend just took it.

Harvey, with growing and undisguised glee, tapped open the attached photo and stared at it.

There was Nell—his Nell—as beautiful a woman as he could ever hope to dream of; blue-eyed and fair-skinned and with long, straight golden hair splayed over freckled shoulders. Beside a short skirt and a peasant blouse half off her left shoulder, she was wearing a lovely smile, an enigmatic smile that was more of a puckish grin than a smile. Nell was a vision of loveliness, one that immediately imprinted itself on the huge space available in Harvey's lonely mind and heart.

His feeling of pure joy came at least partly from noticing—he couldn't help but notice—that Nell was holding a vertically positioned yardstick planted on the ground next to her.

She towered over it by almost a foot.

The Witches of Kimmelman's

It was Yom Kippur, the Day of Atonement, our highest of high holidays. But I was about as far out in the diaspora as a Jew can get. Decades back I'd given up attending services, fasting on Yom Kippur or observing any Jewish holiday in any way. And I hadn't been a member of a temple since my youth.

But I'd been through a lot lately. I'd recently lost my beloved wife of fifty-six years, she who, though not Jewish herself, had sat in patience beside me as curiosity sent me to Yom Kippur's heartrending Kol Nidre service in varied cities—Paris, Stockholm, Bristol, England—during our traveling days so very long ago. That was in better times when I could afford to travel.

Now as I got to thinking of those Kol Nidre services, and of my wife whom I think of and grieve for daily, I was determined to attend another. Not for its intrinsic meaning, but in honor of her.

So I decided I would take myself to the Kol Nidre—it means "All Vows"—at the temple nearest me, a behemoth name of B'nai Jeshuran, but long known to its congregants as Kimmelman's Temple because Rudolph K. Kimmelman was its founding rabbi.

Came the eve of Yom Kipper, I brushed the dust off my last remaining suit, a spiffy black pinstripe number I'd found for $129.95 on the sale rack at Macy's, and showed up at Kimmelman's's wearing it, along with a blue necktie with little sperms wriggling around all over it, a birthday gift from my son-in-law, a lawyer in Eugene, Oregon, who had once been on the national board of Planned Parenthood, forgive my boasting.

Arriving early, I saw so many people there before me, I thought I'd arrived late. I had to stand in line behind them in front of a table covered with a rose-colored cloth, set up next to the doors of Kimmelman's massive main sanctuary. Behind the table sat three matronly women who looked remarkably like the ones my mother used to play mah-jongg with in the mid-1900s.

Signs suspended from the front edge of the table bore the letters "A-K," "L-R" and S-Z," respectively. Each woman had a clipboard in front of her and would inspect it as congregants showed their credentials and tickets to prove who they were and that they had actually bought *and* paid for their tickets and, I suppose, were current on their dues and their pledges to Jewish Welfare. My turn to face the women came at last.

"Gut Yontif," I said to the woman behind L-R, as I placed my yarmulke on my head hoping to impress her with the seriousness of my devotion and thus my right to be there.

"Your name, please?" she demanded, offering a false-toothed hint of a smile. I gave it to her. "May I see your ticket?" she said.

I gulped, knowing this question would be asked. I was too embarrassed to tell her I couldn't afford a ticket. The damn things were going for one-fifty a pop, but that, of course, included Rosh Hashanah. "I don't have a ticket," I admitted, in practically a whisper, but not softly enough to avoid being heard by all three of the women who suddenly turned into Shakespeare's three prophetic witches of Endor. The table, in my red-faced mind, began to burn with an eerie orange glow.

"You don't *have* a ticket?!" screeched the green-faced L–R witch, a hairy wart, flashing red like a stoplight, seemed to pop up at the tip of her endless nose, while a conical black hat appeared atop her head.

"I'm sorry, I replied, "I decided to come at the last minute and was hoping you might have an empty seat, maybe in the last rows of the balcony and—"

She stopped me. Never mind that Kimmelman's sat virtually empty three hundred and sixty days a year. "Sir, every seat is sold. This is our busiest evening of the year. There are no empty seats. You should have planned ahead."

The woman was acting like Kimmelman's Kol Nidre was a hotter ticket than *Hamilton*. I became furious. I needed to answer this witch with a comeback that would put her in her place; that would not leave me feeling as though I had no place here. Would I walk away too late to think of one and say it, as I usually did under such circumstances?

No, not this time.

I leaned across the table and wagged my arthritic finger in front of her grimacing face and spit these words right into her bubbling cauldron: "You just wait till God hears of this!"

And, with that, I spun around and hobbled away as fast as my eighty-seven-year-old legs would take me, practically tripping over my Malacca cane.

The China Incident

I'm a good listener. This helps when you're a psychologist. I've heard a lot of stories in my time but none like the tale told me by the stranger—I'll call him Henry—who sat next to me once on a flight home to San Francisco. Henry's in his late 60s. He's a freelance journalist who's also written a couple of novels which he admitted went quickly to the remainder bin.

I found his story most compelling and will tell it as best I remember it.

Seems three years back Henry met his daughter's teammate, Marie, at a lesbian league softball game. Marie's partner Helen was there with their nearly two-year-old daughter, Nola, an abandoned child she and Helen had adopted and brought home from China a year earlier.

Henry and his wife hit it off well with Nola's two wonderful moms, and they fell in love with the beautiful child. Within a year they'd became fast friends, visiting back and forth and sharing meals regularly.

One day, Marie and Helen declared that their year-and-a-half wait for approval of their application to adopt another abandoned Chinese baby girl had just been approved.

Marie, knowing that the Chinese attitude toward gay adoptive parents had been changing for the worse, decided to make the trip this time as a "single mother." That's the way she and Helen wanted the Chinese officials to look at her anyhow, and besides, Helen had to remain home to care for Nola. So Henry, out of their friendship, agreed, when asked, to accompany Marie to China and help her bring home the new baby.

The agreement was that Marie and Helen would pay for Henry's passage and meals in return for Henry's hauling the luggage, handling the video and digital cameras and occasionally overseeing Lotus—that was to be the baby's new name—when Marie needed rest, a gym workout, time to shop, whatever. Henry would be the helpmate who would replace the homebound Helen. Henry and Marie shook hands on it and the two of them were off to China to bring Lotus home.

After a day in Guangzhou—the old Canton—on China's southern coast, Marie and Henry flew, with seven other adoptive families, to the central China city of Xi'an, known best for the terra cotta images of its fourteenth century founding emperor, Xin's army, that had been unearthed in the 1970s as the "Eighth Wonder of the World."

Henry was assigned the task of videotaping and photographing their remarkable first day in Xi'an. He did this with an inspired flair, capturing everything from the presenting of Lotus to her new mother to the many priceless moments of bonding between the two during their remaining days in Xi'an. This included a visit by the three of them to the site of the terra cotta army where, as did many visitors, Marie and Henry each bought heavy boxed two-foot replicas of Xin's soldiers by which to remember the city of Lotus's birth.

It was on the final day in Xi'an that the shattering "China Incident" took place. The group of families were gathered at the small, suffocatingly hot Xi'an airport lounge, waiting to return to Guangzhou, their city of departure for their return home. It was the beginning of August. All were laden with their newly adopted baby girls and the trappings of baby-care, luggage and souvenirs, when their evening departure announcement came. There would be a long, unexpected and unexplained delay. The mood of the disappointed, overwrought and exhausted group became ugly as the hours dragged on, surly, even, by the time the flight actually departed at midnight.

Henry, overweight and out-of-shape, toting the camera bag, a childcare bag and the two heavy, handle-less boxes containing the soldiers, was sweating profusely, feeling the full burden of his bulky packages and his sixty-six years. After stowing his carry-ons on the plane, he fell into a stuporous sleep, to awaken only a few minutes before the flight ended.

Still groggy, dazed by exhaustion, and having the writer's pre-occupative disease of often forgetting anything other than what he was writing about at the time, Henry did his best to quickly gather his belongings and stagger down the steps from the plane and into the stifling bus that would convey them to the terminal in Guangzhou. After they left the bus and were walking into the terminal, Marie looked at the overloaded, wavering, half-awake Henry. He now had only the childcare bag slung from his shoulder, and a large box under each arm.

She noticed what was missing at once. "Henry," she screamed, "where . . . is . . . the camera bag?"

Henry could only stare back in dumbfounded confusion, the fog of sleep clearing enough for him to realize that he'd left—he *must* have left—the camera bag on the plane. Fully awake now, and pan-icked, he instinctively attempted to climb back on the emptied bus, loudly demanding of its non-English-speaking driver that he be re-turned immediately to the plane for a thorough search. A guard intervened and backed the distraught Henry into the terminal.

With the help of those in charge of the group, Henry and Marie then made inquiries of the proper airport officials. The plane was searched by other officials, but to no avail.

The camera bag was gone. And it was to remain gone. Lost? Stolen? What did it matter? It was gone.

Marie was livid. She said to Henry, "I paid thousands of dollars to bring you here and now you've lost the only thing in your charge that really mattered."

Henry could well understand her harsh attitude and was himself devastated—virtually sickened—by his act of carelessness, not just by the loss of the cameras, but much more by the fact that he'd lost

Marie's irreplaceable memories of her first moments with Lotus; priceless images that could never be recaptured.

His first response was to blurt, "I'm so very sorry . . . I can't believe this . . . I'll replace the cameras . . . I don't know what else to say."

But much more was happening in his befuddled mind. He was in shock. He was also deeply embarrassed by appearing so incompetent; to the other families as well as to Marie. And he was finally beginning to recognize that this incompetence may have been of long standing. This total failure of his ability to focus on a given task had become chronic and, because of it, something drastic like this was bound to happen, and it did. The awareness of his repeated memory lapses hit him like a bingeing drunk finally waking to the stunning fact that he was an alcoholic. His remorse and his feeling of worthlessness in this fateful moment were almost palpable. Marie had counted upon him. He had betrayed her. It was that simple.

At this point in Henry's woeful story, his heavily lined face clearly showed the depth of what he was feeling. He looked older than the man who had sat down beside me just several hours before. Although the incident had taken place some years ago, it was obvious he'd relived its nightmare reality repeatedly. Even now, in the telling, he looked as though he might almost cry.

I waited a moment for Henry to compose himself. Then I asked what I'd often had occasion to ask my clients upon hearing their sad tales: "What, in that moment, did you feel most strongly?"

He blinked a few times to bring himself back to the present. Pondering the question awhile, he said, "For the first time in my life I felt like an old man." Silence followed.

"What happened then?" I had to ask.

"The next day, after things had calmed down a bit, we went to a department store in Guangzhou and looked at cameras. She didn't like the digital cameras, preferring to look for one when we returned to America. But she did find a good video-cam for about a thousand dollars and I bought it for her, and that was that."

"How did the rest of the trip turn out?"

"It was okay, I guess," he said, listlessly. "Although Marie reminded me of the incident a few times, she appeared to accept me, or, at least, to accept the situation. Others in our group promised to supply her with whatever earlier footage and shots they had of her receiving Lotus. We got along, after that, but we didn't talk much. Then, after staying in Guangzhou to fill out the endless adoption paperwork for a week—a long, remorseful week—we flew back home."

"When we arrived in San Francisco," Henry added as an afterthought, his voice growing softer, "Little Nola ran up to Lotus and kissed her and called her 'Mei-Mei.' That means 'little sister.' It was very touching."

This last statement brought a smile to Henry's face, the only time on our long flight that I saw one. "And that was the end of it?" I asked.

The smile disappeared. "Hardly," he replied. "She told me the cameras hadn't been insured for loss, only for theft. I told her if they were my cameras, I'd have reported them as stolen, which they obviously were. But she said she wouldn't do that because she considered them simply lost and had 'too much integrity' to report them stolen. Besides, she told me, even if they were covered for theft and she filed a claim, her insurance premium would likely go up. I offered to pay for the increase if she'd report the loss as a theft but she still wouldn't hear of it." Then Henry stopped.

"Please go on," I urged.

"Maybe a week, ten days later I got a call from Marie. She thought it was time we went shopping for the digital camera I had also said I'd replace. She asked if I had a problem with that." He stopped again. He obviously wasn't comfortable telling his story, but he continued without my urging.

"That," said Henry, "was when I put my foot down. Yes, I told her, I had a serious problem with that and no longer had any intention of replacing the digital camera. She seemed shocked at my refusal. She wanted to know why, after offering to pay, I was now refusing. I told her that, since she had failed to carry loss insurance and wouldn't put in a theft claim and hadn't put an ID tag on the camera to aid in its possible return, she should bear at least some of the responsibility for the loss. I had done my part by replacing the more expensive video-cam."

"Did she agree about the ID tag?"

"No, absolutely not. She said people can lose things even if they have ID on them. I insisted people can also *return* things if they have an ID tag on them. She scoffed at my logic."

"Sounds like you were angry, like you'd recovered some of your self- esteem by then," I said.

"Angry? I was furious," Henry replied. "The truth is, though her partner Helen expressed her gratitude for what I had done, Marie never once bothered to thank me for the help I'd given her during our two weeks there, or for replacing the video-cam without complaining. And she never once showed any feeling about how miserable the incident made *me* feel. She only thought about herself and her loss. You're damn right I was angry."

"And letting out your anger made you feel better?"

"A little. Yes, it did. Anyhow, she hit the ceiling and the argument kept going. Neither of us would budge."

"So?"

"So she sued me."

I leaned toward Henry. "She *sued* you?" My widened eyes pleaded with him to tell the rest of his remarkable story. And he did.

Marie filed suit in common pleas court for the loss of the uncompensated digital camera—about six hundred dollars—plus the cost of Henry's expenses for the trip that he had "ruined," plus an amount, "to be determined," as aggravated damages for the mental anguish the loss of memories had caused her. Henry didn't anticipate there'd be much at stake dollar-wise, even if some amount would be allowed for the "mental anguish," so, since Marie was as anxious as Henry to settle the matter quickly, the two agreed to waive a jury trial and allow a judge to decide the matter.

The judge, Agnes Chilton, was a woman who'd been on the bench for decades. She was a highly respected jurist known for her wisdom and fairness.

Marie's attorney was a young man, Scott Willis, out to make a name for himself. He meant never to lose a case ever, especially not this relatively simple one. His reputation, as well as his client's claim, was on the line. Willis's smooth, fast-talking plea was based upon Marie's having been given ample reason to rely upon Henry and his personal pledge to oversee her luggage, particularly her camera equipment, in consideration for her paying Henry's way. Clearly, he argued, Marie and Henry had what amounted to a lawful and valid contract, verbal and based upon a handshake, though it was.

The young turk, in his opening remarks, claimed that the momentary loss of defendant's memory was responsible for the loss of a mother's priceless first moments with her rescued orphan daughter. This loss of defendant's memory directly accounted for his client's lost memories, the value of which was almost beyond calculation. Almost, but not quite. Those memories could and should be calculated in dollars by the judge.

He added that Henry, a man who had trouble focusing on anything but his writing, had promised he could handle whatever reasonable chores Marie might assign him, and that he'd then broken that promise—that valid contract—by failing to perform. Marie, he concluded, deserved to be compensated for the digital camera, the wasted outlay for Henry's trip and a few other ridiculous things Henry couldn't recall, plus, of course, all that mental anguish.

Marie's case had been made pretty well in Henry's troubled mind, but Henry's crusty, rumpled old lawyer, Alton Crumbacher, a man who had successfully defended countless hundreds of "hopeless" cases, proceeded, in his deliberate, slow-speaking manner, to erode the underpinnings, one by one, of the powerful case that the smug young attorney had built.

Henry, Crumbacher was quick to point out in his resonant bass, had served strictly as an uncompensated friend—a *good* friend—whose costs of travel had been covered in exchange for his valuable services to the Plaintiff. He had agreed to forego his personal comfort by sharing a room with Marie so she would not have to spend any more than she would have spent had her partner been there in his place. But Henry had, most certainly, not been paid anything that resembled a fee and, therefore, should not have been held up to the same standard of performance, the same responsibility, as one who had been so compensated.

The lawyer now, looking first at Marie, then back at the judge," said, "Your Honor, I'd like to call the plaintiff to the stand."

"This is an informal, if binding, hearing," said Judge Chilton. "But I'm conducting it as a normal trial, so please direct your questions to me as a hypothesis." She looked impatient for points to be made and the hearing to wind down.

Henry's lawyer didn't hesitate. "My question goes to responsibility, Your Honor. Had the plaintiff asked my client, as a friend, to, say, drive her in an emergency to the hospital in her own car and my client had an accident along the way, should he be held responsible for wrecking, even totaling, her car? He was merely doing her a favor."

"Objection. Irrelevant," spoke out Willis. "The defendant's lawyer digresses."

"Sustained. Get to the point, please, counselor."

The wily older Crumbacher had already made his point, but he continued. "It is clear that, at most, the doctrine of Contributory Negligence applies here and must be recognized. The responsibility, if not resting fully upon plaintiff's shoulders, should be shared at best, and my client has already put in more than his share by paying one thousand dollars for the video-cam's replacement."

He was on a roll now. "Also, plaintiff had not placed proper identification on the camera bag to help anyone who might find and return it. In Communist China, such honesty is known to be the rule, not the exception. Ultimately, the plaintiff failed to act in the required manner of the Law's classic "Reasonable Man."

Henry's advocate also attempted to introduce the fact that the plaintiff hadn't properly insured the camera, covering it only against theft, not loss. But Willis again quickly objected on grounds of irrelevance and was just as quickly sustained.

Then Crumbacher claimed that Marie, though assured by Henry of his ability to handle the demands of the trip, knew, or should have known through their long friendship, that he was forgetful and often preoccupied by the nature of his work, and that therefore she was again negligent for having placed her reliance upon him.

Marie's attorney, in his summation, stressed Henry's "decidedly moral" responsibility to protect more than just the instruments that recorded her memories, but "the irreplaceable memories the cameras themselves contained, which were now lost forever." He pleaded also that Henry's egregiously negligent behavior had caused irreparable trauma to Marie's psyche. This was more than a material loss, it amounted to an injury that could and should be translated into assessable damages. Treble damages at the very least.

Henry's sagacious old-timer, in his own summation, knew he had his facts right and chose to lean more upon them than any touchy-feely story reliant upon the mercy of the judge. The plaintiff knew of Henry's errant mind yet chose to trust his memory. Defendant was a friend who had acted out of good will, one whose temporary lapse of memory should have been not only predicted but by all means forgiven without moral or legal consequence. Further, though Marie had paid for Henry's airfare and board, this trip was taken not as a vacation but purely as a favor to Marie. He was giving up the comforts of his wife and his home for weeks and was laying out hundreds of dollars of his own for phone calls, some meals and such, and was paid no fee, nor would he, being a close friend, have accepted a fee, and he therefore did not bear the responsibility—the *higher* responsibility—that an independent agent, a paid employee, a "hired hand" would necessarily bear. Marie had been additionally negligent in failing to place proper identification on her property so as to aid in its return. Not to mention, Crumbacher pointedly did mention, Marie's failure to properly insure her camera.

Being summation, no objections to these closing remarks could be raised. Nor could any objection of irrelevancy be made to Crumbacher's final point that Marie was an undeserving ingrate for never —not ever—thanking his client for the extensive service he indeed had performed.

It was, Henry agreed, a tough and brilliant summation.

At this point, Henry stopped telling his story and stared out the plane's window for a full minute. "I can feel the pressure in my ears," he said. "We should be landing soon at SFO."

Startled at his abrupt change of subject, I said, "Henry, please, what did the judge decide?" He turned to me and blinked a few times before replying.

"She threw the case out of court."

"Just like that?" I said.

"Just like that."

I stared at Henry before framing a reply. All I could think to say was, "Sounds like you came out a winner. You must have been quite pleased."

"I guess so," Henry replied.

He smiled wanly before the age began to creep back into his face.

I concluded, to myself, that there had been little for Henry to win.

Robert Jones

Robert Jones was grateful for his nondescript name. His parents had never thought to offer their son a given name of even semi-distinction; a Devon, say, or a Sebastian. Not even a middle initial. But Robert Jones' name was the only thing nondescript about him. He was a granite boulder of a man; a living, walking statue who stood five inches under seven feet tall.

These physical attributes—his height, his remarkable physique and stunning, square-jawed looks—had their advantages. But he chose not to exploit them. Better, he felt, if he didn't even possess them. He wished to be perceived, simply, as a normal human being.

Robert was used to the quotidian trials a man of his height encountered: bending through doors, sitting in a plane or theater, fielding astonished stares engendered by his singular physiognomy.

Though conscious of the awe with which he was met, Robert failed to understand why others couldn't get past his physical self. He was often asked inane questions. To these he gave respectful, if half-hearted, answers: "Did you play basketball or football?" No, track and a little lacrosse. "How'd you get to be so tall?" My parents are tall.

As a child, nurtured by weekly visits to the library where he'd check out a dozen books at a time, Robert's tastes ran less to knights of the round table or comic book superheroes than to little engines that could, or bulls who preferred smelling flowers to goring toreadors. In high school, the basketball coach leaned on him to play but he leaned toward cross-country track because he liked the lonely zone it put him in. He didn't see it as running away from himself, but that's somewhat what it was. The drama teacher beseeched him to play *Of Mice and Men*'s Lennie. He said no, but almost accepted the title role of *The Hairy Ape* because it was about a man like himself, a lonely hulk who couldn't find his way in Manhattan. All told, he was far more comfortable *in* an audience than in front of one.

Robert's love of literature led him to a niche in a world where size most definitely did not matter. He became an editor. And a writer of poems and many short stories, and one long one. He was working on his first novel.

Women—especially strong women not overwhelmed by his striking presence—sought him; wanted him and often boldly said so. But those who made their interest known were disappointed to find him excessively shy and withdrawn. Robert's excuse for putting them off: "I'm too involved in my writing now to be thinking of anything else."

He often pondered what he considered to be his fate. "If I were six inches shorter I'd be just another tall man. The kind other men look up to, no pun intended. Six-one, good. Six-seven, I'm a bit of a freak. You think I don't know that?" This he said to his best—and only— friend, Alvin Sims, a withdrawn freak of sorts himself, but of the computer variety. Alvin had designed the website that would hopefully launch Robert's sci-fi novel, *The Unseen Giant*, about a man born invisible who, when he happened upon a magic mirror that at last revealed his image, was appalled to find that he was not a man at all but a seven-foot simian with the face of a highland ape.

Robert liked women as much as any man did. But he felt that their interest in him had only to do with his physical appearance; his looks, which he'd come to almost detest. How could anyone know him behind his height, body, face? How could he be anything but bitter, shy and self-conscious?

Still, though indeed shy and self-conscious, he was anything but bitter. He was of a good nature. And always hopeful that the right woman, who would see him for who he was, would some day come by.

This Sunday found Robert loping along his usual run around the Central Park reservoir where the other runners were too wrapped up in their own regimen to notice him in his.

Finishing, the sweat pouring off him, he walked a few hundred yards to cool off, then sat down in the middle of the only unoccupied bridle path bench available on this perfect, sun-blessed, early June day.

On the near end of the bench to his left sat a woman. He couldn't help but notice that she was a beautiful woman. Strikingly so. She did not seem to notice him; did not look at him. They sat, he now looking fixedly ahead as did she. Since she was holding a book in her left hand, Robert was unable to see if she were wearing a wedding band. Her right hand rested on the book's open pages. He'd liked to have known its title for what it could tell of her.

Though unnerved by her, he found himself desperately wanting to open a conversation with her. Maybe he could ask about the book. But all he could muster up was, "Hi." Not much of an opening gambit.

The woman blinked a few times then turned toward him. "Are you speaking to me?"

"Yes. I just finished my run and sat down here and you were sitting next to me and, uh . . ." What next? C'mon, Robert. ". . . I, uh, thought I'd say hello. You don't mind, do you?" Stupid question.

But she didn't laugh at him, she just turned to him and smiled. "No, I don't mind. Hello to you."

Saved. "You're alone?" A remarkable observation, he thought, adding to himself, "You idiot." Could she possibly understand that what he really meant, but would never say it, was, "Are you alone in your life like I am?" But before she could answer, he skipped to another question. "Do you come here often?"

Looking into her book again, she replied, "Most Sundays. I love to read and I love the park and the day is lovely and . . . where else *can* one sit and read outdoors in this city?"

"I suppose you're right." Weak. Then he was surprised to find himself saying, "I'm glad you chose to sit here."

She turned again toward him. And smiled again. "Really? Did you sit there *because* I'm sitting here?"

Uh-oh. But the question bode well. "It was the only unoccupied bench available," he explained. "I mean, if I wanted to sit by myself."

"That's not a very flattering answer," she replied, straight-faced. But couldn't hold back the laugh that followed.

"Well," Robert said, "It is the truth. But I also bless the fates that plopped me down here."

Plopped me down here? Did he just say that? Robert mentally smacked his forehead.

No matter, she just laughed again. A very appealing laugh, by the way. "What's your name?" she asked.

"Robert. Robert Jones."

"Right."

"Yeah, I get that a lot. No, really, that is my name. What's yours?"

"Sheila. McCarthy. You know, you have a lovely voice, Robert Jones. Very well-modulated, Do you call yourself Bob or Rob or something? "

"Robert, please. And I actually—really—was about to say the same to you."

"You were going to ask if I call myself Bob or Rob or something?"

This time her laugh melted him.

Red-faced, he said, "Naturally I was referring to *your* voice. How pleasant it is."

"You suppose that means something," she said. "that we're both pleased with each other's voice?"

"No, of course not. No." Then, after a few beats: "I mean, yes."

"Really? Then what *does* it mean?"

"I don't know. But I'd like to find out. Would you, uh, like to—care to—join me for a cup of coffee or something? How about a lemonade on a beautiful day like this? She had referred to him a moment ago as "Robert Jones." He was tempted to ask her what it means when a woman calls a man by his full name.

Sheila looked directly at him but said nothing. Then: "Sounds wonderful and thanks for asking, Robert, but I can't. I'm expecting someone to meet me in a few minutes."

This brought Robert to his feet as he pictured the man—had to be a man—about to prick his fantasy. "Well, if you're not otherwise engaged, may I ask your phone number? Maybe we can meet again. Maybe here again, even if it's not for . . ."

". . . lemonade? Maybe." She hesitated. "Do you have a card? He fished one out of his shorts pocket. She didn't seem to care that it was a little moist from his run. She looked at him, smiled again, reached into her purse and handed him her card. As he took it, she brought her hand up to his face and held it there a moment. Then added a non sequitur that abruptly removed his own growing smile: "You're quite tall, aren't you?"

The tall thing. Never mind. He'd counter it. "And you're quite beautiful, aren't you." Another of her perfect smiles. He could easily get used to them. But who was she meeting? He was now certain it was a man.

This demolition of Robert's hastily-built house of cards continued as a man came strolling up to Sheila. A handsome, impeccably dressed man with a touch of distinguished-looking gray at his temples, and wearing a Panama hat, and wearing it well.

For once, Robert was glad he presented the full package he was.

"Hi, Sheila," the man said, hesitantly, giving her a hasty peck on the cheek. "Sorry I'm late, darling. Hungry for some brunch?" He seemed in an awful hurry to rescue her.

"Sure," she replied. Remembering her manners, she added, "Robert Jones, please meet Harvell Rollins."

Looked to Robert like old New York money. Doing his best to hide his churning thoughts, he accepted the man's firm handshake. Then Sheila took the man's arm and, with a wave and a "Bye, Robert Jones," the two began to walk away. Rollins must have said something funny because she laughed and patted him on the back. Very cozy-looking they were.

Robert was so busy sizing up his "rival" that he almost didn't notice Sheila folding the white cane that must have been at her side throughout their conversation on the benches.

The tall adonis stood in shock, a sequoia about to topple. My God, she's blind. Then a windstorm of awakening rattled his upper branches.

That's why she reached up and touched my face . . . to get a physical idea of me. She can't see me but she *did* see me . . . before she ever touched me. She . . . saw . . . *me!*

But what chance was there he'd ever see *her* again? Their entire conversation hadn't lasted ten minutes. Ten that felt like one.

And so, the tall man with the well-modulated voice, before dragging himself away, aimed a wan, ironic smile at the disappearing couple. Begrudgingly, he had to admit that, walking arm-in-arm, they did look nice together.

"C'est la vie!" he said to himself as he crumpled Sheila's card.

Two days later, Robert was at his desk, his mind regrettably more on Sheila than his work, when his cell beckoned and her name popped up in its window. He stared at it a few seconds before answering.

Would he, she wondered, care to join her for lunch at this wonderful new little bistro near her office on West 86th?

Yes, yes, he would, of course, but, "What about your Harvell Rollins?" he blurted, still shocked at receiving the call.

Here came that lilting laugh again. "You mean my step-father? Are you saying I should invite him too?"

The Phone That Fell From the Sky

Delbert Carmichael sat quietly on the park bench at the edge of the Conservatory Garden in Central Park off East 102nd where he was still living in the apartment, just east of Madison, he'd shared with his Margaret for forty-seven years. As usual, he sat alone. But it hadn't always been "as usual." Delbert often sat there with Margaret or with his many friends, but, at ninety-six, going on ninety-seven, there were no friends of his age left, just their daughter, their only child, Patricia, seventy-two, who lived in Brooklyn, and who had her own problems. Margaret had passed, was it twelve?—no, thirteen years ago—and he was no longer much in the way of making new friends; not anymore. He hardly ever left his apartment except for these rare walks to the park.

Delbert and Margaret had always enjoyed this peaceful spot under their favorite tree—a ginkgo they'd watched grow to maturity, as they had grown to old age. This spot was far from the bustle of the lower Park, the joggers and the bicyclists, and it was here that Delbert continued to quietly contemplate the cosmopolitan life he'd led as a senior editor at Harper Collins.

What he was contemplating at the moment was the baffling circumstance of his being not simply alive at his age, but rather actively so. His walking stick was not a cane. Hardly. It was an affectation that adorned his still almost jaunty stride more than aiding it. He'd done a great deal of walking in his life, mostly in this very park. But lately, he'd been doing a lot of sitting. And thinking. He was slowing down after all.

Why, he often wondered, wasn't he with his Margaret and his friends now? Not that he wished he were; that could wait. Fact is, he was in remarkably good health, considering.

He'd been doing a good deal of this "Why me?" thinking lately. Which is exactly what he was doing when it happened.

Delbert heard it before he saw it. A swoosh of something apparently falling from the tree. Whatever it was, it bounced off the thick privet hedge behind his bench and toppled into an edging of ivy not six feet from him. He looked at the ivy to see if it were an injured squirrel or bird, but nothing moved there. It was almost as if the object had fallen from the sky.

His curiosity aroused now, he walked over to the ivy and groped around in it for a moment until his hand felt a solid object, which he grasped. What he withdrew was—a cell phone. Where had it come from? Perhaps from a child's pocket? He looked up but there was no one in the tree. Nothing up there but the Ginkgo's familiar fan-shaped leaves.

He returned to his bench to ponder the provenance of the phone as he stared at it in his hand. It was one of those old-people flip phones with the big numbers that make it easy to speed-dial your children or call 911. How very odd, he was thinking. But, it not being an iPhone like he carried, there was no way to access any information stored in it. Was it even working? It appeared to be almost fully charged, so he decided to call himself and, sure enough, his own phone rang when he did.

Delbert Carmichael, giving further consideration to it, now felt that he was holding a phone that had somehow fallen from the sky. He was discounting that foolish thought when, at that very moment, it decided to ring. And ring again. And a third time, all the while that Delbert was deciding whether to answer it. Impossible, he thought. But why the devil not? "Hello?"

"Hello, yourself, Del!"

He knew the voice on the very word "Hello." It was that of his lifelong friend and Harper editor, Avery Chastain. The *late* Avery

Chastain, the very same Avery Chastain who died of a sudden heart attack nearly seven years ago.

This could not be happening. Delbert was far too stunned to speak.

"Del, you crusty old bird, speak to me, ask me how I am—say *something!*"

Crusty? Avery had always been the crusty one. But also affable, even lovable, if rather blustery. Delbert gathered himself and spoke: "Hello, Avery. Uh, where are you?"

"Where do you think I am, Delberto?"

"Up or down?" That was all Delbert could think to say.

"Things don't fall up, do they, pal?"

"No, I guess they don't, Ave. Would you mind, uh, explaining what's happening here? Am I a deluded old man? Am I dreaming?"

"Negatory, Delbert. I, my dear friend, am the first one of my, uh, kind ever to have had an object from Here drop through the Barrier. How it happened is very complicated so I won't bore you with the details but it's never happened before and He will be furious when He finds out and might very well send me back when He does."

Delbert could hear the capital 'H' when he spoke of "He." "Back? Back to where, to here? Where I am?" He couldn't believe he was having this conversation.

"Where else?"

"Well, would it be so bad to be sent back here?"

"Are you kidding? All my friends, my Martha, too, they're all up here—except you, you old coot. What the hell is keeping you?"

Now Avery had set Delbert to thinking. "But what if Martha and the rest of you all dropped through this Barrier of yours, same way your phone did? Can that even happen? I'd rather appreciate seeing all of you again."

"You will, Del. Soon enough."

"Do you know when?"

"I'm Avery, Del, I'm not Him."

"Well, all right, Ave. So how may I help you? This phone seems to be very important. Is there a way I can return it to you?"

"Yes, Del, in person, but with you, that could take years. I need the damn thing now, before He finds out."

The more they spoke, the more Delbert was enjoying this little conversation. "I understand that this Him of yours—I guess I have to begin believing in Him now—that He knows everything. But just how long do you think it will be before He discovers this terrible faux pas of yours?"

"Good question. The facts are always there for Him to see but He's been very busy lately, what with global warming and all, and some nasty stuff going on in Africa. I'd say a week, maybe less."

"Well, at my age, Ave, I wouldn't terribly mind joining you sooner rather than later, but I'm still finding it rather pleasant down here so, if you don't mind, I'll just give it some thought for a while. How does that work for you?"

"Not too great, Del. If you change your mind just hit the '5' on the phone. But don't wait too long, there's not much power in those things and they can only be charged from up here because, well, they don't really exist after they've fallen through the Barrier. The only ones who can actually see the little bugger are the one's whose numbers are entered in it, and you're the only number still down there."

"This phone does not exist? How can I be talking on it if it doesn't exist? And how is it that you happened to drop it near me instead of the other billions of people on Earth? And, come to think of it, how can you be talking to me if I have your phone?"

"I told you it was complicated, Delberto. Look, do the best you can, okay, old pal?"

"Sure, Avery." And then he said, without thinking, "Call me anytime."

"How can I without my phone?"

"Sorry, I forgot. Can't you use someone else's?"

"That's what I'm doing, of course. I'm using Martha's."

"Got it, friend. I'll get back to you. Goodbye, then."

When the phone went dead, Delbert slipped it into his side pocket and left the park. Did this really happen? He felt for the phone again and there it was, still where he'd put it. Would he die for his friend and cohort so he could return the phone and insure Avery's stay with his Martha and his friends—*my* friends—in, well, wherever he was? It was a tempting idea now that he knew that a wherever existed. But Delbert Carmichael was not ready to leave this Earth, to leave his idyllic if lonely spot under the ginkgo tree. Not quite yet. Still, what could he do to solve Avery's dilemma? These thoughts resided with him as he did his semi-brisk walk home on this lovely, twilit September evening in Manhattan.

Later that evening, sipping his three fingers of Dewar's pinch bottle scotch, the solution struck him. He'd send the phone back with a dearly departed. A dead acquaintance. Occam's Razor. The simplest solution was the best solution. So, for the next two days, he scoured the Times' obits. Not a recognizable name in the bunch. Everyone he'd ever known seemed to have passed a dozen or so years earlier. He'd have to think of something else. To do this he grabbed his walking stick and headed for the park. He always thought better while walking.

Deeply concerned now for Avery, Delbert, his hand fingering Avery's phone in his pocket, kept walking straight through the park to find himself turning north on Columbus Avenue. It was one of those crisp September days when the trees are just beginning to turn and, engrossed as he was, he was enjoying the very fact that he could, if not actually stride anymore, at least keep up a reasonable pace. As he turned east on Cathedral Parkway to traverse the north end of the park, the massive St. John the Divine Church caught his rheumy eyes. In front of it was a string of cars headed by a hearse and three black limousines. A funeral was in progress.

Aha!

Delbert, dapperly dressed for attendance at such, a silk square in the breast pocket of his Harris Tweed jacket, hurried himself over as best he could. Though not much of a practicing Episcopalian himself, he had attended services there long ago with Margaret when the noted dean, James Park Morton, had presided, so he felt quite comfortable paying it another visit now. As the church doors were already open, he walked right in.

The funeral service was being conducted by the present dean at the east end of the nave. The bulletin board at the entrance had indicated the name of the deceased but Delbert was in a hurry now and hardly glanced at it. Did it matter who was in the casket? It would serve well as the depository for Avery's phone.

As he entered the sanctuary the service had just ended and the mourners were lined up to pay their last respects. He joined the line and moved slowly ahead. But, when it was his turn to view the body, an involuntary shiver ran through him.

The body in the casket was that of himself: Delbert Denham Carmichael.

Delbert looked about him at the faces he could now clearly see. There was his distraught Patricia standing next to the coffin with her two sons. And a few younger colleagues from his Harper days. And Ed and Rose Barnes, his neighbors. And several more he recognized but had forgotten their names.

Delbert Carmichael was attending his own funeral.

He did not know what to do or what to say to these people. Patricia was standing next to the casket to receive the condolences of those gathered. He approached her but she did not appear to see him. "Patricia?" he said, right to her face. But she literally looked through him to the person behind him. He realized at once that if he existed at all anymore, it was only—and literally—in spirit. He staggered out of the church, much in need of the walking stick he was using now as a cane. And fifteen minutes later he was back at his bench in Central Park.

As soon as he sat down, he realized that he had forgotten his purpose at the church: to slip Avery's phone into the pocket of the deceased for safe transport back through the Barrier to him. Collecting himself, Delbert flipped open the phone and pressed the "5" key. One ring and Avery was on the line.

"Avery Chastain here," said Avery, acting his mischievous self by pretending not to know who was calling.

But Delbert was in no mood for Avery's nonsense. He was angry; an emotion he rarely felt. "You tricked me, Avery. You didn't drop your phone by accident, did you? I—or whatever I am at the moment —must have died several days ago. So why didn't I know it? Why didn't you say something when we talked before? What's going on here, Avery?"

"Slow down, pal. Now I can explain—if you'll give me a chance."

"Speak!"

"You've been so in love with life that, when you died, your spirit —that's what you are now, Delbert—your soul wouldn't, so to speak, 'give up the ghost.' Very rare case, the soul not knowing that the body has died. That's why you had to be jolted back to reality."

"You call what I am in 'reality'?"

"I do, indeed I do. And you'd better start calling it that, too. Once you accept it, He can 'beam you up.'" Avery: ever the joker.

Delbert sat there in disbelief. But he was coming around. Avery: always either grumping or joking. A couple pushing a baby stroller was passing by. "Good afternoon," Delbert said. No answer. They didn't see him because he wasn't there. A man came by and sat right next to him. "Nice day," said Delbert. No answer again. That did it.

"Are you still on the line, Avery?"

"I am."

"Then I guess I'm ready to go."

"Good. I'll see you soon. Margaret says hello."

"She does? Let me talk to her."

"Why? You're going to be here in a few seconds."

"I will?"

"Yes. And don't forget my phone."

Please Turn Off the Lights

Lights Off! That's the phrase sewn onto the turtleneck worn by the effigy of Bert, the cynosure of my childhood Sesame Street collection. I loved him because he, like me, collected paper clips. Which is neither here nor there. The same words adorned Ernie's striped T-shirt. Ernie, the wise-ass, sat on the counter next to our kitchen light switch. Big Bird carried this Lights Off message stitched into his image on the curtain next to my bedroom light switch, and Oscar the Grouch graced the waste basket in our bathroom where he belonged.

Two facts should emerge from this litany of the past. I had an abiding love for the Sesame Street of my youth, and I still desperately need a reminder to turn off my lights before going to bed, just as my mother so lovingly reminded me.

These reminders became unnecessary when I began living alone, so I pretty much forgot about Bert and Company because, these days, I can honestly say I've become very good at remembering to not just turn off my lights, but to lock my doors and make certain the gas is off on the stove and the cat has been fed and watered. Yet, even now, when this switching off of the lights has finally become a reliable habit, I occasionally forget and notice a light still on down the hall after I've crawled into bed.

So what's the big deal? I hate to admit that it *is* a big deal. About something that began in as ordinary a way as, well, turning off the lights. One evening I noticed that, after I'd gotten into bed, I'd somehow failed to turn off a lamp in my front-room. I'll tell you where that went—and, boy, did that go somewhere. But, though I doubt you'll believe it. I'll tell it anyhow.

Now, as you know, one does not—*can*not—turn off all the lights in a modern home. Not the little red ones. Not without unplugging *everything*, and sometimes not even that works.

Thinking of this as I had to leave my warm, inviting bed to turn off that front-room light, after I turned it off I had this thought—for no particular reason—that I, for once, was going to turn off every light in every room, never mind the consequences. Every blinking or glowing light, even if it was necessary to unplug its source, even if it took me past my normal 10:30 bedtime. Why? I don't know. It would just be for this one night, just to see if I could do it, if I could accomplish a complete and total *blackout!*

Perhaps it was no more than the bravado I had worked up to see if I could be comfortable in a truly pitch-black home, the kind I lived in as a child when we didn't even have a night light in the bathroom. And when the blackness didn't even bother me because I knew Bert and Ernie and the rest of their gang were out there in the darkness, protecting me.

Call me obsessive, but my curiosity—and the ingrained dictates of my upbringing—had gotten the best of me and I felt compelled to search out every one of those little red buggers. Turn off the lights! Lights Off, as my Sesame gang would say. And so my unplugging trek began.

First there were the nuisance lights, the ones on the three smoke alarms set high on the walls and a few on the ceilings. I didn't think it would hurt if they were de-commissioned for a night. So up on my stepladder I went. Then a couple of land line phone lights. Unplugged. Charger lights? Four of them. Unplugged. The kitchen yielded another four and then I recalled that, so I wouldn't have to feign knowledge of their location in a blackened room, I'd recently replaced all my wall switches with glow switches. And, since I was now in *full* obsessive mode, all of them had to go, or at least be temporarily covered by masking tape. My computer and TVs added up to three more, plus another five on power strips and surge protectors. Throw in several digital clocks, clock-radios, office machines and miscellaneous other devices and the total of little red lights, arrived at just after midnight, using a calculator whose own light needed decommissioning, came to an astounding thirty-four, including my cell phone which I simply killed for the night. Thirty-four little red lights, all glowing at once, mostly 24/7.

Who knew?

My task finally completed, I was smugly satisfied at the engaging, not the least bit daunting, darkness I hadn't experienced in years. I flashlighted my way back to bed, knowing, but not caring, that I'd have at least another hour's work in the morning to reconnect everything. A frivolous whim, I'll admit, but easy to indulge if one lives alone.

I would sleep in *total* darkness.

Lying there on my back, eyes closed, I felt more satisfied *with* my accomplishments than foolish about them. But I was too worked up, by the effort expended, to gain immediate sleep.

Then, some time later, just as I was nodding off, I heard it. A distinct sound not unlike a pin dropping or a tiddly being winked. A few seconds after, came another. Then another. I began counting them. Plink, plink, plink, plink. I opened my eyes as I counted and saw that several of the little red lights had come back on in my bedroom. The clock beside my bed, the clock radio across the room, the smoke alarm light. How could this be happening? Who—what—was doing this? I kept counting the plinks. Thirty, thirty-one, thirty-two, thirty-three, thirty-four. I was about to dash out of bed to check if every one of those little red lights I'd doused had come back on again when I heard yet another plink. Then several more. Then dozens more, way too many more to count. It went on, non-stop. Then the plinking morphed into a clanging, as if someone was banging a sledgehammer on an anvil, the sound soon crescendoing to that of church bells tolling. From both the light and the sound my head was suddenly exploding. Was I dreaming? I couldn't have been.

Then, abruptly, the sound stopped, though its reverberations went on for a while in my head. But, from sheer fright, soon after my count of thirty-four, I'd pulled the covers over my head. This debilitating fear comes from what one feels when one cannot begin to understand what is happening around him. The fear of the unknown. In this newborn silence I sat stiffly upright, unable to move, my duvet still draped ridiculously over my head. A full fifteen minutes must have passed before I could screw up the courage to peek out of my contrived tent. But, though it felt like fifteen minutes, it must have been far more because my well-lighted clock radio now said 4:26 a.m. and the date it showed had somehow jumped three days ahead. This had to be indeed a dream, some hellish sort of nightmare; but I knew instinctively, that it was not. Whatever it was, I was living it, not dreaming it.

My bedroom was now brightly lit, brighter than by the brightest incandescent bulbs, but by hundreds of little red lights, maybe thousands, their source indeterminable. And they covered not just the walls but the ceiling and floor as well. I was now bathed in an eerie, almost palpable red glow. With my heart beating at easily twice its normal rate, I lowered myself from bed, stepped into my slippers, struggled into my robe and forced myself to inspect the rest of my home. If my bedroom had been thus transformed, what might the other rooms be like? And who or what out there was doing this? And why?

With trepidation, I opened my bedroom door, hoping to find some degree of normalcy beyond it, but despairing of doing so. And there it was. If I thought before that I was having a hellish nightmare, I was now certain that I was *in* the bowels of hell. My entire home was drenched in a blindingly bright red, blinking, almost strobe-like light that blotted out every object in it. I could no more make my way through it than had there been a complete absence of it. All I could do was to stumble about, tripping over tables and chairs, totally disoriented.

Finally, crashing into a full-length hall mirror that fell to the ground and shattered, I staggered back and collapsed, stiff with fright, broken by what was transpiring, my wits as shattered as my mirror.

As I lay among the mirror's shards, my hands and face bleeding, I prayed for some semblance of reason so as to determine what really was happening to me. But, looking into my mind's eye, all I could see was—red. The glowing, blinking red of the little red lights, multiplied by what now seemed a million-fold. Lying there, I finally lost consciousness. And when I regained it I found myself here.

Anyhow, there's not much more to tell. There's simply no way to explain what happened in my home that night. I don't know what happened. Fact is, I don't truly know that it *did* happen.

Now, if you'll excuse me, I'm feeling a little drowsy and they'll soon be bringing our bedtime snack. I hope it's not oatmeal cookies again. I hate them! Don't let them know but I stuff them under my mattress.

They're coming, I can hear them, so goodbye now and thank you for visiting me, and, oh, when you leave—please turn off the lights.

Paean to a Coconut Bar

(A Tutorial)

Some late evening, when you've finished lipping your Upmann Churchill and you're hungering for a sweet little post-cigar mouth cleanser, consider the only confection on the Frozen aisle worth the traverse. I speak of the Whole Foods 365 Brand Creamy Coconut frozen fruit bar. I know about Cherry Garcia, I meant the only one with as little butterfat as a prime Havana.

Why does this little bar offer such singular goodness? I am clueless. I also don't know why you love your wife or your inkwell collection. You just do. Anyhow, "why" questions are foolish. Let's talk about "how." To have your way with one.

Since doing so will likely become your nightly ritual—these bars, like any good cigar, don't seem to suckle as well in the daylight—you must learn to seduce one properly. I am here to teach you. I sometimes take a second one to bed several hours after my nightly martini: frozen Gordon's Gin, frosted stem glass, a splash of Martini & Rossi, a dash or two of bitters, a knotted twist of . . .

Where was I?

It should be said that this bar is no puerile Popsicle. It is best indulged by adults and should be eaten in an adult manner. Thusly:

First, heft the package as you would a good novel. Anticipate the quality of its content. Fondle it a little. Read the "introduction." Learn that a single bar—a four-minute orgy—contains a piddling 160 calories. Compared, for instance, to a York Peppermint Patty, a mini-one, no less, which itself, when you consider it, can be rather nice when frozen and nibbled in little . . .

Where was I?

Okay, no one's looking, unzip the box as deftly as you would your girlfriend's jeans, then carefully extract a bar. These few seconds of foreplay will have left it a bit less frozen, a bit more ready for the act you're about to perform. Palm the bar, using your body's rising heat to release it, not from its little black dress, but from its clear cellophane, clearly advertising the curvaceous body within, blatantly eschewing any pretense of subtlety. Then slow down. Resisting the temptation to rip, gently *strip* the wrapper. Slide it off as if it *were* a little black dress, and had asked, begged, to be so handled. Go ahead and kiss it, that's okay. It will then whisper into your ear, "You have lips, you have a tongue, teeth, a mouth. Use them."

Now, in all its naked glory, your little quickie is ready to be "succulated," i.e., contemplated until you can clearly see the Faberge egg that it is, the better to telegraph its succulence to your now tumescent taste buds.

Work with your tongue here. One long lick up the upper half of one side, another up the other to melt its remaining hoarfrost thereby releasing a first suggestion of the intense flavor to follow. Next, slowly place your quivering lips over the entire upper half, close your eyes and, uh, suck for all you're worth.

Repeat until its warmed juices begin to flow and its icy skin has become a sort of coco-slush. Time to bring your teeth into play. Clamp them onto the bar's mid-section, but softly, much as a cat clamps her kitten. Then gently pull, dragging the slush, with its crunchy shards of creamy coconut, into your mouth. Now roll this melted essence over your palate much as if you were sampling a 2005 Chateau Montrose Bordeaux.

Swallow. Breathe in softly. Exhale. After this climactic moment, arrives the denouement. The bar has been weakened and is ready to surrender the rest of its moist, now-limp body to yours.

Place your mouth over what remains and pull, ever so lightly till this remainder resides at the tip of the woody that has borne it. Since you are now in danger of it sliding off, lick its icy sweat from each side gently and lovingly. You'll be left with but a delicate, delicious little morsel.

Ease it off and let it rest on your hot tongue till it deliquesces like the last lazy ice floe on a warming lagoon in spring.

In the afterglow of your fruited intercourse, your mouth will be cool, your body seduced and fully ready for sleep, your mind rested, your libido—*ar*rested.

You've had your Viagra-on-a-Stick. Now have a smoke and turn out the lights.

The Critic

His mind, clouded both by his low opinion of what he was seeing and by the Dewer's Pinch Bottle Scotch he favored, Mason Caldwell fought to keep his eyes open. But, even with his practiced resolve, he slipped into a jerky slumber for a good half hour, knowing beforehand that he was missing very little. He was perfectly aware that the distinguished regulars, in the rows surrounding him, knew very well who he was. They would think he was contemplating, even composing the praising, the belittling, the titillating but always informative words they would read tomorrow about the play they were seeing tonight, one which his readers would rush to or ignore in the days that followed.

Mason Caldwell, longtime drama critic for the New York Times, could open a play or close it with the stroke of his pen, that's the power he had. And here he was, once again, sitting in an aisle seat at yet another Broadway opening, this one a fluffy musical about a young man attempting to rescue his secret lover engaged to marry the sociopathic leader of a cult enclave in Eastern Oregon. Hadn't he reviewed something awfully much like this in the early nineties? These days, most musicals came off as the same to him. This one, costumed differently, might well have been called "The Guru and I" right down to the choreography of its off-key kiddie korps. Mason, this night, would again need to resort to a practice he'd come to detest. He would lie about what he was not awake to observe.

Was it time to stop, to retire altogether? He'd made his pile and, as the hermitic misanthrope he'd become in recent years, he'd spent very little of it. He could afford an early retirement, what the hell. But retire to what? Never mind. He'd endure this evening's travesty, have his usual lobster roll and nightcap or two at Joe Allan's, hit home around midnight, tap out his nine hundred words and send them home; a routine as well-established as his daily traipse through Central park with his schnauzer-poodle mix, Ibsen, the only creature on earth he adored.

This is how it was and how it had been for too many recent years for Mason. In the early years, he embraced the shows, attending a matinee and an evening performance whenever possible. Didn't matter what they were, way off Broadway or on, play or musical, good or bad, whatever they put on the boards, he was there to lap it up. His sui generis voice had kept him tightly wedged into the magazine's top drama slot for well over two decades.

Trained by Sandy Meisner himself as a Method actor at the Neighborhood Playhouse, Mason quickly realized—because Meisner told him so personally—that he was never meant to be an actor. He was too self-conscious and thus unable to lose himself in his roles. The lowest point in his young life came when he failed to be asked back for the school's second and final year. Deeply disappointed but rebounding quickly, he was taken on as an unpaid intern for Playbill. Soon he was writing their program notes, well enough to scratch out a Manhattan living. His review of a modern take on Chekhov's "Three Sisters," submitted gratis, was run by the Village Voice. It was seen by the entertainment editor for the New York Times, who was charmed enough by it to name Mason an Off-Off-Broadway reviewer. His brilliance showed through immediately and, within three years, he was named the Times' youngest-ever front line reviewer, soon to be its No. 1 critic, a legend to this day, twenty-seven years later.

But, at fifty-seven—only the middle of middle age—Mason Caldwell was already burnt out, a cinder of the wunderkind he'd once been. The talent remained, the drive did not. These days, he was fighting off ennui at most of the shows he attended. He wondered what had happened to him. Where had his love of theater gone?

When had he looked forward to Joe Allen's after a play more than to the play itself? The questions were rhetorical.

Never married, Mason had been deeply in love with a woman who'd abandoned him. Janelle Sawyer had been the only woman who'd ever mattered to him. Though he came to see himself and Janelle as one person, marriage had never occurred to either of them. They each had their comfortable upper East Side digs but were never apart except when she was working. She'd spend most weeknights at his place; weekends they were at hers. She'd been at his side for years at the openings. Over cocktails after, they'd talk endlessly about the play they'd just seen, about her work as a creative director at Doyle Dane, about nothing and everything.

And then came the brain cancer that took her within three months, so fast that she never had a chance to fight it. But nothing was the same after that. No, Janelle didn't abandon him. Mason only saw it that way and, until he could get it through his head that it wasn't her fault, he stubbornly resented her abrupt departure.

Family? Mason had only one living relative, an aunt in Montana where he was born, and with whom he'd fallen out of touch these past ten years. Friends? There were practically none. By choice. These days, the bottle had come to be his best friend, if you don't count Ibsen.

Nights off, he'd sit in his East Side apartment drinking with the lights dimmed way down, staring at a lit portrait of Jane he'd commissioned a few years after they'd met. He listened endlessly to the old jazz artists they both loved: Mingus, Coltrane, Chet Baker, Miles and Billie and Ella. Though he finally forgave Janelle her "abandonment," he did damn well miss her. There were nights when, tears streaming down his craggy face, he wished he could be with her in an afterlife he wished he could believe in.

On nights like that, stroking his contented Ibsen, perched across his lap, Mason talked to Janelle out loud, as though she were sitting opposite him. In his imagination, they were still just a working couple taking their day apart just like they once did, fixing dinner at home on his off nights, listening to jazz and then making love, sweet love.

No man ever felt sorrier for himself than Mason Caldwell. And it wasn't going away.

About his work, doesn't everyone, even a critic, go to a theater to enjoy himself? To escape into the play he's watching? Didn't he approach the theater that way in his earlier days? Did any man ever have a better job than his? Mason, knowing the answers, still asked the questions. He hadn't come to hate the stage, it hadn't gone that far, but he knew that he had to make something good happen or something bad would happen to him. He couldn't keep faking his enthusiasm, his vitriol, much longer. He sensed, correctly, that the great Mason Caldwell's job, his being jaded the way he was, was on the line.

Burt Goodman, Mason's editor at the Times—the man who'd hired him all those years ago, and his best, if just about only, friend —had been kidding him lately about "phoning in" his reviews. But the kidding was on the square. Yesterday morning Burt had said to him, "It's a good thing I remember what a great writer you are, Mase, but I have to tell you, my memory's getting weaker." If anyone else had talked to Mason that way, he'd have blown. Still, he knew Burt was right. Mason's fingers, these days, were robo-typing just like the old IBM Selectrics.

His rote reviews kept coming for several more weeks until Burt cornered Mason one morning in his office. "You and I know something's wrong, Mase. Seriously wrong. Nothing's changed. Starting next week I'm putting Barbara Warfield on your column." To allay the expected explosion, Burt added the one-word sentence, "Temporarily."

"What the hell do you think you're doing, Burt? No warning, you're putting Warfield on *my* column?"

"C'mon, Mason, I've been warning you for a month now. You just haven't paid attention. Just like you haven't paid attention to your work."

"How long is this knife going to stay in my back, Burtsy? Until you twist it?

"No, until you pull it out yourself. Look, Mase, you're like a Cy Young pitcher who's lost it. Doesn't mean you can't find it again. But you, my friend, have truly lost it. So I'm gonna help you find it. I'm sending you down to the minors. Single A, if you can stand it.

"Anyhow, I'm putting you on Offies. Off-Offies, even. Review them the way only you can. But find a way to start writing the way only you know how. Now, don't do your volcano thing on me, just get to work. You may actually thank me when you're done. I'm not asking for the key to your office, y'know?"

Mason was too stunned to argue further. His face had shaded to a deep red. But rage wasn't all he was feeling. Something inside him told him that, maybe, just maybe, this would not be a bad thing. Deep down he was ready for it. Maybe. He blew out a lungful of air before replying. "Okay, Burt, you betraying bastard, but when do I get my column back?"

"When you pitch a few good games. Pick your own shows, Mase. Use a pseudonym if you want, and if you think you'll be noticed, put on a false beard or something. Or maybe just tell the truth; that your pitching arm is sore and you're doing some rehab before returning to the Majors."

Neither, staring at each other, spoke for the next fifteen seconds. Then Burt said, softly, "And speaking of rehab, Mason, my friend, have you ever considered the same for your . . . your habit? It shows, you know? I've been there, done that myself, Mase. I'm a recovered alcoholic. I've never told that to another soul around here."

Mason, his mouth in a hard, straight line, had nothing to say. He got up and left, no goodbye, nothing, leaving Burt's door wide open, knowing how much that pissed him off. Minor leagues? Rehab. Where the hell did all that come from?

For the next week, Mason bunkered down in his apartment. He sure as hell wasn't ready for Burt's "Minors." Not now, maybe not ever. Minors! What a crappy metaphor! He'd bought a pile of frozen dinners and four bottles of Dewer's Pinch and was determined to empty the latter, hardly down the drain, as Burt might have advised. He turned the lights low, played his Coltrane and Ella, gazed at and talked to Janelle's portrait, and thought he couldn't possibly feel any lower. Not until he got around to picking up the copies of the Times that had piled up in his ignored mailbox. First thing he turned to was

Barbara Warfield's byline. At the bottom of her column—*his* column —was a twelve-point box informing the reader that "Mason Caldwell is on vacation."

He read all of Warfield's reviews, and had to hand it to her, every piece was beautifully written; better, it choked him to admit, than any he'd done in months. Dammit!

What's next? Mason begged his own question. It was after 9 p.m. A leap off his seventeenth floor balcony seemed a bit drastic. His bottle of Xanax was nearly empty and he was out of booze. Mason Caldwell had never been much of a planner.

Well, if he wanted to achieve some kind of oblivion, he'd have to re- stock. But before that he'd have to shower and shave for the first time since when, he wasn't sure. Then he could walk over to Jack's Liquors four short blocks away. But couldn't he have Jack's deliver his Dewer's? No, that could take a few hours and he'd been dry since yesterday and he did not feel like waiting another minute. So why not hit the Dunsmuir instead? Half an hour later, freshly laundered, he was on the street, headed toward the Dunsmuir Tavern, a fake-Scottish dive where Mario, the barkeep, who didn't talk much and had an admirably one-way wrist, did the pouring. Mason had often spent hours there looking to reconnect with with his lost Janelle.

Three drinks in, around 11 p.m., still more sober than he intended to be, he couldn't help but notice three raucous young couples who'd just burst in. They were talking all over each other about some play they'd just attended. All Mason could piece together was that it was at the Berwin, a few blocks east. They gushed over the play for an hour. They'd never seen such acting, such offbeat plotting, such an odd, satisfying twist at the end.

Mason, while involuntarily eavesdropping, reflected that he'd once felt this way about many—most—of the first plays he'd first reviewed. Their excitement was infecting him. He also realized that he should have seen and reviewed several of these "minor league" plays this past week. His job depended on it. When Mario motioned to him for a refill, Mason stop-signed him, slapping down his Amex. Over-tipping him, he signed and left. His mind was already planning a work day, next day.

The following evening, with only two drinks to fortify him, he ambled over to the Berwin, a small theater he hadn't visited since his early days in the business. Burt had said he could review any show he chose. Mason was still thirsty but he would catch at least a few acts before maybe slipping out to the Dunsmuir at intermission. Two full acts and he could fake any review. Still, standing in front of the theater, he questioned whether he ever wanted to enter this or any other theater again.

But he laid his twenty dollars across the box office counter and entered. The Berwin was an ancient, scruffy, stale-smelling, non-equity sixty-seater debuting the play whose name he'd heard but couldn't recall from the evening before: "Jonas Ain't Around No More." It was five minutes till eight. Maybe twenty-five seats were filled, none by anyone who appeared to be over thirty, and none who appeared to recognize him.

The apocalyptic premise of the two-acter was that not only was Jonas (read "God") no longer around, no one but a young man and woman in their twenties were there, "there" being a seedy, south side Chicago suburb, the only humans left in America after the itchy finger of President Trump, during his second term, resulted in a reciprocal war of the nukes.

Mason, not yet stupefied by the scotch he was craving, was shocked to find that he loved the performance. No, he was knocked out by it. So much did it move him that he neglected to jot his usual notes. For the first time in years he saw the characters as they were, not as the actors behind them. He cared about what happened to them, *cared about what was unfolding on a stage.*

When the play ended, he did something completely out of character. He sprang to his feet and precipitated a standing ovation, wearing out his hands, hardly calloused from clapping. When the actors returned to the stage for Q. and A, Mason sat quietly, listening to intelligent questions answered intelligently. Fifteen minutes into the session, he asked his first. It made the dozen or so people remaining squirm. "Is this theater paying its way?" He was pretty certain of the answer.

The two actors looked at each other. "Does it look like it, sir?"

replied Sara Holtzer, who'd played the young woman. "You may not have noticed but the sign out front said 'final week.' The Berwin is closing next Saturday night."

"For good?"

"For good."

"Who owns the Berwin?" asked Mason.

The other actor, Sam Michaels, replied, "The company, you mean? We do. Most of the people surrounding you do. We're the resident company and the company is folding. Old story. Rising costs, not enough business."

Mason, fully sober, then heard himself say, "What would it take to keep it open?"

The pair looked at each other again. Michaels spoke again. "Are you interested in buying in? Are you a theater person, a producer or something?"

"Looks like an angel to me," said Sara, laughing now. No one was taking this little conversation too seriously. No one except Mason Caldwell.

"Maybe I am an angel. And maybe I'm interested," said Mason, who no longer felt like his brain was connected to his mouth. Why was he doing this? Was he someone else speaking?

"You're pulling our string, aren't you?" said Sam.

"Maybe I am. I'm not sure I even know what I'm talking about but I do want to keep on talking. To you. Look, you two didn't answer my question. What would it take to keep the Berwin open?"

"Our acting company, all we own, our lease included? Maybe a quarter million," said Sara.

"Hold it a minute," spoke up a man sitting near Mason. The man, obviously a company member, had been staring at Mason a while. "I just realized who this guy is. I've seen his picture in the Times. He's Mason Caldwell, their main theater critic. What're you trying to pull here, Mr. Caldwell? I'm Joe Antonovic, the play's director. Most of us here are in the company. What are you trying to do? Are you reviewing us or are you mocking us?"

The air was seeping out of the theater.

"Okay, the truth is I was reviewing you. But don't worry about what I might have to say. I never reveal myself but, since you've outed me, I'll tell you this: I'll have nothing but good to say about your play. It was stunning." Huge grins lit up the faces around him. "The fact is though, I may not be doing a review after all." The grins disappeared. "What's that supposed to mean?" said the off-put man.

"It means I may not be doing much more reviewing. Or *any* more reviewing. You know something? I'd almost forgotten that I'm also an actor like you. Or once was. And I almost forgot how much I love theater. But I'm thinking that I just may have been on the wrong side of the lights for too long. Maybe it's your wonderful performance that's causing this little epiphany in me but—no promises—I'd like to discuss involving myself in your company. So maybe I'm a lot of things. An actor, a producer, maybe even an angel. But a reviewer of plays no more. I believe, suddenly, that I'd rather make 'em than review 'em. Mason finished his manic speech with, "Jeezus, I can't believe I'm saying all this!"

"Uh," interrupted Sam, "aren't you being kind of impulsive, Mr. Caldwell?"

"Mason, Sam. And, yes, I am. And I never felt more sure of myself than I do right now."

"Mr. Caldwell—Mason—couldn't you review 'Jonas' *before* you leave the Times?

Mason busted out with the first laugh he'd laughed in a long, long time. "That just might be a conflict of interest, Sara, but, what the hell, I'll consider it. After all, I haven't quit my job yet." With that, he pulled out a few hundred dollar bills, waved them over his head and added, "Will someone please run out and buy some food and Champagne? This isn't a wake, it's an after party—and it's on me."

Mason Caldwell, it should be obvious, never made it to the Dunsmuir that night. Nor to the liquor store. He sat with the Berwin company till 2 a.m., talking theater, nibbling on sushi and sipping champagne. It was easily the most exciting night he'd spent in a theater since he covered his first play twenty-seven years earlier.

The next morning he broke the news to Burt Goodman. He was finished at the Times. He'd slept on it and was now certain that he was about to buy a theater company. Burt took the news well, saying he wasn't surprised. He'd recognized the irreversible jading of his star reviewer long before Mason did. You love the field or you leave it, was how Burt saw it.

He said to Mason, as his former reviewer was leaving, "Hey, Mase, you give any thought to that rehab?"

"One thing at a time, Burtsy, boy. One thing at a time," said Mason, as he quietly shut Burt's door.

Sürstromming
(A true story)

Swedish cooking, whether from the *hemma* or the *restaurang*, is among the world's best. Thus it is ironic that the world's worst dish is quintessentially . . . Swedish.

Thirty years after first tasting this torturous dish, the only way I know to exorcise its disgusting, revolting, nauseating taste, its even more vile, loathsome and odious odor, and its daunting, downright frightening memory is to tell of it—to tell you of it—and thus, hopefully, to expiate it from my memory forever. It is the devil incarnate and I must speak its name. *Sürstromming.* Norway's much-maligned *lutefisk* is ambrosia by comparison.

I came upon *sürstromming* when my Swedish wife, Mia, our daughter, Anna, and I were visiting the bucolic farm of Göran Waldén, Mia's friend and supervisor during the years she had worked in her native Sweden as co-director of a youth center in Örebro. A dynamic bear of a man with a well cultivated if sadistic sense of humor, Göran not so much offered me the traditional dish, he goaded me into eating it. Its name, I learned too late, translated to "sour herring" or, more appropriately, as he later informed me, "rotten fish."

The chief quality of *sürstromming* is not actually its taste, which is certainly horrible enough, but its distinct aroma; its stench, as it were. The wee herring earns its aromatic reputation by being aged, like good whiskey, in wooden barrels for at least six months. Barrels without taps—and also without tops. After the *sürstromming* is tinned, the ageing process insists upon continuing so that pressure builds, swelling the sardine-like tin to its bursting point.

In America, the resulting bulge would suggest that one quickly bury the can . . . if one didn't fear an EPA citation for toxic waste dumping. In Sweden, however, a swelled can of *sürstromming* tells its patiently waiting owner only that it is ripe for its near-sacred ritual of opening, a ceremony that must be performed slowly and with great care so as to prevent the can's detonation. This latter possibility is not so fraught with fear of bodily injury as loss of the clothes you're wearing, which, if hit by this heinous herring's shrapnel, would themselves require burying.

Göran informed me that some cans of *sürstromming*, at the domed stage and beyond, no longer contain anything but a liquid, a foul liquor prized and drunk appreciatively by the hardy men of Sweden's northern coastal town of Vargön, the only place that admits to canning the nauseating stuff.

If I have almost managed to almost forget the taste of *sürstromming*, I have never been able to get past the smell that blossomed—and I do disservice to that lovely word by inserting it here—blossomed forth when Göran turned the key to roll back the can's lid. The putrid odor airbagged itself, instantly filling the kitchen, and, it would not surprise me, the entire neighborhood. I half expected the wallpaper to strip itself. A skunk would have run from it. And still that offal (sic) smell remains, scorched forever, like forgotten smelts, upon my suffering brainpan. But I willed my nostrils shut and stood my ground. I would go through with this challenge to my manhood.

If you should ever be running through a field of wild strawberries upon a gladed hill on a warm, mid-summer day, and you stumble and fall, head-first, into a forgotten outhouse hole, you shall, in effect, have attended the "opening" ceremonies of a Swedish *sürstrommingfest*.

Wavering, sweating, involuntarily shivering, but indeed standing fast, I stared in nervous anticipation—abject fear—as Göran plucked out the few herrings still intact and laid them on a *sürstromming klämma*, a sandwich composed of *turnbröd*, a flat, pita-like bread, smeared with *messmör*, the dregs from the Swedish cheese-making process, and *potatis* and raw *lök*, onions. Finished, he patted the sandwich flat and handed it to me. To hesitate would be to show weakness. I bit into it quickly, then, posthaste and with eyes shut, swallowed before its redolence could leap from my mouth and reassert itself.

Swedish ipecac, I'd call it. That's when my theory of the real purpose of *sürstromming* was born: *What goes down must come up.*

But I wasn't about to give Göran and his gleeful family—and *mine*—the satisfaction of proving that accurate theory. With determined pride and concentration, I smiled triumphantly and kept the *klämma* down.

To the accompaniment of roaring laughter, I had endured and more than earned my first rewards to follow: a lifting of the windows and a goodly quantity of cleansing Swedish beer and ice-cold O. P. Anderson aquavit. Then, with back-slapping camaraderie, came the Waldén Croix de Guerre: two honorific centilitres of a rare *pontikka*, the potent Finnish moonshine that had been carried over Sweden's northern mountains years earlier by my gracious host. I felt extremely close to Göran in that moment.

Extremely queasy, too.

Göran never quite understood why I refused his generous offer of a half-dozen cans to take with me on the plane—the *pressurized* plane—back to the States. It occurs to me that, if I attempted such a carry-on today, I'd wind up in Gitmo.

Eleven years later we revisited the Waldéns and I survived the *sürstromming* ceremony again, same results. But this time I was to deliver retribution. This was before 9/11. I had secreted, aboard our flight, a quart jar of my special, home-made, ultra-red-hot, kosher dill pickles, liberally laced with garlic, extra pepper seed, cherry peppers and even some dreaded Scotch Bonnets. I proffered it as a gift—and a challenge—to Göran, insisting that he down at least three of these killer koshers, consecutively, without the palliation of bread, water or beer.

And, don't you know it, he did it, loving every damned one.

Taking one huge bite after another, while nearly swooning with pleasure, he whooped with delight, furiously fanning his mouth, then rushing out to share the rest of the bounty with his neighbors. A year later, he told us, he was still nursing the original brine, like it was some kind of sourdough starter, soaking home-grown cukes in it to make his own Swedish-style koshers.

This was retribution?

Gargantua
(For Preston)

"You've got talent, Preston, but it's hiding under a layer of blubber. You're never going to make any wrestling squad of mine until you commit to working harder. Starting with losing all that excess weight. A wrestler needs the least amount of weight he can carry, not the most. But don't let me discourage you, Porter. Do the work, do what you have to do, then come back and see me next year."

That's how Coach McKinnon—a guy who never much cared what spilled out of his mouth—put me down, insulted me and crushed me when I went out, once again, for the wrestling team this year. Well, I guess he was sorta right. But I was damned if I'd admit it.

I didn't fully hear all of his remarks. Didn't want to. All I heard was I was being cut, not as a freshman or sophomore, but as a junior. So I'm not going to wrestle for St. Augustine this season after struggling through two years of pure hell just trying to make the squad. Next year, as a senior, I'll have only one more chance to do what I live for. To wrestle. Which doesn't seem like any kind of a chance at all. Now, I know all about needing to wrestle at the least weight I can effectively make. Still, I feel like I'm trapped in my body. And I'm mad; more pissed than I've ever been before. At the coach, at myself —at the whole damn world! Who needs to be a stupid wrestler anyhow?

Two whole seasons wasted, dammit! Three months until the state championships and now I'm not just on the bench, I'm no longer on the team. A minute later, close to tears that deep anger always

241

brings on me, I find myself in the weight room. Blind with rage, and without donning gloves, I tear away at the heavy bag in the corner, punching it repeatedly until I'm soaked with sweat. My fists are torn and bloody but I don't care. I look at them for a second, then continue my frenzied onslaught until I drop to my knees, completely spent. Better to punch the bag than a locker or, worse, the coach. Who am I punching anyhow? Myself.

Exhausted, I have trouble lifting my "blubbery" body. I stumble into the locker room to clear out my gear. Little Jimmy Abel, my best pal from kindergarten, and the team's assistant trainer, already got the word and is waiting to console me. But I don't feel like any company right now, not even Jimmy. I bark at him to leave me alone. He understands and leaves. After showering, I drag myself home and shut myself up in my bedroom. I start crying into my pillow. Crying! I fight it but can't help myself. I feel deeply sorry for me, why not? I'm ashamed of myself and don't want anyone to hear me. I don't want anyone anywhere near me.

If I was smart I'd have started working out again for next season. But the mood stayed with me for the rest of the school year. The team nearly made it to the state tournament, no thanks to me, of course. I couldn't watch a single match.

Now it's a Saturday, the first weekend of the long summer ahead. I don't want to get up. I feel like staying in bed all day. I've felt this way for a long, long time. The shrink my folks have been sending me to tells me I'm "in a state of deep depression." He even warns me that I'm "at risk for suicide." Thanks, doc, but I don't need you to tell me what I already know.

I wake up at 8 a.m., still groggy from the beers I sneaked in one of our worksheds last night. I look out the window and first thing I see is a huge old tractor tire slowly making its way up the near end of our half-mile long driveway like some kind of a hula hoop gone mad. As it gets closer I see little Jimmy behind it struggling to keep it rolling. Finally I see the tire wobble and topple over on Jimmy. He's totally out of it. Those big tractor tires weigh at least eighty pounds. He tries his damnedest to lift it off him and I don't know whether to laugh or cry. But I'm getting tired of crying.

I throw on some jeans and an old Augies T-shirt and, barefooted, run down the drive and, without thinking, lift the tire and throw it off Jimmy. My pal—my only pal these days—is not hurt. He starts laughing. At himself? At me?

"What the hell are you laughing about, you bozo? I thought that thing damn near killed you." I was ready to flip him like I did the tire. "Too bad it didn't because I cut myself running out here. Whadaya think you're up to?" I add, hopping around holding my cut foot.

"I wasn't gaming you, Preston. The tire really did fall on me," he says. "But you did just what I thought you'd do. Now you're going to do it a thousand more times."

"Do what?" I say, still plenty steamed.

"Here's what I figure, old buddy. You want to make the wrestling squad next year, don't you?"

Do I? I'm not sure how to answer so I just shrug my shoulders. Jimmy ignores me. "And I want to be the Augies trainer. *The* trainer, not the assistant trainer. And I'll tell you a little secret, Press. I mean to someday be a wrestling coach for Iowa. Whadaya think of them apples? So, after I train you this summer, you're going to make the squad and I'm going to make senior trainer or we're both going to die trying. You got that?"

"And just how do we go about dying trying?"

"First, you go on a diet. I mean, you gotta change your whole way of eating. I been studying nutrition, Press. Complex carbs like grains and cereals, no sugar except from natural sources like fruit, lots of protein from lean meat and beans, and lots of water, got it? Nothing white, like they say. I'll talk to your mom about it. We're going to knock fifteen, maybe twenty pounds off you. You're going to wrestle at one-seven-oh, pal, you got that?"

"Great. So I lose 'fifteen, maybe twenty pounds' and suddenly I'm some kind of state champ? Geez, Jimmy boy, I'd be happy just to make the squad again. If I even feel like trying. But screw Coach, he doesn't even want me."

"He will after I'm done with you. The way you eat is just the beginning. Whydaya think I dragged this tire here. It's because you're going to flip this baby, once twice and eventually a hundred times a day until it feels like you're flippin' a quarter. You got that?"

I stare out over our cornfield, trying to picture myself doing what Jimmy just described. I'd just flipped that tire once. It was easy. But my adrenalin was way up because I thought it was an emergency. Now I bend down and try to flip the thing again. I can barely lift it. I let out a huge sigh. I'm tempted to tell him to go to hell. But he's Jimmy. This is the way he gets when he wants something bad. And this time he wants it not just for himself, but for me. How can I not love this guy. Maybe I oughta listen to him. "Guess I got it, pal. When do we get started?" What am I saying? I hate wrestling! No I don't. But I say it to Jimmy. "I hate wrestling."

"No you don't. You just hate yourself because you're not the wrestler you wanna be. Now—right now—pick up this lousy tire and roll it up to your house. We'll begin there. And you'd better pick up some serious iron for your barbells. They're part of the equation. You got that?"

"Okay, okay, I got it. And stop saying 'You got that?' You got that?"

And that's how me and Jimmy spend every one of the exactly eighty-four days before school begins again in the fall. No days off. It takes half a week before I can flip the tire three times consecutively. Then I have to rest, then three more times and that's it for the day. But a week later I do five straight with four reps. Meanwhile, with the new weights my dad bought for my seventeenth birthday, and Jimmy standing over me, I'm pushing up more and more weight, bench pressing 250 and quickly reaching 280, then inching up more as the weeks go by. I begin to believe I can soon bust through 300.

As for my new eating "regimen," as Jimmy calls it, I hate it, but with my mom's full cooperation, my dad's encouragement (and the promise of a hundred dollar bill if I make weight by the end of summer), the weight starts coming off, the baby fat melting away. It helps that Jimmy is on me like flypaper if a pound goes the other way. He hovers over me like a guardian angel—a real, dedicated pain in the butt.

With half the summer gone, and me more than halfway to my target weight and strength goals, Jimmy asks if I'm ready for some instruction. "Instruction?" I say. Whadaya think you've been giving me?"

"A hard time. But I was referring to something called wrestling, Mr. Porter," he says, straight-faced. "Listen, I been studying moves every day, watching videos of Iowa state meets. I didn't want to even mention that to you till I was sure you were committed. So before I do, I have to ask you a question."

"Ask away, amigo."

Jimmy hesitates before answering. "Do you want to be a state champ?"

"Say what? C'mon, James, who doesn't?"

"No, no, no, Press. Maybe I said that wrong. Do you want to be a state champ enough to *believe* you can actually be one? Think, before answering that, rassler man. Lemme put that another way. Are you *going* to be a state champ? Are you *going* to stand on the top step in that arena on the last day of the finals in Des Moines next February and raise your hand? In victory?"

Jimmy paints a nice picture. But I hesitate. What kind of stupid question is he asking? What kind of a dream is he trying to stick into my head? Anyhow, I think about it. How can I not? He's serious. His picture's a little out-of-focus. Then it gets a little clearer. Then—

"Preston! No daydreaming! I need an answer. Now! If it's no then we're both wasting our time and I'm outta here."

Apparently my eyes have been as out-of-focus as the picture I was seeing. I blink and finally see Jimmy. But I see another picture. Myself in the center ring of the Wells Fargo Arena in Des Moines. And my arm *is* being raised. A dream? It seems awfully real. "Yeah, little buddy," I say, softly but firmly. "I do believe I can be state champ."

"You believe you'll be or you *will* be?"

"I will be. I'll be the champ. Okay?"

"Then say it right, my friend. 'I. *Will*. Be. State champ!'" I hesitate. But only for a second. "I *will* be state champ!"

"Louder!"

"It's okay, Jimmy, I get it. I don't have to shout it. I get where you're coming from."

"Good, and you'd better get where you're going because, if you don't, I don't get where I'm going, so we better get going, huh?"

Jimmy looks like he's going to hug me, that's how huge his grin is. Then, dammit, man, he does. He hugs me. Now I'm afraid he's gonna kiss me. Instead, his ugly face goes blank and he says, "Let's get back to work!"

Five minutes later I flip *Gargantua* six straight times. Gargantua's the name I gave the damn tire. Then I do six reps with it. Either I'm getting stronger or the tire is getting lighter. But each time I see the thing, it's always my hated opponent. Not a bad image. It's inspiring a special move that I'm fixing in my mind. I tell Jimmy about it and he thinks I'm crazy. But we practice it at the end of each session. Might come in handy.

I notice that my T-shirts are getting a little tight in the sleeve holes. But my jeans are beginning to fall off. I'd started the summer at 194 pounds, hardly a weight, at five-foot-nine, I could wrestle at. Coach knew that. And he was right. I want to wrestle at 170. I'm already down to 180 and I'd be lower if I'd only been watching my intake closer. But my flips and my workouts are turning fat to heavier muscle so the weight tends to come down more slowly. I know I'm getting there, though. That's something I never thought possible before. Not without Jimmy making me believe it's possible. But then, I never thought I'd be thinking it was possible to be—an Iowa state champ.

Next day, Jimmy starts me on a whole new WML—Wrestling Moves List—moves I never knew existed. I'm not sure Coach knew all of them. Some basics and some tricks Jimmy feels will take me far, take my opponent off his feet or off the mat, put him on his back, take me to the State. He widens my opening stance, giving me a more solid base. The first move he shows me is a Whizzer, a sharply executed spin off my toes to the left, a good way to counter a lower body takedown. And a good old Half Nelson if I'm going for a quick point. And some solid single-leg takedown moves.

Then he shows me a neat Hip Heist I could use if I'm being taken down and have to avoid landing on my hip and being topped. I use my knee to break the fall then heave up and snap into a go-behind where

I can take my opponent down. And a Gazzoni where my opponent is on top of me, slips his arms around mine and locks his hands. I shoot my arm toward the ceiling to break his hold, then flip him. A very neat move if I can bring off. And the Peterson, the Near-Arm-Far-Leg, the Granby, and one of my favorites, the Guillotine, a sort of choke hold, but legal. I'll spare you any further descriptions of all that Jimmy taught me, and what I learned by staring at his bootleg videos with him well into most nights.

We're both being tested. And we're both passing our tests. We both know where we're going and that's to the State Finals in Des Moines in February. How far, I'll find out when I get there, but that's our goal and we inch toward it more every day. And, speaking of inching, I've grown nearly an inch over the summer, lost three inches around my waist and am now coasting down to my sought-after weight, exactly 170 pounds, maybe a pound or two under. Never mind impressing Coach, I'm ready to impress every opponent I face who gets in my way.

Depression? What depression?

Finally it's September. The first day of school I barge into Coach McKinnon's office. "I'm gonna wrestle for you this year, Coach," I blurt.

He rolls his chair back from his old-fashioned wood desk. "Is that you, Porter? I hardly recognize you. Been working out, huh?" He'd have to be blind not to notice. I nod my yes. "Well, you'll have to try out from scratch just like everyone else. It's up to you. Practice starts this afternoon right after classes." He sticks out his hand. I grab it and squeeze hard enough to make juice. His wince shows through the pretend grin he's barely able to manage.

Oh, I make the team, all right. No problem. Partly because Coach must remember my hand-breaker handshake. And when Jimmy informs him of what he and I have been up to this past summer, he names Jimmy his Number One trainer. But ol' James tells me he wants a lot more than that. He wants to be a coach. Hell, far as I'm concerned, he already is. Damn best I ever had, and I been rasslin' since the fourth grade. It's what we do in Iowa.

I do well, exhibiting all my new moves and taking down one

teammate after another, even two of the heavier weights. At the end of the following week, naming his starters, he points to me, smiles and says, "Porter, you're my 170 man." So I not only make the team, I'm off the bench and on the starting mat.

Okay, the season begins. I check out the grapplers I'm gonna face. Several have been regional champs and two made it to the finals last year, losing in early rounds. We have fourteen meets scheduled, most of them duals. I win seven, three of them by pins, then run up against one of last year's finalists and squeak out a one-point win. Coach all the sudden loves me. The next seven matches yield four pins and finally a two-point loss to one of the other state champs. It's a bitter loss because this guy had already lost two duals and I was beginning to think I couldn't lose. But reality bites, and what it bites is ego, which is what Coach tells me I have a little too much of.

I like to think that guy will remember his win as the only loss I ever had as a senior. But maybe my brain is hardening along with my body. The thought drives me to three straight pins to close out the regular season. And I make it all the way through the regional brackets undefeated, a third of my wins, pins.

Looks like I'm going to the finals in Des Moines, the first Augie to do so in the past twenty-six years. Jimmy is so excited that he cobbles together a "State Champ" trophy for me made from one of his father's old bowling trophies. It has a marble base and four fluted wooden columns that support a marble platform that once held a gilded bowler but now carries a wrestler, his head bowed while raising his hand in victory. The wrestler is made out of Legos. Trophies don't come any uglier. Or more beautiful. If you get my meaning. I love it. Jimmy probably got beat up over it because his dad can be a mean old SOB, a traveling seed and fertilizer salesman during the week and, ever since Jimmy's mom died of cancer three years ago, a hopeless and nasty drunk on weekends. Jimmy says he'll present it to me officially when I earn "the real one."

The whole town attends a rally for me in the St. Augustine auditorium the night before I, and sixteen others in my Division Three weight class from all over the state, head down to Des Moines for the first matches on February twenty-second. Five buses will be filled with students, St. Augustine parents and well-wishers along with a caravan of highly decorated cars that carry signs like "Porter for President!" and "Ride 'em, Preston." It's a pretty heady experience for me. Keeping my head on my shoulders at the same time I keep my feet on the mat ain't easy. But Jimmy knows how to handle me. He always comes up with a pin to stick in me when I get too inflated. He told me my butt's so big I could probably sit on an opponent and win.

The name Matt Demshar has been constantly on my mind. He's from Harper City in Northwest Iowa. Demshar made State Champ at 160 last year as a Bulldog sophomore and is returning to seek the Div-Three 170 crown this year. He's undefeated, a cocky kid who has reason to be. Some say he's the best high school wrestler, pound for pound, in the state, maybe the country, Iowa being the best damn wrestling state in the country.

Demshar is the Everest I'll have to climb. But I mean to keep my promise to Jimmy. With the skills and body I've developed, I've also developed a confidence I've never had before. It's not ego—well, not *all* ego—it's just a belief in myself. It wavers at times, but it's growing "Do the work and the rest will come," Jimmy keeps telling me. He's become a better coach than Coach. He works with my head, not just my body. I don't know what I'd do without him. I wouldn't be wrestling without him.

I intend to go beyond high school wrestling. I mean to make it all the way to heaven, mine being that little old college in Iowa City, name of . . . The University of Iowa. Wrestling City, USA.

On the afternoon we leave, I'm up front in the lead bus with Coach. Jimmy's late. I'm about to call him when my cell spits out his special ring. Everyone's singing so loud I can hardly hear him. "Wassup, dude? Where the hell are you, we're ready to leave," I shout.

For what seems like five minutes I don't hear an answer. "I can't make it," he practically whispers. And there's pain in his voice.

"Say again? Speak up, Jimbo."

"I said I can't make it, dammit!" This time he's almost screaming. "I'm not coming. I'm in the hospital. You gotta do this without me, Preston."

I can't believe what I'm hearing. Jimmy sounds like he's almost in tears. He says he was driving over to the bus in his old F-150 pickup and he got a flat tire. When he went to change it, the jack slipped and the car came down on his ankle and broke it in two places. He's having it set and casted and he'll do his damnedest to get down to Des Moines before the games are over, but it doesn't look good. He repeats, I've got to do this on my own.

I don't believe what I'm hearing. "Jimmy, I'm really sorry about what happened but—"

"But what, Preston? You got wax in your ears?" The tears in his voice are tears of anger. "I just said I can't make it. That's what I'm telling you. Let Coach know."

"Just a minute, you little squirt. Why're you telling me you can't do something when you just spent all summer telling me I can do just about anything, including taking the State?"

"That's different, you jerk. I made you believe in yourself, right? I can't make myself 'believe' I'll be healed enough in a few days to get down there. Use your head, man. And your muscle. And your heart. Use 'em all to win, Press."

But who am I kidding? *I can't do this without Jimmy.* I cannot do this without my little buddy filling my head with the kind of positive thoughts and tricky moves I need to beat a guy like Demshar who I'm damn well sure I'd be facing in the final—if I get that far.

"Well, ol' Press, you don't get a vote in this weighty matter," he says. "I'm here and you're going to be down there. And you are going to whup that puppy just the way I taught you, you got that?"

"I got nothing, Jim. And nothing is what I'm gonna wind up with if you don't get your sorry butt down here."

"I don't know what else to say to you, Preston, my friend. Win one for the Gipper. I can't talk anymore, I'm hurting. Break a leg. *His!*" With that, the call goes dead.

I call him back but all I get is his VM. It takes me ten minutes of dumbfounded silence to realize that I have to wrestle without the guy who really taught me to wrestle at my side. I slide over to Coach and give him the bad news. He looks like he's going to faint. He knows very damn well what Jimmy means to me.

Two and a half hours later we reach our hotel near the arena in

Des Moines. There's a dinner tonight for all the athletes that Coach insists I go to, though I don't want to. I'm supposed to get a good night's sleep but I can't.

Next day, the opening ceremonies go on. A minor rock star—an Iowa graduate—sings the national anthem. Badly, or is it purposely, off key. Some high school band plays Sousa's *Stars and Stripes Forever*. I look up at the St. Augustine section in the stands and see eight shirtless Augie guys—some of my best pals—their puffed out naked chests reading, in Augie red and white, simply, *Preston!* I'm too stunned to let it register because I'm only thinking about what I have to do. But I give them half a wave and get back a huge cheer from the entire section. Now I have other things to worry about. Like life—*immediate* life—without pal Jimmy. Damn that friggin' jack!

I'd studied the brackets. Two of them with eight rasslers each. And, wouldn't you know it, I'm not in Demshar's bracket. Which means I have to win three straight matches of three two-minute periods each to face him in the final—the championship match. I know who'll take the other bracket: Matt Demshar, who else? But I'm no longer sure who'll take mine. Oddly—coincidentally?—Demshar's name is listed at the top of the left bracket and mine at the bottom of the right. Are the Fates trying to tell me something? Demshar on top, me on the bottom? I've got to wipe these stupid thoughts out of my mixed up mind.

My first match is no cinch. Eddie Tremayne, a senior at Hartnett High in Waterloo, has, like me, lost only a single match all season. He's a little shorter than me but broader. And plenty mean looking. But I won't let myself judge anybody before I've got my arms wrapped around them; before I can feel them out. I've studied Tremayne's videos with Jimmy. At Jimmy's insistence I've watched everyone's in my weight class. Tremayne has good moves and I'm already down three points after the first period. But a neat escape and a takedown in the second and a nice reversal in the third and I grab the match —barely—on points. The narrow win helps return the confidence I lost by not having Jimmy here. And it tells me something I didn't know for sure: I belong here. Two more to go if I want to meet up with

Demshar. Meanwhile, he sails through his first two matches, including one with a pin in less than a minute of the first period. Scary.

I don't have a pin in my second match, but I overpower my Richfield High opponent enough that he loses a point for fleeing the mat.

In the third match, against a tall, lean kid named Bobo Butler, from Roosevelt in Hellerville, I'm in trouble and nearly get pinned myself. But, needing a strong move in the final period, I make one, getting my points by reversing out of a half nelson and locking Butler in a high bridge to gain a near fall.

I've made it. I win the bracket! And, of course Demshar wins his. In the beginning we were sixteen. Now we are two. Demshar and me. We face each other tomorrow. Meanwhile, I keep looking over my shoulder when I'm wrestling and all I see is Coach McKinnon. I love you, man, but where the hell is *my* coach?!

I've been roomed with Tyler Johansson, a 150-pound junior from Farragut High in a town even smaller than St. Augustine. He's a nice guy who likes to talk but I don't much feel like talking. He must think I'm a real jerk. I'm having a hard time getting my head around the hard fact that Jimmy is 150 miles from where I need him to be. Anyhow, I'm not here to talk, I'm a rassler. Never was much of a talker anyhow.

So I've made it through my three matches, okay? But how am I supposed to get past Demshar without ol' Jim in my corner? My eyes snap open a little past 3 a.m. I call Jimmy but can't wake him. Must be he turned his phone off. I know he's watching on TV. Must be he's hurting a lot worse than me, what with his broken ankle and not being able to be here. Damn! But stop feeling so sorry for yourself, Porter. Give him a break. It's not all about you.

Much as I desperately need my sleep, I don't get back to it till past five. I'm going to be a wreck tomorrow. I wake up in a cold sweat at 6:30 and head down for breakfast with the other wrestlers. I sit by myself, picking over some toast and a bowl of oatmeal and raisins while trying to go over my possible moves. One image keeps popping up. Me, flipping that damn tractor tire in ninety-degree heat last summer while Jimmy stands next to me shouting encouragement. I am in one lousy mood. My match with Demshar is less than three hours away. And, right now, I don't think I can take down a grasshopper with a missing leg.

Nine o'clock. In my sweats, I'm doing my stretches and a little lifting when Mr. Matthew Demshar—the "Valiant Victor from Van Meter"—that's what the Des Moines Register called him this morning—walks—make that, struts—into the workout room, pretty much sucking all the air out of it. His coach, his trainer and a few hangers-on are in his wake like he's Ali himself entering the prize ring. I half expect him to be wearing a mask and a cape. What he is wearing is a grim, determined look, just this side of smug. When he sees me, he breaks into a grin that seems to be saying, "I know who I am, who the hell are you?" Nice to know that he knows who he's going to flatten today. I nod to him, pretending he's a mere mortal, then get a few laughs by giving him a deep bow. But inside, I'm hardly laughing, I'm plain scared. Oh, well, you're supposed to be, aren't you? This is only the biggest match of your life, Preston Porter.

Demshar starts his workout. A few minutes later he has the goddamn nerve to ask me, of all people, to spot him for his bench presses. Sure, why not, I say. He lifts twenty more than I've ever attempted. If he's trying to psych me out, he's doing a pretty good job of it. I turn my brain inward. If I'm going to do what I need to do, that's where it will have to come from. I have to believe in myself. There's no Jimmy standing next to me, to believe in me. But I mean for this fairy tale to have a happy ending.

The match opens with a half minute of circling and feeling each other out. Then it becomes a real struggle. I hold my own as best I can, but he takes me down twice in the first period, both times with the fastest single leg I've ever seen. I gain some ground in the second with a takedown of my own and two reversals but we go into the third period with me down more points that I think I can make up.

Now, well into the third, I'm guessing there are no more than forty-five seconds left in the match. It's also now certain that I'm down too many points to make up the difference. I need a pin and have no idea how to achieve it as Demshar works his way to another point by moving me out of the circle. We restart with him over me.

I notch a point by breaking out with a respectable horizontal spin move. He's still over me with his arms around my belly but now I'm facing him. I know what he's up to. He's looking for a lift back over his head and a slam to the mat for an impending pin.

But, now with only thirty seconds left, I get the miracle I'd been subconsciously praying for. As I'm on my knees fighting off Demshar's choreographed lift, I look through his legs for half a second and see, dead ahead, a wheelchair framed in an entry tunnel just twenty yards away. Backlit, like a guardian angel, is Jimmy Abel. And he's holding up his homemade championship trophy, the ugly one with the Lego wrestler on top. Then it's like someone had just hit Mute on the TV. A word—an instruction—screamed by him, cuts through the din of the arena.

"*Gar-GAN-tua!!!*"

It jolts me back to the vow I made to Jimmy at the beginning of summer. My promise: "I *am* going to be the champ!"

Demshar, I can tell from beneath him, is glaring at me. But it doesn't matter. You don't get points for glaring. Something strange is happening inside my head. A feeling sent as if by a laser from Jimmy's mind. An electric surge. Of what? I don't know, but I have no time to think about it. My counter move is to snap my legs under me, reach up and try to lock my arms around Demshar's waist to prevent his flip. But that's not going to get me the pin I need, that might only prevent his ultimate pin. Still facing him, and with my feet still firmly planted on the mat, I don't reach outward or upward. Instead, I instinctively grab his ankles—leaving me totally vulnerable.

Now I know what I have to pull off. The move I hadn't even thought about till my patron saint Jimmy showed up. The *Gargantua!* The move that's never ever been seen in a video because no one's ever done it before, not even me. But it's one thing to know the move and another altogether to execute it.

Demshar, no dummy, is planted even more firmly than me. He anticipates I'm up to something weird and sets himself, in Zen-like mode, to be unliftable, because, in such a mode, it's said you can practically prevent a shipping crane from lifting you. But today, in this moment, at this very second, with Jimmy's resolve living alongside mine, I am more than a shipping crane, and Demshar, the "Valiant Victor from Van Meter" is no more than a shipping crate.

In my mind's eye, Demshar looks suddenly like a tractor tire—lying on my little buddy, Jimmy. My hands lock on his ankles. He releases his grip for a split-second to get a better one around my body. In that split-second I get an adrenalin rush and lift the dead weight he represents straight up to my waist. I can't lift him higher but I choose to flip him like he's now a half ton pickup resting on Jimmy's ankle. He arcs over, a tiddly-wink doing a perfect imitation of my Gargantua.

A gasp goes up. Not from the shocked Demshar but from the entire shocked crowd. Now he's lying on his back, stunned only for a second. But, in that stunned second, I drop across him like I'm a tractor tire myself. His shoulders go to the mat and, three seconds later, I hear the sweetest sound any wrestler's ever heard: the slap of the ref's hand indicating . . . a pin! First ever against the "Valiant Victor from Van Meter." First *loss* ever.

Everything goes silent for a full five seconds. Then everyone's on their feet, exploding with a roar that practically takes the roof off the place.

Coach has his arms around me. My folks are pushing through the crowd to get at me. My chest-naked friends pour out of the stands to hoist me on their shoulders and drop me right in front of Jimmy's wheelchair, now at the edge of the mat with my father and mother, pushed there by his father who—all the sudden—is looking at me like he wants to be *my* father. Jimmy's all teared up, but no more than I am.

Wincing with pain, he hands me his home-made trophy which I hoist to the cheers of the crowd. The judges are calling me up to the winner's stand—to its highest step. Matt Demshar, trying to be the good loser he's never had to be, joins me on a step lower and holds out his hand in congratulations. I take it with pride, step down and run over to give Jimmy a sweaty hug. By now we're both bawling like little kids. So is half the crowd.

There's nothing left to say. The other trophy I take home ain't gonna have a little old Lego man on top.

"You're the state champ, Press," says Jimmy. "You got that?"

"I got it, James. And I told you to stop saying, 'You got that?'"

Sitting In

For fifteen straight years the writers of Write Now met at the Bonnieview Library in San Harmonica, a tranquil oceanside village kissing the sanded shores of the Pacific. Every week, at the stroke of noon on Tuesday, these dozen or so writers, seniors ranging from their sixties to decades on up, had gathered at Bonnieview to quietly do their writing exercises and read their essays, short stories, poems, memoirs and excerpts of novels and plays, then constructively critique each other's work, never in a mean-spirited way.

Over the years, the women and men of Write Now slowly became not just good but better than good writers. And not just good but better than good friends, enjoying each other's company, celebrating birthdays together and occasionally socializing with each other outside of their writing sessions. For many, these gatherings became the focal point of their writing week. Almost all were retired, among them a radio reporter, a nurse, an ad man, a teacher, a screenwriter, a TV writer, a color-blind photographer, a lawyer, the publisher of a literary journal, a professor, a poet, a judge, an actress and a genuine centenarian.

Naturally, there was some flux. New writers came, old ones went, but every week of every one of those fifteen years looked like every other week in the best, most productive way. The group would nod hello to the librarians, enter the community room that had become their sanctum sanctorum, and work at their writing for two and one half blissfully intense hours, sometimes more when the

257

creativity or the verbosity of a few overlapped the hours allotted. To this cadre of writers, Bonnieview was an oasis where they'd be left to themselves without staff supervision and without rules of any kind except the very few of their own. To mix a metaphor, this oasis seemed as a raft of balsa that would remain afloat forever.

Until one day it didn't. Until the day the raft began to sink under the weight of The Library Board's incomprehensible and draconian New Rules, brought down from on high from the Main Library after having been cobbled together in endlessly obfuscatory and circumlocutional language, and tied around with the sturdiest of red tape.

Suddenly, Write Now would no longer be able to convene, uninterruptus, as before, every week. It would now be forced to compete for space with stamp collectors, knitters, people who like to color in mantras as though they were their childhood coloring books. Worse, they would now be required to fill out a three-page Application for the space that no one ever before had asked to use. This Application would prove, perhaps, that Write Now was capable of doing what they'd been doing, and doing well, for the past decade and a half.

Inexplicably, if approved, the group would then be allowed to meet for ten weeks running, then take a mandatory three-week hiatus, even if the community room lay fallow during the interim. These thirteen-week periods would represent four arbitrary Semesters, each requiring re-approval by re-application and re-submission of the same multi-page Application stating the applicant's re-purposing and thus re-proving its worthiness to re-function as before. Though the Approval Process itself would take four weeks once considered, The Library Board would meet, again inexplicably, just three times a year to undergo such considerations.

Each Semester would require a fresh theme and a librarian would be required to be in attendance at each session to oversee the direction and progress of men and women, all, obviously, past their pre-kindergarten age. And then each Semester might take place at a different branch for reasons even more inexplicable.

Such were the The Library Board's New Rules.

The writers deemed this falderol to be not just forced structure but pure stricture. The New Rules literally choked Write Now from the very day The Library Board's tablets were brought down from the mountain.

At first, the group attempted to comply. It painstakingly filled out the Applications but soon found that the Approval Process was stalled in the bureaucratic dungeons of The Main Library where the Hierarchy of The Board resided. Meanwhile, Bonnieview's community room, now the former home of the possibly homeless Write Now, continued to sit empty on every Tuesday throughout the stall. Three months of emptiness with no fullness of reason.

Write Now's inquiries hit a stone wall. When made of Bonnieview's Manager of the Library to allow use of the room until the Board could meander through its labyrinthine Approval Process, the answer always came back in classic fashion: Only the Library Board could make such a weighty decision. And so the plight of Write Now remained unresolved.

Meanwhile, within the group, resentment and anger were bubbling up like magma. It had dutifully jumped through all the Application hoops set up by the Library Board, only to be refused after first requesting, then demanding, the right to return to their sorely missed home every week as in the past.

Then, one day, all the group's members gathered to ponder their quandary at the residence of its putative leader, the nurse, a founding member.

"We've done all we can to meet the Board's requirements, but they won't nurture ours. That's why we're here today. What do all of you suggest?" said the nurse, in her opening remarks.

"We are not a union exactly," intoned the radio reporter, "but we are a union of writers. I suggest we call a strike vote."

"Is he serious? We're not library employees," said the TV writer. "Then we'll call a vote to picket," replied the radio reporter.

"There's no rhyme or reason to picket," said the poet. "We'd only lose."

"Like hell," said the screenwriter. "We can't lose what we haven't got—and you can print that."

"How might we do this picketing?" asked the professor, analytically.

"In a straight line," replied the radio reporter, with a straight face.

"You're actually suggesting we picket the library?" badgered the lawyer.

"I am," said the radio reporter. "Aren't you people listening?"

"Better run that up the flagpole again," said the ad man. "Never mind, I get it. But first we need to bring in the media for publicity."

"Publicity? Did someone say publicity?" emoted the actress.

"Look, we're writers, not actors," said the TV writer. "But picketing is a form of acting, an acting out. And it's a hell of a lot better than sitting on our duffs waiting for The Library Board to approve us for a 'program' we don't want in the first place. I love the idea." His remarks were echoed by the teacher and the centenarian, then the nurse called for a vote, which passed unanimously.

The picketing began, by ironic design, at noon the next Tuesday. Signs had been hastily scrawled. One said, "NO ROOM FOR WRITERS?" A second, "ASK HOLLYWOOD, HIATUS IS A DIRTY WORD." A third intoned, "CAN OUR LIBRARY TELL WRITE FROM WRONG?" The nurse, the actress, the poet and the teacher led the pickets in a responsive shouting of:

"WHADDA WE WANNA DO?"

"WRITE!"

"WHEN DO WE WANNA DO IT?"

"NOW!"

But, alas, only a few curious neighborhood denizens and one cub reporter for a local paper showed up, and the six straight hours of picketing elicited just a half dozen column inches including one out-of-focus photo and a selfie contributed by the colorblind photographer. The "Writers' Dozen," as the local paper dubbed Write Now, had not succeeded in its mission. If the picketing served any purpose, it was a counterproductive one, further ruffling the sensitive feathers of The Library Board which would no longer acknowledge the group's proposal while ignoring its request for an immediate hearing.

Meeting again, this time at the home of the publisher of a literary journal, the radio reporter admitted that the picketing was an abject failure. No one argued with him. "What now?" said the ad man.

No one answered him. The silence only got louder. Then the centenarian, a wise and feisty woman with unshakable left-leaning political opinions in general and a marked disgust for Donald Trump in particular, spoke up with a single compound word: "Sit-In," she said, in her soft, quavery voice.

"What? Would you please repeat that?" said the slightly hard-of-hearing lawyer.

"I said we should march in there next Tuesday like we belong there, and stay there until we're allowed to be there every week, without oversight, without anyone occupying our seats but ourselves, just like we used to."

Nobody said anything for a while, until the screenwriter said, "That's the best damned idea I've heard yet." Suddenly, everyone was in enthusiastic accord, and a vote was again taken and the outcome was again unanimous. Write Now would engage in its first ever and only—sit-in. What the hell, wasn't sitting, after all, what writers did best?

The following Tuesday, lined up at twelve noon when Bonnieview's doors opened, they all scurried in together, each wearing suspiciously bulging backpacks. The radio reporter had to approach the front desk to ask for a key to the community room, now that the New Rules kept the room permanently locked. He explained that the group wanted to look at it again as it was thinking of renting it at the New Rules-inflated rate of thirty dollars per hour.

This, of course, was an outright lie.

Once in the room, the writers took up their old places around the coupled tables and began their session. The nurse spoke a two-word prompt from which all began to furiously write for five dead-silent minutes which the nurse, something of a wimp in governing the time allotted, allowed to become ten. Today's prompt was "Quo vadis? Whither goest thou?" The group wrote, then recited what they wrote, then went about its other exercises and readings for the next two and one half hours, and adjourned.

But did not leave.

Digging into their backpacks, all then ate a leisurely, if rather late, lunch which brought them to four o'clock, at which time the Manager of the Library burst in to ask just what in holy hell they thought they were doing. Which is what she meant, but she said it in the nicest way.

So they told the Manager of the Library, in the nicest way, just what in holy hell they were doing, and they continued doing it for three more hours during which they leisurely discussed the art of the pen, how to sell their writing and other literary matters, after which they ordered in a couple of everything pizzas and continued the discussion. The media, having been earlier alerted by the ad man, were now in sparse but interested attendance, interviewing individual members of the group.

At the 10 p.m. closing hour, the Manager of the Library, backed up by San Harmonica's Chief Librarian and a phalanx of five Members of The Library Board, called up in panic as reserves, confronted the scriveners and informed them that, "You must vacate the premises immediately or face legal consequences including prosecution and incarceration and the suspension and possible cancellation of your Library Cards for life."

"Don't bandy words with us, you bloated apparatchiks," snapped the centenarian. The group had duly appointed her their sit-in chair for the duration. "You sound like one of your cockamamie proposal forms," she cracked. "If you're saying you're kicking us out, why don't you damn well say so."

The Librarians and The Library Board formed ranks and marched out of the room. After conferring for three quarters of an hour, they marched back in and issued their ukase: "We're kicking you out."

"Well, we ain't goin'," replied the centenarian, in their faces. Just then, four of the group who'd slipped out to pick up the pizza from the delivery boy at the rear door, slipped back in with four boxes full plus a load of sleeping bags. Pointing to them, the centenarian said to The Library Board and its minions, "Does that tell you we mean business? End of discussion. Unless you want to discuss Write Now's returning right now to our weekly, permanent and righteous place in this room."

"We can't do that," said The President of The Library Board. "Our New Rules forbid it. You must first abide by them before we can even consider such an outrageous request. Which we promise you we will do forthwith the moment we convene at out next meeting three months from now. You must stand in line like all applicants, and you must—"

"Yeah, yeah, yeah," interrupted the centenarian. "Your considerations are way past their sell-by date. We want action now. We want in. We deserve to be grandfathered in."

"Great-grandmothered, too," added the centenarian's great-grandson, who happened to be visiting his great-grandma because it was her hundredth birthday week.

"People," intoned The President of the Library Board, "That's it. You are breaking the law. You are trespassing. We have no choice but to have you forcibly removed."

"Begging your pardon," objected the lawyer, "we break no law, sir. It is we, the citizens of this community, who are really the rightful occupants of this building, seeing that it is we whose taxes pay for it. You serve at our discretion. This is public property and we break no law by exercising our citizens' rights to be here."

The President of the Library Board looked about for support from his people standing behind him but none could be found. The reply that came from him was a clearly audible harrumph. He then said, "I'm sorry, I believe otherwise. We will call in the police to remove you, and that is final!"

"Are you sure you want to do that?" said the centenarian. "Maybe you didn't notice, buster, but most of us have chained ourselves to our chairs."

In order to take a closer look, the President of the Library Board stuck out a neck that didn't begin to fill his fourteen-and-a-half-inch collar. The centenarian had not been lying. A field reporter and at-the-ready cameraman for KMA-TV both smiled at the President of the Library Board, as if daring him to act on his threat.

A stalemate for the evening was thus achieved. The Librarians and the bewildered Library Board left, while the Writers' Dozen talked amongst themselves till near midnight then turned off the lights of their community bedroom. Breaking out light sticks to commemorate their at least temporary victory, the nurse also passed around a secreted bottle of Cherry Heering, from which all happy campers took a hearty swig. Then they crawled into their sleeping bags in the hope of awakening to an even better tomorrow.

And when tomorrow came, it was better. An estimated four hundred sympathetic citizens of San Harmonica had lined the sidewalks outside Bonnieview, all offering their full support, some providing whole trays of McDonald's Egg McMuffins. One of them, the defiant daughter of the President of the Library Board, offered to burn her library card if the group didn't get its way.

Boy, did that ever get full media coverage!

The sit-in of the Writers' Dozen sat on for another full day, at which time The Library Board, well, it just caved. It promised to hear what it had promised to hear but wouldn't hear. And Write Now got its way right then.

The Library Board, after its President resigned in what the local media called "disgrace," quickly came to understand that perhaps its Old Rules, themselves more like No Rules, were preferable to its New Rules, which even the media came to see as Too Many Rules. And the New Rules were redacted and re-enacted accordingly.

And the sanctum sanctorum where Write Now thereinafter was allowed to meet fifty-two weeks a year in perpetuity, and for as many hours as they damn well pleased, came to be known, by everyone who used it, simply as . . . The Centenarian Room.

Xerografika

Six a.m.: Kenneth P. Arturian III didn't need the clock to wake him. Asthma forced him to breathe through his mouth all night or breathe not at all. His bone-dry mouth woke him about this time every morning.

As usual, he'd knocked himself out before bedtime the only way he knew how. With a preprandial martini or two (gin, up with a twist) and a hit or three of dear old maryjane. And an Aleve PM and a few Trazodones. The dry mouth he could live with. You just don't get to sleep that easily when you're about to hit sixty. And when you have problems like his.

When the clock hit seven, his damnably impatient cat, Dormus, demanded he once and for all get the hell out of bed, go to the bathroom and turn on the tap so he, Dormus, could slap his own dry-mouthed tongue at its ambrosial flow. Dormus was roughly the same age as Ken in cat years.

Arturian's KenArt Galleries didn't open till ten but he had much to accomplish before Nancy Pemberton's 7 p.m. opening party that evening. He hadn't done well with the etchings of the narcissistic, single-named Arturo, and was lucky to break even with Herschel Koenigsberg's oversized slashes of what seemed like Glidden's entire house paint sampler the month before. But Pemberton's gouached tapestries and fabric art had taken up seven praising column inches in the *Time's* art critic Harmon Terwiliger's "must see" section of his column yesterday. So he was reasonably certain the party would fill with not just the usual empty pockets, but a few serious buyers as well. There was still a lot of wall space left in upper Manhattan.

Ken, often wrong lately, was to be wrong once again.

People just weren't buying these days, what with the disastrous downturn of 2008, last year. His gallery was, saying it straight, tanking. Another lukewarm showing and he might be facing Chapter Eleven. Reality was screaming its presence in this hard, new world and most of his longtime patrons, no longer impressed with impressionism, abstract or post-modernism, were leaning toward realism itself. Photo-realism, the new hyper-realism and, returning after long being snubbed, minimalism. Or they simply weren't buying at all, art hardly being your *de rigueur* Four Seasons meal or an enthralled, gala night at the Met. And damned if Ken would ever dream of cutting expenses by leaving the upper East Side to wallow with the Johnny-come-latelies and pop-ups in SoHo or Tribeca or the chi-chi new Chelsea Piers revitalization.

Ken's longtime friend, then second wife, now ex-wife, Betsy Riviere, managed KenArt. It was Betsy who was holding the gallery together in its rapid decline. It was she who mounted the shows and arranged the openings, all while putting off creditors with panache. Without Betsy there was no KenArt. Face it, without Betsy, there was no Ken. Which is why, after he'd broken off their marriage, he couldn't break the habit of her. So Betsy Riviere was begged to stay on at the gallery, gradually becoming its face while Ken, drinking too much, found ways to stay away, most often traveling, searching for the one artist who would return KenArt to the haute cachet it had under his father's and grandfather's guidance.

Arturo's season opener, as noted, had been a disaster. Virtually all the critics panned the show as "a sham . . . pretentious . . . hardly up to the venerable KenArt standard, however it may be slipping."

"*Slipping* standard?" Ken was apoplectic. And desperate to prove these empty-headed yahoos wrong.

Soon up would be the do-or-die holiday season. His December show would have to kill or he'd damn well have to kill the gallery. Himself too, as he'd recently thought of doing but hastily dismissed. That's how bad things were. Making matters worse, he had no December show in mind. And was being sharply and aggravatedly reminded of this daily by Betsy, who felt it was already late to be just announcing it.

And so Ken found himself culling the art backwaters of Europe, ignoring, on a hunch, its major art centers for Ibiza, Montenegro and where he happened to be at the moment, an art enclave in Limassol on the southern coast of Cyprus.

"Art is where you find it" might have been tattooed on Ken's arm. "Find the artist and the buyer will find you," was another of his fondest sayings. But today, again failing to find anything that even half-pleased him, he was wallowing alone in wine-fueled, full-out self-pity at a table for two on the veranda of La Brezza, a Limassol waterfront café. While picking at his cheese plate, he turned to summon his waiter for another bottle of Tsiakkas red.

As the bottle was being opened and poured, Ken noticed an old man studying him. The man, short and slightly built, was eighty if a day. He was standing on the esplanade, ten feet from the railing that separated them, behind a tripod mounted with a large Rolleiflex camera that looked almost as old as he. The camera was aimed directly at Ken, who did not like his picture taken. Ever.

"What do you think you're doing?" Ken said to the man, surlily.

The man, stone-faced, replied, in raspy, Greek-inflected, broken English, "I give you five Euros, you let me take your picture."

"Keep your money, old man. Nobody takes my picture without my saying so."

"So say so. Unless you are some kind of jewel thief."

Ken did not laugh.

"Come, my good man, you got good face. I compose nice art. Let me shoot you."

The man was well-composed himself, clad, if eccentrically, in an old blue blazer molded to his bent body, an open-necked, horizontally

striped T-shirt beneath it, a red kerchief knotted at his neck, white
linen trousers slightly frayed at the cuffs, huarache sandals and a
big, floppy-brimmed Panama hat he'd removed from his tanned and
tonsured head to shield the sun from his camera. He could have
passed for Pablo Picasso.

Ken was loath to call photography art. But, wine-sotted by now,
and not giving a damn about much at the moment, he said to the old
man, "You call photography art?" The man did not reply. "What kind
of 'art' do you make?" continued Ken, baiting him further.

"Xerografika."

"Is that some kind of a Greek word?"

The old man, stone-faced, shook his head. "Is my word. No more
questions. I shoot you now, okay?"

But, before he could protest, and before the man could begin to
click his camera again, something clicked in Ken's glazed brain. I'm
here to find art, he thought. The man does photography he has the
nerve to call "art." Well, what the hell, let's find out. "Sure, go ahead
and shoot," he said. Which the man did, moving his bulky tripod
around to photograph Ken from different angles until, ten minutes
later, he appeared to be satisfied with what he had shot. He thanked
Ken and began to pack up his equipment.

"What's your name," Ken asked.

"Pantelis. I am Giannis Pantelis. Gianni to my friends, which I
guess you are not. Is okay. But you want I should send you your
picture?"

"No, you want I should buy you a glass of wine, Gianni?" Ken
surprised himself for asking. He wasn't usually so chummy.

The old man cocked his head in appraisal of the invitation. Then
he held out his hands, shrugged his shoulders and said, as he hauled
his equipment bag to Ken's table, "Sure, mister, you got a name?"

An hour later, with the sun settling into the Mediterranean, the
two men, now both mellowed by the excellent red, were seemingly
becoming the best of friends, spilling their life stories to each other
even as they spilled a few ounces of their wine, exclaiming their
points. Ken learned that Pantelis's wife had died many years earlier.

He'd since lived alone and had no children or other close relatives. He was an ex-pat from Greece, 900 kilometers to the west.

"This Xerografika—whatever you call it—what's it about really?" asked Ken."

"What is there to say, Arturian?" (which Giannis pronounced "Ar-TOO-rian). "Why talk about it? It must be seen. You come to my place now, I show you."

And they were off, Ken tottering under his load more than the old man, to a battered warehouse several blocks away. After fussing to open the three locks of the warehouse's heavy steel door, Pantelis led Ken through a darkened passageway into a large, dimly-lit room, an atelier at least forty feet to a side, with a slanted, glass-skylighted, eighteen-foot ceiling. Above one corner of the room was a small loft space accessible only by an elevator just large enough for two people. The loft was occupied by a rumpled, unmade bed separated by a purple velveteen drape from a small space serving as a kitchen. The kitchen contained a card table, two rusted folding chairs, a grease-laden two-burner, tabletop stove, a sink and not much else. Behind another curtain was a bathtub and a toilet. This entire living space could not have occupied more than 150 square feet. But Ken spent little time surveying it because his eyes were mostly fixed on something else.

The something else was everything else cramming every square foot of the sprawling atelier. At its center stood a blocky, three-by-four-foot photocopier. Next to that was a rickety table mounted with perhaps a dozen reams of oversized paper and a huge lit lightbox, its cold, fluorescent tubes casting an eerie glow onto the two men now standing next to it. Beside the lightbox's table was a ratty divan. A bulky gray, oil-stained pillow, decorated with petit point daisies that may once have been yellow, lay askew at one end of the divan.

The man had to rest sometime.

But what Ken was really looking at—couldn't take his eyes off of —was Pantelis's "Xerografika" pictures. Dozens and dozens of them. Maybe more than a hundred, all shot in black and white, lining every inch of wall space to an eight foot height. Most were mounted on bone white mats framed in black steel. The rest just leaned, matted only, one behind the other, against the walls. Many, unmatted, were taped haphazardly to the limited wall space available; apparently not frame-worthy in the rheumy eyes of Giannis.

At first glance the pictures appeared to be nothing more than enlarged photographs. Then Pantelis flipped some switches. The room came alive with the light of two dozen or so pin spots aimed from above at the framed art on the walls. Ken edged closer. It was then he saw that the photos weren't photos at all. They were compilations of odd-shaped paper photocopies cropped and pasted together to form a montage, a single macro image. These images emerged only when Ken stood back and saw them for what they were meant to be. A synergistic whole far greater than its many parts.

The gallerist, art dealer and aesthete in Ken were stunned into silence. Slipping on the latex gloves he always carried with him for handling fine art, he spent a full forty silent minutes, hardly breathing, inspecting—even touching the unmatted ones with Pantelis's permission—these strange, wonderful pictures. His jaw remained open and his mouth became dry as he slowly moved from one to the other, closely observing the details of each composition, then stepping back to drink in its entirety.

Most were faces, photographs from the old man's ancient reflex camera, blown up by the photocopier into pieces he'd fitted into his finished montage, most finish-sized at two by three feet, but several as large as five by eight.

Besides the faces, there was a picture of a house being framed, its two-by-fours casting artful shadows; nature's take on man's work. And one of a cat sitting under a table lamp, contemplating whatever cats contemplate. A third, looking down a row of naked mannequins in a storeroom, one mannequin with its arm missing, others leaning upon each other, as if robotically sympathizing over the lost appendage.

But it was the portraits, some candid, some posed, that grabbed Ken, held him. One in particular, a gigantic, tightly cropped head of a young girl looking off into the distance, her freckles standing out not in black but over-daubed in a burnished magenta. This man was not big on color, didn't shoot in color, didn't photocopy in color. But he knew how to use color. Sparingly. And effectively. His use of color seemed to serve as his signature because, oddly, none of his pictures, his nonpareil masterpieces, were signed. This lack of an actual signature was a form of something—modesty?—not overlooked by Ken. He was entering it as a file in the folder of his still indistinct plan. A plan as desperate as his own situation.

Each of Pantelis's "pictures," he explained, were made in a careful sequence: a subject shot by his camera, the resulting, stark black-and-white photo then enlarged, a portion at a time, the portions then fitted back into a whole by carefully overlapping and aligning them on the lightbox and affixing them just as carefully, one to the other.

In this manner there was no limit to the size of a Xerograf. A single greatly enlarged image might use fifty sheets of archival paper, the halftones of their images purposely lost over several passes through the copier. The final image would then be cropped and touched up, its imperfections dodged and further retouched by hand, as needed. And only rarely colorized by the whim of the still-steady hand of the old man whom Ken was now beginning to see as a consummate genius.

While Ken's eyes locked onto Pantelis's stunning pieces, his inchoate plan began affixing itself to his convoluted mind. Here had been this old man wanting simply to take his picture. And Ken had almost blown him off. Now the art dealer reluctantly turned his gaze from the old man's pictures, and from his innermost thoughts, to the old man himself.

"Gianni, my friend, I don't know why this strange god of irony brought us together today, but I thank him. I thank him twice and thrice." He knew Pantelis had no idea of what he was talking about but he went on nonetheless, taking the better part of an hour to discuss and, finally, to extol the work. Then he got to his point.

"Where have you shown these pictures?" he asked. Having asked, he got the answer he'd hoped for.

"Show them?" said Pantelis. "To who I show them? I am too busy making to show them."

"I meant show them at a gallery, maybe at a one-man show. Have you ever sold one? Ever *tried* to sell one?"

"I make, I not sell. I have plenty money already. Why you ask, you want to buy one?"

"Sure I do, Gianni," Ken heard himself saying, But what I really want is to take everything here on consignment—everything!—to show at my gallery in New York."

Pantelis peered at Ken as if he were looking at the inmate of an asylum. "What is consignment? Never mind. Why you want to take my work away?"

"I like your work, Gianni, that should be obvious. If you let me sell it at my gallery, I will give you half of what it sells for. And I believe your larger pieces will go for many thousands of dollars. Each. Do you understand that? All of New York comes to my gallery. You might just wind up a very wealthy man. Maybe even a very *famous* wealthy man."

Pantelis burst into a hacking and uncontrollable laughter. Laughter that Ken saw as mockery and did not appreciate. Was this fool making fun of him? Then Pantelis's sallow, wrinkled face became serious. "Look, my new friend, I do my Xerografika for me. I do not care if others to see it. What I do is good but is called 'graphics.' Some do not call it art even. I like—how you say it?—the process. The *doing* of my pictures. I finish one, I move on to next. This is what make me happy. You say you want to take my work—my *graphics*—to New York? I think you are a crazy man."

"What are you saying, Gianni? You think I don't recognize great art when I see it? Have you never heard of me?" Wrong question, thought Ken. Pantelis, had no more ever heard of him than he'd heard of Pantelis. "Are you telling me no? Have you any idea what I can do for you?"

"I telling you no, Arturian. Absolute no. I am old man. I die soon. What can I do with more money, with fame? Also, please to understand, I cannot empty this room of my work. *Any* of my work. It would be to empty my life. Some people like to live with books, I live with my pictures. My pictures keep me alive, you understand *that?"*

The two discussed the matter for another half hour but Pantelis was adamant. Nothing Ken said would budge the old man. To Pantelis, no was no.

Xerografika would be the salvation of KenArt. The saving of Kenneth Arturian himself. He had to have these marvelous pictures. And have them now. This Pantelis was indeed old. If he wasn't outright lying, his pictures had never been sold, never even been seen by anyone who mattered but Ken. Apparently the foolish old man had few if any friends and had said he had no living relatives. And he was as unknown as his magnificent pictures, even locally.

So—if he went missing, who would miss him?

Ken's plan shifted to a higher gear, then exquisitely clarified itself. If there were suddenly no creator of Xerografika, he could create one himself, an artist—a persona—who existed only as limned by Ken in, say, an offshore bank account in Ken's name. Which would allow him to collect not half but *all* the proceeds of the sale. But then, if there would be no more Pantelis, there would be no more pictures. But there wouldn't be anyhow because Pantelis would never let his pictures go to begin with. Well, what the hell, he reasoned, wasn't a dead artist worth more than a live one?

So that was the plan. His great, good and new friend, Giannis "Gianni" Pantelis, needed to be dead. Now.

Ken was reasonably certain no one had seen him enter the building with Pantelis, so no one knew he was there. As the man, sitting on the filthy divan, prattled on about his Xerografika, Ken eyed the ratty pillow next to him. Desperate does what desperate must do. He grabbed it and, with almost the same move, shoved the old man flat, avoiding his shocked, widened eyes, then pressed it over his face, holding it there a full two minutes as the panicked man feebly kicked his feet until his breathing stopped. And his heart. There had been almost no struggle and it took nowhere near as long as Ken had anticipated.

He had no idea that killing a human being was such a simple task. When he realized what he'd done, a certain, inexplicable feeling of exhilaration came over him. A good feeling. He'd crossed some kind of impossible boundary. But, to Ken, it wasn't impossible at all.

Collecting himself, fully sober by now, he texted Betsy that "All is well. Found Dec. show, shipping same asap. Details to follow." The next call he made was to Lavar, a local shipping service advertised on Google. Yes, they could send a truck over almost immediately to do the packaging and arrange the shipping. It would be expensive, explained the agent, quoting a little over five thousand dollars for the entire job, shipping included. "Just do it," okayed Ken.

Then he dragged Pantelis's limp corpse to the elevator, got him up to the loft, laid the old man on the unmade bed, covered him and returned to the studio. There, he awaited the Lavar people while sitting on the very divan where he'd murdered the man whose highly valued pictures Ken now saw, unequivocally, as his own. He'd done more than any other man would dream of doing to obtain them because he had his own dream to fulfill. To his way of thinking, he'd earned his ownership.

The Lavar truck arrived an hour later. Ken spent the next four hours overseeing the packing of most of the pictures. When the truck left, he brought Pantelis's body back down and laid it to rest on the divan. He arranged it to look as if an old man had died taking a nap. Of what? Of old age. A slight problem was the rictus of fear that could not be removed from the dead man's face. Oh well, doesn't everyone fear the spectre of death?

Ken, a man who appreciated irony, took his dinner that night at La Brezza where he'd met Pantelis earlier in the day. He celebrated his coup with another bottle of Tsiakkas.

Next morning, at 11:30, he was safely aboard British Airways Flight 210 headed back to New York. As he sat in his first class seat he chuckled to himself. It occurred to him that, unintended, his spur of the moment crime may just have come off as the perfect crime. Two perfect crimes. Murder and theft. But his smirk of satisfaction left him when he realized he was counting his chickens too early. He figured that, if he didn't hear from Cyprus within a week, only then would his crime attain that "perfect" status.

Twelve days later—with no word at all from Limassol—every

picture filched from Pantelis's atelier was safely tucked away in the lower, hermetically sealed storeroom of the KenArt Gallery, awaiting mounting for the December fifth first showing of . . . *Xerografico: The Black & White Mind of the Late Lorenzo Pantelone.*

Ken thought it rather droll to Latinize the surname of his accommodating benefactor, Giannis Pantelis.

Several more weeks passed. The Saturday of the Xerografico opening night party arrived. It ran from seven to ten, a huge, jam-packed success. Betsy couldn't shoo out its stragglers till well after eleven. Ken was half drunk as he usually was at openers. Everyone loved Pantelone's pictures. Nine—a good number for an opening night—were sold on the spot, including the $36,500 girl with the freckles. The numbers boded well.

Boded well, that is, until Monday's specially called 8 a.m. post-mortem meeting. Ken, Betsy, their curator, Cecil Barnes, the KenArt sales staff and interns—twelve in all—were congratulating themselves over their coffee and Danish when one of the interns arrived with a stack of late edition Times containing Harmon Terwiliger's review.

Terwiliger might have been God himself to the gallerymeisters of New York. It had been said his word was worth more to a painting than any film reviewer's was to a Hollywood epic. He'd made the fortune of many of Gotham's top galleries. And drained a few on the way. But Terwiliger had been generally kind to KenArt in the past.

Silence prevailed as Barnes, in his flutey voice, read the review out loud.

"The venerable Kenneth Arturian calls his ambitious new show 'Xerografico.' It flaunts a name someone Arthurian claims to be, if recently dead, a 'new discovery,' one Lorenzo Pantelone.

But, for a show of discovery, it has discovered nothing new.

Yes, it's a lovely show. Of graphics! Artful graphics, to be certain, though hardly rising to the dignity of true art. This column has seen fine poster art. Cassandre, Mucha, Erte and a fellow name of Lautrec come to mind. These Pantelone posters, however, belong not in an important art gallery but in a convention hall exhibit. It's as if the emperor wore no panteloni . . ."

There was more. But Barnes, nearly in tears, had to stop. The staff and interns silently filed out of Ken's office, leaving Ken, Betsy and Barnes to stare into themselves, afraid to look at each other.

"The man is an ass!" hissed Barnes, the best he could come up with before walking out. The silence that followed was broken suddenly by the old-fashioned overhead bell that tinkled shortly after the gallery doors were unlocked at 10 a.m. The TV monitor told Ken it was Nathan Armbruster carrying a hastily-wrapped Pantelone xerograph under his arm and a scowl on his face. They knew why he was there. There was no question of refusing a refund to a patron like Armbruster.

Ken had to come forward to greet him as Betsy sat, unable to move. Armbruster wouldn't be the last one returning a purchase that morning. He left with an Amex refund receipt for $22,500. Ken reached into his desk for his single malt Glenfiddich. But, before he could pour a few fingers, his phone rang. It wasn't another disgruntled patron.

The call was from . . . Cyprus.

A Brief History of Paper

This absorbing history of paper, if totally spurious, is absolutely true and completely, if deniably, verifiable. Its facts are abundant, but do not outnumber those which are other than facts.

There was no such thing as paper until 105 B.C. There was your parchment, of course, and your sheepskin, and, before that there were your wax tablets and your Ten Commandments, but we're talking paper here.

The first paper was not, as believed, invented by that Chinese tavern keeper, a retired shogun named Tso. Tso was seeking a new way to prepare chicken and accidentally burned down his tavern, in the process inventing General Tso's chicken. Wait a minute. That's not where I meant to go.

Paper.

Four centuries later, in 312 A.D., Georgy Bogdanov, a butcher in Smolensk, Russia, happened one day to be offering a nice special on pork chops at just seven kopeks a kilogram. Soon, a Mrs. Yessikov, a constant complainer if ever there was one, came in and informed Bogdanov that Petrov, the butcher across the street, was offering the very same cut of pork for five kopeks a kilo.

"So why didn't you buy Petrov's pork chops?" asked the exasperated Bogdanov.

"Because he was out of them," she replied.

Bogdanov, his eyes rolling, then replied, "Well, Mrs. Yessikov, if I was out of pork chops, I'd offer them at five kopeks, too."

That also is beside the point.

Where was I?

Paper.

Our Bogdanov would show Petrov what was what and who was who.

He would load up on pork chops, drop his price to four kopeks, damn the consequences, and likely gain a nice chunk of Petrov's— that thief's—regular customers.

And so Bogdanov boldly posted his four-kopek pork chop special in his window. But, while sawdusting the floor of his shop on the morning of the posting, as he did every morning before opening, he managed to slip and, while trying to right himself, toppled two huge wooden barrels, one containing beet borscht laden with sour cream, the other with creamed pickled herring, and before he could mop up the mess, his first customer came in for the four kopek special. Then another, then several more and, before you knew it, the place was packed and stayed packed, with no fewer than a dozen customers slipping and occasionally falling upon the sloppy floors but quickly rising to keep their place in the line that serpentined the place. This went on for nine more hours till closing at which time there wasn't a pork chop left in Bogdanov's ice-cooled cases.

I'm getting to the paper.

What was left on the floor at closing was a god-awful mish-mosh. The borscht and herring spill had been spread by the crush of the feet and bodies that had walked and slipped and fallen upon it, and was now coating the entire shop floor. Bogdanov, exhausted from the endless onrush of customers, could only stare at the mess, wagging his head before it drooped onto his desk. He desperately needed rest before he could even hope to begin the clean-up.

So exhausted was he that he slept the whole night through. Upon waking, he discovered, in addition to a terrible crick in his neck, that the mess had dried and hardened. Poor Bogdonov concluded that this strange coating would now be impossible to mop up and would now have to be literally peeled off. And so he got to work. In the act of peeling off this miserable sheet of dried sawdust and sour creamed beet borscht and pickled creamed herring, he noticed that it resembled nothing so much as a purplish version of papyrus, the pricey stuff the tsar used to print his frequently posted ukases.

The man pondered for days upon his serendipitous finding. He reasoned that this odd substance could very well be used to write upon and would be infinitely cheaper than papyrus or the skin of sheep, currently in vogue, because there were few things cheaper in Fourth Century Russia than borscht and creamed herring. Well, maybe vodka; but go try to write on vodka. If he could just find a method to mass-produce his wonderful borscht-based aggregate, he could possibly become a wealthy man. But this would be difficult to bring about, as mass production would not be invented for another fifteen centuries.

Anyhow, Bogdonov would call this material "paper" because it resembled papyrus. However, several problems presented themselves. Bogdonov's new "paper" had a spongy surface so that when one wrote upon it using the usual blackberry juice, the juice would run like it was the Volga River itself. Not only that, this was ten centuries before the printing press would be invented so books were hand-written and thus rare and only for the rich. Few were able to write books. Or write at all. Or read, for that matter. Thus there was little demand for the hapless Bogdanov's newly discovered "paper."

But the man would not be discouraged. He tried dozens of combinations of borscht and herring and sawdust, sometimes using a finer sawdust, other times substituting yogurt for the sour cream, adding onions to the herring, even throwing in a little chicken fat as a binder. And he successfully introduced a form of whitewash to his mixture to make his paper whiter. Also, he took to rolling his meat wagon back and forth over his new invention to make the paper flatter and harden its surface, but it was still too soft to properly accept juice, which, in the Russian language, translates to *ink*. Nothing, however, would bring his remarkable paper up to snuff. He was beginning to think that perhaps it was not so remarkable after all. And frankly, it didn't smell so good either.

So it came to pass that our deeply saddened butcher fell into despondency. He knew there was a place for his "paper" in this pre-medieval world. But he was ready to give up. As he sat at his crude wooden desk one gloomy day, he held up a sheet and inspected it to see if there was anything more he could do to improve it. It was white enough and thin enough, and a little rosewater thrown into the mix solved the stench problem, but it was still too soft to write upon without running or smudging.

Tears welled up in his dark brown eyes and slowly rolled down his generous cheeks and onto his jowls. He rubbed his head with both hands to erase the growing ache inside until, suddenly, his anger and his gorge rising, he wiped the tears from his eyes, crumpled a batch of his troubled paper into a tight ball and flung it into an empty meat box across the room, crying, out loud for anyone to hear, "This miserable garbage isn't good for anything but wiping my—"

Oh, my goodness!

Georgy Bogdanov had just invented something far more used, and by far more useful, than any mere writing paper before or since. Something soft and gentle and absorbent.

He would, of course, have called it toilet paper but toilets would not come along for another twelve centuries. Instead, he called it "wiping paper," which, in the Russian language, translates to "*Charmin.*"

A Note on the Type

The text of this book was set in Castrati Capon, designed in 1719 by the type designer and editor, Ernest Mispell, in response to a need for a typeface more readable than the Campbell's Condensed then in vogue.

Mispell's posterity was preserved by his invention of both the serif and the swash which he saw as a boon to mankind and a way to market more ink. Mispell was both a kleptomaniac and dipsomaniac, traits which led him to steal the bold designs of Bodoni, whose strokes were upright, something Mispell, in his cups, rarely was.

Mispell's skewed letters became the laughingstock of English readers. Particularly his capital E which lay practically on its side, as, too often, did he. The name he gave this letter design was *Italics* inspired by a tower he saw in the town of Pisa. Until the form came into popular use, users were seen to read it by tilting themselves eighteen degrees to the right. Mispell incorrectly predicted that his *Italics* would eventually replace the quote mark and its spawn, the air quote, in common use at the time.

Due to his errant ways, his wife left him for the noted pederast, Eugene Dombey. The whole sordid affair was chronicled in Thomas Wiggins' moving if squalid bildungsroman fin de siècle roman à clef *The Back Door* (Houghton Mifflin, $29.95), the text of which is set in a digitized version of Schminkle, designed by Hiroshi O'Brien, a Leipzig used car salesman.

The typeface for *A Note on the Type* is Locavore Modern, and is available in both organic and artisanal.

The index is set in Comic Sans Cute, introduced by Shecky Greene at his foundry in Las Vegas, known for its quirky typography in an age when what people printed there stayed there. Greene designed Comic Sans Cute to serve those who dot their I's with a circle.

No tree was spared in the processing of this book's paper. The glue is made from dead horses. The binder is K. O. Pectate. This book will soon be available at Amazon.com/books for one cent, a price that might encourage you to fill your shopping cart were it not for the damn $3.99 shipping charge which is probably a lot more than it costs to ship but let's not go there. In the two years this book was in gestation, four hundred and thirty three mom-and-pop bookshops were forced out of business, like you give a hoot.

This book is currently remaindered at the *Free, Take One!* bookcase just outside of Betty's Reborn Books in Bayonne, New Jersey. It will also be available at a buck a bag on the final day of a library sale near you and in the third bin from the left on your neighbor's tree lawn next pick-up day. It may also be found coverless, on a curbside card table just south of Houston in the Village, sold by those goniff booksellers who never paid a royalty to no one in their entire miserable life.

This treatise on *A Note on the Type* will appear in the soon-to-be-released compendium *The Best of Notes on the Type* (Harvard Press, $27.95).

The text of *The Best of Notes on the Type* will be set in Concrete.

Made in the USA
San Bernardino, CA
06 May 2017